Into the Dust

A Novel of the Many Roads West

By
S. Ruth Ely

PublishAmerica
Baltimore

© 2008 by S. Ruth Ely.
All rights reserved. No part of this book may be reproduced, stored in a retrieval system or transmitted in any form or by any means without the prior written permission of the publishers, except by a reviewer who may quote brief passages in a review to be printed in a newspaper, magazine or journal.

First printing

All characters in this book are fictitious, and any resemblance to real persons, living or dead, is coincidental.

PublishAmerica has allowed this work to remain exactly as the author intended, verbatim, without editorial input.

ISBN: 1-60474-778-1 (softcover)
ISBN: 978-1-4489-0880-6 (hardcover)
PUBLISHED BY PUBLISHAMERICA, LLLP
www.publishamerica.com
Baltimore

Printed in the United States of America

Dedicated to all those who have looked forward with faith to imagine what could be and all those who look back with wonder and try to imagine what was.

Acknowledgments

I have a multitude of people to thank; it would take almost another book just to do that. I would, however, like to mention a few. My list would start with the Kruger family, who introduced me to the beautiful hill county of northeastern Tennessee many, many years ago. Then the various historians, researchers, genealogists and families who graciously listed their research information on the internet as well as several well-written books full of material about my time period that helped ground my fiction in the fact of the times. And of course the home team: The Heritage Museum in Independence, Oregon; the Salem Public Library's wonderful collection of newspapers from this era; and my personal inspirational team, the Polk County Historical Society at the Polk County Museum in Rickreall, Oregon; Researchers Nancy Noble, Lynn Mack; Archivist Nita Wilson; The Brunk House crew—the Society still maintains the 1861 farmstead that has a prominent role in my story; Rita Montgomery, encourager and great speller; M. Jean Harvey who knows how to wield a semi-colon; and Arlie Holt, historian, whose passion for Polk County history is hard to resist being caught up in; and all the volunteers who daily come to share their knowledge and love of history.

Into the Dust
A Novel of the Many Roads West

Introduction

A death in a family is often the opening chapter of a mystery. Historical societies and museums across the country are brought boxes containing photos, letters, and artifacts with no idea of whom the people in the pictures were, who wrote the letters or owned the items. They see the same scenario all the time; as occupants come and go in a house, things are left behind, sometimes even moved to new houses by other than the original owners. Over the years the artifacts languish, buried under boxes of outdated Christmas decorations, until there is a death. At that time, some distant relative comes and starts going through everything, to see what to sell and throw out. Some items go into a box labeled "might be of historical value." The following week that carton is given to a local museum or historical society. How exciting it is to find a name, or a little history written on the back of a photo now and then! But quite often there isn't a clue. Researchers try everything they can, short of carbon dating, to figure out who the people were or connect them with a family. But sometimes the stories of the people who lived, loved, suffered and helped build our country are sadly, simply lost into the dust.

In 2002 a box, containing letters and small artifacts, was dropped off at the Polk County Muscum, to see if there was anything of significance to save. I just happened to be one of the volunteers on duty that day. I sat down to read a few letters to see what I could discover. One small envelope seemed a bit thicker than the others. The name on the outside of the envelope had faded to the point that only one or two words were legible. I gently opened the letter. From its condition, it appeared that if it had ever been opened, it probably was read only once; the letter itself was in pristine condition. I held my breath as I gently unfolded the little treasure. To my surprise, there in the center of the letter lay a beautiful, ten inch lock of auburn colored hair. The tress was as bright and silky as the day it was put into the letter, which, according to the date on the paper, was well over a hundred years earlier. The letter brought tears to my eyes. A young wife and mother was begging her husband to forget his dreams of making his fortune in Oregon, to remember her, and to return to their home state back east. Her loneliness and pain were spelled out in every word. After reading the letter, I felt as though I'd stepped into a someone's private world, yet there was no way to know who these people were, or what actually happened next. Many came west in the years following the great first wagon trains, they came with dreams but often those dreams became a new reality.

As a writer, once a door has been opened, I like to see what's inside and beyond. It's like visiting an open house at a new building site, you look in every room, check the closets, imagine how you would live there. Reading this letter gave me much the same sensation. It felt like a story that needed to be told. It was so typical of the tantalizing little pieces of information that can push your imagination to wonder and research the possibilities. And it was, as is so much of the rich tapestry of the history of our country, a little story inside the bigger stories. I set off to flesh out what might have been. And I took a most fascinating journey across our land and around my own beloved Oregon.

My story is pure fiction, inspired by this one letter, but many of the places in the story did exist, and special events happened. Many of the people in the story really did exist and crossed paths with people like my fictitious ones. It was much like the history we are forging right now. Our story goes on too, each time we meet someone, we add another thread to the fabric of life that's being spun around us. It's something to think about each time we take a photo or write a letter. Will someone wonder about us in 150 years?

S. Ruth Ely

Chapter One
Northeastern Tennessee—May 1866

Zachary Grant yawned and rubbed his lean side where a bullet had grazed him during the war. Sometimes after the morning chores, that spot would ache, reminding him of what he so wished he could forget. At twenty-one, he already felt like an old man after only a few hours of work. He had just sat down for a cup of coffee when a loud knock on the door brought him instantly to his feet. In one quiet move, the squirrel gun he always kept by the door was in his hand. He motioned for his wife Lydia, to stay back and be silent as she started toward the door. She went pale and stopped, shaking in fear as she watched her tall, dark haired young husband. "Who is it?" he asked as he stood to one side of the door.

"Jake Bly," the low voice called from outside. "I'm a friend, Zack."

Zack went to the window and looked out; there was only one horse so it appeared the man had come alone. He cautiously put the gun back down and opened the door. Zack knew the older man standing on the porch, but only by reputation. "Jake Bly," Zack said, without offering a hand, "What are you doing out this way?"

Jake stepped inside the door and threw his hat into a chair. "Oh, just thought I'd ride out and see how you and the missus were doing." He looked at Lydia and smiled. "Seems that you're doing pretty well." Jake looked at Lydia, who was obviously expecting. "Morning, ma'am."

Lydia smiled politely and tipped her head. She'd heard of Jake Bly and he was just what she thought he'd be—a small, balding, skinny, evil-looking man with tiny eyes. She felt a chill thinking of what Jake might want with her husband. She was glad when Jonas, their hired hand, followed Zack's mother, Rose, into the main room with supplies from the root cellar. Somehow she felt safer with the whole family around.

Jake took a long look at Jonas through narrowed eyes. "I see you still have a slave on the place?"

Zack shook his head and waved Jonas out of the room, patting him on the shoulder as he went. "Jonas is not a slave, never has been one here. He's a hired hand, and a good one at that. I trust him, and my mother needs him to do the garden and maintain the place since my pa died. I got to earn our living with my tack and horse shoeing work, and I just don't have time to keep up the farm. Besides, it's the law. No slavery allowed any more."

Jake scoffed, "The law you say? What about the other law they passed? That Civil Rights law they call it? Everyone is equal? Colored folk can own property and have the same rights as anyone else? You want a colored family living next to you? I sure don't. The next thing you know they'd be hiring you to work for them, shoe their horses. How'd you feel about that?"

Zack shrugged, "I hadn't thought about that, but we've been living next door to them all our lives. Only they never had the chance to own the places they lived on. Seems a man should be able to work for a living and own a home if he can. As far as working for them, I suspect their money is as good as anybody's."

Jake shook his head, "I don't trust any colored myself."

Zack changed the subject, "What do you want here today, Jake?"

Jake sat down without being asked to sit. He looked around, hinting he'd like to be offered something but no one moved to oblige. "Several of the boys from Elizabethton have been thinking of forming a militia to protect the interests of the area from some of the northerners trying to take advantage of us."

"A militia?"

"Yes," Jake leaned toward Zack as if to be more convincing. "We got about 20 men so far. All experienced soldiers like me and you. There are several other militia groups around, but we want one for just our valley and these surrounding hills."

"I've done my fighting. I don't want any more." Zack stepped to the fireplace and added a small limb. It was chilly in the mountains even in May. He looked at Lydia and saw fear in her eyes. He smiled to reassure her, but he wasn't feeling anywhere close to happy.

"Jake, I'm sorry you rode all the way out here for this. I'm not interested in serving in any more armies. I've had my fill of killing, being shot at," his hand involuntarily rubbed the spot on his rib, "And watching people die. I won't be party to any militia."

Jake shook his head and stood up, grabbing his hat on the way to the door. "Well Zack, I hope this isn't a decision you'll regret. You can't trust those Yankees or the freed colored who are moving in on us all over the place."

"The Good Book says we should love our neighbor. I would be happy if I could just figure out a way to live in peace with my neighbors for a little while in this world."

Jake glared at him. "Peace? How can you talk about peace after the way we've been humiliated by the Yankees? How'd you feel when they gave you that "pardon" and sent you home with your horse and saddle but nothing else? Did you think you'd done something wrong to be pardoned like a criminal for? They wouldn't even let us have our own good hunting rifles. What did they think we'd feed our families with?"

Zack swallowed the bitterness that welled up immediately when being reminded how the war had ended for him and so many others. "That was nearly a year ago. I've learned to live with it and go on. You'd do well to do the same."

Jake shuffled his feet. "And who was it that killed your pa? It was some of those so-called neighbors of ours who wanted to stay with the Union. They are the same ones who are proud as peacocks that we were the first southern state back in the union."

"We don't know for sure who killed my pa," Zack said sternly, "Just that he was shot on his way home from the valley by some lowlife."

Jake shook his head. "Everyone knew your pa was going to join the

Confederate army and knew you would, too." Jake crossed his arms, "And you did, remember. You pledged your loyalty to the South!"

"That time has passed. I am an American, first and foremost, and we are trying to live as a re-united country. President Johnson has promised us…" he started to say but was interrupted.

"Johnson? Can't trust him any more than you could Lincoln. And Grant? He was there at the end for Lee. Remember those pardons they gave us. How can they do anything right for us?"

"I can see there is just no talking to you, Jake, and you're wasting my time by being here. I got work to do and you'd best be on your way." Zack opened the door and waited. He put his hand on Jake's bony shoulder for a moment before he left. "Jake, try to learn to live with the way things are now. It will do no good to keep hate in your heart, always boiling away."

Jake swept Zack's hand off his shoulder. "Heaven help me never learn to live with the way things are now." He tipped his hat toward Lydia and Rose before going out the door. Without another word, Jake stomped off the porch. Zack could hear him whipping his horse into a fast gallop as he rode off.

Zack let out a deep sigh and sat down in the closest chair. He looked across the room and smiled as his pregnant wife eased herself down onto the willow rocker his father had made for his mother years ago. Lydia was only a few months along, but clearly showing. "You look like you're getting ready, darling." He watched her, overflowing with love. She was still the prettiest girl he'd ever seen, little swollen belly or not. Her chestnut red hair gleamed in the early morning sunlight beaming through the big window in their main room. Her skin was as pale and delicate as ever, yet she was robustly healthy. Zack counted himself a lucky man.

Lydia frowned at him, "I'm a long way from time to have this baby, husband." She adjusted a little pillow at the small of her back. "I wish it were today. This baby is going to be a big one. Your ma tells me big babies run in your family."

Zack smiled, a little more than pleased about the baby. He tried to forget the encounter with Bly but he could tell it had affected his wife and his mother. It worried him that so many just wouldn't let go of the war.

It was a dangerous time and he knew it. The times of joy were always bittersweet, mixed with fear.

Lydia tried to put on a brave face, like Bly's visit hadn't shaken her at all. She looked at Zack's mother, Rose, who was just as frightened as she was. Rose was older than Lydia's mother would have been if she'd lived through her fourth pregnancy. Lydia smiled at her mother-in-law. The older Grant's hair wasn't completely gray yet, but she was tired. It was the kind of tiredness that comes with losing too many in her life. Zack's father been killed just before Zack went off to war. Her only remaining son, Joshua, had gone to war on the Union side when he was only 16 and hadn't ever been heard from since. All her other children, three boys, died of childhood illnesses. Zack was all she had left. It was easy to understand Rose's pain, and Lydia, too, had lost a lot because of the war.

She'd been born in Greenville. She had a wonderful life, full of parties and pretty dresses. Lydia was born Lydia Louise Beaumont, and was the youngest of three, her brother, Will, was six when she was born and her sister, Ellen, four. But it was Lydia her mother had doted on. But that all came to a halt when her mother and a newborn sister had both died. Much to Lydia's distress, her father had remarried shortly after that and she was no longer the center of the world. They moved to Knoxville. She had a nanny who fed her, bathed her and made sure she was quiet at all times in her stepmother's presence. Her father had a nice farm and a profitable livery business. Things changed with the start of the war. Her stepmother was from Ohio and decided to go home to her father, a widower who was ailing. It broke her father's heart, but he stayed in Tennessee. Shortly after her stepmother's departure, her father had a heart attack and died. Lydia's brother ran the livery stable until that awful day the Confederate army ordered the business burned rather than give it to the Yankees who were coming. Her brother was disgusted with all things southern and left for New York to find work.

Her sister, Ellen, had married just before the war began and had two children by the end of the fighting, followed soon by one more. She and her husband, Roy Jackman, had stayed on the family farm. Lydia was forced to live there too, penniless like many. It was a time of meager food, little hope and damaged pride, but somehow they got through.

Zack had visited her brother at the livery several times, buying horses and sometimes shoeing them as his unit passed through town. He'd made a point of talking to Lydia whenever he could. He'd even come to the farm for dinner a couple times. She had known then that he was the one, but she didn't get her hopes up too high because so many were being killed every day in the war. She prayed for him but knew the odds were not in their favor.

When the war was over, she practically held her breath waiting to hear from him. The day he rode into the yard at the farm was one of the greatest days of her life. She eagerly accepted Zack's proposal and was glad to be leaving so many bitter memories behind.

Now Lydia was worried that her world was going to collapse again. She knew that thought was going through Rose's mind, too.

Zack was tired, emotionally and physically, and had just started to nod off when Jonas came back into the room. "Do you want some tea, Miss Rose?" He brought the teapot and a cup to her.

"Jonas, you are too good to me." Rose smiled, at the small gray haired black man who spoke with a decidedly British accent. "How is it that you've never lost that accent, even after all these years, Jonas?"

"Lord Bently, whom I worked for first, taught me the King's English so that I would not embarrass him in front of his friends." He winced, and smiled slightly, "I was sort of a trained monkey for him. He liked to show me off and demonstrate how well I could be trained. Reading and writing were not expected of a person of my station. He considered himself a genius for being able to teach a person like me."

"I doubt if he realized who the real genius was." Zack laughed softly, "I wouldn't know how to read and write if it hadn't been for you. You're the best teacher a boy could have had."

"Thank you, Mister Zack." He bowed slightly and brought the tea tray to Zack.

"Are you ever going to stop calling me Mister Zack? It makes my skin crawl. I've always thought of you as my friend Jonas."

"Thank you for that, Master Zack. But it's safer for both of us if I never forget how the world sees me. In your case, calling you Mister Zack is a sign of respect. In other cases, calling someone mister is a sign of contempt. You and your family are truly the best of people. Your father, God rest his soul, rescued me as much as I rescued him. I will serve this family with my last breath, not because I have to but because I want to with all my heart."

Rose laughed, "Sometimes I think you don't know us at all, Jonas. You pulled my husband out of the water during the flood, it's true, but you've given us so much in return. You owe us nothing. We're not the best of people, but I can say we do love you. We consider you family, not hired hand or anything else."

Lydia didn't know what to say, but she knew it was true. Jonas, black or not, was family and would give his life for his kin. She adjusted the pillow again and prayed silently that he wouldn't have to. She looked out the window at the hillside trying to ready itself for another spring. The flowers were budding and the trees leafing out. Surely everything would work out and they would be happy here forever.

* * *

After the morning chores, Zack sat down on the woodpile and watched Jonas stacking more rocks into the wheelbarrow. "We are going to have the most fences in Tennessee at the rate you're putting them up, Jonas."

Jonas laughed lightly, "Well, at least they're good for something. They keep the cows in and the neighbors out."

Zack looked around at the farm his grandpa had carved out of the hillside. It hadn't been easy. The only level piece of land was where the front yard was. The garden plot behind the house was slightly sloped up to the storage barn, which sat into the hillside at the back and on stilts in the front. The livestock were kept in a small barn slightly down the hill in front of the house. His grandpa and pa had cleared about ten acres for a pasture over the years. Zack had been working at clearing another five, selling the wood off for cash. Jonas' little cabin was near the small storage barn in the back. The necessary was on the east side of the house and slightly down the hill; it had been moved several times over the years, resulting in narrow, well worn trails here and there. Zack smiled, they looked like rabbit trails. He loved his home yet never really liked farming, but it had always seemed safe until the war. He couldn't suppress the restless feeling he had, the nagging fear that things were going to change in his life, the way he'd felt just before his pa was killed. He tried to shake that feeling off.

"So, what did you think of Jake Bly?" Zack asked Jonas.

"He is a bully, like a lot of scared men." Jonas came and sat down on the woodpile by Zack. "I have seen a lot of them in my time."

Zack hesitated a moment, "I know it's not any of my business, but you never talk much about your life before here. Do you mind my asking?"

Jonas wiped his brow. "I'm not sure I remember it all. Seems so long ago," he looked at his hands thoughtfully. "I don't remember much about my mother and father. I think I was only eight or nine when I thought I was going on a great adventure with a great man, Lord Bently. My mother and father were pleased too, I think. I wasn't a slave but a cabin boy on his fine sailing ship. I left Cape Town with him and sailed for England. It was hard work, and he was strict with me, but I learned quickly and he seemed pleased. At fifteen or sixteen, I was sent to one of his plantations in South America. There I was put in charge of the inventories. Then just after I turned eighteen I was allowed to marry. Lyssia was her name. It wasn't until she became pregnant that I learned the true nature of Lord Bently. He raised more than cattle on that plantation. He bred his slaves, too. The plantation overseer, a disgusting old sot named Ridley, sold Lyssia one day on a whim to another plantation owner. When I protested, he informed me that I had grown too smart for my own good. He threw me into a cell for four months, with nothing but bread and water. Then he sold and shipped me to a friend of his in New York. I was sent off in chains to my new owner, who was originally from Georgia. When the slavery issues heated up, he decided it was politically unwise to own a slave so he "gave" me, as a gift, to a horse breeder in Kentucky, which is where I was when I was given to your father, who freed me at last."

Zack looked toward the house and thought how awful it would be if someone took Lydia from him. "What about Lyssia and your child?"

"I heard from someone in New York who had been on the other plantation once that she had a boy; she named him Jonas after me. They were sold again shortly after that. I never heard any thing else about them. She was sixteen when we married, so she'd be about thirty-five now. The boy would be a grown man." Jonas looked toward the sky and watched a hawk soaring overhead. "Maybe someday, when the world is a little less hostile I will go look for them."

"When the world is a little less hostile? Lord grant that day be soon!"

"Amen, Mister Zack, Amen."

Jonas looked at Zack, "You have asked me something about my past, may I be so bold to ask you about yours?"

Zack looked surprised, "My past! You've known me since I was a boy."

"What about that wound on your chest bothers you so. I've seen the look of pain on your face when you touch that spot. It goes far beyond an old wound that healed a long time ago."

Zack sighed, he didn't know if he could tell anyone one about that, but maybe it would be good to say it out loud and not carry it like a rock in his heart. He looked down at his feet. "Normally I was not in any battles, I took care of the horses in the staging areas but towards the end we all were in the fighting. It was about three days before the surrender. Don't even really know where we were. The battle had been really fierce. I'd killed five or more people in a matter of minutes, when this one Union soldier ran out of a thicket and just fired point blank at me. Lucky for me he wasn't a good shot, just grazed me. He was so close I could just reach out with my knife and slice his throat! So I did. As he went down, he fell against me. His weight, and my fatigue, sent me sprawling. I landed with him in my arms. He turned and looked at me. He was just a boy, maybe fourteen or fifteen at the most. The kid had the palest blue-gray eyes. He whispered, "I wish I could have seen my momma one more time." And then he died. I sat there and held him for a few minutes. It kept going through my mind that this boy would never see his mother again or have a family of his own. I just couldn't remember what we were fighting for anymore. I might have become a coward, I don't know, I just didn't want to fight anymore. I was grateful that I got to go to the rear of the fighting because of my wound and the blood I had lost. As it turned out I didn't have to kill anyone else, the war ended and I got to come home."

Jonas patted Zack on the shoulder. "You are no coward my boy. Sometimes being a survivor is the hardest thing to live with."

Both men quietly got up and returned to their work, lost in their own thoughts and fears.

Chapter Two
South of Independence, Oregon—May 1866

Seventeen-year-old Cleveland Taylor stood next to the grave long after the last of the few neighbors left. The women folk had left food enough for his supper in the house before they left but the boy had no appetite at that moment. He felt so alone in the world. He had two older married sisters, but one had moved back to Ohio and the other moved on to California. Neither had been home nor written in years. It was just he and Cork, the collie mix that had just showed up one day, a couple years back. No telling how old the dog was but she was a good dog, always at his side. With his ma laying by his pa, Cork seemed his only friend.

The world felt so big and as much as he wanted to be a man, at the moment he felt like a lost child. People always thought he was younger than he really was too, which didn't help. His hair was a mass of light-colored curls giving him a boyish look. He wasn't big in stature either, only about five foot seven. His father had been described as a short, stocky man so Cleveland expected he'd not be too tall. But he could take care of himself and the farm. He studied his hands, not big but strong from working with wood and doing heavy work.

He looked at the grave of his father and remembered the day, just two years ago, he and his mother had stood in the same spot together. He'd vowed that day to be the man of the house. Tears flowed, unnoticed, down his cheeks as he remembered his promise to take care of his mother and make a good living for both of them. He had done what he said, worked as a carpenter by day and kept up with the farm at night. Cleveland even went to Church on Sundays with his mother.

But now Cleveland felt so helpless. He just couldn't believe his mother was dead. She thought she had just a cramp in her stomach but by the time the doctor said it was appendicitis, it was too late. There was nothing her praying church nor he could do but accept it. He shivered as a cold breeze penetrated his wool coat. It seemed fitting somehow that even though it was spring and daffodils were popping up everywhere on the hillside, the weather had turned cold for the last couple days and heavy clouds threatened rain before the day ended. The dreariness of the day fit his mood. He put his cap on and headed for the house. When he reached the front porch he turned and looked to the other side of his field, to the oak trees that marked the edge of the property. He felt comforted somehow that he could see where his mother and father were. He wiped his wet face on his sleeve and went inside with Cork.

Cleveland shared some of the food left by the neighbors with his dog. He was disgusted with himself at how hungry he was suddenly, even though he'd just buried his ma. He sighed and dug in, eating almost everything that was on the table. Even Cork was full by the time Cleveland wrapped up the leftovers and put them in the milk can to hang up outside to keep cool.

Someone had thoughtfully stacked the fire in the fireplace for him. All he had to do was light it. He moved his cot from the alcove so it was in front of the fireplace and settled in as the darkness came. Cork lay down by his feet and sighed contentedly. Cleveland stared at the flames but felt no warmth. This was the first time in his whole life he was alone, without his father and mother. It was so strange.

He looked around the room and all the things in it, each reminding him of his family. His father had been a master woodworker. How many times he'd sat at the polished table with its three matching chairs. He thought about eating meals with them both, then just his mother, and now... He looked at the long, wide, wooden parlor bench with a back and arms on it. His mother had made a nice thick pad for the seat and back, that made it fairly comfortable to sit on.

He looked at the old wood stove in the corner, and at the flour bin built into the work table where his mother made bread and pies for him just last week. Cleveland ran his hand along the edge of the willow cot his father had fashioned for him. How long had he slept on that cot? Was it ten years? More? He couldn't bear the thought of going into the back room that was his mother's yet. It was almost too overwhelming to consider.

What would he do? One of the neighbors, Mr. Porterfield, had offered to buy the place and even offered him a place to live. What did he want? What should he do? Nothing seemed clear now. He reached down and stroked Cork, who responded by rolling over on her back without even waking up. That brought a smile to Cleveland's face for the first time that day. He remembered what his mother always said, "Have faith and trust God in times of trouble." He felt his faith was very small and his trouble was very big. He slid back onto his cot and watched the flames dancing in the fireplace; he soon fell fast asleep and didn't notice the fire dwindle and die away.

* * *

Cork made it known she needed out just before dawn. Cleveland didn't realize he'd fallen asleep. He let the dog out and built a fire in the cookstove. He had a pot of oatmeal going before Cork came back in, begging for her breakfast which was a biscuit left from the food last night and a cup of oatmeal. Cleveland ate the two remaining biscuits with his oatmeal, then headed for the barn to take care of the old jersey cow, her calf, and his two mules. He stopped for a moment and looked across the field at the graves of his parents, then continued to the barn to tend his animals. He stopped again and realized that the farm, the animals, all of it was now his. Cleveland stood and turned slowly in a 360 degree circle. He could see his whole farm: The cleared, plowed center of it, a lane of sorts, running up to the main road; the oak trees on the hillside to the west where his family were buried; the willows along the creek that marked the back side of his pie shaped farm. The side where the house was. His mother's kitchen garden and root cellar just behind the house and the outhouse hidden in the fir trees beyond that over a small rise. Then the barn, half for the animals and half a carpentry shop of his pa's, then the fenced five or so acres of pasture in grass on either side of the rutted road to the house. He was alone, but he wasn't without means. He had a farm and he knew how to work and support himself. He might be young, but in that moment he found the strength and the will be to be a man on his own.

After the chores were done, Cleveland saddled up his favorite mule to ride up to Buena Vista to visit Mr. Porterfield and tell him of his decision. He had to turn Cork back twice, but he finally got her to stay on the porch. The world seemed like a different place to him that day. Cleveland looked at everything he passed with wonder, like he was seeing it for the first time. He didn't hurry his mule along, he let her take the hill into town at her own speed.

Cleveland was a grownup now, that was for sure. This was his home and he had family roots here. He rode into Buena Vista with his head high. He only had a quarter in his pocket, but he decided he'd buy a cup of hot chocolate at the hotel café.

Cleveland tied old Molly to the hitching rail outside the two story building, dusted himself off a little, and strolled inside. He sat down at a table close to a window. The waiter came over and eyed him suspiciously. "What can I get you, son?"

Cleveland nervously looked at the menu written on a black board behind the counter and felt relieved when he saw the prices of things. "I'll have a bowl of your soup and a cup of hot choc…"he hesitated—hot chocolate was a child's drink, "I'll have coffee."

The waiter smiled knowingly, "Yes sir. I'll bring that right out for you."

Cleveland enjoyed looking out the window at the bustling little town. There were wagons coming up from the ferry, some empty, some full of supplies for the big pottery factory down by the Willamette. When summer came, it would be grain in the wagons being taken to one of the two big warehouses.

Across the street people were going into the drugstore or greeting friends as they passed.

The Porterfields were the only people Cleveland knew around Buena Vista because he had worked mainly in Independence when he did carpentry work. And there was plenty of that kind of work after the big flood of '61. Most people chose to rebuild on higher ground after that. Even out where he lived, some of the folks closer to the river than the Taylor farm had suffered heavy damage. The Willamette could get mighty angry sometimes.

Cleveland enjoyed watching people. He tried not to be caught staring as the ladies in their sunbonnets and the girls with pretty calico dresses walked by. A couple girls his age passed by his window, their hair flowing freely in the gentle breeze. Everyone seemed to have a family or friend to be with. His heart stirred, thinking of his mother and how alone he was. Somehow, being in a place full of strangers made it even worse. He wished for a moment he knew where his two older married sisters were. Cleveland had had two more older sisters but they had died on the trek to Oregon. His ma had talked about them sometimes. His ma would lament about not being able to leave a headstone or any markings so the Indians wouldn't find the graves. She'd get a faraway look in her eyes and talk about how awful it was they weren't buried proper. Cleveland was glad he was able to bury her and his pa proper. His ma would have liked that.

"Here you are, son," the waiter had returned unnoticed. He sat a large bowl of soup in front of Cleveland, followed by a generous roll with butter and then the mug of coffee. He smiled as he offered a small pitcher of cream and a couple lumps of sugar. "Our coffee is awful strong, thought you might like to sweeten it a bit." He also put a small slip of paper down and waited.

Cleveland looked at the paper and realized the waiter wanted to be paid before he ate, just in case. He knew he must look like a poor farm boy. He fished out the quarter and laid it on the paper. The waiter smiled and within a minute, was back with his dime in change. Cleveland breathed a sigh of relief when the waiter finally left him alone.

The soup turned out to be delicious. It was a rich, dark stew of some kind, full of carrots, potatoes and beans. Cleveland decided the meat was probably venison. He was grateful for the sugar and cream when he tasted the coffee. Even though he probably could have eaten more, Cleveland was very content when he finished the last of the roll and headed out the door, pausing to thank the waiter. He strolled out into the warm, sunlit street and smiled. It was a better day.

Cleveland left Molly tied at the hotel while he walked down the hill to a place where he could see the ferry and the river. Today the wide Willamette was calm and smooth as silk, looking much like the coffee with cream he'd just had. He knew it was deceptive, though; many stories went around about foolish men who'd tried to swim across it, or were turned over in a boat and then drowned in the unseen swift current. From his viewpoint about 50 feet above the water, he could see downriver at least a couple bends and up river to the next. It was beautiful. He stood for a few minutes watching the ferry make its way slowly across the Willamette and marveled at how modern, and civilized the town was becoming.

It was a little harder walking back up the hill than coming down had been but the young man made it easily. Molly was nearly asleep on her feet when he reached her. He led her over to a watering trough and let her have a long drink before they continued on. She rewarded him by nearly peeing on his foot. Mules!

Cleveland walked his mule out to the edge of the town before jumping into the saddle, then continued on to the Porterfield farm. He stopped to look around when he reached the top of the ridge, just at the southern edge of town. From that vantage point, he could see all the way east to Mt. Jefferson and north to the hills on the other side of the river. Looking west, he could see over the rolling farm lands to the coast range. Sometimes he wished he could have land up here. He envied the Porterfields because their land was on a slope ahead and they had a view of the valley. Cleveland's place was in a small hollow almost halfway between Buena Vista and Independence, just off one of the roads to Corvallis. His father had purchased twenty acres from the corner of a bigger farm. It had taken a year or so to get all the oak and fir cleared out of the level part of the land for the pasture and the house area, but with Cleveland's help, it had gotten done. His pa had said they didn't need a big place because he was a tradesman, not a farmer. Cleveland understood that and felt proud because he, too, was a tradesman. Well, almost. He gently nudged Molly on.

One of the farmhands pointed to the barn when Cleveland arrived. Mr. Porterfield was just finishing brushing down a horse when Cleveland walked in.

"Well, Cleveland," the older man said with a smile and an outstretched hand, "good to see you, boy. I'm glad you came by today. Can you stay for dinner? We'll be eating in a couple hours or so."

"I just ate in Buena Vista, thanks all the same," Cleveland returned the hearty handshake.

"Well, what brings you over, son?"

Cleveland stood up as straight and tall as he could. "I just wanted to thank you for offering to buy my place and take me in, so to speak. I have decided that I want to stay on my farm and keep it in the family. I think my mother and father would be comforted knowing I did that. It was their dream and now it's mine."

Mr. Porterfield looked questioningly at the boy before him. "How old are you, Cleve?"

Cleveland made a conscious decision and lied, "Eighteen, sir. Well, almost."

Mr. Porterfield shook his head, "Didn't think you were quite that old, but I guess you have a right to make your own choices." He shrugged, "If you ever need any help, son, you just let me know. Your dad and I were good friends, and my cousin came out on the wagon train with your dad. When I came a few years later, your dad and my cousin helped me build this place," he motioned to the barn. "House, too, of course. Your dad was a very good carpenter."

Cleveland relaxed a little, "He taught me carpentry. I may not be as good as he was yet, but I'll get there."

"I'm sure you will, son, I'm sure you will." Mr. Porterfield lead the horse to a stall. "There you go, girl. Good as new." Then he turned and put his arm around Cleveland's shoulders. "Just times in our life we all got to step out on our own. Guess this is your time, Cleve. I have faith that you'll do just fine."

"Thank you, Mr. Porterfield." Cleveland felt vindicated for his choice.

"If you can't stay for dinner, you could at least stay for some lemonade and a piece of apple pie."

There was no argument offered!

It was nearly dark by the time Cleveland got back to his farm. The cow was upset and needed milking, and the mules needed to be fed. Cleveland got all the chores done, even fed a grateful Cork before he ate. It didn't matter that his dinner was just a cold piece of chicken, a cup of warm milk and a slice of bread, it was enough. He lit the evening fire and settled down for the night. He might only be seventeen but he was ready to face whatever came. He no longer felt alone, he was a part of the universe now. Tomorrow he'd go to work. Cleveland had already missed Tuesday and Wednesday of this week. His boss had given him until Monday off because of his mother, but he didn't want to wait. This was his life now and he was ready to live, every moment as his own man.

Chapter Three
East Tennessee—June 1866

Neither Lydia nor Rose could contain their excitement as they rode along the rutted roads in the family wagon. It was almost a full day's drive into Elizabethton, but it didn't matter. Going to town for supplies was a treat! Money was very tight for the family. Usually Zack made only twenty or so dollars a year shoeing neighbors' horses and making bridles or tack. Most everything they needed they either grew or bartered for. Most of the time Zack bought flour and tea at one of the small settlement stores in the valley, but today they were going all the way into town. Zack had more than ten dollars he'd saved up for the occasion from the sale of some firewood he'd cut, dried and sold to a family in the valley.

They came into town just before suppertime. Zack found a livery that would keep the team and wagon for the night before escorting the ladies to a small hotel nearby. He secured a room for his mother and a room for himself and Lydia just down the hall. Once that was done, they decided to look the town over before dinner.

As they walked along, Lydia felt very homesick for the life she'd known in Knoxville, but that passed quickly because she knew it was only a memory. It was fun to walk on the board walkways and look into store windows. Rose pointed out pretty things and commented how nice this or that would look in the sitting area of their one big room. Lydia smiled;

it was the happiest she had seen Rose in a long time. She took Zack's arm and he smiled down at her. It seemed to be the most pleasant of days.

"Well, look who's come to town, boys," a jeering voice floated venomously in the air.

Zack whirled around, putting himself between the women and the unknown threat. Eyes narrowing, he recognized Jake coming up behind them, along with two others still wearing their Confederate uniforms proudly. "Well, Jake, how are you?"

"Fine, Zack, just fine." Jake motioned to the two with him, "This is Garrett Laken and this here's Aggie Portain, boys from Mississippi who came up to be a part of our militia. They got the right idea, unlike some we know in these parts."

Zack looked at the two straggly looking men; neither of them could have been much over twenty. "Didn't you boys hear that the war was over a year or more ago?"

"Some people think that, yes sir, some people," Aggie smirked.

"Can't cause anything but trouble for yourselves and everyone, else don't you see that? Jake, there just isn't any sense in trying to keep the war going with your militia." Zack tried to reason with the older of the three.

Jake glared back, then quietly said, "If you think you can run from the trouble that's coming, you're a fool, Zack."

"There'll only be trouble for you if you keep this up," Zack stated flatly.

Jake just shrugged, tipped his cap towards the ladies without a smile, walked around them, and continued on down the street with his friends.

"No good can come from knowing that man," Rose said to Zack.

"I know, Momma, but you wouldn't believe how many still try to keep the old fires of hate going. The war isn't over for some fools. And it's not really about slavery anymore, it's about pride and ignorance." He was almost shaking with anger.

Lydia had never seen Zack so outspoken and distraught. A warning bell sounded again in her heart. She tried to lighten the moment by pointing out a restaurant ahead, "Zack darling, I'm mighty hungry. This baby of yours takes a lot of energy to carry. Think we could forget Jake for a bit and enjoy a little supper?"

Zack looked at Lydia with concern in his eyes. "Sure honey, I'm sorry. I hadn't realized how long its been since we ate last. Guess we really haven't had anything since breakfast." He looked at his mother, remembering that she wasn't all that well either, "Sorry, Momma. Guess I'm not very good at taking care of my womenfolk."

His mother walked over and hugged her boy, "You do just fine, son. Liddy and I are as hardy as the hills around here." She put her arm around her daughter-in-law and smiled, "And this one might be the strongest of us all."

They all laughed and walked to the small café where oilcloth covered tables were scrubbed clean and inviting. The jolly, heavyset waitress was also the cook. She came to the table with a pitcher of water and three glasses.

"Evening folks, name's Frances" she stood by as they made themselves comfortable. "I got three choices for you tonight. I got roast beef with rice and peas, or fried catfish with green beans, or ham and scrambled eggs with grits. Would you like a minute to think about it?"

Zack looked at his mother and wife, who both shrugged and looked to him. "I think we'll all have the fried catfish. We don't get catfish in the mountains very often. And a pot of tea, if possible." He was pleased at the reaction he got from both Lydia and Rose. He could see he'd made a good choice. Frances nodded and headed for the kitchen.

It only took a few minutes before Frances was back with a plate of biscuits, butter and the pot of tea and three mugs. "We don't get much call for tea out here." Frances said smiling, "Must be an acquired taste."

Zack hadn't thought about it until now, but they had acquired the taste from the English member of their household. That brought a smile to his face and as he looked at his mother sipping her tea, he knew she must be thinking the same thing.

The catfish dinner was a good choice. Frances had breaded the generous portions of fish lightly and fried them in butter. The green beans were excellently cooked with a little onion and bacon. Luckily for them, she had also made a berry cobbler for dessert. It was well worth the two dollars it had cost.

After dinner, they strolled to the end of the wooden walkway to the park near the beautiful Doe River Covered Bridge. It was a magical night with the moon clearly visible on the horizon, but not quite ready to shine on its own. They sat for a few minutes listening to children playing near the river, then laughed when they heard them being called in. In the stillness of the evening, they became lost in their own thoughts: Lydia of the sound of her own child someday playing outside and having to be called in at night; Rose was thinking of the children she would never hear playing again; and Zack was thinking of his son—would there be a war in his lifetime that would cause him grief long after the last shot was fired?

It was nearly 8:00 when they got back to the hotel and settled in for the night.

They didn't mention the encounter with Jake at all.

* * *

It was sprinkling lightly when the family stepped out the next morning but it didn't dampen their spirits. The women shopped for enough material to make a couple smock dresses for Lydia, who was quickly outgrowing her clothes. They bought a book of poetry for Jonas, who seemed to like that sort of thing. They bought combs and a new toothbrush and powder for everyone in the family. Rose and Lydia were almost giddy; Zack had given them each two whole dollars to spend at the general store and it was hard to choose with so many options. Finally they had a sizable haul and were pleased to have thirty-five cents between them left to return to Zack.

Zack went on a small shopping spree of his own. He'd been at the hardware store buying some leather straps and fancy harness rings to make better halters with. He also bought a couple gallons of whitewash, and two panes of glass for windows in Jonas's small house, which at one time had just been a shed. The windows in the building now were only covered by shutters in the summer and heavy blankets in the winter. A few nails, bolts, wire and a tool or two completed the shopping. Zack carried his purchases to the livery stable to hitch up his horses to the wagon.

In a few moments, he pulled up in front of the general store and helped the women get their wrapped packages tucked safely in the wagon. "Did you buy the store out?"

Lydia laughed, "We tried, husband, but there just wasn't enough time."

"I have to say I don't know when I've had such fun," Rose said contentedly. "Thank you Zack. That was most generous of you."

Lydia hugged Zack as he lifted her up to the wagon seat, "Hey woman, you're getting heavy." He laughed and whispered in her ear, "And never more beautiful."

Lydia blushed and whispered back, "You are the beautiful one, my love."

Rose allowed Zack to help her up on the wagon, another sign she wasn't feeling all that well. There was a time when Rose could have worked all day, driven the team to town, hauled hay or whatever, but not now. She wasn't all that old, just forty-six, but she had trouble breathing sometimes, and it made her tired. She still worked in her garden and kept the house with Lydia's help, but she was definitely slowing down.

Lydia sat close to Zack as they rode out of town. She could feel the warmth of him against her leg and side. She could also feel his muscles go taut as they passed Jake Bly and his cronies standing in front of a house at the edge of town. Zack never looked at them but she could tell he knew they were there. She could feel the heat of his body rise and anger showed in the set of his jaw.

Rose sensed what was going on because she reached out and patted Lydia on the knee. The two looked at each other. A knowing look passed between them. Women always know when their men are tormented by something out of their control. Silently they headed off into the day and towards their mountain home, high above the troubles in the lowland, wishing the trouble would stay in the valley but knowing it wouldn't.

Chapter 4
Independence, Oregon—June 1866

Every muscle in Cleveland's body was aching from six straight days of hard work. The work had begun on a two story house on Monday, and now on Saturday afternoon they were finally going to have a day off. The boy was glad that people didn't work on Sunday. He rubbed his neck with his handkerchief. The week had been the hottest of the summer so far, making the work seem even harder. They started shortly after sunrise and worked till an hour before sundown, so after the ride home he still had to feed his stock and the dog. He was really looking forward to Sunday.

The job boss paid the workers every weeks' end in cash. He let the two carpenters and their helpers, Cleveland and Moss Reiber, leave at 4:00 p.m. so they would have time to get to the stores before they closed at 5:00 p.m. Cleveland felt renewed by the feel of money in his pocket. He was excited when he stopped at the general store because he had quite a list of things he needed. He bought two jars of peaches and three of vegetables, two pounds of bacon, and five of flour and coffee, a ten pound sack of potatoes, five pound sack of carrots, three large onions, two cans of condensed milk and large bag of oatmeal. As an afterthought, he bought a small piece of rib steak with a good sized bone in it for Cork. The butcher threw in a soup bone with quite a bit of meat on it out of kindness. Just before Cleveland left the store one more thing caught his eye. He just had to have a stick of hard candy to tide him over until he got home to cook his dinner. Molly complained about the extra weight on the way home but Cleveland took it slow and walked along side of her the last half-mile.

When Cleveland got home he quickly fed the barn animals, then swept the floor of the main room and the porch. He threw a stick for Cork a few times, but the dog tired quickly in the lingering heat of the day and just wanted to lay on the porch panting. Cleveland went inside and built a fire in the stove. In no time he had a pot of coffee brewing and his steak sizzling. He added a couple slices of onion, carrot and a potato and cooked them to just right. He fetched down one of the three tin plates he'd used all his life and scooped the pan of food onto the plate. Cork had come inside and was nervously waiting to see what she would get.

"So this smells good to you, too? Well, sit and wait." Cleveland laughed. He found the old pie plate he used for scraps for Cork. He dropped a thick slice of bread into the drippings left in the fry pan and mopped it dry. He tore the bread into bite-sized pieces, added a couple pieces of potato, a carrot and the fat he trimmed off the steak. When it felt cool enough, he slid the plate over to where Cork obediently sat. It took the dog about two seconds to devour her meal and lick the plate until it was shiny clean.

Cleveland took his plate outside and sat on the bench his father had made. Cleveland had also made a bench that flanked the other side of the door. To a visitor, they would've looked just alike. But Cleveland knew, and he always chose to sit on the one his father made. He slowly ate his dinner, enjoying each mouthful, always aware that just beyond the end of the bench Cork watched every movement he made in case he dropped a crumb. She would never insist but she was always hungry and lived in hope. Cleveland was secretly delighted thinking of the treat that was in store for her. He left a good piece of meat on the bone when he called her over and presented her with her special surprise. "Don't get used to such fancy treats as this." He patted her on the head as she joyfully trotted to the end of the porch with her treasure.

It was a pleasant evening and the twilight lasted a long time. Cleveland was new at thinking of the future. Since his father had died he had only lived in the now, the today of chores and obeying his mother. But now he was on his own, and suddenly he realized there was a whole new set of possibilities for him. What did he want to do? He had never asked himself that before.

He looked across to where his mother and father were buried. What had their dreams been? They always said they came to Oregon to have land of their own, and to start a new and better life for their children. But now? They were dead and he was alone. Cleveland felt sad, thinking that this hadn't turned out to be what they had dreamed of at all. Their daughters were either dead or far away and their only son was left on his own. But then again, they had raised him well. He had a trade and he knew how to take care of the farm, and maybe someday that better life would be the one he'd make for his own family. That thought startled him. Having his own family would mean he'd have to get married.

Even sitting in the near darkness, he knew his face must be red as a hot coal. He'd seen girls he thought were cute, and some even smiled at him. He'd had strange thoughts, too, wondering what it would be like to share a bed with a woman. He knew of such things; his pa had told him early on how it was with men and women. He smiled when he remembered the day they had taken a heifer to a neighbor's farm to have her bred. One of the hands on the other ranch had made some crude comparison to a woman he once knew then added, "'Cept the heifer doesn't expect the bull to marry her in a church first." His pa gave the man a stern look, "Watch your mouth! There are just some things you ought not say in front of the boy." The other men around laughed, but Cleveland understood most of what he was saying. He also caught the gist of the remark about being married in a church. His ma made sure Cleveland understood what a decent man would do in all circumstances, and one of the most important was the subject of honorable intentions and marriage. He'd been warned over and over to avoid the saloons in town and the kind of women who hung around them when he grew up. "That's the fastest road to ruin, my son," his father had agreed with this mother. "Rum and loose women." For a moment he wondered about how old a man might have to be to go into a saloon and take a look at a loose woman. Cleveland couldn't tell if the thought of that brought on a chill or if the night breeze had started blowing, but he decided to put the cows inside the barn and go inside himself. He heard the plaintive cry of a pack of coyotes on a neighboring hill and decided to put the mules in the barn for the night, too. The mules could handle themselves, but in a pack those critters were apt to cause mischief.

Cork came in with the last of her steak bone and finished it off in front of the fireplace. It was cool enough for a small fire before bed. Cleveland sat on his cot and looked at the pictures in an old Frank Leslie's Illustrated Newspaper. He hadn't any idea how his mother had gotten several back issues of the newspaper but she had kept them from going to the outhouse. He read them over and over, looking for new things to think about. He was fast asleep in no time. It had been a full day.

* * *

After chores in the morning, Cleveland went to the creek and bathed as he did every Sunday. It felt good to use the soap his mother had used on him and the laundry. While he was at it, he washed his two work overalls, two work shirts, spare longjohns, and two pair of socks. He laid them all out on the bushes to dry. He put on his best clothes and was headed for the house when the Porterfield family pulled their wagon into the yard. "Would you like to ride into town to church with us, Cleve?" Mrs. Porterfield called out. Her elderly mother sat in the back of the wagon, seemingly unaware of where she was, just looking off into the distance. It made Cleveland a little uneasy, so soon after losing his mother.

"I'll just ride along with you, if you don't mind. I've got the mule all ready to go. I'll just put my dog in the house and catch up with you."

Mr. Porterfield tipped his hat and snapped the reins over the back of his two big pulling horses. Cleveland hurried and got the cows into the pasture along with the other mule. As usual, Cork had to be reprimanded at least twice before she would remain on the porch while Cleveland left. He and Molly caught up with the Porterfield wagon and made their way easily into Independence.

The church service was quite lively. A visiting preacher put fire into to his sermon and had everyone yelling "Amen brother!" as he made his closing points. Cleveland wasn't sure he understood what all those points were, but he knew this man really believed what he was saying. Cleveland admired people who had a lot of faith, and he wished he had more himself. After the service there was a big picnic in honor of the visiting preacher. Cleveland felt a little uncomfortable because he hadn't known about bringing anything. Mrs. Porterfield assured him she had brought enough potato salad and fried chicken "to feed an army." Reluctantly Cleveland was talked into staying. And did he enjoy it! There were platters of all kinds of things he hadn't had in a long time: deviled eggs, ham rolls, sweet bread that would melt in your mouth, and desserts of all sorts with loads of whipped cream. There was even sarsparilla to drink.

Reverend Murphy, the regular preacher, talked quietly to some of the women who looked Cleveland's way. Cleveland swallowed hard, maybe they were mad at him for not bringing anything. Maybe he had been rude and eaten too much. He felt shaky as the reverend's wife came over to him. Even though she was smiling, he thought he was in trouble.

"Mr. Taylor, my husband was just telling me that you lost your mother a short time ago. I'm so sorry to hear that." She looked concerned. "I want you to know that if there is anything we can do to help out, you just let us know," she smiled. "And today, when you leave, I want to pack a nice basket of food for you. I don't imagine you have much time to cook, managing a farm as well as working in town." She started to go, then turned and looked him up and down. "You know, Alice Myers's was saying her son just had a growing spurt and outgrew all his clothes. I think they'd fit you just fine. I'll talk to her about bringing you some new clothes."

Cleveland was embarrassed and didn't quite know what to say, "I really have enough clothes, thank you, Mrs. Murphy, but I would appreciate the food. You're right, I don't have much time, nor talent for cooking, what with working and taking care of my farm."

She seemed satisfied with his answer, nodded and walked over to a couple ladies with instructions. Within moments Mrs. Murphy was back with a wooden box full of things that "would keep well over the next few days." Cleveland could hardly believe his good fortune.

"Thank you, Mrs. Murphy," he looked beyond her and said a little louder, "And you ladies."

Mrs. Murphy smiled and patted him on the shoulder before walking off, happy to have done a good deed. Cleveland looked around, sure his face must be crimson. He was shocked to see a girl watching him, smiling. She walked over to him and introduced her self as Lizzy McBee. Cleveland stuttered through his name, feeling like a schoolboy. She was a pretty girl in a way, beautiful long brown hair, bright eyes and a warm complexion. Her nose was a little too long and her two front teeth that were widely spaced but she had a great smile. He was immediately distressed, however, by the fact that she was a good two or three inches taller than he and probably twenty pounds heavier. He really looked like a child next to her.

"I'm sorry about your mother," she said seriously. "My dad works as a bricklayer at the house you're working on and he told me about her dying. He said your dad died a couple years ago too. That must be so hard, to be all alone."

Cleveland was at a loss for words—had he become an object of pity to everyone? "I'm doing all right on my own. I work and take care of the farm. It's hard, but I'm strong and young and I can do it." He was surprised to hear anger in his voice.

"I've been told that, too," she said with admiration in her voice. "I think you must be about the most mature boy in town." She coyly played with the end of a piece of ribbon on her dress, then looked straight into his eyes and smiled.

"I'm sixteen, how old are you? Do you have a girl here in town?"

Cleveland gulped, realizing that this girl was clearly flirting with him. His knees felt weak and he thought maybe he might faint. This was all too much emotion for him, he needed to escape. He was rescued just in time by Mrs. Porterfield. "Cleveland," she called from a few yards away.

He turned to her, grateful for her intervention, "Yes, Mrs. Porterfield, I'll be right there."

He returned quickly to Lizzy, "I'm sorry, I have to go," he started to move off but stopped long enough to see disappointment in Lizzy's face.

"But it was certainly nice to meet you." That brought a smile back to her face.

He quickly joined Mrs. Porterfield, "Yes, Mrs. Porterfield?"

She looked over his shoulder at the young girl walking off the other way, "Oh dear, I hope I didn't break up an important conversation," she said with a smile. "We're getting ready to go home, and I just wanted to say good-bye and invite you over to our house next Sunday for lunch after church."

"Thank you, Mrs. Porterfield. I'd be happy to come for lunch next week."

Cleveland immediately tucked the large box of food under his arm, got on his mule, and was out of town before the Porterfields. Cleveland was confused and perplexed by what had happened that day. He would have to think long and hard about how to change his image. He wasn't an orphan, he was a man.

He had no idea any girl would come after him so boldly. He had to be careful about giving the wrong signals to someone who might have him in their sights. He had to think about the kind of woman he might consider for a wife. For some reason that was scary.

Cork was beside herself with joy when she smelled the box of food that Cleveland brought home. She seemed a little disappointed when he put on a kettle of vegetables with the big soup bone from the day before. When the stew was finished Cleveland fished the big bone out and gave it to her. She acted like a puppy, leaping around and barking at the bone before bearing down on it for the first time. Cleveland laughed as he had a piece of chicken from the basket. He poured himself a bowl of the rich soup he'd made. He put a cupful of soup into Cork's dish to cool. When she could tear herself away from the bone, she ate her soup and the meat off a chicken leg. They shared everything, feast or famine. She was the only one he really understood, and she made his days go by easier.

He walked down to the creek and got his laundry off the bushes. Then he stayed out on the porch for awhile. Cleveland listened to the sounds of the evening: Quails on the hillside making their funny little sounds; a coyote talking to others somewhere in the valley; an owl beginning his nocturnal hunt; and the cows moving around getting ready to be put inside for the night. Somehow, on a man's farm life seemed understandable and right. Cleveland headed for the barn to do the last chores. He had to go to work early in the morning so he needed to get some rest. Pa always quoted the Bible, Matthew 6:34 to be exact, "Therefore do not worry about tomorrow, for tomorrow will worry about its own things. Sufficient for the day is its own trouble." Cleveland saw the truth in that now. Today had had plenty of its own trouble!

Chapter 5
Northeast Tennessee—July 1866

Rose was feeling poorly. The cough had been real bad the night before and she hadn't slept much. Jonas had laced her tea with honey and a few herbs. It seemed to be helping, she wasn't hacking so much. Zack had helped her get to the front porch swing where she could enjoy sitting in the sun for awhile, and she seemed better. Lydia came out to check on Rose throughout the morning, bringing her more tea or keeping her company for a few minutes at a time between airing bedding, beating rugs and making a stew for lunch.

Lydia brought a tray to the front porch at noon. "Momma Rose," she said quietly to her mother-in-law, "Here's your lunch, darling."

Rose looked at the tray through half-opened eyes, "Oh thank you Liddy," she said sitting up straighter, "I must have dozed off a bit. The sun is so warm and makes a body sleepy."

Lydia sat down in a chair near Rose. "It is so nice out here. I can see why you and your husband liked it here."

Rose smiled, "I wasn't as old as you when I married and came here. My husband was born here. Was his folks that built the house. Well, most of it. We put in the stove and the back two bedrooms. We built Jonas's shack and the barn." She looked around, "It is pretty here but the land is poor, hard to grow a decent garden."

"Where did you live as a girl?"

"I was born in West Virginia, but my family moved to Tennessee when I was just about nine. We lived over by Limestone. My husband had come looking for work but instead he found me." She smiled and for a few moments sat lost in her memories. "We stayed in Limestone until our first child was born. By that time Zack's grand-daddy had died, his grandma was already long dead, so we got the farm, my husband being the only child left. My husband had two brothers and a sister, but they all got the smallpox early on and died. Didn't have many doctors when this was the frontier. We are so lucky now. We got a doctor in almost every town these days."

Rose looked across the valley, her eyes seeing the little cemetery on the other side of the hill where three of her babies lay. She sighed and thought of her other son, Joshua, the one she had no idea of what happened to. He'd only been sixteen when he went off to fight with the Union Army three years ago. She hadn't heard from him or about him since. "Joshua loved this farm. I always thought that he'd be the one to take over the farm after his daddy died." She shrugged and looked at Lydia, "I always thought Zack has been a little too restless to be a farmer. He never did talk of what crops he was thinking on putting in or dreaming of building the place up." She nodded, "He's a good boy though, gets things done. I have no doubts that he'll take good care of you and your children."

Rose could hear Zack hammering on metal in the barn. "He was such a creative boy, always had been. Loved working with his hands. He and Joshua were just about complete opposites. They looked like they couldn't possibly have had the same father, but they did. Zack was tall and willowy, and Josh was four inches shorter, but broad shouldered and strong looking. Zack had an easy smile but Joshua was all business most of the time. Joshua was an outdoors man, loved hunting and fishing, like his father did. He brought home game and all kinds of good eats. Zack could get rabbits, squirrels and an occasional deer but he preferred to barter his tack work for sides of beef, hams and chickens." Joshua often reminded Rose of her husband but Zack never did.

"Momma Rose," Lydia gently intruded into the older woman's reverie. "Would you like some more stew?"

"No, child, it was very good but I don't have much appetite. The squirrel was a little tough, didn't you think? They're still pretty lean this time of year. In the fall's when they're best, all plump and more tender."

Lydia nodded, she knew she wasn't being criticized. Everyone loved her cooking and said so often. Rose was right, the squirrel was a little tough. Rose made a mental note—no squirrel stews before August. "I'm going to get the menfolk their lunch. Do you want to stay out here or go in and lay down for a bit?"

Rose reached out a hand, "I think I'll go in and take a nap," she laughed, "well, another nap."

Lydia helped Rose to her feet then followed her inside. Rose went on to her room and Lydia went to the back door, leaned out and yelled, "Food's ready, you men."

She had two bowls of steaming hot stew waiting on the table for Zack and Jonas. She'd baked bread that morning so there was a couple thick slices of the heavy white loaf by each plate. Rose had made jelly from some berries earlier in the month, so it was quite a feast. Zack and Jonas smiled as they looked at the spread.

"Miss Lydia, you always make the most pleasant of food," Jonas said with honest appreciation.

"Don't go bragging on her cooking too much," Zack chided with a wink to Lydia, "She'll get the idea she's a great cook."

Lydia threw a dishtowel at Zack and headed outside, smiling all the way.

"You're a lucky man, Master Zack," Jonas said as he ate.

"I know that I am," Zack said wistfully, "I just wish the world outside our property was a friendlier place. I'm almost afraid to go into town anymore." He looked at Jonas, "You probably should not go into Elizabethton. Bly and his cronies are evil and no telling what they might do."

"I've no need to go to town. I can get the few things I need at the valley store and they've always been nice to me. They knew your father and treat me well out of respect for him, I think."

Zack nodded, that was true. The two men finished their meal and were about to go out the back door when a knock on the front door stopped them. Zack motioned for Jonas to stay where he was and then got the rifle and put it by the door before opening it.

"How do, Zack," a friendly voice said.

Zack recognized Rooster McGill from two hills over. He had a small farm that Zack had visited many times to shoe a horse or chop firewood for the family since McGill was quite elderly and his sons still quite young. "Why Rooster, what brings you up this way? Would you like to come in for some spring water or tea?"

Rooster stepped back and pointed at his wagon, which was loaded with everything he owned. His wife stood by the wagon with the their boys. "We just stopped by to say good-bye and ask a favor."

Lydia had heard the wagon pull into the yard when she was in the hen house gathering eggs. She joined Zack on the porch. Zack introduced Rooster who in turn introduced his wife, Sophie, and their young sons, eight year old Brandon and ten year old Mitchell.

"Where you going, Rooster?" Zack said, still surprised that the older man and his family were pulling up stakes.

"We're going to California. Maybe do some mining, but mostly hoping to buy a farm and start over in a place that's a little more civilized."

"What do you mean?" Zack asked with concern.

"I said something at the store about being glad that the war was over and glad that we overturned slavery cause it was against the Bible. Next thing I know some men in white sheets ride into my place, burn down my barn and threaten my family. They yelled something about I didn't fight in the war so I don't know what I'm talking about. They said the next time I open my big mouth, it will be the house."

"Did you see who it was?" Lydia said in fear of knowing the answer.

"Didn't see any faces because the cowards covered up themselves with sheets but I knew who it was, at least one of them. The guy was riding a pinto pony with one white leg. Only horse like that is ridden by a ruffian named Laken. I've seen him in town a couple times, hanging out with some other no goods."

"Yeah, I know who you're talking about," Zack said in disgust.

"I hate to see you leave, Rooster, you've been a good friend and neighbor. Are you sure this is what you want to do?" Zack said as he shook his head.

"It is. They say the land out there is fertile, not like our hills here.

Maybe I can grow corn or wheat, and not just rocks. The Hicks from the next valley over bought my farm, so it's all settled. We're going."

"You said there was a favor you wanted to ask?"

Rooster looked at Lydia and then Zack, "Well, my wife, Sophie, is a little sentimental over her pet cat. We can't take the animal, no place for a cat on the trail but she loves it and wants it to have a good home. We always let it come into the house so it's not clever enough to survive on it's own if we just left it in the barn for the Hicks. So we were wondering if you and the Misses would consider taking the cat in?"

Lydia looked at Zack, she had never had a pet. Zack talked of having a dog once that they had but it was a hunting dog, not a pet. And a cat? What did you do with a cat? She'd seen a couple cats as a child but never played with any. She smiled and shrugged, "Guess we could take the cat in if it takes to us."

Jonas walked out on the porch. He had met Rooster once or twice when he helped Zack cut wood. "Mister Rooster, it is truly sad news that you are leaving. You will be missed."

"Thank you Jonas. You're a right good man and I hope you do well."

Jonas walked up to the wagon, "Could I see the cat?"

The younger boy, Brandon, jumped up on the wagon and fetched down a reed cage.

Jonas took the box, then reached in cautiously and began to stroke the animal. Everyone smiled as a loud purr started. Gently Jonas lifted the frightened animal out of the crate. It was a beautiful cat. It had long yellow fur and large round yellow eyes. It was big too, probably weighing over ten pounds. "Lord Bently had three cats. I used to love them. They always slept on my bed during the day and I fed them. Of course, they weren't mine, but I didn't know that at the time." Jonas swallowed as he recalled the pain of those memories of his childhood. "I would count it a great honor if you allowed me to take the cat." He looked at Sophie.

She smiled, "I can see that Goldie would have a good home with you. Thank you."

Jonas looked at Lydia and Zack, "Would that arrangement be agreeable with you, Mister Zack?"

Zack loved Jonas like a brother, and letting him have a cat seemed too little to give but it was something. "Of course it's agreeable. You'll have to teach all of us how to live with a cat, though. None of us have ever had one so we don't know anything about them."

Jonas put the cat back in the box and bowed, too overcome with emotion to say anything. He walked around the end of the house carrying the cat to her new home.

"Well, I hope everything works out as well for you on this journey," Zack said putting his hand out. "I wish I was going with you, my friend. I'd like to find a friendlier place, too. I hope you find it somewhere." The older man shook his hand then turned and helped his wife back into the wagon. No one said anything. The boys and Rooster walked ahead, leading the horses pulling the wagon. California was a long way away, but they knew it was one foot in front of the other. And they were off.

Lydia stood watching them as long as she could, fighting back tears for a reason she couldn't put into words. She had heard what Zack said to Rooster and wondered if he had meant it, or was it just talk. He'd never talked of leaving the farm, but she too had sensed the restlessness Rose mentioned. She was a person who wanted a place to call home. Lydia felt the creeping coldness of fear begin to invade her body. A sudden movement just below her belly button broke the hold of the depression she was working herself into. She rubbed her stomach were the baby had just kicked.

Zack stood watching the wagon disappearing around the bend down the hill with a clenched jaw.

* * *

Goldie turned out to be a breath of fresh air. Joy in a tense time, laughter in the gloom. Jonas brought her into the sitting room in the evenings, and everyone took turns pulling a string or tossing a yarn ball for her to chase. She would leap into the air or pretend to be stalking prey, creeping slowly then bounding across the floor. Everyone truly enjoyed her antics. When she was tired, she would choose one of them to curl up on. At first Rose wasn't sure, but it took Goldie about a minute to win her over, first rubbing her face along Rose's chin, then turning several times in her lap before easing down into a sound, purring sleep. There was something therapeutic about stroking that long, soft, delicate fur. Running one's fingers through it and the resulting soft vibration was delightful. It was hard to equate the loving, soft creature that had so beguiled all of them with the one that regularly dispatched mice and the occasional rat in the barn with no mercy. But she had made a family of converts. Jonas acted like a proud parent.

One rainy night, the four of them sat around by firelight and watched Goldie play with a goose feather tied to a string hung from the back of a chair. She was so joyful and full of life. Lydia looked at Zack, he was watching the cat but his mind was far away. She wondered if he was still thinking of Rooster moving his family to California a couple weeks back. Did he want to leave Tennessee? She shuddered, did he want to leave her? She looked down at herself. Was it really her he wanted to leave? Did men really think pregnant women were desirable? She tried to get interested in Goldie's antics but she had caught Zack's melancholy mood.

Rose puffed the last two times on what was in her pipe and decided it was time for bed. She walked over, scratched Goldie's ears for a moment then said good night and went off to her room. Jonas picked up Goldie, who started purring immediately. He said his good night and left Lydia and Zack alone.

"You want some buttermilk before you turn in, darling?" Lydia asked quietly.

"No, nothing for me," Zack said watching the fire that was dying down. "Think I should put a log on the fire for the night?"

"It's not that cold, honey, it's the middle of the summer. We all still have good covers on the beds. We'll be alright. Tomorrow might be a hot one so, we don't want to start out with the house hot. We'll be baking bread and canning peas."

Zack nodded. He didn't know why he felt so unsettled but he did. "You go on to bed, I'm not tired yet. I think I'll sit here for awhile."

Lydia came over to Zack and sat on his lap, "Am I getting too heavy to do this?"

Zack laughed, "You'll never be to heavy to sit on my lap, wife." He pulled her face down to his and kissed her soundly.

"Maybe we should go to bed now, while you're not tired," Lydia whispered in his ear.

Zack was surprised but willing, "I guess I am ready for bed after all." He picked her up and started toward the bedroom, hesitating near the candle long enough for Lydia to blow it out. She hugged him tightly as he quickly carried her to their room and closed the door.

Chapter 6
Polk County, Oregon—July 1866

Cleveland had a bad week. Twice Lizzie McBee happened to drop by where he was working. Once she brought him a sandwich and lemonade. The next time she brought her younger sister with her, who invited Cleveland to supper that night. Cleveland declined because he had to get home and tend to the stock. He was grateful for that! He didn't want to hurt Lizzie's feelings, but he wasn't ready for courting yet. She must have thought he was much older, when in fact he was just a year older. Somehow he felt he needed to keep that secret to himself.

As if Lizzie's attentions hadn't been bad enough Mrs. Murphy, the minister's wife, brought by a box of cookies and breads on Wednesday, just before quitting time. Her friend had sent along a bag of clothes too, just in case. Cleveland thanked her but felt humiliated again. It seemed Mrs. Murphy had decided to make him her good deed for a long time. He didn't know what to say to make her understand he could take care of himself. What made it worse was he really liked the baked goods she gave him, they were as good as his mother used to make. He was really torn. He chided himself, that part of him was still a child, after all, and only part of him a man yet.

He had thought about throwing out the clothes Mrs. Murphy had brought him, but as he looked at them he realized that some of his things were ripped and torn in many places. He'd patched them as best he could, but he realized they must look shabby. He tried on a pair of overalls. They fit pretty good and the only tear had been deftly mended. He looked at his own two pairs of work pants. He decided which was the worst looking and that he'd only wear those around the farm. With the overalls there was one flannel shirt, two pair of socks, darned at the toe and a nightshirt. He'd never slept in a nightshirt before, always slept in his long underwear. He tried on the nightshirt and it was comfortable enough, but he folded it and put it on the shelf in his mother's bedroom for some other time. The flannel shirt fit fine, and he was in need of socks, so that worked out well, too. Cleveland guessed he was a prideful man. His pa always said that pride was a sin, thinking of one's self too good to take the lesser portion or stand at the back of a line. Cleveland knew the townsfolk meant well and he wanted to be grateful, but it felt very much like they were looking down on him with pity, which was not what he wanted. He wanted their respect for the fine way he was taking care of himself and his home. He wondered if people ever change their opinion of someone.

* * *

Sunday came again with all the same obstacles to run. Cleveland joined the Porterfield family in a pew and sang with gusto, all the while keeping an eye on Lizzie McBee, who seemed to be looking at him every time he glanced her way. He knew his face must be flushed because he felt so hot. He hardly heard a word of the sermon, but nevertheless he thanked the minister for a rousing talk as he left the church.

Lizzie waved and Cleveland waved back but continued on to his mule. He passed the Porterfields who reminded him he'd promised to come to lunch. He promised he'd be there by two that afternoon, then he hurried out of town, successfully avoiding Lizzie's attentions and Mrs. Murphy's fussing. He felt like a coward, but he didn't know what else to do. He rode home and played with Cork for an hour or so before heading off to the Porterfield farm. This time he allowed Cork to come with him. The Porterfields always liked her and she played well with their old hunting dog, Tracker.

It only took half an hour going overland to get to the Porterfields. He took the shortcut when Cork came along. He didn't take her into Buena Vista. There were a couple feisty dogs that liked to fight there and he didn't want her getting hurt, so he took the rougher but shorter route.

Molly complained several times about the rough ground or the steep slopes of a small ravine they had to cross. Cork thought it was all just great fun. Occasionally she would spook a quail and tear off chasing it. But she would come quickly back when Cleveland called her.

Lunch was a festive affair at the Porterfield's. Mrs. Porterfield cooked for the farm hands all the time so she was used to preparing big meals, which was good for Cleveland because he was always hungry. The kitchen table where the family ate could hardly contain the bowls of mashed potatoes, boiled eggs, green beans, platters of sliced lamb and fried chicken. It overflowed to a sideboard table where fresh bread, jam, cookies and a couple pies waited. Cleveland filled his plate at least twice. Then he had two pieces of pie and a cookie before pronouncing himself full.

"You are a real good eater," Mr. Porterfield laughed, "Haven't seen six foot farm hands eat any more than you can. Must be still growing, boy."

Cleveland looked embarrassed, he wondered if he'd been rude. "I'm sorry, but it was all just so good."

"Don't tease the young man," Mrs. Porterfield swatted her husband playfully with her handkerchief, "I like it when people take to the food I cook. I take it as a compliment."

Cleveland relaxed a bit and smiled. He wondered at what Mr. Porterfield had said. Was he still growing? He would make a mark on the porch and start measuring himself against it everyday. Oh, how he hoped he was still growing. He couldn't remember how tall his father had been, he'd only been fifteen when he died. He daydreamed a moment of being tall and mature looking, almost opposite of what he was now. At that moment Cork and Tracker came into the kitchen leaving a trail of mud on the floor.

"Out of here you!" Mrs. Porterfield jumped up and pushed the two dogs out the door. She laughed and grabbed a mop and quickly cleaned up the tracks. "They must have gone clear down to the creek. Crazy animals."

Cleveland stayed and helped Mrs. Porterfield stack the dishes by the sink before going outside and sitting with Mr. Porterfield for awhile. Cork and his playmate tired after awhile, then slept together at the men's feet while they visited. Cork seemed reluctant to leave for a moment when Cleveland got on Molly and started for home, but was happily running along with them in a minute.

Mrs. Porterfield had sent home a small bag of food for Cleveland's supper, which he ate most of on the way home. By the time he got the evening chores done, he only had two hard boiled eggs and a piece of pie left. He gave Cork one of the boiled eggs and the top crust off the pie. She had not been left out of the lunch; Mrs. Porterfield had given both the dogs a fair amount of scraps, so Cleveland figured she'd had enough for the day and so had he. He went to bed contentedly that night, after crossing the field and saying good night to his ma and pa.

* * *

It was raining the next day when Cleveland rode into work. It was miserable to work in the rain but luckily he could work inside. They were nearly finished with the house, all that was left was putting up the inside doors and finishing the floors.

It looked like he might have a week off, the boss, Harve Bauer, announced on Friday. He was waiting for a family to decide on the style of the house they wanted before ordering the lumber and supplies. At first, having a week off sounded bad, with no pay coming in. But on the bright side, he could do a lot of the work around the farm he hadn't been able to get to. Cleveland had quite a list: He wanted to whitewash the house; build a new padded chair for the living room; maybe even get shoes on the mules; and get some more hay for the winter for the stock. He had already a little hay in the barn but it wasn't nearly enough, especially if he got a beef cow, and maybe a horse. He wanted to build a chicken coop so he could have a few chickens, he really liked those boiled eggs. When you owned a farm, the work was never done.

One blessing the rain brought was that it was too muddy for Mrs. Murphy or Lizzie McBee to come around the construction site.

Cleveland had a much better week, in spite of the weather being so disagreeable. On Saturday, when he drew his pay he headed to the general store to buy supplies for his many projects. He was smiling all the way.

***

It felt funny on Monday not to be going to work but it was nice. Cleveland slept until sun up. The cow and calf were irritated at not being let out to the field as early as usual, but seemed happy to see him nevertheless. He took a look at the mules feet and decided they could wait a few days before serious tending. Cork was bouncing around everywhere he went, and occasionally he'd stop working long enough to throw her a stick but mostly he kept working. He fixed a little portion of the fence around the gate where the cow had pushed a board off. He gathered up all the spare boards he could find and started to fashion a chicken house in the style the Porterfield's had. It was quite clever with a back board they could lift up and get the eggs out of the nest boxes without going into the cage. His coop wouldn't be as big as the huge one at the Porterfield's but it would work for half a dozen or so chickens. He put up posts where he would put the chicken wire that would protect his flock from the coyotes and racoons. He looked at Cork. She'd never chased the Porterfield chickens, but he wondered if he could trust her around chickens in her own yard. His pa had always said a dog is just a few generations away from being a wolf. Cleveland wondered about that.

While finding the wood for the coop he also found a couple pieces of wood that would be sturdy but pretty enough for the chair he wanted to build. He was tired of sitting on the bench his dad had made. It was well made and padded, yet it wasn't very comfortable and weighed too much to move around. He mostly sat on his cot, or chairs at the eating table. He'd seen a large chair with broad, flat arms and a tilted, high back in the church parlor that looked simple enough to build. He modified the plan he'd seen a bit by putting rocker legs instead of straight legs on it. It took him several days to finish but when it was done he thought it looked handsome. He used a nice dark stain on the wood and sanded it to a feathery smoothness. He didn't have anything to pad the chair with, so he just used a small braided rug his mother had kept by her bed. It made the chair much more comfortable, so much so that the first night he sat in it in front of the fire after dinner, he fell asleep.

When he woke up, he had to go out into the dark and get the cows into the barn. The mules were edgy and didn't want to come in, so he had to chase them down by the light of a small oil lamp. He was cursing them and himself for being so foolish. He thought for a moment about not putting them in the barn, then decided he had better make the effort. It took another fifteen or twenty minutes but finally he and Cork got them in and the door secured.

He was sitting on the porch to rest a minute before going in and getting ready for bed when the hair on Cork's back stood straight up. She crouched low and bared her teeth, letting out a menacing low growl as she stared into the darkness. That scared Cleveland, she had never done that before. He jumped up and dashed into the house to get his father's old Sharps rifle. He put a bullet into the chamber. Then he lit another oil lamp that he hung on a hook at the edge of the porch. He stood straining to see what Cork did. Cleveland sensed the seriousness of the danger because the dog hadn't moved at all. The night was dark with clouds, covering a nearly full moon. Just as the clouds parted a little Cleveland saw a crouching shadow moving towards the barn. He lifted his gun and fired. He immediately loaded another bullet. He was a good shot and thought he'd hit whatever it was. But when it got up and started towards him, he fired again and was greeted by an agonizing howl. He only had one more bullet but he didn't hesitate, he loaded again and taking dead aim, fired again. Just feet from him the shape dropped, finally still.

Cleveland quickly got a large knife from inside and picked up the lantern. Slowly he inched towards the still figure. He nearly soiled himself when he saw it was a mountain lion and it was still breathing. He quickly bent down and cut its throat. Instantly the ground under the animal turned black. In seconds the raspy breathing stopped and Cleveland uttered a sigh of relief. Cork, still growling, carefully came over and sniffed the dead cougar. Even by lantern light Cleveland could see the beast was huge, probably near a hundred pounds.

"Looks like we got the stock inside just in time, Cork." Cleveland said petting his friend, "Thanks for warning me of the danger. We make a good team."

Cleveland worked into the night skinning the animal. Cleveland kept the head and hide. He hoped they would net him a little money and maybe even a little respect when he took the pelt into town.

Once the cat was reduced to pieces and in an old feed bag, Cleveland put a saddle on Molly and drug the remains to the top of the ridge on the far side of his property near the road. He knew by morning the coyotes would be all over it. That was the way of nature.

One thing for sure, he had to go into town first thing in the morning for more bullets. This was still wild country and a man had to be prepared for anything. He felt he'd faced his first physical danger and survived, he was proud of himself. He only wished he had someone to share it with besides Cork.

* * *

It was mid-morning by the time Cleveland and his dog went to the site where he'd left the cat. They found that coyotes or some critter had been at the remains but there was a good bit left that already smelled. He decided to bury what was left. He dug a fair sized pit and then found several big rocks to cover the spot with. When finished, he sat down on the pile of rocks and wiped the sweat from his brow. He looked back toward his house and realized this was the same view you saw from the road just a dozen yards south of where he'd been working. It was a pretty view in the morning light. "I think I'll build a bench and put it right here somewhere," he said aloud. Cork turned her head trying to understand what he was saying. "Maybe I'll plant a tree right behind here for a little shade. It would be good to come here in the morning sometimes and look at the place. From here I can see my home, where I know I'm meant to be." He petted the dog, "Don't you feel that, too, girl?" She wagged her tail and barked at her master and friend. He threw a stick and she happily chased it. Cork enjoyed the romp all the way back to the house in the warm morning sun. Her joy was catching as Cleveland ran and played with her.

INTO THE DUST

When the two got to the barn the game was over. Cleveland hitched up the two mules to the wagon and threw the hide in the back. He let Cork come with him and she proudly sat on the front seat of the farm wagon with her master.

Their first stop was just two farms away. Old Fred Wiggins was a hunter and had hides all over his place. Cleveland hoped his neighbor would tell him how to care for the pelt of the cat. Although Wiggins didn't visit much with the other neighbors, Cleveland just thought it was because of his age. The boy didn't have much experience guessing other peoples ages, but he thought the man must be in his sixties or better. His wife had died years ago and his children moved away, so the man lived alone and kept to himself mostly.

Wiggins was sitting on his porch when Cleveland pulled up in front of the house. He didn't smile until he recognized who it was. "Well, young mister Taylor." He got up and came off the porch and stood by the wagon as Cleveland got down on the ground beside him. Cork looked at Cleveland for permission to get down too, but she didn't get it. With a sigh, the dog laid down on the wagon seat and waited.

"Mr. Wiggins, how are you, sir?"

The old man scratched his white stubble of a beard. "I'm doing fine as can be expected I guess." He extended his hand to Cleveland, "Sure was sorry to hear about your ma, boy."

"Thank you sir," Cleveland felt suddenly lost for words.

"You can stop calling me sir, everyone just calls me Wiggins to my face," he winked. "Don't know what they call me to my back."

Cleveland smiled, "Thank you, si...Wiggins."

"So what brings you by today?"

Cleveland walked to the back of the wagon and uncovered the hide of the cat. "Shot this last night just as it was making for my barn. I was wondering if you could tell me what to do with it. I've seen the hides you have sometimes drying outside your barn and wondered what the trick was to curing them out?"

Wiggins took a step over to the wagon and stood open-mouthed, "You shot this, boy?"

Cleveland nodded, "Yeah I did, but it took me three shots. Finally had to cut it's throat."

"This is a big one, boy," Wiggins looked at the claws, "A real prize." He took the hide and laid it out on the ground. "Tell you what I'll do, I'll dress this hide for you for $2.00."

Cleveland looked at the man and thought "Maybe this is how he makes a living. This looks like a pretty poor farm and he's not been working it much." He'd really been planning to do it himself but maybe he would be helping a neighbor. "Done." He extended his hand, feeling like a grown up. The older man smiled and the deal was sealed with a handshake.

* * *

It didn't seem like a week had gone by at all when Cleveland reported back at work. He took his lunch time to take his hide to the general store to see if it would be worth anything. The boy was embarrassed by the fuss they made over his killing the mountain lion. Someone even took a picture of Cleveland with the hide. Cleveland gave Mr. Wiggins full credit for the fine job of curing the hide.

The store owner offered Cleveland $25 worth of merchandise on account for the pelt, which thrilled the young man. Cleveland agreed and hurried back to work. He could buy all the things he needed for winter now, maybe even a few luxuries like a pair of Ab Crider boots he'd seen, possibly a haircut and dinner at the café in town. He couldn't help but hum happily as he worked that day.

Chapter 7
East Tennessee—Early August 1866

The heat of the day lasted until well after dark. The whole Grant family sat out on the front porch enjoying the little night breezes that pushed the warm air around.

"I didn't get much done today, it was just too hot," Jonas said apologetically to Rose.

"Don't think a thing about it. You work too hard as it is. Neither of us are young chicks anymore. We got to pace ourselves, especially in this heat," Rose responded.

Lydia swayed gently in her favorite rocker on the porch. Her eyes were half closed as she relaxed, while little beads of sweat still formed on her brow. "It would be nice to be a child again and go down to the creek and just jump in buck naked on a night like this."

Zack laughed, "You did that when you were a child?"

Lydia laughed, "no I never did that but my brother and his friend did once. They didn't know I was following them. I watched from the cattail bushes. Sure surprised me."

"Bet it surprised them!" Rose laughed.

"I never told anyone til now about that. It was my little secret. Thought I'd wait until a time when I could embarrass my brother with the tale but I never got the chance. The war came along and changed everything."

Zack nodded, "War changes everything for everybody, no doubt about that."

Jonas changed the subject, "The stars seem especially bright tonight don't they?"

Rose scanned the sky just as one streak, then another at a slightly different angle appeared in the sky. "Look at that! Two shooting stars at one time. I think that means that someone is coming to visit. That may not be a good omen."

"Ma, we see lots of shooting stars about this time every year. It's not an omen. It's just something natural." Zack said quietly.

"I think you're right about that, Mister Zack," Jonas said in agreement. "I read once that bits of meteors actually break up in our atmosphere and cause the shooting stars, as we call them."

Rose scoffed, "I think it's an omen."

Lydia laughed, "You're not going to convince Rose of anything with your scientific talk, gentlemen. I think we should all just enjoy the beauty of the sky tonight and count our blessings."

"Amen to that, darling," Zack said with a yawn. "I think I'm beginning to get sleepy. Anyone else ready to turn in?"

Before anyone could answer a clatter of hoof beats could be heard coming up their road. "Get a lantern quickly, Jonas," Zack said quietly but sternly. Jonas jumped up and fetched the light from inside the house. Zack put the lantern on a hook on the edge of the porch so he could see who was coming to the house.

"Everyone back inside, now!" Zack backed up to the door once everyone did as he commanded. Jonas brought him the rifle and stood behind Zack with his own squirrel gun.

Within moments the yard in front house filled with riders draped in white sheets, each bearing cut out eye holes. "Zack Grant," one of the riders yelled. "Come out and talk with us, Zack."

Zack walked out on the porch a couple steps, rifle across his arms. "State your purpose for showing up like this, scaring my Missus and mother."

"We come to ask you to ride with us, Zack. We got some people in the valley that have been spouting off about how we lost the war and we deserve what we got. They're talking about starting a community for colored folk, letting them buy land here. We want to show these trouble makers that we're not going to just stand by and take such an insult. Are you with us, Zack?"

Rose walked out on the porch beside her son. Zack tried to push her back inside but she wouldn't be pushed. "Is that you, Jake Bly?" she asked.

"Ma'am, this isn't a thing you should be mixing in," the voice yelled.

"Zack served his time in the war with honor. You are now asking him to serve in a cause with no honor. If it was honorable you wouldn't have to wear a sheet over your head to hide your shame." She looked over the men and saw the pony with the one white leg. "I see Laken is with you. All you no-account boys think no body knows who you are, but you are known and if you hurt someone, you'll have to answer for it with the law."

"Ma'am, your husband was a good man and out of respect for him we are not interested in you and your family. But that might change if you don't watch what you say. These are dangerous times."

Zack stepped in front of his mother, "Jake, are you threatening my mother and me?"

"You've been warned," the man pulled the reins hard and his horse reared. He pulled the animal around and sped off, followed by the rest of the riders.

"Ma, you go in and go to bed," Zack hissed, "Don't ever do that again. Those bullies wouldn't hesitate to harm you or Lydia. Don't rile them like that and give them any excuse."

"Sorry Zack, they really aren't interested in me though. Can't you see they're just trying to put pressure on you to get you to join them." She reached out to touch her son.

He shook his head and took his mother into his arms. "I'm sorry ma, I didn't mean to get so angry at you. I just was so scared for a minute there. They're just scum." Zack kissed his mother on the cheek. "You go to bed now. I'm going to sit out here for awhile and make sure they don't come back. Jonas can keep me company. Now ma, go make sure Liddy gets in bed."

"Don't stay out here too long, I really don't think they'll come back." Rose said as she turned and went into the house. "All-fired heathens."

"Ma, don't swear, it isn't like you." Zack said with a laugh.

Jonas come out and sat down on the step next to Zack. After Rose was out of ear shot he asked, "Do you think they'll come back?"

"Never know about crazy people, especially in a mob. A man might seem normal when he's by himself, but get him together with three or four others," he shook his head, "You never know. One gets a mean thought and everyone thinks it's their own thought and they act on it."

"I've lived with a little nagging fear all my life, that I might die a violent death."

Zack put his hand on Jonas' shoulder, "My friend I think we all have that fear. Sometimes it seems more likely than other times."

"Surely does, Mister Zack, surely does."

The men stayed out another two or so hours but finally decided it was time to turn in. The night had began to turn cool, but the coming day would be hot again so they needed to get their rest while they could.

* * *

When the family gathered on the front porch the next morning there was none of the beauty they had enjoyed the night before. Someone had killed one of their cows and left it in the front yard, just in front of them. The poor animal's throat had been cut and then coal oil poured over it.

Jonas scoffed, "What a shame. Can't even use the meat."

Zack gritted his teeth and went to get a horse. In a few minutes he had pulled the dead animal down the hill to the edge of the farm. He and Jonas buried it whole, since the meat had been ruined. No one even asked the question of who might of done such a thing. They knew exactly who it was.

Rose and Lydia stood on the porch watching the men silently do what had to be done. "What are we going to do?" Lydia said fearfully.

Rose shook her head, "Don't know. Just don't know." She bit her lip. "I do know that as long as Zack is here they will continue to pressure him in any hateful way they can."

Lydia wiped tears away from her face, "maybe we should have gone with Rooster and his family." She looked at Rose for a reaction, "you know to California?"

Rose walked to the edge of the porch and stood thoughtfully looking around at the farm. "I've been here a long time, all my babies were born here," she said softly. "But I'd leave in a heartbeat to save my son." She looked down at her hands and then sat down in a rocker. "I don't think I could go in winter though, my lungs just ain't strong enough." She shook her head, "Maybe in the spring I could go."

Lydia looked down at her own changing shape. "I couldn't go until spring either. This baby is going to be born in the winter for sure." She sat down on the porch steps and buried her head in her arms.

Both women couldn't help the tears that flowed. When Lydia was able to control herself again, she turned to Rose. "Do you think we could manage here, you, Jonas and me?"

"What are you thinking, child?"

"Well, the crops are all but in, we've canned enough to see us clear through to spring. Jonas could go to the valley store for us if we needed anything. Zack has already laid in enough wood for the winter."

"You can't be thinking of sending Zack away?"

"Not away exactly," Lydia tried to sound hopeful, "He could go out to California and find a place for us, and then come back and get us in the spring."

Rose shook her head, "I don't know, but I think it might take more than four months just to get there. He might not get back before summer." She looked at Lydia, "You want Zack to be gone when you have that young one?"

Lydia shook her head. "I'd rather he be gone than dead." She got up and hugged Rose. "I am so afraid of what might happen."

The tears started all over again. The women managed to pull themselves together by the time they heard the men coming back up the hill. Zack took the horse back to the barn and Jonas walked on up to his cabin. From the slump to his shoulders the women could see how upset he was about this turn of events. He, like all of them, realized what was happening.

"Will this war ever end?" Lydia sighed. "The war between the states is over, but not the war between people. How do we change people's minds and hearts? That's a lot harder than changing borders or laws."

Rose patted her daughter-in-law's hand. "Help me up child. I am so tired and angry I think it best if I lay down for awhile. I don't want any breakfast, don't think I could face food right now."

Lydia helped Rose get on her feet then stood and waited for Zack to come to the house. But he didn't. Rose saw him take the axe and head for the trees they'd fallen for firewood. Chopping wood had always been a way to let off steam for Zack. She smiled sadly, thinking, "That's probably why we already have enough wood for us for the winter and enough to sell in the valley, too."

Lydia walked off the porch and down to the little flower garden Rose had put in. The roses and sweet peas were still in bloom. Their fragrance reminded Lydia that there was still beauty in the world even if she couldn't see much of it. She sat down on the bench under the wistaria vine and just let her mind go blank for a moment. It was balm to her soul to hear nothing but the birds darting about the garden, the wind in the trees and smell the soft headiness of summer. A sharp crack of metal splitting wood rang across the hillside, jolting her back to the reality of the day.

She gathered her skirt up and made her way through the woods to where Zack was.

When he saw her coming he stopped battering the tree limb he was working on and sat down on a stump. "Should you be walking out here on this uneven hillside, Liddy?" He said with concern.

"I'm being careful, husband," she said, a little out of breath.

Zack smiled at her and came to her, picking her up easily to take her the last few steps to the stump. They sat together silently for a few moments. "Why did you come out here, Liddy?"

It was harder to say than she had thought when she rehearsed it over and over in her mind. "I was talking to your ma, and we were thinking that it might be good to leave here."

Zack looked shocked, "You and ma want to leave here? Now?"

Lydia shook her head, "Well, not now…well, not all of us." She looked at him fighting back the tears, "You my husband…. We were talking about you going on to California, find us a homestead." She could hardly go on, "Then come back and get us."

Zack sat open-mouthed for a stunned moment, "I ain't scared of those bullies that were here if that's what you're thinking."

"You aren't, but we are," she felt braver now, "We figure they'll just keep up on you till you join them." Her throat felt so tight she could hardly force the words out. "If you're not here, well, we're of no interest to them."

"Hadn't thought of it that way," Zack stood up and walked a few feet then back again. "Why would you want to go to California?"

"I don't know nothing about California. It was just you seemed interested when Rooster was going there, so I thought you'd at least know someone out there."

"I actually do know someone who went on one of the wagon trains. Just before the war friends of the family went to Oregon. Reverend Elder and his family it was. They said they'd heard you could grow anything you wanted to in the rich soils of the Willamette Valley. I remember my pa was tempted to go with them, but ma didn't want to leave all they'd done here." He looked around, seeing the whole farm in his mind's eye. "I reckon ma would never leave here."

"She said she would if it would save her son," Lydia said softly.

Zack walked to Lydia and hugged her to him. "I don't know what to do," he sobbed, "this is my home. I don't want to be run out by some no-accounts."

"The war will never be over here," Lydia sobbed. "At least not while these ruffians are around. Maybe we could just go for awhile. Not sell the farm, but rent it out for a year or two."

"That sounds better than selling the family place," he was shaking, thinking about leaving his home. "What about you and ma? Are you up to going?"

Lydia freed herself from his arms and looked him in the eye, "No, husband. We'd wait until you either send for us, or come back and get us. Neither of us are really up to a trip like that going into winter and," she looked down and then smiled at him, "Like this."

"But the money," he protested.

Lydia put her hand over his mouth. "I know about the old coffee pot under the back step. I don't know how much you've saved up to build us a house of our own but I know it's enough to get you to California or Oregon, whichever you want to go to. You can build us a house there."

He gathered her into his arms again. She pressed herself against him, feeling completely spent. Lydia was glad when he picked her up and carried her back to the house. She didn't have enough strength to get there under her own steam. Her world had just collapsed again and she had lied convincingly enough to make her husband think she wanted him to leave her and their unborn child. "Lord," she prayed silently, "help us get through this and let this be the right thing to do. Give me courage and strength, because I have neither." She clung to Zack as they neared the house.

Rose had come back out on the porch. She looked down at Lydia as Zack put her down on her feet at the base of the steps. Lydia managed a weak smile, "Mama Rose, Zack is going to Oregon. He's going to build us a house there."

Rose bit her lip and looked at Zack's worried face. "Well then, I guess we need to get some planning done. Lydia and I will get your clothes washed and mended son." She put her arm around Lydia as they came together. "We'll be all right, the two of us. We're tough." She tried hard to keep from crying because she knew that Lydia was on the edge of breaking down, too. "Why don't we have lunch. I've got some turkey with rice soup in the kettle. Zack, go fetch Jonas and we'll all eat."

Zack didn't say a word, just went around the side of the house. Lydia finally let out the breath she'd been holding for so long and Rose staggered to her rocker. The looked at each other with fear and dismay but Rose nodded, it was the right thing to do. Lydia dried her eyes on her smock and put her shoulders back. Rose got up and joined her. Arm and arm they went to fix the men lunch.

* * *

Three days later all the plans had been made, even a neighbor and his wife had volunteered to look in on Rose and Lydia to help when needed.

It all seemed to be going smoothly until that final morning, just as the sun crept over the trees. To Lydia it felt like all the air had been sucked out of the valley. She was having a hard time breathing regularly, her heart seemed to want to beat in a new frightening way. She stood on the porch watching Zack try to find a place in his bulging saddle bags for the lunch Rose had just packed for him.

Jonas brought a poncho to Zack, "Are you sure you won't take a pack horse, too?"

"No, I'll be taking the train part of the way and I can't afford to pay passage for two horses and myself. This gelding is young and strong. Besides, I'll be trying to hire on with a wagon train in Memphis. Or I'll be taking the stage, if I can afford the fare from there to California. I've heard it runs pretty regular. Gets a person there in just 3 weeks."

"That doesn't sound too bad, just three weeks from Memphis." Rose said, trying to reassure herself and Lydia that this wasn't that dangerous, even though she'd heard stories about robbers and Indians raiding those stage coaches.

"Once I get out there I'll see what it looks like and try to find the best place I can for us. I might have to work a little and meet some folks, but I promise it wouldn't be any longer than necessary to get a start for us." He looked at each one of them, his family, gathered there on the porch. It was a chilly morning, giving just a hint of the fall that would come shortly.

Jonas shook Zack's hand but couldn't say anything more. The black man turned and walked back to the porch where the women stood arm in arm. Even Goldie had come out onto the porch. Jonas picked up the cat and stroked her absent-mindedly.

Zack came back up on the porch to hug his mother. He then bent down and kissed Lydia firmly. It was hard to tell whose tears were flowing down their faces. As much as he wanted to, he couldn't say a word, and neither could Lydia. They just nodded and held hands for a few moments. Zack quickly turned and got on the horse and started down the hill. He stopped just at the bend of the road where he could get the last glimpse of the house. Lydia and his mother were side by side, watching him. He would carry that image with him the rest of his life as he rode on out of sight.

As he eased the horse forward, a bitter feeling came into his soul. He felt like he was reliving that awful day when he used his wound as an excuse to leave the battlefield. Was he truly a coward? How far would he have to run to redeem himself, he wondered.

Chapter 8
Monmouth, Oregon—Early August 1866

Cleveland found the extra three miles to get to the job site annoying but his boss had shortened his hours to compensate. He arrived at the Christian College at about 7:30 a.m. instead of the 7:00 a.m. in Independence. It took just a few minutes for Mr. Whitson, the President of the Board for the college, to show Cleveland the area that was still needing repairs. They'd had some work done but it was far from finished. The school was due to open in October for the fall term.

Throughout the tour, Cleveland measured and jotted down the supplies he would need to do the work. There were several doorjambs to replace, and some windows that had been improperly put in that would need new sills. Some floors in the ground level rooms would need to be replaced because of a water damage from a summer wind and rain storm that first blew out a few windows and then let water in. Then there was painting and putting in moldings. Cleveland noticed that there were several desks in need of repair, too, including an instructor's.

By mid-morning Harve showed up and asked "Well boy, what are we going to need for this job?"

Cleveland was ready and handed him a list. "This is what I have found so far. I noticed that some desks were damaged here and there. I think I could fix those, maybe even build a new one for the teacher."

Harve looked at the young man, his face registering surprise, "Well, I guess we could figure that into the cost of the project. You sure you can do that kind of furniture making and repair?"

Cleveland nodded, "Made myself a pretty nice chair recently. Turned out nearly as well as my pa could have made and he was a great hand at making furniture," he said shyly.

Harve nodded, "I didn't work with your dad but Old Bill Brown did and said he was a very good woodworker. I think that was the reason you got hired to this crew of builders and carpenters, but you don't have to ride on his coattail anymore. You've more than proved your own merit, boy." The boss smiled and offered his hand.

Cleveland smiled and shook the man's hand. "What now, Mr. Bauer? Do you want me to start working?"

"Let me talk to Whitson with a figure on what this work will cost and see if he wants us to do the work. Always got to work out the deal you know." He patted Cleveland on the shoulder and started to leave to find the board president, "Why don't you take a half an hour, go into town and find yourself some lunch." He reached into his pocket and fished out a fifty cent piece and tossed it to Cleveland, "Even if you brought your lunch today." He smiled and walked off.

Cleveland playfully tossed the coin in the air and then caught it. He strolled out of the building and down the dusty street to the business section of town. The main street was a pretty combination of several buildings with wooden sidewalks out front. Somehow it was a more refined feeling town than the raw hustle and bustle of Independence. There were no boats or ferries coming and going, no big grain elevators or noisy saloons. There was a café in one of the storefronts near the far end of the shops.

Cleveland dusted himself off a bit with his hat before going in. It was a hot day and stifling inside. He chose a table near the open side door so he could be as cool as possible. The menu was posted on a large placard near the front door. Cleveland laughed, the sign simply said, "Today we have turkey pie, with bread pudding thirty-five cents." So much for any kind of choice. But it was all right, he loved turkey pie.

A tall dark haired young man about Cleveland's age came to the table to take his order. "Are you having a meal sir?"

Cleveland smiled, no one yet had ever called him sir. "Yes, please."

"Would you like coffee or milk to drink?"

"Do you have cream and sugar for the coffee?"

"Yes, we do," the young man smiled, "That's the way I like it, too."

Cleveland nodded, "That's what I'll have then."

In just a few moments the young man was back with the coffee pot, mug and fixings.

"Are you a student at the college?"

Cleveland looked surprised, "No, I'm a carpenter. I think I'm going to do some work over at the college, though."

"Oh," the boy looked disappointed. "I'm starting there this term. I want to be a teacher someday. Do you go to school somewhere?"

"No, I went to school until I was 10 but then my dad needed me to help him. He died when I was 15 and I had to take over the farm. My mother was a good teacher, though, and she continued to teach me about reading, writing, and math."

"That's good, everyone should know how to do those things," the young man extended his hand. "I'm Tad Crocker."

"Cleveland Taylor," he responded. "I live on the other side of Independence."

"I'm from Albany, but I've got a room with a nice family here in Monmouth."

"Do you and your mother come over here often?"

"My mother died this past spring, it's just me living on the farm. Well, me and my dog Cork."

"Oh, you have a dog?" Tad started to say something else but a gruff voice cut him off.

"Order ready," came the anonymous command.

Tad shrugged and disappeared into the kitchen for a moment. He came back with Cleveland's lunch. He put the food down and then left him alone while he waited on a couple other people who had just come into the café.

It only took Cleveland a few minutes to finish off the plate of food. Other customers came into the café, so he didn't have time to talk to Tad anymore except to say "thank you" when he paid his check. In moments, he was headed back to the college

Harve was waiting on the front steps for him. "Good news, Cleve," he said. "Whitson gave us the go-ahead. I have the things we need at the other site, so I want you to ride back with me and pick up what you need and haul them over. You can use the company wagon and then bring it back when you have unloaded everything. I think this might take two or three weeks so plan on showing up over here tomorrow. Since this is further for you to come, let's say you start at 8:00 a.m. and quit at 6:00 p.m. That way you'll be leaving home and getting back about the same time you do now. Whitson said you could work on that teacher's desk too. They have other student desks so they weren't worried about those."

Cleveland thanked the boss for being so considerate. By the end of the afternoon the wood and tools had been delivered to the school and things were in place to start work the following morning. Cleveland was a little surprised and more than a little pleased when Harve told Luke Sutton, the newest hired laborer, that he would be helping Cleveland on the school job. One of the journeymen carpenters would come in mid-week and check everything but otherwise, Cleveland was lead on this new site.

It turned out to be not so pleasant, though. Luke Sutton was only about thirty years old, but he was worn out. He'd tried his hand at mining in California before coming to Oregon. Nothing here had seemed to work out for him either. But in spite of how he looked—tall, thin and tired out—he was surprisingly strong, lifting boards into place with ease. Some of his problems caused Cleveland a lot of worry. Luke often came to work smelling of alcohol and in a foul mood. He swore constantly and flew off the handle when even the smallest of things went wrong. One time he narrowly missed hitting a window when he threw a hammer.

Cleveland knew Luke had a family, he'd seen his skinny wife and kids, three of them, come on Saturday when Luke and everyone else got paid. Nobody in that family ever smiled. They just sort of followed after Luke as they went to the store, bought a few things and went home. Cleveland had never seen them at his church or anywhere around town. He knew the job, or at least the pay, was important to Luke. He was torn about whether he should say something to Harve about the things Luke did while they were working. He felt obligated to help Luke because of his family, so he chose not to say anything.

But his resolve was for naught because the day Luke didn't come to work, Harve visited his house and found him too drunk to work. Also Luke's wife bore evidence of a beating at Luke's hand. Harve had no choice but to fire Luke. He gave the money Luke had coming to his wife.

That was the way Cleveland heard it the next day, from Truit Jens, the journeyman carpenter who came to help Cleveland finish the work. He'd heard, too, that Luke's wife took the mail boat to Portland that very day. When Luke finally came around sober he was frantic. He'd confronted Harve, who had to fire him all over again. When Luke found out Harve had given his wife his final pay, he flew in a rage. The deranged man had to be restrained after throwing several punches at Harve and threatening him with a gun. The county sheriff was sent for, and within hours Luke was locked up in the county jail for assault and attempted murder.

* * *

The work at the college went very well after Luke left. Truit was a quiet, hard working older man, just the opposite of what Luke had been to work with. Truit worked on the details of the doors and Cleveland worked on the floors, helping each other as needed. Two or three times a week Cleveland would go to the café to have lunch and visit with Tad. They had become friends over the bowls of soup or whatever the course of the day had been. It was nice to have someone his own age to talk to. In the evenings Cleveland worked on the teachers desk in his workshop at home. He had it done a few days before the work at the college was to be finished. He brought it in one morning when he came to work.

He had used the body of the original desk but had inlaid it with some new hardwood, repaired and added some drawers. Then he'd refinished the entire piece, sanded and varnished it. It looked better than new to Cleveland, and he hoped Mr. Whitson would think so, too.

He needed not have worried. Mr. Whitson was astonished and delighted when he saw the work. "My boy," he said with his hands on his face, "You are an artist."

Cleveland beamed, "I'm glad you like it, sir."

"Well, well," Mr. Whitson said thoughtfully, "You have created a problem with this desk, though."

"Sir?" Cleveland said, getting nervous.

"Well my boy, if I give this to one of the professors, they will all want one like this. That would cost the school a lot of money." He smiled, "So I think the only solution is I take this desk for my office and replace this one in the classroom with my old desk."

Cleveland felt relieved. "I guess that sounds like a good solution, Mr. Whitson."

Mr. Whitson laughed and walked off down the hall. Cleveland was pleased, it made him feel good to do things that other people liked. He hummed happily all day as he worked.

That turned out to be a good week for Cleveland. On Saturday he found himself staring at a two dollar bonus, his first ever, with his pay. If that hadn't been enough, his boss had made a big deal out of the work he'd done on the desk, saying that he was going to assign him cabinet making duties, which everyone knew was journeyman carpenter work. In a way without saying it in words, Cleveland had been promoted. No one else doubted now he was a man, now all he had to do was completely believe it himself.

* * *

Cleveland was slightly sad to see the work in Monmouth ending. He'd come to like having lunch and talking with Tad. Working with just Truit also had been pleasant. They got on fine and it made the days go by easy. Now they would be done in another day or two.

He hadn't thought once about Luke until that day when he showed up at the college. When Cleveland saw him his first thought was how changed he looked. He'd been forced to be off the liquor for three weeks. His color was better and he might have even gained a few pounds by eating regular. But his attitude had not changed.

"Did you tell old Bauer about my drinking, boy?" he yelled.

"No sir! I did not," Cleveland said honestly.

"Well, someone must have," Luke stamped his foot and shot a hostile look at Truit. The older man just scoffed and went on working.

"No one had to tell him, Luke," Cleveland said quietly. "He found that out for himself when he went to see why you didn't come to work. He thought maybe you were sick or some of your family was. He didn't know he'd find you drunk and your wife all beat up."

Luke's eyes narrowed, "Don't you talk like that, boy. I never hit my wife in my life. If she said I did, she's a liar."

Cleveland shrugged, "Well, what you do is your affair. What are you doing here anyway?"

Luke shifted his feet, "I don't know, just wanted to come by and see how the work was going." He looked around, "I haven't been able to find another job so it's been a little tough since I got out of jail. Bauer dropped the charges against me, so I suppose I should thank him for that," he snorted. "But firing me put a mark against me."

"You put that mark against yourself with your drinking, Sutton," Truit finally said. "Harve is a fair man. If you look, you'll find others who'll give you a chance. You just got to prove yourself again. We all do stupid things when we drink." He crossed the room and put his hand on Luke's shoulder, "That's why I don't drink anymore. Takes courage to step away from the bottle but if you really want to you have to make something else more important to yourself." Truit looked at Luke and then said softly, "You need to seek the Lord, my friend. That was my answer, faith in someone more powerful over demon rum than I was." Truit turned and walked back to where he was painting.

Luke looked at Cleveland and Truit. The anger seemed drained away, he had that worn out look about him again, like someone too tired to stand much longer. "I guess I'd best go."

Cleveland remembered the two dollar bonus he'd been carrying around for the last few days. He walked over to Luke, and took his hand and put the money into it. "Someday when you've got a job and your life is good again, you can look me up and pay this back to me. But now go into town to the restaurant and have a good meal. Take the ferry over to Salem and find yourself a room for the night, then get up and find work. One thing at a time. Just one thing at a time. Don't try to think about anything but the task at hand. That's how I got through my folks both dying when I was still wet behind the ears. You'll get through this, do what Truit says have faith."

Luke looked at the money then Cleveland. "How old are you boy? You sound like my father. He had a lot of faith, didn't get him much but an early grave in Missouri when I was 16."

"Was he a good man?"

Luke nodded, "Yeah, not like me."

"Why don't you give yourself a chance? Allow that you've made some mistakes that you're not going to make again. Truit's right: everyone makes bad deals sometimes."

Luke sighed, "I will pay this back. Thank you, Cleveland, I don't deserve your friendship and consideration, but thank you anyway." He held out his hand and smiled as Cleveland took it.

Nothing more was said. Cleveland walked to the door and watched as Luke walked towards town. Sadness seemed like a visible cloak over the man's slumped shoulders. Cleveland wanted to keep that memory of what a mess Luke had made out of his life by just a few wrong choices. He was a man now, and men could take simple seeming steps that would lead them to ruin. Life wasn't easy at best, one had always live with caution. His pa always had said on the wagon train to Oregon, they slept with one eye open and the rifle under the blanket. You had to be ready for anything. Cleveland felt like very little had changed except the nature of the enemy. It had been Indians, wild animals and robbers that worried the pioneers, now it was one's own self you had to watch out for. He wondered, in the end, which was more dangerous?

Late the next day Harve came by the college to take a look at the finished project with Truit and Cleveland. He looked around and smiled stiffly, complimenting both men on a job well done but the look on his face showed there was something else entirely on his mind.

He had some bad news. "There isn't any way to say this but out plain. Luke Sutton has been found, drowned, in the Willamette just south of Independence. He'd been drinking yesterday in a saloon in town and that was the last time anyone saw him." Harve shifted his weight from one foot to the other, obviously uncomfortable. "People say he might have tried to swim the river. I'd like to think he was just trying to sober up, or clean up, and accidently fell in," Harve said quietly. "He'd had a troubled life."

Cleveland and Truit looked at each other, "He was here yesterday and he said he thanked you for not pressing charges against him so they didn't keep him in jail," Cleveland said, trying to ease his boss's conflict.

Harve scoffed, "Well, I guess I didn't do him any favor. He'd be safe and alive sitting in jail if I hadn't tried to be a forgiving man. Lord, did that backfire!"

Cleveland thought about his bonus money. If he hadn't given it to Luke, the man wouldn't have had enough money to go to the saloon. Had it been his two dollars that really killed him? He could understand how Harve was feeling because he felt the same. But what do you do about it?

Truit stepped over and offered his hand to Harve, "You are a good man and Luke's death is not your fault. Sometimes you just can't help someone who can't find it in themselves to look for other ways out of their problems. Luke made his own choices. You did not put a bottle in his hand. He did."

Harve took the hand offered in friendship and support and nodded. He took a deep breath. "Well, that's all water under the bridge now. Pick up the tools here and get ready to take them back to the other work site. I'll get Whitson to sign off on the work and we'll be out of here. Can I buy you men pie and coffee before we head back?"

There was no argument with that. Life went on despite the hard times you had to go through. Cleveland had learned that lesson early in his experiences.

Chapter 9
Knoxville, Tennessee—August 1866

Zack took a detour so that he could arrive at Lydia's sister's home without having to pass through town. He'd been riding for four days and knew he probably looked like a hill country bumpkin. It occurred to him he should stop and tell the family about what was going on at home and about his moving his family west.

Roy Jackman, his brother-in-law, was clearing a stump from a field when Zack came into the lane that ended at the Jackman farm. "Hey Roy," Zack shouted, "It's me, Zack Grant."

Roy stopped his team of big plow horses and jumped down off the one he was sitting on and ran to the lane. After a hand shake and hug, Roy sent Zack on to the big two story white house while he finished with the stump. Zack offered to help, but Roy wouldn't hear of it, pushing him on toward the house.

Ellen, Lydia's sister, was standing on the porch as Zack rode up. "Zack Grant, what a surprise. You're all alone, though. Is there trouble? Where is Lydia?"

"She's fine, couldn't travel because she's having a baby soon," Zack said as he got down from his horse and tied it to the hitching post. He smiled as he noticed Ellen was also expecting. "Looks like that runs in the family."

Ellen blushed, "You'd think after three, we'd figure out what causes it and stop."

Zack laughed, "Well, it obviously agrees with you. You look just great." He walked over to Ellen and leaned down to kiss her on the cheek.

"Can you stay for awhile, Zack?" Ellen said as she opened the screen door into the house.

"Just maybe a night or two," Zack said dusting himself off a little. "I really am filthy. Could I wash up before I come into the house?"

Ellen pointed to the side of the house. "Got your choice. There's a wash basin on the back porch, or about 100 yards into the woods there's a creek for washing more than just your hands."

"I'm dirty enough for the creek. Might even wash my clothes while I'm at it."

"In that case, there's some good soap by the washstand you might want to take with you." She started in and called back to him, "I'll put a couple of towels on the back porch for you."

"Thanks Ellen," Zack called to her. He walked his horse over to the lean-to shed outside of the main barn and took the saddle off. He turned the animal loose in a small corral that had a watering trough. "I'll be back, boy, to take care of you. You just rest."

Zack found the soap and towels and headed off to the creek. It was a nice warm day so the creek felt cooly refreshing as Zack stripped down to bare skin. It wasn't a big amount of water running down the stream at this time of year, but he found a pool that came up to his chest if he was sitting down. He chased a crawdaddy away and lathered up. His hair took two washings to get the dust out of it. After a few minutes the clothes he had worn for four straight days got a taste of the soap. Zack laid the wet wash on the bushes around the creek and jumped back into the cool pool he'd chosen. He let the water take his weight and he half floated. It felt so good he nearly fell asleep. Finally the water's coolness was no longer as refreshing as it was cold. A shiver signaled it was time to get out.

Zack changed into his dry clothes and headed for the house. He could smell dinner already cooking as he opened the back door and went in. "That smells great, Ellen!"

Three children came running and hugging, nearly knocking Zack down. "Unka Zack," they shouted shrilly in unison. "Whoa kids let me sit down and then we can have a group hug."

Zack sat on the floor and hugged his two nephews, Toby and Virgil, and his niece, Darcy. A wave of remorse tore through him, thinking of his own child who would be born before he came back. For a moment he thought of turning around. He had to fight back tears as the children quickly lost interest in their uncle and went back to playing in other parts of the house.

Ellen came over and helped Zack to his feet, "Those three are a handful. But they are precious. You said that Liddy is expecting? When does she think it will come?" Ellen said.

Zack sat down at the eating table, "Don't know rightly, maybe early December."

Roy came in from the back porch at that moment, he had just washed his hands and face at the washstand outside. He walked over and patted Ellen on the stomach, which brought a big smile from Ellen. He laughed and came over and sat across from Zack.

"So what brings you to Knoxville?" Roy asked.

Zack took a deep breath and poured out the whole story. Roy and Ellen listened intently to what he was saying, nodding and looking at each other. When he was finished, Ellen got up and brought the coffee pot and mugs to the table. Roy poured each of them a cup of the strong black brew before he said anything.

"It ain't any different here Zack, I'm sorry to say." Roy said disgustedly.

Ellen shrugged, "We don't go into town anymore than we have to for that reason. I've read the local papers and they are all politics. Everybody seems so on edge. And the Yankees having troops here riles people. You never know when shots are going to whiz by your head."

"I don't set no store by those politicians," Roy scoffed. "They talk about fixing things but they don't fool nobody but themselves. They do whatever makes them rich. Like the railroads, the people who owned them can't even manage their own companies now. The government," Roy spit into the fire in contempt, "is going to think on that while they control the rails. I tell you, it's a real bad situation everywhere."

"People got nothing in a lot of places still. I know the war's been over for a year or better but folks whose homes or businesses were burned out by Yankees or, like us, by our own," Ellen sighed, "Just haven't got money or supplies enough to build their houses again or start their crops. Everyone is just able to do enough to scrape by. And then there's the scallywags coming in from everywhere to buy up land from desperate folks. Lordy, there's not a fleshy cow or sheep left on anyone's farm." Ellen shook her head. "This is more about people just never forgiving and forgetting."

Roy gave his wife a stern look, "How can you forget and forgive when they ain't asking you to forgive them and they don't want to forget anything?"

Ellen looked at Zack. "I guess some folks just move on then." She got up and went about finishing preparations for dinner.

Roy nodded, "I guess that might be one answer." He ran his hands through his hair and then rested his chin on his palms. "I took care of your horse Zack. Gave him some grain and put him into the pasture for awhile. He took a dust bath right away. Guess horses know when they're dirty, too."

"I sure knew I was. I turned your little creek out back as brown as spring run off."

Roy and Ellen laughed and the heaviness caused by their recent conversation seemed to lift. Zack went back to the creek before dinner and brought his almost dry clothes up to the house. Roy told him to hang them in the barn to finish drying. They had a cot in an empty stall for visitors to sleep in so that worked out well for Zack. He hung the clothes over the stall door and went to eat.

Ellen had fried chicken, grits, steamed collard greens and biscuits on the table by the time they all sat down. Roy said a quick grace then began dishing up the children's plates. There wasn't much talking during the beginning of the meal, as everyone was too busy eating. It was the first real meal Zack had since he left home. Not knowing what he might need money for later on, Zack had been just eating the things his mother and wife had packed but he'd run out that very morning.

Zack smacked his lips, "Ellen, you really know how to fry a fine chicken."

Roy laughed, "She'll do."

Ellen smiled proudly, "You want coffee now or after dinner, Zack?"

"After dinner would be fine," Zack replied.

Roy reached across the table and wiped little Toby's cheek which was covered in grits. "Boy, you got more of that on you than in you."

"Sorry, pappa," Toby said quietly.

Ellen got up and got a wet cloth to wash the child's face. "You pa is right, honey. But its all right. Everybody is messy sometime." She kissed her son as he excused himself from the table and headed outdoors. The other two Jackman children did the same. It was suddenly much quieter at the table.

Zack had one more piece of chicken before calling it quits. He sat back in his chair and patted his stomach. "That was a fine meal, Ellen. Thank you."

"You're welcome, brother-in-law," Ellen said with a curtsey. In a few moments Ellen had the table cleared and went contentedly about washing the dishes. She put on a big white apron over her dress and got two pans down. The wash water had been resting on the back of the stove as they ate and was just hot enough for her. She put half of the water in each of the pans, got the soap from the wash stand and began to hum as she made short work of the stack of plates.

Roy and Zack strolled out onto the front porch. There were a couple rockers and a bench to sit on. Zack took the bench and leaned back against the house. It was a pretty, soft evening, all sorts of purple, pinks and blues in the sky. The frogs, crickets and night birds filled the air with pleasant harmonies. Fireflies delighted the children who raced from one bug to another, trying to catch one.

The Jackman place was in the valley, not on a hillside down in a steep hollow like his place was so you could see for what seemed like miles across the cleared fields. "This was Ellen's family farm before you married. Did you have a place of your own?"

"My mother and father are still alive and on our home place. I got four older brothers, two of them live with the folks still. Both are married and have children, so there really isn't any reason for us to be there. When Ellen and Lydia's brother left, we just fell into taking care of the place, so I guess it's ours for working the property." He looked at Zack, "Does Liddy have a claim against the place?"

"No, no." Zack had never thought about that. "She'd never want to come here. She wasn't really happy with your step-mother and was glad to leave here. It's a mighty nice house though."

Roy laughed, "We thought it was huge when Liddy left and we only had two kids, now with three and another on the way, it don't seem big enough."

Zack snickered and thought about his own three room house. They would have had to add a room when their baby came, too. This house had four bedrooms upstairs and a parlor, kitchen, dining room and a storage room downstairs. That Liddy's family had once been quite wealthy was obvious. Now Roy worked like a man possessed just to keep it up.

Roy was quiet for a few moments and stopped rocking. Zack looked at him in the dim light of the evening, then smiled. Roy was snoring softly. Zack went out into the yard with the children putting his finger to his lips, "Quiet children. You can play until your ma calls you but do it quietly, your dad's taking a little nap. He worked hard today."

The youngsters did as they were told and played quietly until Ellen stepped out on the porch. She saw her husband sleeping and walked over and kissed him awake, then called the children. "Time for your baths and bed. Say goodnight to Uncle Zack and get in here."

A chorus of "goodnight Uncle Zack," rang out across the yard to where Zack sat on a stump.

"Goodnight children," he called back.

Roy stretched and stood up and walked over to Zack. "Sorry. I guess I dozed off. I'm getting to be an old man, can't stay awake long after dinner."

"You're not much older than me, so you're not an old man yet."

"I'll be twenty eight my next birthday. Seems old these days." Roy sighed.

"I feel old myself."

"Well, sun-up I got a whole field full of stumps to tackle. You can help, if you're planning to stay a day or two."

"I aim to leave in the morning after breakfast. I want to get to California before the winter sets in. I figure I'll either hire on to a wagon train out of Memphis or take the stage. I have no idea what that costs, do you?"

"No, I know it's running both ways now, the stage line from Memphis to California but I don't know what they charge for the ride." Roy rotated his shoulders and rubbed his neck. "I can't say I'd take that stage though, it goes right through Indian country. Apaches, I hear they do awful things to a man if they catch one."

Zack shuddered at that thought. "I reckon it's not so dangerous if they do that coach run twice a week. They couldn't keep it going if they were having that much trouble."

Roy shrugged, "It only takes one arrow in your gut."

Zack shook his head, "You really want me to stay and pull stumps, don't you?"

Roy smiled broadly, "I think we could get that one field done in three days."

"Okay, three days, but no more." Zack laughed.

Roy slapped Zack on the back, "Good to have your help." Then he walked into the house talking to Ellen in a voice loud enough for Zack to hear, "Honey, good news. Zack is going to stay until Friday and help me with the stumps. Isn't that great?"

* * *

Friday came quickly. At dawn that morning, Zack bathed in the creek and put on the freshly laundered clothes Ellen had laid out for him. She'd also washed all the clothes in his pack. "Never can tell how long you'll have to go before you find a place to wash clothes again. None of us have ever been further West than Knoxville 'cept Roy." That was true, nobody in Lydia's family or Zack's family had been past Knoxville. Roy had been to Nashville once as a boy but didn't remember much about it. All of the time Zack served in the confederate army he'd been in Georgia or Eastern Tennessee.

Ellen and the children stood on the porch as Zack finished packing his saddle bags. She insisted he take a bag of biscuits and jerky. "Never can tell how far it will be between places where you can hunt or find a meal.

Not much food in some places." She couldn't help the tear that slid down her cheek. "Be careful, Zack, watch out for ruffians, and write us will you?"

"I'll try to do that," Zack gave her a hug and shook hands with Roy. He knelt and hugged each of the unusually quiet children. Darcy started to cry and Zack stroked her hair as he picked her up, holding her for a moment before handing her to Roy. There wasn't anything else to say. He got on his horse and trotted slowly down the long lane to the main road. When he looked back for the last time the family had all gone on to the day's activities.

Zack turned around and looked at the rutted road that ran east and west before him. His gut ached and his stomach churned. East was his wife and own family. West was the unknown. Could it be better than what he knew lay to the east? Why was he really doing this? Was he a coward who ran from trouble? It took him five or six minutes before he could bring himself to decide what he was going to do. Slowly he turned the horse, taking him to a fast trot into whatever fate had in store for him. "God willing, this will be the right thing for everyone," he said out loud to the horse. "Come on boy, we got more than 2500 miles ahead of us."

Chapter 10
Independence, Oregon—August 1866

It was nearly a hundred degrees in the shade at four o'clock when the boss finally called it a day, "Boys it's hot…. Let's start again in the morning."

There was a general sigh of relief from the three men who had spent most of the day tarring, papering and hammering in that heat. One other man had started out with them, but he got a bad sunburn by noon and had to quit for the day. Cleveland's eyes ached from the glare of the intense sunlight.

Once they were all on the ground, everyone headed for the water bucket. It was nearly bone dry by the time they'd all had their fill.

"Hope it cools down soon. I can't see, the sweat's running in my eyes so bad," Truit said.

"You're getting old," one of the other men laughed.

"I must be getting old, too," Cleveland said before Truit had a chance for a comeback. "I've probably sweat off a couple pounds today alone."

"Well you work hard I have to say, young'un," the other man laughed again, then walked off towards his horse.

"Are you headed straight home, or do you have time for supper at my house," Truit asked Cleveland.

"I should go home, but if I'm not too long at your place I could eat with you." Cleveland's mouth watered at the thought of a home cooked meal. He ate regular but he wasn't much of a cook. "Is that going to be all right with your Missus?"

"Emma loves company! She always cooks like the boys were still at home." Truit spoke over his shoulder as he untied his horse from the hitch pole. "Follow me."

The two men walked along, leading their animals and talking. It was a pleasant walk, the mile or so to Truit's house near Ash Creek. His wife greeted her husband with a kiss on the cheek and when her husband introduced Cleveland, he got a quick peck too. Somehow it wasn't embarrassing. The men washed up outside while Emma hurried around inside to fix a meal.

Truit motioned to a table with benches under an oak tree at the back of his place. "We eat out here when it's so hot."

Emma came out of the house with a pitcher of lemonade and some glasses. "I put some ham on to fry and some potatoes. Should only be a few minutes." She smiled and went back into finish cooking the meal.

"You said you had boys?" Cleveland asked.

"Yep, Corbin and Truit Jr., a daughter too, Lillith."

"Do they live around here?"

"Well, Lillith married and lives in Oregon City. The boys both live east of Sacramento, went to do a little mining but stayed even when that didn't work out. Corbin's got a job in a bank and Truit Jr., well, he's a farm hand on a small place. He's always talking about going to Texas though. Probably will someday." Truit looked at his young friend, "You got any family?"

"Two living," Cleveland sipped at the tart lemonade, "Two sisters, both married. I have no idea where they are. Had two more sisters that died on the way out to Oregon in '53."

"Those were tough times, the wagon trains." Truit nodded. "My family came by boat into San Francisco and then came up from there. Not a pleasant trip, but I was only 9 so I thought it was a great adventure. We've been here in Oregon nearly 20 years now, came up when I got my certificate in ships' carpentry. Never went on a ship though." He laughed.

Emma came out of the house carrying a large tray. Truit jumped up to help, "Woman, you should of said something," he scolded her with a smile. "That's way too heavy for you."

Cleveland was struck by the tenderness he witnessed between the Truit and Emma. He realized that he'd forgotten that about his parents. They were hard working people, but they always cared about each other. There had been a soft, unspoken commitment between them that they would help and care for each other for as long as they lived. He sighed when he thought, "they just didn't live very long." Life didn't seem fair sometimes.

Emma sat down across from Cleveland next to her husband. She looked to be about the same age as Truit, slightly gray hair, wrinkles at her eyes and mouth but she was still remarkably beautiful with bright brown eyes, dusky skin and white, straight teeth. There was something in her face he couldn't quite identify but she was unique looking.

Emma bowed her head, "Would you say grace Cleveland?"

Cleveland's mouth fell open, he'd never been asked to do that before. He swallowed hard, "Lord, thank you for the food we are about to eat. Amen." He found himself sweating again just like he was on top of that roof.

Emma smiled, "Thank you." Then she handed him a plate and dished out a portion of food from the fry pan she'd brought out. She gave Truit about the same amount as she'd given Cleveland, and that left just a small amount for her. She sat a bowl of apricots on the table between them as well as a plate with thick slices of bread.

Cleveland looked at the food, it was a mix of ham, potatoes, beans held together with some sort of cheese. He carefully forked some and tasted it. To his delight it was wonderful. He made short work of two pieces of bread, three pieces of fruit and the mixture on his plate. "That was a mighty tasty dish, Ma'am." Cleveland said to Emma.

"That was something my mother used to make in California."

"Did you come on the same boat as your husband?"

Emma laughed, "No, I didn't. My people were already here."

Cleveland looked confused for a moment. Then he realized Emma was Indian. "What tribe are you from?"

"My early people were from a small tribe in Mexico, but we migrated into California and there my grandmother was married to a Spanish land owner. Then my mother married a Portuguese sailor. He didn't stay in California and couldn't take her with him. After I was born, she never saw him again. So I am Indian, Spanish and Portuguese, quite a mix?" She laughed.

"Well, I'm not as sure as you are about my ancestors," Truit laughed and patted his wife's hand, "But I'm sure there's not anyone as beautiful as you, my love."

"You flatterer!" Emma got up and gathered the dishes into a pile, "I'm going inside and do up these dishes."

The men smiled as they watched Emma go into the house. Truit turned to Cleveland, "You know it's a damnable shame that people round here don't take to that woman. There are a few people who are polite, but nobody really friendly."

Cleveland looked surprised, "Why is that? She seems like a very nice lady to me."

"It's not whether she's nice or not, it's that she's part Indian."

Cleveland nodded, "Guess there will always be that kind of folks who can't just let people be people. I was reading the Salem Oregon Journal the other day. There was a front page article where this guy was ranting on about the Democrats, calling them all sorts of names. Just a few weeks before that someone was calling the Republicans the same thing, or it was someone going on about colored people. I just don't understand it myself. If God created us all equal, why can't we accept that?"

"There's no power in being equal, son, and it's all about power. If you can control what rights people have by laws or social status then you got power, and that's worse than any drink a man can take. Wanting power will lead to the killing of your soul."

Cleveland sat back and thought on what Truit was saying. He listened to the sound of Emma stacking pans and dishes inside the house. How could anyone fault her just because her great grandmother had been an Indian? Who knew how many people in this town really had Indian or colored blood somewhere in their families? Did it really matter? Cleveland realized that he'd heard talk from some of the men on the job that now made sense and clearly told him where they stood. He vowed to himself to be careful around those men from now on. He might have to work with them but nothing else. One of the men went to the same church he did. How could he sit and listen to the sermons on brotherly love and acceptance, and then make jabs at Truit because of his wife? Thinking of that brought a sour taste to Cleveland's mouth, and he spit off towards the tree.

"Don't seem fair," Cleveland said quietly.

"Life isn't fair son, but you have to go on. You just got to choose your friends carefully." Truit smiled, "You're the first one I ever asked home to supper with us."

Cleveland smiled, "You may regret that. Emma's a powerful good cook and me being a bachelor, I might wear out my welcome."

Truit laughed out loud then called to Emma, "Hey woman, this young man thinks you're a pretty good cook. You want to prove him wrong? How about we have him over on Saturday after work?"

Emma leaned out the door, "Sounds good to me. Can I fix some spicy dishes?"

Truit shrugged and looked at Cleveland, "Ever have Mexican food?"

"Not that I know of but I would try it."

Truit smiled and responded to his wife, "He's game for it but maybe not too hot at first."

That made her laugh, "Okay, easy on the chili peppers. See you next Saturday, Cleveland." She closed the door.

Cleveland stood up and shook hands with Truit. "Thanks for asking me over, supper was real good. I look forward to dinner on Saturday too." He turned and untied Molly, then walked her to the edge of town before getting on. It was beginning to cool down a little, so the ride home was easier.

The minute they reached home Cleveland took Molly to the creek. He let her stand in the water and get a drink while he stripped down. He tied her to a nearby bush while he waded into the calf high water and sat down. Cork joined him but didn't come into the water, choosing instead to chase grasshoppers. The water was freezing initially but in moments felt nothing but refreshing. He immersed himself several times, then got his clothes and rinsed them out and draped them over the bushes. He felt a little foolish running for the house in his birthday suit, but he did it anyway.

He only put on pants, no shirt or shoes, then he went back and got Molly. She was happy to be free of the saddle and blanket. She rolled in the dirt for a few minutes before seeking out the shade of a tree. The General had slept through their homecoming.

After evening chores and a light supper of biscuits and gravy, Cork and Cleveland went back to the creek. Both of them sat in the cool water until it was almost dark. Cleveland gathered his clothes from the brush and put on his work shirt against the first evening breeze.

Cleveland and Cork sat on the porch as they liked to do in the evening. He waited until bed time before putting the stock in the barn. It had been so hot in the barn during the day that he wanted to let it cool off before suffering the animals to go in there. But he had learned the importance of putting a wall between them and the things that stalked the night. He'd heard of a man in Dallas, a Mister Staats, who'd shot more than ten bears and cougars, so they were around that was for sure.

About an hour or two after sunset Cleveland felt tired, so he and Cork made their trip to the barn and fetched the animals in. The General wanted his grain, Molly wanted to sleep. The cow and her half grown calf laid down and contentedly chewed on their cud. Everything seemed right with their little world, so Cleveland secured the pasture door and then the shutters over the glass less windows, then the main door.

Even Cork seemed done for the evening, she was waiting at the front door of the house to go in. She looked disappointed when Cleveland detoured for a stop at the necessary, but followed him up and over the little hill behind the garden.

In a few minutes they made their way back to the house. Cleveland left one of the windows open a few inches, one on either side of the house so they'd get the benefit of the night breeze. It was still hot in the house from the heat of the day so he didn't sleep in his usual long-johns. Instead he got the lightweight nightshirt he'd been given. It was hard to get used to at first, feeling the air moving about on his legs and under the garment next to his skin, but it was a lot cooler than his drawers had been. He fell asleep in no time, dreaming of eating Mexican food for the first time, wondering what chili peppers tasted like.

***

All week Cleveland found himself waiting for Saturday to come. When it finally did he was so excited about going to Truit's for dinner almost forgot to collect his pay. Harve chased him down just as he was getting on Molly and handed him the money. "Oh thanks, Mr. Bauer," Cleveland said, red faced.

Truit smiled and motioned for Cleveland to follow him. They both stopped at the store and picked up several things. Then they headed off towards the Jens home. Cleveland had to hold himself back, he had the urge to nudge Molly into a trot but Truit was just going at an easy pace. It only took a few minutes to reach the house.

Tonight they were eating inside since it was a much cooler day. The air was heady with aromas as they walked through the doorway. The room was unusually dark, there were only two large yellow candles burning in the center a table. It was hard to see much about the room, except it was fairly small with two small windows on either side of the front door and two on either side of the back door at the other end of the long narrow room. As his eyes adjusted to the dimness, he could see a wood stove and dry sink with cupboards by the back door.

The table was in the middle of the room. There were four large stools placed around it. There was a colorful table cloth on the table and bright pretty plates set for three people. The candlelight danced on the table. He'd never seen anything so fancy.

Emma came out of a room to the side of the big room and hugged her husband, then Cleveland. She was wearing an off the shoulder dress of pretty reds and pinks, looking like someone in a ladies magazine. She smelled of flowers somehow, and the feel of the skin of her neck pressing against his was a sensation he'd never felt before. Cleveland felt himself go hot in the face. He was grateful it was dim in the room so he could hide his embarrassment.

"Please, gentlemen, go wash up then come in and sit down. Supper is ready." She took the supplies that Truit had brought in and put them in the dry sink. The men dutifully made their way to the back porch where a wash basin and pitcher of water awaited them. Cleveland had noted the two or three big pots simmering on the stove as they passed. He couldn't imagine what was being served but it sure smelled inviting.

In moments they were back and, as instructed, sitting in anticipation. Emma didn't disappoint them. She brought several serving bowls and a tray of a flat bread to the table, then asked Truit to say the grace, which he did quietly.

"All right Cleveland, I hope that you like these," Emma handed a platter to Cleveland.

He hesitated a moment looking at the mound of something rolled in what looked like corn husks, carefully he lifted one onto his plate. It was surprisingly heavy. He handed the platter to Truit who took two or three. Cleveland watched as Truit opened a husk and scraped out a spoonful of the filling. Cleveland did the same. He couldn't believe how good the mixture of corn meal, meat and beans inside was. It was a little spicy but not bad. "This is wonderful, Emma," he said around a second mouthful.

"Those are tamales," she smiled and passed another item, "These are frijoles." She waited until Cleveland had taken a large serving and passed the bowl on. Then she handed him the last bowl, "And this is my version of fried chicken."

The spicy bean dish brought tears to Cleveland's eyes. Truit saw the reaction and got up to fetch a glass of water for him. "I guess you know what spicy means now huh, Cleve?" He laughed.

Cleveland gratefully accepted the water and downed half of it then and there. "Yes," he said half choked. "I surely do. It's good though."

He found the chicken easier to eat. It had been boned and rolled in flour with spices before being cooked and it was very good. "Never had chicken so tender," he remarked. "I'm making a chicken coop so I can have some chickens out at my place. Maybe you could tell me how to cook a bird this way."

"I'd love to," Emma beamed.

Everyone laughed and joked over the supper, lingering until the last bean was gone. Cleveland thanked them for the wonderful dinner and was pleased when they offered to make it a standing invitation for the first Saturday of every month. Cleveland didn't hesitate in accepting.

Happily he rode off towards his home. It wasn't until about an hour after bedtime that he realized just how spicy that meal had been. Cleveland spent a miserable night running between the house and the outhouse. On his last trip just before dawn he vowed never to eat spicy food again, no matter how good it might taste at the time.

The next day he didn't go to church and went back to bed after tending the stock. Cork was truly confused, but stayed quietly by his bed until just after noon, when a wagon pulled into the yard.

Cork's barking got Cleveland up and on the porch by the time the Porterfield wagon came to a stop in front of the house. He walked over next to their wagon.

"Morning, boy, we missed you at services this morning so thought we'd stop and see if you were all right."

"I am fine, just ate something that didn't agree with me."

"Are you sure you don't have food poisoning, son," Mrs. Porterfield said with concern. "Maybe you ought to see the doctor in town? We could take you."

"No, no nothing like that, it was just spicy Mexican food. Hadn't ever eaten any before and you know how I like to eat. Well, I just ate too much of it for a first time." Cleveland managed a little laugh and rubbed his stomach. "Worked better than any laxative I've ever heard about."

The Porterfields both laughed, "Well I guess that's something to remember if you ever need one again." Mr. Porterfield said.

"Where'd you get Mexican food," Mrs. Porterfield asked.

"Oh, I ate at the Jens' last night. I work with Truit and he invited me." Cleveland answered.

"She's an Indian woman, isn't she?" Mrs. Porter raised her eyebrows.

"Not really, more Spanish I think. Sure can cook that way, but boy, spicy." Cleveland rubbed his stomach again. "They're really nice people, both of them," Cleveland added for some reason.

"Well, you have some buttermilk, it will cure that right up." Mr. Porterfield said smiling. "You come over next Sunday for dinner at our house. It will agree with your stomach much better."

"Yes, dear boy, please come next Sunday. We haven't seen much of you for quite some time. And you be careful about what you eat," she hesitated for a moment, "And who you eat with." She reached down and touched his cheek. "I do miss your ma. I know you must get lonely here. Are you sure you don't want to come live with us?"

Cleveland stepped back from the wagon. "That's a right nice offer, Mrs. Porterfield. You know I like the two of you a lot. You are decent, God fearing people and I count myself lucky to have you as friends. But this is my farm, I work for a living and take care of it and myself. I am grown now, no matter what I look like or how old I am." He nodded and smiled, "I will come to supper next Sunday. Sounds really good, thank you."

"Okay then," Mr. Porterfield slapped the reins on the back of the horses pulling their wagon before Mrs. Porterfield could say anything else. She had to settle for a wave as they drove off.

Cleveland stood on the porch watching them go. He pondered about what Mrs. Porterfield had said about watching who he ate with. He'd never heard them talk about anyone in a negative way except folks who drank too much or put on airs, but how did they really feel about people of different cultures? It just never came up before. He shook his head and looked at Cork, "How do you really know what people are like? How do you know when to speak up and when to not? What's really important anyway? This being a grown up human being is harder than you'd think, dog."

Chapter 11
Nashville, Tennessee—End of August 1866

It had been a hard ride from Knoxville to Nashville. Two or three nasty thunderstorms had converted the easy going, hard packed roads to slippery primitive paths, riddled with mud holes. Wagons were stuck every few miles. Lending a helping hand caused him delays and a sore back. Zack found himself caked with mud every night it seemed. He'd stopped early several times to camp beside a stream so he could wash up and rinse out his clothes. The one little bar of soap he'd brought along was already gone so he used sand to clean himself. Sitting in the stream soothed his aching muscles. To make matters worse, two days before he reached Nashville he started coming down with a fever.

By the time he got to the railroad station, he had a full blown cold. He was grateful that he had money enough for a ticket for himself and the horse. The train was at the station already so he got his ride loaded into the stock car then found himself a seat in the back of a passenger car. It was noon but he didn't feel like getting out and buying something from the vendors that were on the train platform. He needed just to sit down. It was just a wooden bench but it was better than a saddle for him right now. He pulled his jacket up around his neck and within moments fell fast asleep. He was unaware of the train whistling or bumpy start. The train soon reached a rhythm that felt like a rocking chair just a little off kilter.

Zack slept for hours without moving. When he did awake, he realized it was dark outside.

Zack looked out of the window and could see they were stopped to take on water at some little station. The rail car was dimly lit by two gas lanterns, one at either end of the room. There were about six or seven other people in the car with him. There was a man and woman with three half grown children, an elderly couple, two men in business suits and two more who were in Union uniforms. Zack felt a twinge of anger but let that go, reminding himself that the war was over. He turned back to the window and watched the crew working outside.

Zack coughed several times, his nose was running too but in all he thought he felt better. The sleep seemed to be what he needed most. A porter came by with a pot of hot coffee and a jug of water. Zack opted for the coffee in hopes it would loosen the tightness in his chest a bit. It did seem to help. After the porter left the elderly woman came over and gave him a couple pieces of horehound drops to coat his throat. That helped, too. Soon he was asleep again.

When Zack opened his eyes again streaks of daylight were appearing over the trees on the horizon. He shook himself fully awake. He couldn't believe how much he'd slept. The train came to another stop for water and supplies, allowing the passengers the chance to use the toilets near the station. Zack felt a little unsteady on his feet at first but as he walked around a bit he found his strength returning. He still had a cold but he was much better. His cough was merely annoying now.

He felt very hungry, having not eaten anything but a biscuit and piece of jerky for breakfast the day before. There were two choices at the depot. A big woman with a dirty white apron was offering a meat pie and coffee for fifty cents, and an Indian man was selling smoked fish and flat bread for fifty cents. Seemed high to Zack but he was hungry. He looked at both of the sellers one last time before deciding. He thought the Indian man looked cleaner than the woman, so when he got back on the train he was having smoked fish and flat bread for his breakfast. It turned out to be a good choice. He'd never had better fish or bread.

Just before noon the train rolled into Memphis. Zack could hardly believe how much ground they'd covered in twelve hours. It had taken less time to get from Nashville to Memphis than getting to Knoxville had from home. He stepped off the train and got his horse.

The first order of business was to find a place to stay for a day or two while he figured out his next step. Memphis was bigger than any city he'd ever seen. He wandered a few blocks from the train station. There were hotels and saloons everywhere. Some looked pretty rough, so he decided to get away from central downtown.

At the edge of town he found a small boarding house that had a restaurant on the main floor and rooms on the upper floor. The elderly proprietor said for fifty cents a night he could have a private room, breakfast, and a bath, twice a week. It would be twenty five cents a night if he wanted to share a bed with another gentleman. The fifty cent room seemed reasonable to Zack.

After finding a nearby stable for his horse, Zack walked around a bit, looking for information about the stage or the wagon trains that were being assembled to go to California. As the day wore on Zack began to feel sick again so he returned to the boarding house. He decided he'd eat before he went up and lay down. It was too early for dinner, but the cook had chicken vegetable soup left from lunch that she willingly heated up for Zack. After two bowls of thick, rich soup Zack was ready for bed. He paid his bill and dragged himself up to his room.

He slipped off his shoes and his shirt but left his pants on over his longjohns. He was fast asleep in less than two minutes. He wasn't aware of anything until he awoke to someone gently stroking his forehead with something cool.

Zack tried to open his eyes but the light hurt. "Who are you?" He felt surprisingly weak.

"I'm Clara Frothman, remember me? I'm the landlady here. You're at my boarding house."

Zack tried to sit up, but was unable to. "What's the matter with me? What happened?"

"You've been really sick, Mr. Grant, we had the doctor out two days ago. Said you got pneumonia. You're on the mend now though, lots of rest and good food. Your fever broke yesterday, so you'll be right as rain soon."

"How long have I been here?"

"A week tomorrow." She helped him sit up enough for another pillow to be put behind his head. "Don't rush yourself, son," she eased him back on the pillow. "We've been taking good care of you. Miss Lambert, our cook, has been up twice a day giving you soup. My caretaker, old George Brown, has come in every evening and bathed you."

Zack forced his eyes open and looked at Clara Frothman, "I don't know how I can thank you all. I hadn't realized I was that sick."

"Well, you've run up a little bit of bill with us and the doctor but we'll work that out when you're well." She smiled, "That's what's important, young man, that you get well." She got up and opened the window a bit. "These rooms get a little stuffy when they aren't aired regular. Mind you we'll shut this before dark. Don't want you getting a chill and taking a turn." She left the room.

Zack moved his arms and legs. They were stiff and his body ached everywhere from inactivity. He willed himself to sit up on the edge of the bed. It was painful and his head spun but he was determined to make himself sit up as long as possible. That turned out to be only about five minutes. He was utterly exhausted when he flopped back down onto the pillows. In moments he was either asleep again or he had passed out, he wasn't aware of which.

When he woke up again he could tell he'd been bathed and put into a clean nightshirt because it was the middle of the night. How could this be happening to me, he thought. How indeed. He rolled over and slept the rest of the night.

In the morning when Mrs. Frothman came in she was surprised to see Zack dressed and sitting in the chair by the window. He smiled at her weakly, "I got this far."

"Are you sure you should be up? You look so pale, my dear."

He held up his hand and shrugged, "I really am much better. I think I'll stay in my room today but hopefully by tomorrow I'll be able to come downstairs. I have to check on my horse."

"I sent George over the day you got sick and they know you'll come when you can for him."

"You've been so kind, Mrs. Frothman," Zack felt close to tears, "I don't know how to thank you for your all you and your staff have done for me."

"It's just what good Christian folks do for one another," she looked around as if someone might be listening. "We southerners stick together. My husband and son both, God rest their souls, served under General Lee. I saw from the markings on your saddlebags you served The Cause too."

"Yes, ma'am, I did," Zack answered weakly.

Mrs. Frothman crossed over and kissed Zack on the top of his head, then left the room overcome by her memories and emotions. Minutes later the cook, Miss Lambert, arrived with some scrambled eggs and oatmeal. It tasted like heaven to Zack.

* * *

A week later Zack was finally well enough to continue on his journey. The only problem was his sick spell had set him back by costing half of the money he had with him. He no longer had the option of taking the stage to California. He was going to have to find a job to pay his way. After tearful good-byes at the boarding house, Zack headed into downtown Memphis to look for work.

There didn't seem to be any shortage of help wanted signs in saloons or hotels but he wanted a job that would take him west. He stopped two men in a huge hauling wagon that was just pulling out of a warehouse. "Excuse me gentlemen," he smiled, "do you know where a man might get a job on the trail to California or Oregon?"

The two men looked at each other and then at Zack, "Are you some sort of mind reader man?"

Zack looked surprised and confused, "What do you mean?"

"We was just talking about wishing we had someone to ride along with us for safety's sake. You can't have too many guns when you're guarding supplies."

"Does it pay?"

"Ten dollars a month and found."

"Sounds good to me. Where do you go?"

"We'll be working our way close to Independence, Missouri. Lots of wagon trains go through there so you'd probably be able to hook up with one of them." The older of the two men reached out a hand, "I'm Bill Zumwalt, this here's Ten Trees LaClair."

"Zack Grant," he shook with Bill. "Ten Trees?" He looked over at the blue eyed man with fair skin.

"His father and grandfather were both French Canadians and his mother was half French too. Makes him the whitest Indian you've ever met. Speaks French, English and German, plus a couple Indian languages, comes in mighty handy."

Zack nodded, sounded like an impressive young man. "Good to know you, Ten Trees," Zack tipped his hat, bringing a smile from him. "If you're offering me a job I'm of a mind to take it."

"Throw your saddle bags on the back there and lighten your load. We got a long way to go before dark." Bill snapped the reins against leads of the four mules pulling the wagon and they slowly began moving off. Zack quickly deposited his saddlebags and bedroll into the back of the wagon and fell into an easy lope behind them. He kept his rifle with him though, he understood what Bill was saying about safety. There were a lot of desperate people in these parts after the war and even more evil people than ever preying on the weak. A man just had to stay on guard.

Just before sundown, Bill pulled the wagon off the main road near a small stream. He moved the rig far enough up the creek as not to be seen from the main road. "This looks like a likely place to camp for the night," he said, motioning to Ten Trees.

Ten Trees jumped down from the wagon lightly and began unhitching the four horses. He walked them down to the creek and let them have a short drink. "Not to much yet, boys," he said as he pulled them back toward the wagon. He found a nice little meadow just a few yards beyond the camp site and tethered the animals so they could graze awhile. By the time he rejoined Bill and Zack, Bill had a small fire going and the coffee pot on.

Supper that night turned out to be rabbit stew. Ten Trees had killed the rabbit from twenty feet away with a rock as they had traveled earlier. He'd then jumped down, got the rabbit, gutted it and was back on the wagon in just minutes. Zack had never seen anything like that before. He'd made a mental note to ask him how he did that, and over their meal seemed like the time. "Ten Trees, if you don't mind me asking, how'd you hit that rabbit from the moving rig like that?"

"Practice," the young man laughed, "Used to do that from a pony when I was a kid. My father trapped animals all the time but I could kill almost any of them quicker with a rock. Used to drive him into a rage sometimes."

"Your father still hunting somewhere?"

Ten Trees shook his head, "No, died four years ago when I was about eighteen. My mother had died five or six years before that, so not much reason for me to stay in the mountains. I guess I could have gone to a reservation. Some of my mother's people wound up on one not far from here in Kansas. She was of the Fox Sac Nation."

"A reservation?" Zack pondered that a minute. "I've heard they are pretty rough places."

"Yeah, I heard that too," Ten Trees laughed, "Your 14th amendment freed the colereds and supposedly gave them rights but the Indians were not included in that." He shook his head, "We didn't understand white men and how ruthless they could be. We were like that rabbit in the stew, easy to knock off with a rock."

Bill waved his hand, "That's enough politics for tonight. Let's not sour the stew." He passed the coffee pot around and then settled back to enjoy his meal. Everyone did the same. Quickly it became apparent everyone was tired from the hard ride that day, they were all yawning within minutes of finishing their food. "Zack, you get your bedroll over there under that tree and," he pointed to a spot on the other side of the wagon, "You over there, Ten Trees. And I'll take under the wagon, just in case we get company during the night. We'll tie the horses on the back of the wagon here."

Zack got up and fetched his bedroll and put it where he was assigned and tied his horse nearby. "I got to go to the creek and wash off a little dust before turning in." He quickly got his towel and new bar of soap and headed downstream. In a few minutes he'd stripped to the waist and began washing himself. Up-stream he heard a soft splash and saw Ten

Trees sitting naked in the middle of the two foot deep water. "It's cold but great," Ten Trees said quietly. He splashed himself with the water then jumped out quickly, covering up with a spare blanket and heading back to the campfire. Zack finished his partial bath and joined the others at the campfire.

Bill assigned each of them a watch during the night. Zack took the first two hours. He sat close to the fire and found it very hard to stay awake. When it was finally time to let Ten Trees take over, Zack could hardly get to his bedroll before he was fast asleep. He was still in the same position when Bill gently shook his shoulder. "Time to break camp, Zack."

Zack sat up, surprised that the sun was nearly up. Bill had coffee made as well as some biscuits and gravy. "You've turned out to be a pretty good cook, Bill. Where did you pick up that skill?"

The older man laughed and smoothed his gray hair back before putting his hat on. "Well, I was married back in Maryland. Was for about 20 years. My wife was an invalid for the last seven years of her life. She'd been a right fine cook in her day before the accident. She'd fallen from her horse and broke her back. She'd sit in her chair and tell me what to mix, how to cook this and that. I think I must have done all right because she never complained about the results."

Zack watched Bill sip his coffee. He'd never thought about Lydia getting hurt and needing someone to care for her. He looked back in the direction he thought Tennessee might be and that ache in his gut returned. Again he had grave doubts about what he was doing.

Ten Trees took the cooking gear to the creek and rinsed everything off, drying them then on a questionable looking piece of cloth. Once everything was packed back in the wagon, they hitched the horses up and headed off again. Today they would make it to Osceola, Arkansas, according to Bill. It would be their first real stop. The river boats came up the Mississippi bringing trade goods, so they would pick up another load after dropping off the one they had.

The Mississippi was an impressive river to Zack. They took a ferry across to the west side and then drove on into town. It was another busy place, with saloons and hotels along the river. Bill had made this trip often so he knew just where he was going. They pulled into a big yard near a warehouse and Bill went to see the shipping clerk. In a few moments two husky men came out and began unloading the crates. They didn't ask for help from Zack or Ten Trees, so they just sat and watched. Bill came back out in a few minutes.

"Well, gentlemen, we have to wait until day after tomorrow to pick up our next load so I suggest we find a place for the horses and a nice rooming house for ourselves." He looked at Zack and then Ten Trees, "Just to be on the safe side there are a couple things we should and shouldn't do. Let's not mention your Indian connection Ten Trees, we'll just call you Ted LaClair while we're in these parts. I'm sorry, I know you aren't ashamed of your race. I'm not either, but there are hot heads that like to make life miserable so just to keep the peace let's let them think you're one hundred percent white. The other thing is not to flash any money around. We're just poor drifters like most everyone else here."

Ten Tree's face registered his disgust at the idea but then he shrugged and nodded his agreement. "Ted LaClair? Sounds like a New Englander to me. Should I have an accent?"

"Don't be cute, Ted," Bill said with a laugh. Then he looked at Zack, "You in?"

"I'm in," Zack said in agreement. He knew only too well people's attitudes about other races.

It didn't take long to find a place for them to stay in and a nearby livery to board the horses. The hotel for the men wasn't fancy but it was clean. Zack and "Ted" were to share a large double bed and Bill had a cot in the same room. When it actually came to sleeping though, Ten Trees preferred the floor in his bedroll. "No sense getting used to something soft when you just got to go sleep on the ground again."

Zack figured he was right but really enjoyed a bed when he could find one. There would be plenty of nights to sleep on the ground before he reached California or Oregon. He wasn't sure yet where he was going. His journey so far hadn't worked out exactly as he'd planned.

Zack took a walk around the city the next day. He stopped and had lunch in a café near the river. He had some beans with small sausages. It wasn't very good but he ate it anyway. After eating, he watched the steamboats on the river for awhile. It was strange to have leisure time, something he'd never really had before. He wrote a short letter to Lydia and mailed it in the post office in town before heading back to the rooming house.

The next morning they got their new load and were back on the road headed for the St. Francis River and Missouri. Zack felt like he and his young gelding were inching their way west instead of galloping there, as he had thought he would. He had no idea where all this was getting him, and doubt was his constant unseen companion.

Chapter 12
East Tennessee—Early September 1866

Lydia filled her days with work. It seemed to help the time pass and keep her mind off Zack. Sometimes she felt sad that he'd left, sometimes angry. She also found herself irritated at the baby. If she hadn't been pregnant she could have gone with Zack. Her emotions swung in lopsided circles nearly making her dizzy at times. It was not unusual to find tears running down her cheeks for no reason. It was a miserable time. Her back was hurting so carrying this baby, this huge baby. She had begun to have fears she would die trying to birth it.

On one bright morning Jonas and Rose had gone for supplies at the valley store. Lydia found riding in the wagon just too uncomfortable in her condition. She watched them drive off, then sat on the porch and had a good cry. When she could stop feeling sorry for herself, she went out back and picked the ripe squash. She took them to the underground root cellar near Jonas' cabin, and put them in corn husks to save for winter. Getting back up the steps into the cellar gave her more trouble than usual. After just one step, she had to go back down. It panicked her a bit to think she was all alone and might get stuck in a place like this. With a little more effort she made it out. "Guess that's the last time I go down there for awhile," she said out loud.

After airing her bedding and remaking her bed, she swept the main room and emptied hers and Rose's chamber pots. Neither of them liked to go to the outhouse in the dark. She scrubbed the containers and put them back in their cabinets. The chores seemed to take longer every day. In no time it was time for lunch. She wasn't very hungry so she just had a piece of bread with jam and a piece of cold ham, left over from breakfast.

Lydia got a cup of coffee and took it to the front porch. It was cool enough for a light shawl even though the sun was shining. The leafy trees had started their annual dance of color. Among the pines on the hill across from the farm were splotches of reds and yellows. It was a pretty time of year, but for all their beauty, the turning of the leaves was a sign that winter and hard times were coming. It was a kind of pleasure before pain time. She shuddered, thinking of the pain of having her baby. As if sensing she was thinking negatively about it, the baby kicked hard and moved in a jerky motion. Lydia shifted into a more comfortable position and the tossing stopped. Lydia warmed her hand with her coffee cup then gently massaged her stomach. The baby seemed to like that and she could feel it almost move toward her hand. "You little dickens, you already got me doing just what you want. You're just like your daddy." She sighed and looked out over the yard. "I wonder where your pa is now, sweetheart. He's only been gone a month and I already miss him like it's been a year." She sipped on her coffee. "Do you think he might get back before you come into the world, baby?" Shaking her head, she said, "Neither do I."

Lydia leaned back in the rocker and unintentionally dozed off. She dropped the coffee mug she was holding and it hit the porch with such a thud it woke her up. She cursed herself for being so clumsy. The coffee had splashed up on the edge of her dress, making a nice stain on her as well as a mess on the porch. She got the mop and cleaned up the porch. Her dress was another story. She only had one other workday dress and it was dirty, too. She'd planned to wash it the next day. She took water and rinsed out the stain as best she could. Hopeful that it would dry better than it looked at the moment, she was fanning the dress dry on the porch when Jonas and Rose returned.

Jonas brought the wagon up to the house and helped Rose down before taking the wagon to the barn. Rose hurried to the porch and looked at Lydia with concern. "What did you do, child? Your water didn't break, did it? It's too soon."

"No, Ma Rose," Lydia laughed, "I just spilled a cup of coffee all over me."

"Did you get burned, honey?"

"No, it was cold by that time. Tell the truth, I fell asleep in the rocker."

Rose sighed, relieved. "I have some good news for you my girl." She reached into her pocket and took out two small squares of paper. "You got two letters."

"From Zack?" Lydia squealed in excitement.

"One, and one from your sister Ellen I think." Rose handed the letters to Lydia who took them gently and walked to the rocker. Lydia just sat looking at the two letters in her lap. "Well, girl, aren't you going to see what they say?" Rose said impatiently.

Lydia looked at her, ready to be cross, but then she realized Rose was missing Zack as much as she was. They both needed to know what he had to say. Lydia opened the one from her sister first and started to read it aloud.

"Wait for me," Jonas yelled, running as quickly as he could across the front yard.

Lydia motioned to him, "Okay, hurry up." Once Jonas was on the porch he sat down on the top step and listened intently. Rose drew her rocker closer to Lydia. When they were all settled she began to read.

"My Dear Sister Liddy,

We had quite a surprise this week. Your man spent three days with us. He looked real good. Helped my Roy pull some stumps out of a field we're clearing. He tells me you are having a baby. That is so wonderful, sister. It is that I am too. Our 4th baby will be here by Christmas. After our baby is born, Roy will see about making a trip to see you. Times are a little hard here but we manage. We have kept the farm intact even though about once a week some carpetbagger comes by wanting to buy it. We still have several cows, a couple pigs, plus the horses, and chickens. The garden did pretty well this year, root cellar is full.

Zack told us about the trouble there. Things of that nature are not much different here. It is a troubled time. Zack left here for Nashville. I washed his clothes and sent jerky and biscuits with him for the road.

Said he would take the railroad train from there to Memphis then hoped to take the stage coach to California. Hope you are all safe. God bless you and yours.

Your loving sister,
Ellen"

"Well we know he got to Knoxville safe." Rose said, biting her lip and fighting back the tears. Lydia was not doing that well.

Lydia turned away and gulped back the tears. When she finally could breathe again, she took the other letter and carefully opened it.

"My darling wife and family,

I am in Nashville today, I just got my horse into the stock car and found a seat for myself. I got caught in a rainstorm on the way here and seem to have caught a cold but I'm all right. I miss all of you and have several times doubted my decision to do this. I have seen that the misery we are suffering is wide spread. There are lots of folks who had their houses, crops and even animals burned. They have nothing. Plenty of people on the road with all their belongings. It is kind of sad. The country is beautiful and even though it is hot during the days the nights are bearable. I have slept out most nights to save my money for the stage in Memphis.

I stopped in Knoxville and had a few pleasant days with Roy and Ellen and the children. Those kids made me realize what I am missing by not being there when our child is born. Forgive me my darling Liddy.

I will close and put this in the post box on the train platform before we leave in a few minutes.

I remain your loving husband, son and friend,
Zack"

Even Jonas was in tears by the last words of Zack's letter. "I miss that boy, but I am glad to know he's safe." He got up and walked toward the barn, shoulders drooping.

"Any of that coffee left, Liddy?" Rose asked.

Lydia swallowed hard, "I think so," she croaked. "I set it on the back of the stove so it should be hot still, maybe a little strong though." She got up and tested the front of her dress, "I guess I'm dry enough to try another cup." She managed a weak smile.

Rose got up and hugged her daughter-in-law for a full minute. The two of them stood, gaining strength from each other. The moment was ended by a sharp kick that even Rose felt. "Whoa," Rose laughed, "that baby is a jack rabbit."

"Sometimes I think he's trying to get out through my belly button." Lydia laughed as she rubbed her bulging stomach.

Rose studied her for a minute. "Child, I know you aren't due until sometime in December but I'd be real surprised if you went that long. You are getting so big. It ain't all that good to have too big a baby."

Lydia smiled bravely but she understood what Rose was worried about. Too big and the baby would be unable to be born. Death would take both of them. Lydia felt a bead of cold sweat run down her back. "I need that coffee now, too. It feels like it turned colder. Maybe we'll have an early snow?"

Rose looked at the valley. "The trees are turning color a little early this year. Even seen a couple trees losing leaves on the ride up the hill. You might be right, it might be an early snow this year." Rose motioned to Lydia, "You go in and get us a couple mugs. I got to see if Jonas is all right."

Lydia nodded and went inside. Rose walked off the porch and down to the barn. Jonas was brushing down one of the horses. "Jonas," Rose walked over to him, "You doing fine?" He nodded he was. "Good. Listen my friend, does Dr. Mitchell still come through the valley once a month?"

"I believe he does. The people at the store keep a list of who's ailing so he can visit them."

"Well, the next time you go to the store put us on the list. You can say it's me, my poor lungs, if you want but I really want to have him check

Lydia. That baby is going to be a big one and I think she might have trouble. Will you do that, Jonas?"

"You know, I think I forgot to get some extra coal oil for the lamps. I'd better go back down tomorrow." Jonas smiled.

"I think that's a right fine idea, sure wouldn't want to run short of coal oil." Rose hugged Jonas. "You're a saint, my friend."

"Easy to be a saint in the company of angels." He smiled.

"You old soft talker!" Rose slapped him playfully on the back and headed back for the porch where Lydia was waiting with the coffee.

"He okay?" Lydia said, concerned.

"He's fine, just getting old like me. He forgot to get extra coal oil so he's going back to the valley store tomorrow. He thinks you're right, we might get an early snow. Do you need anything at the store that you can think of? How about some calico to make a quilt for the baby? It would give us something to do in the evenings."

Lydia nodded, "that sounds like a fine idea. Maybe something in yellow since we don't know if it's going to be a boy or girl."

Rose nodded her agreement and smiled. Her little conspiracy was going to work out just fine.

* * *

Dr. Mitchell came to the farm about two weeks later. It was about midday when he arrived. Ominous clouds loomed over the valley, adding an air of worry to his visit. Lydia watched the tall, rough looking, old country doctor first examine Rose. First he listened to her chest, both in the front and in the back with his stethoscope. He stood thinking a moment and listened again. "Rose, I hear a slight rattle in your lungs. It's not serious yet but I'd recommend you avoid sitting to close too the wood stove and give up your pipe."

Rose stammered, "My pipe? I don't..."

"Yes you do, I can smell it on your clothes and on your breath. You'll be just fine if you give that up." Dr. Mitchell turned to Lydia. "Now let's take a look at you, young lady."

Lydia opened her mouth to object but Rose practically pushed her over to the doctor. "Let's have you lay on the couch here. I need to listen to your heart and your baby's." Lydia reluctantly did as he asked. She hadn't been to a doctor since she was a child in Knoxville. It somehow seemed indecent to have him running his hands over her body, even if he was a physician.

"This is a big baby," he said as he felt the movements just below Lydia's skin. He put the cold hearing devise under Lydia's blouse and listened. He lifted her skirt and found the top of her under slip pulling it down to expose her extended abdomen. Lydia squirmed uncomfortably.

Rose took Lydia's hand as the doctor first put the scope on one side of her belly then the other. Several times he went back and forth, thought a minute and then repeated his route. Finally he pulled up her under garment and helped her to sit up. Rose and Lydia clung to each other, fearful of what the doctor might say.

"Well," he said slowly, "you are in good health. Your eyes are clear, so are your lungs. Your heart seems young and strong. You obviously don't smoke a pipe." He gave an accusing look at Rose. "However, I am concerned about you and your baby." He hesitated, then smiled. "Actually, I believe it would more correct to say "babies" my dear. I am sure you are having twins."

Rose gasp and Lydia went pale. They looked at each other in stunned silence. "Are there any twins in either of your families?" the doctor asked.

Rose shrugged, "My husband had a twin brother who died right after they were born. I hadn't even remembered that."

"Well it does tend to run in families." The doctor put his tools away. "One thing this does mean is that you will probably not go to full term with them. That poses some health risks for your babies. What I want you to do is send for me when your pass your water. I might not make it for the birth but I'll be here as soon as possible to make sure the babies are healthy." He reached over and touched Lydia's cheek, "And you too, young lady." He prepared to leave. "They have a telegraph now at the valley store so you can have them send me a message."

Just before he went out the door he turned to Rose, "No pipe!"

Rose laughed and shrugged. The two women followed the doctor out on the porch and watched him as he drove his little rig down their road.

Jonas came to the house just as the doctor went around the bend. "Well ladies, what's the verdict?"

Lydia hugged Jonas and then Rose, tears were in her eyes again. "Are you all right, Miss Liddy?" Jonas asked quickly.

"Well, yes and no. I thought I was having one awful big baby, but what I'm really having is two regular sized ones. You're going to have to add baby tending to your list of chores, Jonas. This will be more than Rose and I can handle alone."

"Lord have mercy," Jonas said, putting his hands on his cheeks. "I can't believe it. We're going to have two babies running round the place!"

Rose laughed, locking arms with Jonas and dancing around. "I'm going to be a double grandma! I always wanted a lot of grandchildren, just didn't know they'd come two at the same time."

Lydia sat down in her rocker feeling joy, excitement and fear all rolled into a swirling mass of emotions. Rose and Jonas whooped around on the porch in delight. They were all brought back to reality in an instant when the heavens opened up and it started to pour. Thunder reverberated off the hillside and lightning lit up the sky. Everyone went inside to wait out the storm and hope that the bolts wouldn't hit the house or barn. Fall storms could be deadly.

Chapter 13
Polk County, Oregon—September 1866

It had rained a little, early on in the month but then it turned mild and dry. This was Cleveland's favorite time of year. The vine maple turned all sort of oranges, the poplars silvery yellow and the sweet gum danced in shades of red. The rich green of fir and spruce made dramatic backgrounds for the spectacular display. There was also a freshness to the air. Every breath just invigorated a person, especially a young man in his prime.

Cleveland had been working on a house in Independence for the last two weeks and was glad his part was finished. It was a three story home for a wealthy businessman and his family. The fellow was an unpleasant sort and made all kinds of demands. He'd often criticize the work being done, no matter who was doing it. But more often than not, he would question Cleveland's work. Harve reassured him over and over again that even though he was young, Cleveland was the best carpenter he'd ever hired on.

On the day they drew their pay, Harve told them he didn't have another project lined up yet, but as soon as he did he'd send word to each of them. There was some grumbling but not from Cleveland. He'd worked steadily all summer, except for one week between houses. He had enough money saved for at least a couple months, if need be, so he wasn't too worried.

When Monday came he felt a little strange staying home but he had a project or two in the workshop. He'd decided to make a chair for the Porterfields as a Christmas present. He also wanted to finish his chicken coop.

Truit had given him some scraps of really nice walnut wood. It was enough, Cleveland figured, for a smaller version of the rocker he'd made for himself. He smiled as he thought how Mrs. Porterfield would like that. He'd all but forgotten the questions in his mind about her attitude about other people. He'd had dinner with them since then and nothing more had been said.

Cork chased squirrels in the pasture while Cleveland sawed and banged around in the shed. She came back to help when he started digging holes for the posts around the chicken coop. "Girl, you are just not helping me," Cleveland laughed, pushing the dog back out of the pit he'd just dug.

"We're not chasing gophers this time."

Cork acted insulted that he wouldn't let her dig. With a great sigh she went and lay down on the porch, never once taking her eyes off Cleveland. Finally the tactic worked and Cleveland gave in. He picked up a stick and threw it across the yard. With a happy bark she dashed after the prey. Several more tosses finally made her happy and she went back to chasing squirrels, butterflies, mice or grasshoppers. If it moved, she chased it.

Cleveland laughed at her antics as he dug, "Thank you Lord for that dog. She does keep my spirits up."

It took the morning and half the afternoon to get six of the ten post holes he thought he needed for a twelve foot by twelve foot yard for the chickens. He'd finished the chicken coop, so all he needed was to fence the area now. "Oh yes," he said out loud, "I got to get some chickens and find out how to raise them."

"Talking to yourself nowadays, Cleve?" a familiar voice surprised him.

"I didn't even hear you come up, Tad," he said offering his friend his hand. "I was so intent on getting this done."

"I let my horse into the pasture at the far end and walked in so that's why you didn't hear me," he said. "Hope that was all right?"

"Of course it is." Cleveland dusted himself off a little, intending to stop working but before he could Tad took off his jacket and shirt.

Tad picked up a shovel and looked around. "Where do you want the next hole?"

Cleveland laughed and marked off the remaining holes. By suppertime all the holes were done and the posts in solidly. "Can't thank you enough for helping with this, Tad." Cleveland said as the two of them washed up by the back door of the house. "What brought you out here today? I can't imagine you were just looking for work."

Tad wiped his face and hands dry on a rough towel and smiled with a shrug. "I came to tell you that I'm leaving. My dad lost his job last week and just can't afford the tuition for me to go to school after all. And at the same time a small miracle happened. My Grandfather died in the spring. We didn't know he even had anything to leave anyone but my father got a fair amount of money, so he wants to use it to open a little grocery store and wants me to come help get it established." He looked down at his feet, and sighed. "I have to go."

"Well, Albany's not that far, I could probably come see you sometimes and you could come visit me too."

Tad shook his head, "My folks want to move to where they have more friends and family. It's been rough for them the whole time we've lived in Oregon. My father's not a farmer, he's been a shop keeper all his life. He was working in a grocery store in Albany, but he didn't like the people he worked for."

"You were born in Missouri weren't you?"

"Yes, I was, but my father and mother lived in San Francisco before here and that's where they want to go."

"Oh," Cleveland said, trying to keep the disappointment he felt to himself. "I've heard that's a right interesting place. My oldest sister and her husband went to California after they were married, my ma told me."

"I did want to finish school here though," Tad sat down on the porch. "I'd hoped that I'd have a career of some sort, maybe be a teacher."

"I imagine they'll have schools there, won't they?"

"I suppose," Tad nodded.

They sat in silence for a few minutes. "You want some biscuits and gravy? That's about the only thing I really cook good enough for company to eat."

Tad laughed, "No, I got to get back to the boarding house. I've got to be out first thing in the morning so I have to pack my bag. Can't take my books on my horse so I brought them over for you." He pointed to a small satchel lying on the ground by the fence.

"I don't know if I can read college books," Cleveland said in half protest.

"Sure you can, you are one of the brightest guys I know. Probably could be a teacher yourself." Tad said as he jumped up and ran over to fetch the books back to the porch. "There's only three of them. One on penmanship, one on mathematics and one is a novel we were to read and make a report on, *Moby Dick*. I'd started to read it but won't be able to finish it now. You'll like it though, it's about whalers on a tall sailing ship."

Cleveland smiled, "Thank you Tad," he took the books and looked at them. "I'll keep them for you just until you get settled and send for them."

"All right," Tad smiled, "but they are yours. Get rid of them if they get in your way."

Cleveland walked his friend to the pasture gate and helped him saddle his horse again. Then they walked together to the main road. They shook hands again, then after a moment hugged like brothers. Neither could say the fatal sounding words of good-bye so they didn't. Cleveland stood watching Tad ride up the hill towards Monmouth. That old feeling of loss swept over him again. He'd lost so many people already in his young life.

Cork sensed his mood and didn't insist on playing anymore that day. She was content just to stay beside him as he worked through his grief, one more time. She gratefully shared his plate of biscuits and gravy, seeming to enjoy it more than he did. They walked through the evening chores together then Cleveland built the night's fire in the fireplace. The dog sighed and settled in on the braided rug in front of the fire, watching her young master thumb through the newly acquired books. Occasionally something would catch his interest and her ears would go up but then he'd go on and she would relax again. Finally he laid down on his bed and fell asleep. She then did the same.

* * *

It was just four days later when Cleveland's friend Truit rode into the yard in his old heavy farm wagon. He had a load of assorted pieces of finished wood besides firewood in the box. "Howdy Cleve," he called as soon as he was within earshot.

"Truit, good to see you." Cleveland said.

Truit climbed down off the wagon and shook Cleveland's hand. Cork bounced up and licked the visitor's face then ran off to play. "How about some coffee?" Cleveland offered.

"Sounds good, kind of nippy on the ride out." Truit dusted himself off a bit as they headed into the house.

Cleveland poured two mugs of the strong black liquid and the men sat down at the eating table. "This a table you made?" Truit asked as he ran his hand along the smooth top of the wood. "It's a beauty."

"No, my father made this and the chairs." He pointed with pride across the room, "He made that sitting bench." Then added after a sip of his coffee, "I did make that chair there though." He nodded toward the chair by the fireplace.

"That's right handsome, too," Truit nodded.

"So, my friend, what brings you out here? Did Harve find us another job?"

"Well, I did hear he was offering a bid on a project but that's not official yet. No, I came out to bring you some lumber and more firewood."

Cleveland was a little confused, "That's mighty nice of you. But aren't you going to need those things?"

"Well me and the Missus are thinking of pulling up stakes and heading back to California. She got a letter from her people and they've got a place for us if we'd come. She's missed them a lot, and I think that it would be good for her." He looked down sadly, "Especially now."

Cleveland's eyes widened, "What do you mean especially now?"

Truit looked at Cleveland and managed a slight smile, "You know I told you that I used to live quite a different life. I was a bit of a hell-raiser if you want it put straight. Well, seems maybe that's all catching up with me. The doc in town tells me that I got a bad heart and maybe even something wrong with my liver. He thinks I'm going to have to take it easier from now on."

"So what are you thinking?"

"Well, first off we'll move down close to the boys so they can help us around the place. Then should something happen to me, Emma has two sisters and three brothers still living in the San Diego area so she won't be alone. We don't have many friends here, only you and Harve. Seems like the thing to do." He sighed and finished his coffee.

"So when are you planning to leave?"

"Within the week. We got to go before it snows on the passes. Can't trust them Siskiyou mountains after mid-October to be clear of snow, so we will go soon."

Cleveland felt overwhelmed. He had already lost Tad, now in the same week we was losing other friends to California. "Well, I hope that turns out to be a good thing for you." His stomach was turning as fast as his mind was whirling.

Truit shrugged, "I am sure it will be." He got up and walked to the door, "Let's get that wood off the wagon for you."

It only took a few minutes to stack the lumber in the workshop and the wood with the pile that Cleveland had already begun amassing for winter. They sat down on the porch for a moment when they finished the work. Truit was clearly out of breath and tired. Cleveland had seen that more and more lately on the job but hadn't realized his friend was really ill. He felt nauseated that he hadn't recognized the danger Truit had been in. It had been a heart attack that took his own father.

For the second time in a short span of days Cleveland stood at the end of his property waving good-bye to a friend. He couldn't help the tears that came uninvited.

* * *

Friday, Harve sent Butch McCready, one of the day laborers, out to tell him to report for work on Monday in town. "We're going to work on building a store front for a new shop in town." Butch said with a laugh, "I think it's going to be a shop for ladies hats."

Cleveland looked at the small, rough man in his mid-thirties. He had teeth missing but it didn't stop him from smiling ear to ear. He was a happy go lucky type of guy, made lots of mistakes but everyone liked him in spite of it. He was married to a minister's daughter and they had two sons both in their teens, probably about Cleveland's age but they always seemed younger because they were so unruly. They were very much like their dad, a nice guy, just different. It perplexed Cleveland that some people could be tolerated well even if they were different and others couldn't. The world didn't seem too fair at times. He could remember his mother saying, "Son, the world isn't fair but you just got to remember what God wants each of us to do, to do justly, love mercy and walk humbly with Him. When we look down on another for any reason we are putting ourselves above God who loves everyone." He was proud his momma taught him well.

Butch didn't stay any longer than it took to let Cleveland know of the coming week's work. He and his tired sway back horse were gone from sight in just a few minutes. Cleveland wondered who would be the head carpenter now. Truit had been, he knew two others who worked off and on for Harve, but neither of them were half as good as Truit.

* * *

On Monday Cleveland was in for a big surprise. At the work site Harve gathered all the men around, all five of them working on this particular building. He went over the general plans and began making the assignments of work to be done. He looked at each of them and then at Cleveland, "and Cleveland will be the lead carpenter." Harve looked at the face of each man. "I know he's young but he really knows his work. Is there anyone here who will have a problem taking directions from him or going to him for help?"

Each of the men looked at Cleveland and smiled, "No problem," was the chorus they all sang.

"Well then, let's get to work." Harve said and handed the plans to Cleveland, "Let's get this building up this week."

Cleveland swallowed hard and took the papers from his boss. "Okay, let's do it," he said trying to sound confident when his knees were shaking so hard he wondered if he'd be able to walk.

Within minutes the crew had fallen into the routine of the work. Cleveland smiled as he realized what an honor he'd been given. True, this was a small two room, one story, building but it might as well be a castle for the way Cleveland felt. He vowed to himself that this building would be the prettiest and strongest in town.

Chapter 14
Missouri Territory—Early October 1866

The travel had been fairly easy but the work tedious to Zack. Each little town site they visited seemed to blend into each other after a few days. Sometimes they'd pick up horse shoes, wagon rims or apples, sometimes they'd drop off supplies of pine soap, blankets or yard goods. There didn't seem to be any end to the variety of things to haul. Many times Zack had no idea where they were. After they had left Osceola, the trio had meandered through the Arkansas countryside to the St. Francis River. Then they followed it north, veering off to small townships and isolated stores along the route. The only really good thing about the trip so far was that the three of them got on well together.

They were within a day of the Four Mile Settlement at Chalk Bluff when a broken wheel caused some problems for them. It took more than three hours to fix, and by that time it was close to supper time. Since they were all tired, they decided to call it a day. The area was heavily wooded with willows and birch trees. The road ran along a small stream at the bottom of a fairly steep, narrow valley. They found a likely looking spot and pulled the wagon off the main road. Zack took his horse and started up a gully to look for some fresh game while Ten Trees and Bill set up camp. Zack hadn't gone too far when he heard the sounds of other horses coming. Just to be safe, he moved around to the top of the ridge where he could see who was nearing where they'd pulled off. Two riders came into view riding very slowly. They were looking around. One waved, and then Zack saw the third rider hanging back in the shadows. The first two cautiously made their way to where Ten Trees and Bill were.

The men at the camp site had been caught off guard and were nowhere near their rifles. Zack could see the third man get off his horse and move, hand gun drawn, into the trees just below him. Without a sound, Zack got down off his horse and quickly followed the fellow. In a moment a well placed rock took the threat from that man out of the mix. After tying the man up with his own belt, Zack went back and got his horse and went around to the road.

He let his horse gallop as to assure being heard. Zack put on a little act for the benefit of the two unknown men. "Hello the campfire," he called from the road. "Got a little coffee you'd share with a traveler?"

Bill caught on immediately. "Sure, stranger, come on in. We just got two other visitors here too."

Zack had his rifle laying across his arms as he came in cautiously. The men were still on their horses so Zack didn't get down either. The man closest to him was a rough looking red-headed fellow in his early forties with a full beard. He sat atop a beautiful Palomino horse with a long, flowing white tail. Zack knew horses and that was an expensive one. He wondered about how this fellow came to have the animal. The other man was younger, maybe even the other's son, he just sat slouched in his saddle silently. Both men looked like they hadn't had a bath in months. Zack noticed the young one glancing towards the hillside once or twice. Zack smiled to himself, the help they were expecting would not be coming. "You wouldn't happen to have a bandage. I cut myself earlier today when I was hitting a critter with a rock," he asked Bill, still playing the game and trying to create a little diversion.

Bill nodded to Ten Trees who silently moved off into the wagon as Bill walked over to Zack, "You better let me have a look at that son. Some cuts can go septic in a hurry."

Zack leaned over and offered his hand to Bill who looked at the hand first then reached behind Zack and took the pistol Bill knew would be there. At the same time Ten Trees appeared at the back of the wagon with his rifle in hand. "You gentlemen want to step down from your horses or do you want to ride on?" he said calmly.

"Now, that's no way to treat strangers, son," the red head said in a menacing tone.

The younger man looked at the hillside again, Zack followed his gaze and then smiled. "If you're waiting for the fellow on the hill I'm afraid you'll be disappointed. He had a little accident and won't be joining us for dinner."

The red headed man jerked his head around in surprise and anger, "You kill him? That's my other boy."

"No, I didn't kill him but he may have a headache. He's tied up there until we get things settled here."

Bill aimed his gun at the redhead, "So this was to be a bushwhack, huh?" He laughed, "You'd been mighty disappointed, I'm afraid. All we got on the wagon right now is nails and tar paper. We're headed to Greenville where they're building a church."

The red headed man scoffed, "We were not planning a robbery. We just wanted some food and company."

"Didn't look that way with that boy in the woods with a gun."

Bill pointed up the hill and motioned to the younger man, "Go get the boy. Is that your brother?" The young man nodded as he slipped off his horse and ran up the hill.

In just a few minutes the young man called out, "I found Jacob, Pa. He's alright." Within minutes the two were back at the campsite. In the light of the campfire, Zack could see that the one he'd hit was young, too, no more than fifteen or sixteen. He felt a little bad about hitting him but then reconsidered. If he was old enough to hold a gun and sneak up on people he was accountable for what happened.

Bill looked at the trio and then walked over and put some biscuits and a few pieces of jerky in a sack. "If you truly are only hungry this will get you to Four Mile Settlement. It shouldn't be far down the road. As for the company, you won't find any here. So move on."

The older man glared, "I thank you for the food. But should we meet again, you best be wary of me. I don't forget when someone's hurt one of my boys." He whirled the horse around and his sons fell quickly into step behind him. Before they reached the main road the old man threw the bag with the food into the brush.

Ten Trees ran and fetched the still full sack of food. "So much for just wanting food." He said disgustedly when he came back to the fire. "That was an all fired lie. They were robbers."

Ten Trees walked over and slapped Zack on the back, "That was good. You really knew what to do."

Bill nodded and sat down by the fire. "How'd you catch that boy on the hill? We didn't hear a thing."

"Anyone in Tennessee can hit a squirrel's head with a rock from thirty feet, a man's noggin is a much bigger target." Zack laughed.

"Well, I said it before and I'll say it again," Bill said as he handed out the coffee mugs, "It's good to have you with us on this run, Zack."

"This sort of thing happen often?" Zack asked.

Ten Trees smiled, "Not often, usually no more than once or twice a year."

Zack sighed. "Oh."

They all laughed, but Zack had learned something that unnerved him that night. Just when things seem peaceful it can turn in an instant. It was like he was back in the war. You never knew what tree might be shielding an enemy just waiting for the chance to kill you. Zack felt that cold fear and anger return. It galled him that even as a child, he never was afraid sleeping in the woods even though there might be bears and wild cats. Nothing in nature was really to be feared as much as his fellow man. Animals were much more likely to leave you alone if you were careful. People, on the other hand, would kill another person just because of the way they looked or what they thought.

That night Bill doubled the watch and only one of them slept at a time. Even at that, Zack had a hard time really sleeping.

* * *

It was late in the afternoon when they reached The Four Mile Settlement. It had been raining so the travel that day had been pretty miserable. They reached the general store just an hour before they were to close. Joe Tonne, the owner, greeted them heartily and helped them unload the items they had for him.

"Run into any trouble on the run? We kind of expected you a couple days ago." Joe asked once they were done.

"The roads were pretty bad today and yesterday we had trouble with a wheel." Bill said then shrugged. "We also had a little incident yesterday with a man and his sons. Thought they might be trying to rob us. They acted mighty suspicious like."

"A man with red hair?" Joe asked quietly.

Bill's eyebrows went up. "You know of him and his boys?"

"We've heard there was someone with a young boy raiding farms here about. They stole a prize horse from one of the more wealthy farms."

"Was it a palomino?" Ten Trees asked.

"Yes I think it was, pretty gold colored horse with a long white tail." Joe nodded.

"That was him," Bill said, "The boys looked to be his sons."

"Well, seems you were lucky fellows, they shot the man they stole the horse from. They might well have shot you, too, for the goods in your wagon."

Bill smiled and pointed at Zack. "We got us this new escort. He did a right good job of controlling the situation. He got the upper hand right from the start."

Zack was embarrassed for being singled out. "We all took care of ourselves."

"It's closing time, men. Are you staying in town tonight? They serve a good steak over at Martha's Café. I'd be happy to treat you all to a good dinner."

Bill looked at the other two, "Well, that sounds like a great offer. I think we could be persuaded to stay for that. We'll go find a place to put up our horses and wagon. Is there a good hotel?"

"Don't know how good it is but there's one at the end of the street. The livery is just beyond that a quarter of a mile. Martha's is just across the street from here. Why don't I meet you boys over there, in say an hour?"

Bill shook Joe's hand and they headed out. Everything was just where Joe said it would be. The hotel was old but seemed clean. Again Bill got one big room for the three of them. It had bunk beds on both sides of the room, so each of them would have a bed of their own. Other than the bunks it had a wash stand with a pitcher and basin but no chamber pot. The owner had mentioned the outhouse was out the back and to the left. He also said that the back door was left unlocked at night for the convenience of the guests, so he advised to be sure and lock the room door.

The livery stable was one of the biggest Zack had ever seen. Instead of just stalls for animals, they practically had rooms. It was easy to put the wagon in a big stall and lock the gate to it. Bill felt safer doing that than any place he'd put the wagon before. The mules got to stay all together in another big stall. Zack's horse even got a big stall of his own. Luxury even for the animals.

Dinner turned out to be more than they'd expected, too. Martha, the owner and cook, was a real knockout. She was probably forty but still beautiful. She had flowing blond hair that she twisted up into a large bun on the top of her head and held there with a Spanish pin. Her eyes were deep blue and her smile revealed perfect teeth. Even in her big cook's apron, it was obvious that she had an amazing full figure. Zack smiled as he watched Bill's eyes follow Martha around the room as she served meals to the six or seven other people in the room. Zack and Ten Trees enjoyed the tender beef roast and potatoes, but it seemed Bill wasn't even aware he was eating.

"So how's the food?" Joe said around a mouthful. "I come here at least once a week. My wife can't cook worth a bean."

Bill looked at Joe, "I didn't know you were married, Joe. You never mentioned that before."

"Yeah, I've been married about fifteen years now. Got five kids, Rachel six, Becca nine, Lissy ten, Jane eleven and Alice thirteen. It's a lot more work having girls. Always got to be watching out for them, keep them safe especially as they get a little older."

Zack laughed, "All girls?" He sobered then, what if his baby was a girl? Would she be safe without him to protect her?

"Yes, I kept hoping the next one would be a boy but never happened. We gave up trying for that boy for fear of having another girl." He smiled, "Well, almost."

Everyone laughed. It was a very good evening. On the walk back to the hotel everyone's mood was considerably lighter than the night before. Before they reached the hotel Bill had decided that a little rest from the trail would do them all good. He decided they'd stay on an extra day. Zack and Ten Trees looked at each other. "I think I'd like to see what Martha serves for breakfast and maybe dinner again too," Zack said trying to keep from showing any undue levity.

"Yes, that sounds good to me," Ten Trees joined in the fun. "I especially like pie. Maybe she'll have an apple pie on the menu tomorrow."

Bill nodded, "She is a great cook." He laughed and slapped Zack roughly on the back and shoved Ten Trees off the board sidewalk. "I see what you two are doing. You're trying to play matchmaker. I wouldn't mind it but I'm a man on the move, no time to settle down. Martha looks like a woman you'd have to stay home with or some young buck would be there while you were gone. She's too attractive not to have plenty of men step in if given the chance. Women like her need a man who's there to tell her she's pretty, admire her cooking and see to her personal needs on a regular basis, you know what I mean. I'm a wandering man, not for the likes of her." Somehow each of them knew the truth of that and the fun went out of the game.

Ten Trees and Zack fell in behind Bill as they quietly approached the hotel. That night as Zack lay in his top bunk, he thought of what Bill had said about a woman's needs. What had he done to Liddy? Would someone come along who'd take her away from him? He stirred uncomfortably, could someone take her away from him? Had he ever considered her needs? "Oh Lord," he thought to himself, "What have I done?"

The next morning Bill woke the other two up just before sunrise. He'd been out already and brought back some biscuits, sausages and coffee. "You boys deserve a good breakfast before we hit the trail again." He offered the food with a smile.

"I thought you wanted to rest the mules and stay an extra day," Ten Trees said grumpily, as he stretched and tried to wake up. "Damnation, that was awful," he said tossing his pillow across the room. "Should have slept on the floor, this bed is so full of lumps it was like sleeping on the bank of a rocky creek."

Zack looked at Bill as they all ate sitting on their bunks. "What made you change your mind Bill?"

Bill shrugged, "Well, you know I thought about Martha a lot last night. I figure if we stay here too long I might get some crazy notion that would, in the end, cause me a lot of grief. You against heading out?"

Zack shook his head, "I'm headed west, any step in that direction suits me fine."

Bill nodded and quietly finished his meal. By eight that morning the men were back in the wagon and off again. Once or twice Zack noticed Bill glance back. He understood how his older friend felt, he'd done his share of looking back in the last month. Doubt rode every step of the way with him, as palpable as the air around him. Zack was never completely convinced that he was making this journey for any other reason than his own selfish desire to run from trouble no matter what. It started in the war, feeling that way, trying to stay out of the main parts of the battles, trying to be brave yet wanting very much to run and hide, save his own hide at any cost. Never-the-less he'd fought when he had to. After he'd been wounded he had been grateful to be sent to the rear of the battle, to the field infirmary. He often wondered if those who died had been braver than those who somehow lived. It was a bitter memory for him, one he'd ride thousands of miles to forget.

Chapter 15
East Tennessee—October 1866

There had been a heavy frost the night before. When Lydia stepped out onto the porch that morning her breath sent a warm fog before her where ever she went. It was beautiful, all the trees covered in white, here and there a few fall colors clung to a branch. There were a few small birds still about but not many. The time of hard living had begun for most wild things. People who were prudent fared a little better, especially in the valleys, but here in the hills life was hard to wrestle from the land.

Lydia went to the barn and found Jonas getting ready to take care of the stock. Their three cows and small herd of goats were all clamoring to be fed. "I'll do the goats," she said as she walked by him. She had been helping Jonas with small chores since Zack left.

"Don't lift anything too heavy now," Jonas cautioned.

"Like I could if I wanted to," Lydia laughed and patted her bulging belly.

Jonas smiled, "You look like having babies agrees with you, Miss Liddy."

Lydia groaned, "Tell that to my back. I can't imagine going another two months at the rate I'm growing."

A goat jumped up and put its feet on the edge of the stall. Lydia petted it for a moment then looked down at the goat's extended sides. "I think this one is going to have twins, too."

"Goats do that more often than people." Jonas walked over and patted the side of the goat.

"Yes, I think you are right. We'll have several fine animals to sell in the spring."

The two of them worked for several more minutes in the barn, putting feed out and then opening the door to the pasture so that everyone could go out when they were done eating. Then Jonas took two horses out to the far pasture. Lydia returned to the house to help Rose with breakfast. After breakfast they would air all the bedding, then while the linens were hanging outside they would make bread. Lydia liked that, a regular routine and lots of work. It made the long, lonely days pass more quickly.

When she reached the porch she turned around and stood looking out over the farm yard. There were very few days she didn't find herself standing on the porch looking down the road, hoping to see Zack riding back to her. Some days it made her angry, other times she would have to fight back tears, today she just felt as cold inside as it was outside. She scanned the horizon and then looked at the sky. The sun was beginning to make it's way over the top of the ridge. It would be a little warmer in a bit, but the pleasant fall days were past now. In the valley below the days would still be fair, but up here there would be a bite to the air and coats or shawls were always required attire. A kick from one of her children reminded Lydia that she need to think of more than Zack now. She moved quickly into the house.

Rose had coffee and biscuits with ham all ready. "Jonas with you?"

"He'll be in right quick," Lydia said as she plopped down onto a chair by the eating table.

"I swear that walk up from the barn is getting harder everyday."

Rose laughed, "Darling daughter, it's going to get worse before it gets better. Not only when you are still packing those young'uns inside you. When they're born and growing you'll be packing them for the first year of their lives and they'll get mighty heavy as they grow. It's going to be a challenge then, too."

"Well, I'm counting on you and Jonas to help carry them around when they're hatched."

Jonas came in and sat down on the bench across from Lydia. He rubbed his hands vigorously, "My it's cold out there already. Think we're going to have some snow early this year."

Rose put the coffee pot on the table and the mugs. Lydia got up and helped her bring the rest of the food to the table. Jonas poured coffee into the mugs and then waited until the women came back and sat down.

Rose took Lydia's hand and Jonas' then they all bowed their heads, "Father God, we thank you for another day and food to nourish us. We pray for Zack on his travels that he is eating well and safe. We pray for all those we love where ever they are. Help us Lord to serve you and do thy will. Amen."

Lydia appreciated Rose's morning prayers. There were many times in the last few months that Lydia's own heart was so conflicted she didn't know what to pray for. She was ashamed of it but often found herself angry at God for allowing Zack to go away, for leaving her alone and a list of other offenses in her life. Lydia often admired, maybe even envied, Rose's faith. She always felt hope no matter how bad things had gotten for her. Through all the losses in her life, Rose had continued to maintain the attitude that all things work to God's will. She might not understand it at the time but in his good time he will set things right, wipe away her tears and restore her hope. Lydia shook her head and thought to herself "That would take a lot for me."

"Liddy, you look a little pale this morning," Rose observed. "And you haven't been eating enough. Why don't you let Jonas and me air the bedding and you sit for awhile."

"I'll be fine," Lydia said as she started to eat. "I'll eat more. I forget sometimes I need to since I have two others to feed."

Jonas shook his head, "I cannot imagine what it must be like to have a baby," he laughed, "Excuse me, *two* babies moving around inside you."

Rose looked at Lydia and they both giggled. "Well Jonas, my dear friend, it's not what you'd think. It's sort of enjoyable most of the time. Towards the end when they feel like they're going to burst through your skin it's not pleasant, but it's the closest you'll ever be to another human being."

"I wonder about my mother," Jonas said quietly. "She was still very young when I left home. I had three younger brothers and a sister at that time. I wonder if she had more children and if she and my father still live. I wish I could remember more about the way they looked and my home."

Rose patted his hand, "This is a difficult world. We all get separated from those we love sometimes. Not everyone is lucky enough to find them again..."she stopped mid-sentence when she noticed tears forming in Lydia's eyes. "I'm sure someday you'll see them again if that's God's will."

Jonas took a deep breath and silently finished his meal. Rose and Lydia did the same.

* * *

Two days later things got really complicated. Jonas was in the barn throwing some hay down out of the loft for the horses. Somehow he got tangled in the rope that he'd been using earlier to move the bales around and fell from the loft. He lay unconscious for over an hour, until Lydia came down to tell him it was time for lunch. "Jonas, noon meal is ready," she called cheerfully as she entered the barn. In the dim light she didn't see him at first, but then as her eyes refocused she saw him laying there in a muddy part of the barn, blood covering his pants and he was so still. Her screams brought Rose on the run.

The two women struggled to get Jonas onto a clean mound of hay. Lydia hurried to the house for blankets, supplies, and bandages. In a few moments she was back and in some distress herself. Rose had examined the nature of Jonas's injury. "He's got a broken leg for sure, can't tell about any ribs or internal things yet." She looked at Lydia, "Child, you go over there and sit down on that bale of hay for a few minutes and get calmed down."

Lydia didn't have to be told twice. Her back was killing her and she could hardly breath. Any exertion these days just took everything she had. Tears welled up in her eyes and she began sobbing, "What are we going to do? Is he going to die?"

"No, he's breathing regular," Rose said as she cut away Jonas's pant leg revealing a nasty hunk of bone protruding from the calf. She held her breath as she gently moved the leg into position so the bone went back into place. Jonas moaned with pain and his eyelids fluttered but didn't open.

"We got to get the doctor up here." Rose said looking at Lydia. "Saddle the horse, I'll ride down the hill."

"Can you ride that far?"

"I won't go any further than the Goss's place. Ernie can come help us get Jonas into the house."

Lydia hurriedly saddled the easier riding of their two horses. Rose didn't bother to get any heavier wrap than the sweater she had on, so at the last minute Lydia threw her own shawl around her mother-in-law and Rose sped off.

Lydia slumped down beside Jonas and kept the pressure over the open wound steady. She was thankful that the bleeding had eased off. The sight of the blood was turning her stomach, and throwing up was the last thing she wanted to do. She wrapped an extra blanket around herself as she started bandaging the leg. She put a large pad over the wound and wrapped it tightly. Jonas's eyes opened for a moment then he passed out again. "Hang on Jonas, hang on, dear friend."

It seemed like hours before Rose, Ernie and Betsy Goss came thundering into the yard in their wagon. Rose came running, showing the way. "Here he's in here."

Lydia heard them approach and was immediately crying again. "Rose, he's passed out again."

Betsy Goss, a gray haired, small, plump lady, threw her arms around Lydia and let her cry on her shoulder until Betsy's dress front was soaked. Ernie Gross was a short but stout man who had no problem picking Jonas up and carrying him into the main house. Rose drug a couple quilts out and they laid them on the floor near the fireplace. After Jonas was as comfortable as possible Ernie looked at the wound and was pleased to see the bleeding had all but stopped. "I sent my boy, Eddie, to fetch the doctor. It may be tomorrow before he gets here, so I guess the most important thing to do is just keep him warm and not moving around. This leg will most likely have to be set again." Ernie ran his hand around all parts of Jonas's body and found no other places that seemed painful but the leg. "There's a knot on the top of his head, probably hit it on the ladder as he fell. Might have a whopper of a headache when he finally wakes up. If you got any corn liquor it might ease the pain he's going to have. Just a little probably wouldn't hurt him."

Betsy took Lydia to the eating table and looked at her. "Child, you are so huge! And you're awful pale."

"The doctor tells me I'm having twins," Lydia said with a shrug.

"Twins!" Betsy laughed, "I always worried about that running in my family because my cousin Mary Sue had a set. Must have been in her husband's family, cause after her man's death she married again and has four singles." Betsy hugged Lydia. "You sit there and let me bring you some tea. I know you all drink that here." Betsy walked over to the sideboard and found a tea pot. In moments the fragrance of tea brewing filled the room.

Lydia shook her head as she sipped her drink. "Can't tell you how grateful we are to you folks for just dropping everything and coming to help us."

"We told your man that any time you needed help he could count on us," Ernie said with a wave of a hand, "You'd done the same for us."

"Lydia's right though, we appreciate this so much." Rose hugged both Ernie and Betsy.

"God's ways are so mysterious," Betsy said thoughtfully. "We had been talking just last night about getting up early and going to the valley store. We've been out of coffee for two days." Betsy looked at Ernie, "then this morning as I was moving stuff around to find some baking soda I found a small sack of stuff we'd been given by the Lockleys from the next ridge as a Christmas present last year. The apples were shriveled up beyond recognition and the walnuts were questionable but the small bag of coffee was as good as new."

Rose gasped, "Had you not found that bag, you wouldn't have been home when I came!"

Lydia couldn't help crying again, a tragedy and a miracle in the same day? She put her hands over her face and began to shake.

Rose came to her immediately, "Liddy honey, why don't you go lay down for a bit? We'll call you in a few minutes for lunch. I'm going to add some vegetables to the soup and we'll have something to eat before the Goss's go home."

Lydia smiled weakly and got up to go to her room. She was surprised at how shaky she felt. The room was trying to spin around her and she was afraid she might faint. Betsy sensed that Lydia was unsteady so she hopped up and put her arm around her. "Let me help you get there, Lydia. I think a rest is overdue for you. Too much excitement for one day." She looked at her husband, "Why don't you take care of the stock before you leave today honey. I think I'm going to stay here until the doctor comes." She looked at Rose and saw the strain on her face. "Don't you think that would be a good idea, Rose?"

Rose nodded, "I would really appreciate that, Betsy. I can't ask you to do that though, with all your own…"

Betsy put her hand up and smiled, "You'd do the same for me." Betsy continued on with Lydia to the back bedroom. Lydia hardly said a word as she slipped onto her bed and took a couple deep breaths before falling into a deep, dreamless sleep.

* * *

Ernie and his teenaged son Eddie took turns coming every day to take care of the stock. Betsy helped with the cooking and washing as things fell into a strange new routine. It was three days later when Dr. Mitchell finally arrived. Rose and Lydia had washed and bandaged Jonas's wound twice a day. It looked good to them but they would not be convinced he was going to be all right until the Doctor said so. Jonas was able to open his eyes and talk, but he was too dizzy to sit up so he just laid there for the most part. He could lift his head enough for Rose to spoon soup or broth into him.

Dr. Mitchell kneeled down on the floor and examined the break. "Yes sir, Jonas, you did a fine job of breaking that bone. We'll have to align the bone, then wrap it real tight, then set it with a splint. You'll be able to get up on a crutch in a couple days but no lifting or heavy work for six weeks." He set about moving the leg into position while Rose held Jonas' hand. It was painful but Jonas took it without comment.

The doctor examined the bump on the patient,s head next, "Looks like you got a concussion to add to your misery, son." He turned to Lydia,

"Hand me that pillow please." The doctor pointed to a small pillow on the settee. Lydia fetched it immediately. Dr. Mitchell put it under Jonas' head. "Now every half hour or so I want you to sit up for a few minutes. Then I want you to lay back down but not flat. Keep your head elevated. It will help with the dizziness until you are able to sit up and be moved to a chair. You'll be very sore for a few days but I expect a complete recovery." The doctor got up and then looked at Lydia.

He motioned for her to come to the eating table and sit in front of him. She did without question. He took his stethoscope from his case and listened to her heart and lungs. Then he put his hand to her face and pulled down her eyelids and looked thoughtfully at her. "Hum," he said more to himself than to her, "Little light colored."

"You need to be eating more red meat," he advised, "And is your back giving you a hard time when you walk?" She winced and nodded. "Well then, my dear, I am prescribing limited bed rest for the rest of your term. You can go out to the necessary with someone's arm as support and get up for your meals but otherwise, it's bed for you."

"That's just not possible now," Lydia said shakily.

"I know there is a lot going on here," he said, putting his hand on his chin, "I am going to help you all. I have a nephew, Mark Fellowes, he's been minding my farm while I do my practice. Right now you need him here more than I need him there. I'll send him to help out until Jonas is back on his feet and these babies are born."

Rose started to protest but the doctor put his hand up,. "These are extraordinary circumstances and you have to accept help. You are an independent woman, but you can't do this alone, Rose."

Rose shut her mouth, she knew the truth of what he was saying. "Then thank you Dr. Mitchell."

"We'll stay until your man gets here and help out as much as we can," Ernie offered.

"You've all done a good job for Jonas," the doctor smiled at each of them. "Good neighbors are hard to find." He walked over again to Jonas and helped him into a sitting position. Jonas could only take it for a minute or two and then wanted to lie down again.

Rose went out to the root cellar and got two dollars for the doctor's fee. "Is this enough, Dr. Mitchell," she asked, extending the money to the man.

He looked at the money and then at Lydia and smiled. "More than enough. I'll only take half of that. You've fed my horse and I am hopeful you will give me a little something to eat before I go today." He took one of the bills and put it into his pocket.

Rose smiled, "Why, of course, doctor. We've got a nice ham that we cooked yesterday. Would you like potatoes, too?"

"Actually, if I could just have a piece of the ham and a slice of your wonderful brown bread I could take that with me to eat on the way. Mrs. Jenkins on the other side of the valley is having trouble with bleeding gums. I really want to stop and see her before dark."

Rose hurried and got the food the doctor had requested. Within minutes he had said his good-byes and was headed off in his little black phaeton buggy to other homes. Rose breathed deeply as she stood with the others on the porch in the crisp fall air. "We are so lucky to have a good doctor in these parts."

"Amen, to that sister Rose," Betsy said. She turned to Lydia, "Well my dear, now the hard part. Bed rest for you!"

Lydia shook her head, "I really don't think…." she started to say but Betsy just turned her around and gently pushed her into the house and to her bed.

Two days later Mark Fellowes arrived. Lydia wasn't sure what she was expecting but he wasn't it. He was a handsome, tall, blond man in his mid-thirties. If he stood just so, the sunlight revealed little flecks of gold in the green of his eyes. He was by far the most fair man Lydia had ever seen. If she could have described a Norse god, he probably would have looked like Mark. Rose seemed unnerved by his presence as much as Lydia did. The first day he joined them was awkward. Rose and Lydia seemed unable to say anything intelligent between them.

Late in the afternoon Rose brought a cup of tea in for Lydia. Lydia sat up in the bed and Rose sat on the side. "What do you think of our new farm hand?" Rose asked quietly.

Lydia leaned over as far as she could and whispered, "Did you see his eyes? They are a color I've never seen before."

"He's strong too, makes me wish I was twenty years younger," Rose laughed quietly.

"We best remember you're old enough to be his mother and I'm married and about to have twins." Lydia bit her lip to keep from laughing out loud.

"I think he's married too," Rose said with a sigh, "Can you imagine being married to a man who could have anyone he wanted? What kind of a beauty she must be!"

Lydia shrugged and looked down at herself, "I don't think I was ever really pretty myself and now I must really be a sight."

Rose put her tea cup down and hugged Lydia. "You are and always were the prettiest girl around. My son knows he is a lucky man."

Lydia clung to Rose. She desperately wanted to believe that Zack thought he was a lucky man. But would a man who thought he had everything he needed, leave her when she was about to have his child? She pulled back from Rose and exhaled, "I think I'm tired again." Rose nodded, took the tea cups and left the room. Lydia lay back and let the tears flow yet again.

Chapter 16
Polk County, Oregon—October 1866

It had been two weeks since Truit left and a week since Harve had sent for Cleveland. It worried Cleveland a little, not knowing when the next work would come his way but he was frugal and could stretch his money to cover the down times, at least so far. He'd tried to put in a garden but he hadn't been altogether successful with that. His little root cellar would have some potatoes, onions and carrots, maybe a few turnips but they weren't his favorite. He'd traded some turnips with old man Wiggins for apples so he would have a fair supply of those for the winter. Meat was another matter. He wasn't much of a hunter so his main supply would be rabbit, with an occasional duck or goose. He hadn't been able to get his chickens yet. They turned out to be pretty costly to buy.

To pass the days, Cleveland had turned to making small dressers and chests. Some he used in his own home and some he took into town. One of the stores bought a couple to see how they'd sell. Cleveland was thrilled when the store owner asked for three or four more. He made enough to cover the cost of the wood and still have a few dollars to help buy supplies. It was enough to tide him over during the layoff's. He was glad, however, when he saw Harve ride into his yard. "Morning, Mr. Bauer," Cleveland called out as he walked off the porch to greet his boss.

"Good morning Cleve," Harve slid off his horse and offered his hand with a smile, "Ready to go to work tomorrow?"

"Sure am boss," Cleveland grinned, "would you like some coffee?"

"Sounds right good," Harve looked at his hands, "Better wash up before I come in."

"Wash stand's around back," Cleveland said, "I'll go make sure the coffee is ready. Come in when you're ready."

They nodded and each went a different way. Cleveland had made coffee early that morning but had set it to the back of the stove. He felt the side of the old pot and it was just barely warm. Cleveland threw another stick into the woodstove and set the pot right over the hot spot. It was hot again by the time Harve came through the back door.

Cleveland poured two cups of coffee and took them to the eating table. Harve followed and plopped down in one of the chairs Cleveland's father had made. "This smells strong, just the way I like it."

"I'm not much of a cook so I just do what it says on the bag, boil the beans until it smells like good coffee." Cleveland laughed.

"You do just fine, son."

Cleveland sipped his coffee for a moment, wishing he had a little cream and sugar for it. He'd run out of those luxury items several days ago. "What's the job this time, boss?"

"You ever been over Eola way?" Harve asked.

"I've been through there on my way to Bethel. My mother had a friend that went to church over in Bethel. We visited her several times after my pa died. But I don't remember too much about it. It's about two hour ride in a wagon, isn't it?"

"Well, maybe an hour from town." Harve looked thoughtful, "You could stay at the job site if you want to pitch a tent. You could bring the dog I think."

Cleveland looked at Cork. He wasn't sure he'd want her running around a countryside she didn't know. "I think she'd be alright here if I could get home by six or so."

"Daylight's getting shorter now. You could work nine to five if you want to. Kind of banker's hours. Your pay would be a little less, of course, but it would get you home at a better time."

Cleveland thought a minute, it would mean he'd leave about seven-thirty and be home by six-thirty. "That sounds workable."

"We're going to be building a barn for the Brunk family, ever hear of them?" Cleveland shook his head. "Nice family in Eola. Got a beautiful two story house with front porch running the length of the house and a balcony over the porch. It sits up high so you can see quite a distance. I always wanted a house like that. I think Harrison Brunk has a lot of kids, needs a big house. He's got lots of land around the place, some orchards, cows, other stock. He has a small barn now but he wants a nice one with a good workshop for his tools and work. That's where you come in. I want you to build that workshop area and tool bins. He's paying us well, so I want quality. Might help us get more of those kind of places to work on."

"Do we have a design to follow?"

Harve shook his head and smiled, "Nope. I thought you'd have a good idea what a workshop would look like, the kind of shelves and places a man would need who wanted to do woodwork and repair his farm equipment."

"I'll have to talk to him and get his ideas about what he's going to be working on. I'll size him up too, how tall he is, how strong. All those things make a difference in how high to put shelves," Cleveland said confidently.

Harve reached over and patted Cleveland on the shoulder. "I knew you were the right man for the job."

Cleveland smiled, it was pleasant to have his boss think of him as a man. It was slowly growing on Cleveland that he was the only one with any doubts anymore.

They finished their coffee and Harve headed off to notify the rest of the crew. There were a couple projects that Cleveland needed to finish before he started working away from home again. He happily headed off towards the barn with Cork right at his heels.

* * *

It was going to be a beautiful fall day Cleveland could tell when he stood on his porch just before sunrise. The air was crisp and clean. There wasn't any frost but it was close. Cleveland saddled Molly and the two of them headed off. Cork was disappointed that she didn't get to come along this time but she understood and went back to the porch to wait the day through for her master.

Maybe it was the fresh air or the road was better between Independence and Eola, what ever the reason, they made the entire trip in only an hour. When Cleveland slid off his mule at the Brunk farm, he congratulated Molly for a job well done with one of the carrots he'd brought along for their lunch. She readily accepted the prize. He tied her on a long lead and headed up the hill towards the farm house. When he was a few yards from the house, he stopped dead in his tracks. He involuntarily let out a long gasp. On the balcony of the house was the prettiest girl he'd ever seen. She was sitting there brushing her long, light brown hair. After each stroke she would run her hands through the tangle of silky locks. Cleveland's knees felt like rubber as he was held to the spot.

Sunlight danced around the girl. The colors of her hair reflected and absorbed the light in fascinating waves. He could have stood and watched her for hours but then something awful happened. She realized he was watching her. "Oh," was all she mouthed before she disappeared into the house. Cleveland gulped and looked around to see if anyone else saw him watching the girl. He was dismayed to see Harve walking towards him with a silly smile on his face. "You look thunderstruck, boy." He laughed, "Close your mouth and follow me."

"Who is she?" was all Cleveland could say as he fell breathlessly into step with Harve.

"That's one of the Brunk girls. Mary is her name, I think," Harve shook his head, "Don't get ideas though, boy. You haven't met her father. That'd be enough to scare me off."

Cleveland looked back at the house one more time before it was out of sight. The girl had not come back out on the porch. He sighed and hurried to keep up with Harve.

Harrison Brunk was waiting at the work site. He was a stern looking man with a full face beard that made him seem bigger than he was. He didn't smile and he didn't offer any pleasantries. He told Harve what he wanted and how long he expected it to take, no more than a month. When Harve told him that Cleveland was in charge of creating the workshop space Harrison turned his full, frightful gaze on the young man. "This young lad?"

"I assure you, Mr. Brunk, Cleveland Taylor is a first rate carpenter. If you want references we can supply them." Harve reached into his pocket and produced a letter. "This is from Mr. Whittson at the college in Monmouth."

Mr. Brunk took a moment and read the letter, then nodded, "Says here you're a mighty fine worker, son," he said to Cleveland with a half-smile. "We shall see."

"Mr. Brunk, sir," Cleveland tried hard to talk without a shaky voice, "I would like to ask a few questions, if you wouldn't mind, about your preferences."

Mr. Brunk nodded and motioned for Cleveland to follow him. Harve watched the two walk over and sit down by an apple tree and smiled. Then he turned his attention to the others standing by. "Come on men, let's get most of the walls up today and the roof on by Thursday. We have work to do for Mr. Brunk."

The days flew by. The walls and roof were on the barn and the first of the inside stall walls and storage areas were laid out. The shop area would be almost as big as Cleveland's house. It would be a challenge but he knew he could do it. Mr. Brunk had been very specific in what he wanted making the job easier for Cleveland. Surprisingly, what Mr. Brunk wanted was exactly what Cleveland had drawn out ahead of time.

Several times during the first couple of weeks Cleveland caught a glimpse of Mary Brunk as she shook rugs or worked in the garden. He never got close enough to say anything to her, though, until the end of the third week as they were all getting paid. She came down to the barn site with a basket of apples and gave each of the men a couple apples to eat on the way home. As she handed him his fruit, Cleveland thought his heart might stop. For the first time Cleveland could see her dark blue eyes. Her skin was flawless and her nose turned up ever so slightly. Mary Brunk smiled at Cleveland and he stammered something like, "Thank you Miss Brunk, I will really enjoy these apples because you picked them for me." She looked a little surprised but just laughed softly and moved on to the next man.

Harve came up quietly and lightly pushed Cleveland towards his mule. "Time to go home, son."

Cleveland caught his breath and started walking away with Harve, yet his eyes couldn't help but follow Mary as she smiled at each man and waved as the last of them got on their rides for their trip home. Cleveland waved but he didn't really want to leave. Harve nudged his mule with his horse. "Going to be dark by the time you get home, Cleve. You'd better get into town quick if you want to stop at the store."

Cleveland finally heard him and urged Molly down the evergreen lined path in the direction of Independence. He took one more look at the Brunk house as he rode off. Mary was no where to be seen. He resigned himself to heading home and suffering through Sunday before he could come back. It would be a long weekend.

* * *

It was pouring rain on Monday. The roads were a muddy mess. Molly had thrown up enough mud with her hooves to coat Cleveland. He was soaked by the time he got to the work site. Luckily the roof was on the building and he was working inside. When he got to the Brunk farm he tied Molly under a tall oak tree for a little protection from the driving rain. "Nasty day, old girl," he said as he petted her one last time. "Maybe we'll go home early today if it's all right with the boss." Molly nickered softly as if she understood what he'd said. He laughed and headed off to the barn.

Cleveland started where he'd left off on Saturday. He measured out the shelves he was going to build for the work bench. Mr. Brunk had ordered some pretty heavy timbers and it took all his strength to work with them. He sawed several boards to length, measured them by fitting them into where they would go, then used the saw again to make a perfect fit. For the final fit he used his chisel, then planer, creating a smooth edge and top. He then used a fine grit sandpaper and as a last step, oiled the surface until it nearly gleamed. He was so caught up in his work that he didn't notice Mr. Brunk was watching him. Finally Mr. Brunk cleared his throat.

Cleveland jumped a bit but tried not to act surprised, "Mr. Brunk, how do you like it so far?" Cleveland didn't really know what else to say.

"Well, son," Mr. Brunk said sternly, looking at the shelves, the work table top and the tool hanging racks. "I know I questioned your boss about your ability to do this job when you started last week, but I have come to appreciate that Mr. Bauer was right. You do know what you are doing. Carry on boy." Mr. Brunk turned to walk away then stopped, "I'm told you are an orphan."

Cleveland was shocked, orphan? Who calls a man an orphan? "My mother and father have passed, sir, it is true, but I do fine." Cleveland felt instantly that he needed to defend himself. It was clear Brunk still saw him as a child.

Mr. Brunk shrugged, "My wife feels that it would be good if you came to dinner with the family for Thanksgiving."

"Thanksgiving, sir?" Cleveland couldn't remember when that was.

"That's about three weeks hence, on a Thursday. There'll be no work that day."

"I'd be honored to join your family, sir," he stammered. Did Mr. Brunk know of his feelings for his daughter? Then he remembered what he was saying, "For Thanksgiving dinner."

"Good, good, we'll be eating at one o'clock. Don't be late and wash up before coming into the house." Mr. Brunk walked off, hands behind his back. He inspected other areas of work as he walked.

It was hard for Cleveland to concentrate on his work the rest of the day. Visions of passing a biscuit to Mary Brunk danced in his head and a couple times he dared think of maybe touching her hand as they exchanged a plate or cup. His head spun as he thought of maybe being able to come courting, maybe kissing her. Suddenly he was embarrassed, he'd been so preoccupied with his day dreaming that he'd sawed a board over a foot short. He shook his head with disgust and started over. He'd use the short board for another project.

Right after lunch Mary came to the barn where Cleveland was working. "Pa told me you're coming to Thanksgiving dinner. I thought I'd ask you what kind of pie you like so I can make it for you."

Cleveland felt like his tongue weighed ten pounds, "Pumpkin or mince is good, but apple has always been a favorite, or cherry." He shrugged and smiled weakly, "Truth is, I don't get pie very often so I like them all."

Mary looked thoughtful for a moment, then turned around and left without saying anything. Cleveland was puzzled but in just a few minutes she was back with something wrapped in newspaper. "Here! You take this home and try it. If you like it, I can bake another for Thanksgiving. It's my own version of Dutch apple pie with currants."

"Miss Mary, you didn't have to do that,"Cleveland smiled, as he took the package from her.

"Oh, you know my name?" She laughed, "I guess that's only fair since I know yours too, Cleveland Taylor."

"How'd you come to know my name?" Cleveland felt like soaring.

"I asked my father to find out who the cute young boy working on the barn was and he said he already knew, Cleveland Taylor."

Cute young boy? Cleveland's heart seem to fall a hundred feet. "I'm no boy! I'm a man. I make my own living, own a farm, work it, too."

Mary put her hand over her mouth, "I am sorry. I know that your folks both died and you're on your own. That must be hard. How old are you, Cleveland?"

"Old enough," he barked. Then he realized how gruff that had sounded and decided to be honest. "I'm seventeen, almost eighteen, so you can see I'm not a child anymore."

Mary looked at Cleveland's strong hands and muscular arms, "I'm very sorry, Cleveland. Yes, I can see that you're not a child anymore. I ask you to forgive me, you look much younger from a distance. I thought you to be fourteen or fifteen or so, not almost eighteen." She smiled. "Will you forgive me?"

Cleveland was lost again, there would never be anything he wouldn't forgive her for. "Of course, I forgive you. Will you forgive me, for losing my temper? It's just that I get that so much. I can't help looking so young."

"That might be a good thing when you really are older. People always are trying to look younger than they really are." She started towards the open side of the barn, turning one last time. "See you at Thanksgiving, Cleveland."

Cleveland watched her walk all the way to the house before turning around and facing Harve who had quietly come up behind him. "Boy, what am I going to do with a carpenter with calf eyes for the owner's daughter? I hate to burst your dreams, my son, but Mary Brunk is way out of your reach. Her father would never let the likes of you, or for that matter, me, come courting her."

"They've invited me to Thanksgiving dinner," Cleveland said smugly.

"Don't read too much into that," Harve looked around and then out at the rain that was still coming down in sheets. "We're going to stop early today. Pick up your tools and get everything under cover. I think we may be having a windstorm by night fall. Don't want to lose anything."

Cleveland did as he was told. In two hours the work site was in order and everyone headed home. Cleveland hardly felt Molly slipping around under him on the rutted road. He wasn't fully aware of the stinging rain that often contained bits of ice. He was warm inside and happy. He was going to have Thanksgiving dinner with Mary Brunk, what else could matter?

Chapter 17
Stone Hill, Missouri—October 1866

The weather had turned decidedly cooler and the once beautifully colored trees were dropping their leaves in showers of orange and red. Zack longed to see the hills around his home. This was the best time of year for hunting and filling the smokehouse with meat for the winter. He often wondered if Jonas would get enough game to see them through.

Through one small community after another they traveled. After awhile they all seemed to blend together and he stopped trying to remember their names. They stayed over in Greenville for a couple days during a really bad stretch of rainstorms. They hadn't found a very good place to stay, just a bunkhouse at a farm that no longer had ranch hands. It had been cold and drafty, but with enough wood in the small wood stove, they got by. The owner's wife had provided them some meals that were barely passable, biscuits and salt pork for breakfast and lamb stew for dinner. It had felt good to get back on the road after that. At least Zack had time to write another letter to Lydia and get it mailed.

Other than that one stop over, they kept moving along at a steady pace. It was long days of tedious work, picking up this here and dropping off that there. This day they would be coming into Stone Hill. Bill said they'd be picking up a heavy load, which worried him considerably since the roads were nothing more than ruts in this part of the country.

Zack was amazed that Bill always knew where he was going. He could find the most remote of outposts, small township or even a ranch like he'd been there hundreds of times. Today was no exception. The sign on the gate they passed said "Stone Hill Winery." Zack had heard about wineries but had never seen how wine was actually made. He had made hard cider once or twice with his neighbor, Mr. Goss, though.

"You ever drink any wine?" Bill asked Zack as they got down from the wagon in front of the big main building.

"No can't say as I really have," Zack shook his head, "my friend Jonas said that his old mas…" he stopped himself and searched for a better word, "Employer always served wine with dinner. Sometimes three kind at one meal. He made some once, wasn't very good. Must be like a rich man's kind of drink."

"It's not bad, but give me corn liquor if you give me anything at all." Bill laughed.

Ten Trees shook his head, "Strong spirit drink was one of the worst things the white man brought. It really made a lot of Indians so dependant on the white man for a supply that he'd do anything. Some even sold themselves into slavery for it."

Zach shuddered, "That's probably why my mother always rants and raves about the evils of corn liquor or even hard cider."

"There are some who really can't stop once they start," Bill said quietly, "I can see the wisdom in not taking any at all."

Zack smiled. "Still I wouldn't mind trying fancy wine, never having had any before."

Bill patted him on the back, "We'll see what we can do about that. Let's go find Lasitter, he's the foreman here."

Lassitter turned out to be a tall, skinny, older man. He nervously counted and recounted the twelve barrels he was having Bill take. "We usually have our own wagons to take this to the rail head; but this last spring we lost one wagon in a flood and the other has a broken axle. We've got an order in for a replacement but this shipment must be delivered before Thanksgiving."

"We'll get it there for you, Lassitter, don't worry." Bill tried to be reassuring. "My friend here, Zack, has never tasted wine. Don't suppose you keep a sample bottle around for that purpose?"

Lassitter looked through squinted eyes at Zack, "Yes, I believe we do have something. We always test the kegs before we certify them and so there is a little bottle drawn off. Follow me."

The three wagoneers followed the man through a door. They were surprised to find a set of stairs leading down on the other side. There were lit candles along the walls of the stairs. Once they had made their way down the stairs, they found themselves in a long tunnel lined with kegs. More candles lit the way. At the back there was a small table, several chairs and a cabinet with several small half full bottles. Lassitter put a candle in the middle of the table and brought over one of the bottles with four small, delicate glasses. "I don't suppose you know what kind of wine this is?" Their blank looks told him they didn't. "It's a nice, sweet wine." He poured a little in each of the glasses. The others watched as he first sniffed it, then swirled it around in the glass, sniffed it again and took just a sip.

They all tried to do the same, with mixed results. Ten Trees sloshed the wine into his mouth and instead of a sip, Bill downed his. Zack tasted his cautiously. It wasn't bad, but it sure wasn't sweet. It smelled pretty good, though. He declined when offered another glass. He'd tasted it and that was enough to satisfy his curiosity. Bill, on the other hand had a second glass, and so did Ten Trees. Lassitter put the bottle back on the shelf after that. Zack could see that Bill would have finished that bottle off given the chance.

It took all four of them to load the barrels into the wagon. It left very little room for the other things they were carrying. No riding in the back of the wagon this time for Zack. He saddled his horse to ride along side.

"We'll have to make straight for Rolla. Can't take chances with this cargo," Bill said quietly to Zack. Zack knew, there were those who would think this consignment was worth stealing. He took his place next to the wagon and they started out. He kept the strap loose on his rifle, just in case. For the first time he really understood how dangerous hauling goods was. It took miles before he was able to relax enough in his saddle to start looking at the countryside again. He tried to look casual but he was still tense as a board. Rolla seemed a long way off.

* * *

A two days later they pulled into the railyard in Rolla without incident. Zack breathed a sigh of relief as they found a porter who helped them check the barrels in and load them into a box car. Bill got a bill of receipt from the station master and put it into an envelope addressed to Lassitter. "He'll be happy about this," Bill said. He walked over and handed the letter to the clerk at the depot window. "See that this gets mailed, will you?" The clerk smiled and nodded, taking the letter and putting it with a stack of others waiting pick up.

Bill stretched and walked back to the wagon. "We can pick up a few things here in town at a warehouse. I don't have anything specific that's been ordered so we'll just get some general merchandise to sell as we go."

Zack started to get back onto his horse when he noticed another horse tied up in front of a saloon a half block away. A beautiful palomino with a long white tail. The horse looked a little thinner, but there just couldn't be two like that in this country. Zack looked around and then alerted Bill. Bill went to the clerk at the depot counter. "Who's the law around here?"

"We got a district Marshall and a sheriff. The sheriff's office is just one block over on the corner. Can't miss it. You got trouble, mister?"

"No, no, just wanted to chat with the man."

Bill told Ten Trees to stay with the wagon, then motioned Zack to join him. They walked briskly to the sheriff's office. It wasn't much of an office, just a couple rooms to the side of another building, but the back room had bars over the windows. Once they were inside they saw the back room was closed off by a set of iron bars.

The sheriff was sitting at his desk working on some paperwork when they came through the door. He leaned back in his chair and quickly give them a stern look, obviously sizing them up. When he felt they were no threat he leaned forwards, "Something I can do for you two?"

Bill spoke up first, "Sheriff, we just saw a horse we know to be stolen from down around Four Mile Settlement on the St. Francis." He shook his head, "At least we think it's the same horse. It does look a little underfed, but I can't imagine the guy taking good care of the animal. He's a red-haired guy traveling with his two sons."

"I think I have a notice about that here somewhere." The sheriff dug through his papers for a moment, "Yes, here it is. One of them was shot and killed during a robbery in some little town in Carter County. The other two got away. Says here the one that got shot was between fourteen and sixteen in age,." He shook his head. "You say it was his father he was riding with? What a shame." He stood up and reached for his hat, then strapped his gun belt on and tied it to his leg. "I'm going to get a couple deputies in case you are right about this. You go back to your wagon. When we come over there, if you see the guy just tip your hat and ride on. Don't want you to get involved in what might happen here."

Ben and Zack hurried back to the wagon and joined Ten Trees. The horse was still tied up down the street. The three of them tried to make it seem that they were just fixing rigging, getting ready to go, but they kept an eye on the scene. Within five minutes the sheriff and two other men came around the corner and spotted the horse. They made some last minute comments to each other and one went around back as the other two went in the front door. When the sheriff entered the saloon, people started leaving before one shot rang out. Zack held his breath. The door of the saloon opened and the deputies came out, shoving a man in front of them. The sheriff looked up the street, and Bill tipped his hat when he saw the red-headed man standing next to the deputy. Then he got in the wagon with Ten Trees and they slowly pulled away from the train depot.

The three men leaving in the wagon didn't noticed that the red-haired man also recognized them. He squinted and muttered some threats towards them but was quickly silenced with an elbow across the mouth. The boy with the man just cried.

Zack had an uneasy feeling about the whole incident. He kept looking back over his shoulder all day. He stayed on his horse, in a state of readiness, while Bill and Ten Trees made deals for merchandise at the warehouse and a couple other outlets. It wasn't until they camped that night a good twenty miles from the town, that he began to breathe easier.

"Hey, take a look at these," Bill said after they'd finished their supper. "These are trade beads I thought I could sell to the outfitters going on the trail. They can trade these for food with the Indians." He opened a small cask of brightly colored glass and stone.

"I've never understood that," Ten Trees shook his head, "Why anyone would give up food for something you couldn't eat."

"You are one cynical Indian, Ten Trees," Bill laughed.

He smiled and shrugged, then looked at the barrel of beads with Zack. Zack ran his hand through the mix and spotted something interesting. "What is this?" He picked up one of the stone pieces. It was yellow with a dark line up the middle that made it look like an eye. The light of the campfire seemed to reflect inside the rock. "Looks like the eye of a cat."

"I don't know," Bill took a closer look at it, "You want it though, it's yours. Anything else you want out of that, too."

Zack smiled and fished out a dozen or so blue beads. "You know, I think I'll take you up on that. I used to make tack all the time so I think I'll make a halter piece for my child's horse."

"Your baby isn't even born yet and you're getting him a horse?" Ten Trees laughed.

"It will give me something to do in the evenings," Zack said wistfully thinking about his son having a horse someday. He took the beads and put them in his bed roll. The next town they came to he would buy some leather and get started on his new project. He looked up at the stars and wished he could kiss Lydia at that moment. His heart was full of love for her, but his mind was full of shame for leaving her just when their child was coming into the world. What kind of a man would do that? Had his life been so unbearable? He didn't know who he was anymore. Again, he felt lost. "Oh Lord, let her be all right! Don't let any of my foolishness cause her pain," he prayed silently to the dark sky.

* * *

The weather cooperated in their travels for the next few days as they wound around the countryside from village to lonely country outposts. Everyone needed something different and Bill had been a good judge of what to buy and bring. In a few days they pulled into Warsaw. They stopped at a mercantile store and sold three bolts of calico, several casks of nails, hardware and several cases of canned goods. Bill was more than pleased as they found a small café for supper that night. "We could do with a day or so of rest before heading on to Independence," he announced cheerfully.

It didn't take long to find a boarding house and livery stable. "I'm going to stay with the wagon," Ten Trees said, looking around the open space the wagon would be in and at the owner.

Bill looked with narrowed eyes and saw the same things. The man was small and nervous, his eyes darting to each of them but they always went back to the wagon. Bill wondered if he was thinking that there might be something of value in the wagon. "Good plan, Ted," Bill switched back to calling Ten Trees by his "white" name. Ten Trees just scoffed and smiled.

"We'll be leaving in the morning after breakfast," Bill decided. "We're about out of supplies anyway, and the wagon is nearly empty so you'll have plenty of room to put a bedroll down." He said that mostly for the benefit of the livery owner. It seemed to work, the man turned and went out of the barn.

"We're not staying over?" Zack said.

"Guess not," Bill said, "I got an uncomfortable feeling here. Let's go to the boarding house and turn in. We'll be back early, Ten Trees."

"Bring some breakfast when you come, I especially like bacon." Ten Trees called after them, "And a pot of coffee."

Bill waved over his shoulder, "I really like that Indian but he does make demands."

"How'd the two of you hook up?" Zack asked as they walked the few blocks to the hotel.

"I was making this run two years ago and I came through the town he was living in. He was working in a store. My partner had just quit me so I was trying to do the run on my own. Ten Trees and I got to talking and he said he'd like to travel around with me, so I hired him on the spot. It's been pretty good, not too much trouble, but lately we've heard about more and more robberies. That's why we decided to hire a shotgun rider."

"What did you do before you did this?"

"Oh, I've been making runs through this country for years. Used to haul supplies for the Union troops. I'd take things from St. Louis all over this area and north. Just started going to Memphis this last year."

"You were a Yankee soldier?"

"Yep, I was." Bill smiled and looked at Zack, "And you were a Reb?"

"Yes, I was." Zack said grimly.

"Hard to forget sometimes, isn't it?" Bill said as he stomped the mud off his feet at the door of the boardinghouse. "Does it make a difference between us now? Here?"

Zack looked at him and shook his head, "No, it doesn't, Bill, not here and now."

Bill put out his hand and Zack shook it. For once in his life his past didn't seem to matter, this was all about the future now. They went into the building and found the small room they'd been given. It had bunk beds so Zack took the top one. In no time at all he was fast asleep.

* * *

It was pleasant traveling along the Flat River into Sedalia over the next couple days. They passed a couple herds of cattle being driven into town. It wasn't a problem for them; although, there were rumors at the stores about farmers not liking the cattle drives. There was reportedly shootings over property lines and the situation was tense for the locals. "County's getting too settled, too many people," Bill said as they pulled out of a small general store in Benton County. Zack was riding in the back of the wagon and Ten Trees was sitting next to Bill in front.

Zack nodded, "Yeah, saw the same thing in our neck of the woods."

"That's what my people have been saying for a long time." Ten Trees laughed.

Bill playfully pushed his Indian friend on the shoulder, "You want to walk the rest of the way?"

Zack decided to take a nap and found a more or less comfortable place in the back of the wagon between two grain sacks. It wasn't easy to fall asleep in the bouncing wagon but in moments Zack was out. He slept dreamlessly for awhile, then he began to have a nightmare; he could almost hear shouting and gunfire. With a start, he realized that there really was shouting and gunfire. Bill was yelling at the horses and whipping them into a fast trot. Bullets whizzed through the thin canvas over the wagon. Zack grabbed his rifle but a rut in the road sent him sprawling and he hit his head on the side of the wagon. His head swam and he fell down among the goods, practically out of sight. He was out cold.

When he awoke he heard angry voices outside the wagon. "What do you want?" Bill growled.

"You caused me a lot of trouble," an unknown but vaguely familiar voice roared back. "Where's the other one?"

"There's just the two of us now. Our run's about over," Bill said.

Zack got the message and eased himself and his rifle out of the wagon, lifting the canvas and going over the side. His head still hurt but he knew what to do. He dropped quietly to the ground and looked under the wagon. There was only one horse and no extras standing on the ground. He could see that Bill was on the ground, blood oozing from his leg. Ten Trees was kneeling over him. Zack silently walked to the back of the wagon and peeked around. He recognized the horse and rider, it was the palomino and the red-haired man.

"I'm Jesse McCord and you've crossed me for last time," he said angrily. "You cost me my last son. If you hadn't pointed us out in Rolla, he'd still be with me."

"How did you get out of jail? Did your son die there?" Ten Trees asked.

"We broke out when they came to feed us," Jesse laughed malevolently, "Nobody better than me in a fight. My boy ran off the first night we camped after the break. I imagine he's half way back to that worthless mother of his in Ohio. I could have made a man out of him but he was too much like her."

"Like you did your other boy?" Bill said through his pain.

"Shut yer mouth," Jesse hissed, "Don't bother, I'm going to shut it for you permanently." He leveled his shotgun at Bill.

Zack saw the imminent danger and stepped out from behind the wagon, "No you don't." He yelled. Jesse swung the shotgun towards Zack. They pulled their triggers at the same time, but Zack dove to the ground and Jesse's shot caught only the edge of Zack's coat. Zack's shot found it's target and Jesse swayed back and forth in his saddle for a moment then fell to the ground, dead.

Zack rushed to take Jesse's gun, but there was no need to hurry. Jesse McCord's days of terrorizing people was over. "His boy is probably lucky to be on his way to Ohio."

Bill let out a groan. Ten Trees was examining the wound when Zack joined him. "Looks like it went through the knee cap itself," Ten Trees observed.

Zack got some bandage material from the wagon. "We'll get you into Sedalia as quick as we can. There's got to be a doctor there."

They put Bill into the back of the wagon and tied Jesse to the Palomino. It took most of the day and into the night to reach Sedalia but they finally got there. The doctor was in bed but their banging on the door of his home got him up. He lead them to a small exam room at the back of his house. Bill had lost a lot of blood initially but the bleeding had stopped. Fortunately Bill had lapsed into unconsciousness. The doctor took a few minutes to probe the wound, remove a couple bone fragments and then cauterize a couple small bleeding spots. He looked the work over one last time, then splinted and bound the leg. "If he is going to walk again, he will need several days of bed rest and then limited duties for several weeks. I suggest you find him a good boarding house, because he certainly doesn't need to be bounced around in that freight wagon for awhile. He can stay here for the next two days. Come back on Thursday and we'll transfer him to where he's going to stay."

Ten Trees and Zack stood dumbfounded, this was not what they expected. "What we going to do?" Ten Trees asked.

"Well, first let's wake up the sheriff here and give him our other charge." Zack led the palomino down the street until they found the sign saying "Sheriff's Office." They knocked, and a deputy answered the door.

"Little late, gentlemen," the gray haired, heavy set man said as he adjusted his glasses. "What do you want?"

"We got a man here," Ten Trees pointed to the horse, "Tried to kill us out on the Flat River. He's wanted in Four Mile Settlement for stealing that horse. He had a grudge against us for turning him in Rolla. We'd seen him before when he'd attempted to rob us, so when we saw him in Rolla we told the sheriff there. He said he escaped from there and came looking for us."

"He shot Bill Zumwalt, the owner of the freight wagon we ride with." Zack said, "Bill's over at the Doctor's right now. Got a shot out knee."

"You don't say," the deputy came outside and looked at the man draped over the horse. "We got a wire about him escaping from Rolla." He looked around, "Said he had a boy with him?"

"His son. This guy, Jesse McCord, said the kid run off. I don't think you'll be hearing about him anymore. I don't think the kid was ever really a part of what this man did."

"Hum-m-m," the deputy said.

"Did you know there was a reward for his capture?" The deputy said with a smile.

"No, we didn't," Ten Trees answered.

"Yep, two hundred and fifty dollars," he motioned for them to follow him inside, "I'll send a wire first thing in the morning. Where will you boys be staying?"

Ten Trees looked at Zack and shrugged, "We just got here. Is there a good boarding-house?"

The deputy looked thoughtful, "Well with all the cattle people here now, most of the best places are full but we have one lady on the edge of town, Hope Grandville, who sometimes rents out her barn. Got a couple bunk rooms off it. Doesn't keep anything but a couple horses now since her husband died."

"How do we find her?" Zack asked.

"What're your names?" the deputy asked.

"I'm Zack Grant and this is T…Ted LaClair," Zack said as he extended a hand.

"Tom Marks," the deputy returned. "Sheriff Oroville will be here in the morning, so I'll set him straight about all this. He'll be the one probably taking care of the details."

Within a few minutes Zack was knocking on the door of the Grandville home. Martha was still up reading by candlelight.

"What do you want?" she asked through the closed door.

"We just got into town ma'am and the sheriff told us you might have room in your barn for us and our mules. We've had a bit of bad luck on the road. We're freighters. There's two of us. Our partner was shot during an attempted hold up and we're going to have to stay in town for a couple days." Zack spoke loudly, fearing the woman might be elderly.

The door creaked open and Zack was surprised by the woman he saw in the candle's light. Hope Grandville was a very tall woman, probably near six foot. She was big, too, not heavy exactly, but built like a man and she was wearing work pants with a man's shirt. Her hair was long and worn in a heavy braid wound around her head. She had a pleasant face. Zack found it impossible to guess how old she was but he figured she wasn't over forty. She looked them up and down with a critical eye. "Well, I guess I could let you have the barn rooms. You got horses?"

"We have four, ma'am." Ten Trees said with a smile, "And a freight wagon to store."

"All right, there should be enough room for that. I'll get a lantern and show you the way."

In moments they were walking toward the barn that was a few hundred yards from the house. "There's the outhouse," she pointed in one direction, "remember to knock before opening the door." A few feet further she pointed again. "There's a small creek just over the rise there, plenty of water in it for washing your clothes or yourself. If you want a hot water bath, there's a place in town where you can have a bath and a shave for two bits. There's also a Chinese woman in town who'd do your laundry. As far as meals go, I'll bring you out breakfast in the morning and then we'll talk about how long you're going to stay and what else you might need. How does two bits a day sound for the horses and the same for you boys?"

"Sounds fair, Mrs. Grandville," Ten Trees said with a nod from Zack.

"Please call me Hope," she put her hand up, "Everyone does."

The two rooms off the main part of the barn were adequate. The larger one had a set of bunk beds on either side of the room, a table with four chairs in the middle and a small wood stove near the back. The smaller room was just a large closet off the first, it was only big enough for a cot like bed and an old wardrobe.

"That little stove puts out plenty of heat and you can make coffee in the mornings on it. Do you have a pot in your gear?" Hope lit a candle that was on the table. It sputtered but finally put out a nice light.

"Yes, Mrs.....Hope, we do," Zack said looking around, "This will be just fine.

"I'll be here just after sunup with some breakfast. Wood's out back of the barn. I got horses in the first two stalls. There's enough stalls for all your mules. We used to have lots of horses. I don't bother now. There's hay in the loft. Bedding for you boys is in that wardrobe." With that Hope turned and left.

"I'll get the wagon." Ten Trees quickly went back to the front of the house and drove the wagon to the barn. It took only a few minutes to get the mules set up for the night. It was a luxury for them to have a stall for themselves, a water bucket handy and hay in the stanchion. The wagon was inside the barn so they just closed the doors. It was nice to be inside, even if you had to sleep on wood slats.

"Hope was right," Zack said as he and Ten Trees sat near the little wood stove, "that does put out a lot of heat." Zack had brought in the coffee pot as well as some jerky and biscuits. They ate their cold, late supper in silence. Ten Trees was the first to head for bed. He used his own bed roll rather than Hope's. Zack did the same. He was exhausted by the time he blew out the candle and piled into his covers. The little stove's warmth filled the room and soothed their troubled minds. Yesterday things had seemed clear, today everything had changed again. Zack was puzzled by the twists his life had taken; his last thought before sleep claimed him was of Lydia and the baby.

Chapter 18
East Tennessee—November 1866

Lydia hadn't slept well the night before. Like many nights these days, she found it hard to lie in one position very long. The babies were restless too, kicking and competing for space for themselves. When Lydia woke up, she lay there debating whether to try to make it to the necessary or just use the chamber pot. She decided to make a try for the outhouse. The sun was shining through the windows in an encouraging way so she swung her swollen legs over the edge of the bed. She stood up and for a minute thought the gust of water down her legs meant that she'd peed herself. Then she realized what it was and screamed for Rose.

Rose burst through the door and looked at the water all over the floor and gasped. "Mark!" she screamed, but she hadn't needed to raise her voice because he'd come running from the barn when he hear Lydia's cry. He whipped past Rose, grabbed up Lydia and laid her gently back on the bed.

"You're going to be just fine, Lydia, don't be afraid," he said comfortingly. "Eddie is at the barn. I'm going to send him to the store to wire my uncle to come right away." Mark turned and ran for the barn. Rose gathered all the things she had already prepared in a basket.

Rose stroked Lydia's tear stained face. "It's too soon, Momma," Lydia whimpered.

Rose shook her head, "Daughter, babies know best when it's time. Have you been having cramps?"

Right then a big one hit and Lydia cried out, then it passed. "I thought it was the babies kicking. Guess I didn't realize what it was."

By the time Mark came back to the house Lydia's contractions were coming in regular intervals. Each one of them brought a new reminder of the danger Lydia and the children were in, but Rose reassured Lydia that everything would be fine. "What can I be doing?" Mark asked.

"You can make sure we got plenty of hot water for keeping everything clean and then for washing the babies."

Mark went to the well and brought in three large buckets of water. He filled all the teakettles and a couple of pans full of water and put them on the stove. He was surprised how nervous he was. His own three children had come into the world easily. No complications what-so-ever, in the same week his uncle had said they would be born. His uncle had delivered them all. All healthy babies; he was so blessed to have his children. But it wasn't all joy. He thought about his wife, Mercy. She'd gone into a deep depression for months after the last baby, Tyler, had been born five years ago. They had not slept as man and wife since because she was deathly afraid of getting pregnant again. He shook his head; seeing the ordeal it was for a woman to have a baby, he wondered how the world got to be so full of people. His thoughts turned to Lydia, here she was alone without her man, delivering her babies a month early with only her mother-in-law and him for support. "Well, I'm here for her," he vowed. He checked his hot water supply and went back to see what else he could do.

Jonas was up on crutches now and hobbled into the house. "Did I hear Miss Lydia scream?"

"Looks like those babies are trying to come today, Jonas," Mark said on his way to Lydia's room with the first teakettle. "Might be a good time to pray."

"I can do that," Jonas followed him to the bedroom door. "Miss Lydia, I am going to be praying all day for you and those babies. Don't think there's much I can do to help, but I'll try to do anything I can."

Lydia smiled weakly and waved at her friend, "Praying sounds good,

Jonas, thank you." She couldn't say much more. Rose spooned some cold water into her mouth then put a cool cloth to her forehead. Mark put the teakettle next to the basket on the bureau. He looked at the knife, scissors, thread and big needles. He cringed; he'd heard about women tearing really bad during the birth of one big baby. He couldn't imagine what might happen with two. For a moment he felt like he was going to throw up.

"You need anything else right now, Rose?" He was grateful when she shook her head. "I'll finish up in the barn and be back. Just yell if you need me." He rushed out of the house and ran down the hill to the barn. He went around back and sank down on a bale of hay. It took several minutes for his stomach to stop pitching.

Mark threw himself into the work. After awhile he was able to put what might be going on in the house out of his mind until the Goss wagon came flying into the yard. Betsy jumped out of the rig before Ernie had actually stopped. Mark ran back to the house to greet Ernie. He was glad to see the couple. Somehow their presence was reassuring.

"Babies here yet?" Ernie said with concern.

"Not yet, but she's trying," Mark said, then leaned close so no one else would have heard, "It doesn't seem to be going very well."

Ernie looked at the house. "What's say you and I get some breakfast ready for the women for a change. This might be a long day. I'm pretty handy with a skillet."

"About the only thing I can make is coffee," Mark admitted.

"Well then, we'll have bacon, eggs and coffee."

"I think Jonas is a fair cook. Maybe he's got a specialty." Mark laughed, feeling the pressure lifting a bit.

Within minutes the men had made breakfast. Rose and Betsy took turns throughout the morning sitting with Lydia. The pains were just about on top each other by noon. Lydia was as limp as a rag doll by that time. She no longer reacted to each pain but held a steady grimace on her pale face. Then during one long, sharp pain, she screamed for Rose. By the time Rose got under the bed sheet to see what was happening, the first baby was well on the way into the world. Rose yelled for Betsy who came running into the room.

"Grab that towel, woman, we got a baby here."

"Lord God Almighty," Betsy shouted as she leaped on the bed to retrieve the red little human being. She stuck a finger in the mouth to clear the airway then rolled him over on the towel and patted his buttocks a couple times. The hoped for result came in a heathy bleating sound.

Out in the main room, Mark nearly choked on his coffee when he heard the wail of the newborn. The men held their breath and waited. They didn't have to wait long because a second chorus of new life rang out in less than two minutes.

Betsy ran to the door and asked for more hot water, which Mark and Ernie supplied in duplicate. "She alright?" Mark asked quietly.

"What'd she have?" Ernie said excitedly.

"Boys, pretty as they can be," Betsy said with a laugh.

"Liddy alright?" Mark questioned again.

"Surprisingly so," Betsy whispered as she took the water, then closed the door.

Ernie shook his head, "Amazing things women are, aren't they? They have babies like it wasn't nothing at all."

"It didn't look like nothing at all to me." Mark said, his voice slightly quivering.

Ernie looked at Mark with a question in his eyes but he didn't ask it. "Let's get some more coffee. Nobody going to sleep for days with two new babies in the house."

Lydia hardly noticed when Betsy and Rose kneaded her stomach, forcing the afterbirth out, then wrapping it and taking it away.

Rose gently cleaned Lydia up and brought over a clean night gown for her to put on. Lydia sat on the side of the bed while Rose changed the bedding. Once everything was clean and fresh, she helped Lydia lay back on a stack of pillows. Then she brought each of the baby boys over and laid them on either side of Lydia, helping her to move them into position at a breast.

"Oh," Lydia said in surprise as the first one found a nipple.

Rose smiled, remembering those first few moments with her own babies, "You get used to it. It's not all that bad."

"They're both boys?"

"Yes, both boys." Rose pulled the light sheet up over the babies as they suckled for modesty. "What names do you have in mind?"

"Zack and I had agreed on a list. We didn't know we were having two babies, so I guess we'll take the two off the top."

Rose got a couple pieces of colored yarn. "This is how we'll tell them apart for awhile until they come to look different from each other. So what do you want to call this baby?" She tied a small red band around a tiny ankle.

Rose looked at the little baby with lots of dark hair, "We'll call him Samuel." She kissed the tiny head nestled against her chest.

Lydia looked at the other baby, he had less hair than the other and it wasn't quite as dark, "It may not be that hard to tell them apart. I already see little differences. We'll call this one Peter."

Rose laughed, "You are the boys' mother alright. A mother can recognize her child immediately."

"It's easier than that," Lydia said pulling the cover back from the babies. Look here," Lydia pointed to the baby's neck, "This one, Samuel, has a little birthmark. Looks like a tiny ladybug right on his collar bone."

Rose looked over to see what Lydia saw, "Well I'll be, it does look like that in a way. I wonder if it will grow as he grows. Does Peter have one?" Rose gently lifted the baby and looked his shoulders over, "No, no birthmarks at all that I see."

Lydia looked at her boys as Rose put Samuel back in her arms. Both looked perfectly fine, though pretty small. They drank their fill and fell fast asleep. Lydia let Rose take the boys and put them into the cradle that had served as first bed for all the Grant children, for four generations now.

It was just before supper time when Betsy came in with a tray of soup and bread for the new mother. Lydia was surprised how hungry she was. She finished her meal and then at Rose's urging, lay back down for a little rest. Without realizing it, Lydia fell into a deep sleep. She hardly awoke during the night when Betsy or Rose laid one or both of the babies in her arms to nurse. Daylight was streaming in the window when she finally woke up. She felt amazingly good, sore but good.

She got up a bit unsteadily at first, but within moments she was alright.

She peeked in on her boys. Both babies were sleeping soundly, arms around each other. "Must have been that way for months," she thought with a smile, "Sweet little angels. Thank you, Lord!"

She put on her robe and went to the kitchen. No one was up yet except Mark. He was surprised when he saw her. "Are you sure you should be up?" he asked with concern, pulling up a chair for her.

She motioned him away and headed for the back door. He intercepted her before she could step outside. In one easy motion he picked her up and carried her to within five feet of the necessary. She was embarrassed but thanked him anyway. "I am just fine, Mark. I can make it out here now on my own. I may not look it, but I feel like I've lost a ton of weight." She went on to the building. In a few minutes she came out. Mark was still standing there. She put her hand up, "I can walk back under my own power." She saw the look of worry on his face, "Just give me your arm so I don't fall and I'll be fine."

Mark held her around the waist as she held on to his arm. Somehow it was uncomfortable to have his hands on her now, where it hadn't just two days ago. She couldn't put a finger on the reason, but she knew there was something. "Your wife is a lucky woman. You're very good in a crisis."

Mark didn't say anything. Lydia wondered about that. He never mentioned his wife and only rarely, his children. Did all men forget their wives so easily? She wondered if Zack could sense she'd had the babies? Would he care? Did he ever think of her? She shook her head and tried not to think about all the questions that nagged her. Today she had her babies and they were calling to her now in the way babies let their needs be known. She hurried on toward the house.

* * *

Two days later Dr. Mitchell was surprised to see Lydia cooking a stew when he arrived. "I can't believe my eyes, child. You look like a young girl again." He pulled her away from the stove by the arm and asked Betsy take over the cooking chores. He asked Rose to accompany them to Lydia's room for a full exam. Lydia didn't want to go but Rose urged her on. It was humiliating to have to let him look at her private areas but mercifully he was brief. "Everything here looks fine. You're having no pain, I take it?"

"I'm still sore and pass a little old blood now and then, but nothing to worry about I think."

"I think you're right, nothing to worry about." He turned and looked at the cradle. "Let's bring the boys over here on the bed so I can take a look at them." Rose gently picked up Peter and brought him first.

Dr. Mitchell listened to his heart, checked his lungs and then carefully examined his genitals. "Can't see any hernias or problems with his innards. Bring the other one over." Rose put Peter back and brought Samuel. Samuel put up a fuss at the doctor's touch. "This one must be the first born." He performed the same exam despite the baby's protest. "You have two really healthy babies here, Lydia. They are on the small side because they were a little early, but not too much. We probably had the due date wrong. You were probably only a week or two early from the development and size of these boys. Nice job carrying them to almost full term. Pregnancy seems to agree with you." He reached over and patted Lydia's shoulder with a smile, "I imagine I'll be making trips out here on a regular basis when your man comes home."

Lydia looked at Rose and they both managed a smile, but it was clear that both of them wondered the same thing. Would Zack ever come home? Lydia thanked the doctor and then went back to relieve Betsy at the stove.

"I knew I was fine," Lydia said to Betsy but Mark and Jonas were waiting to hear the verdict just as much. "Boys too!" Everyone breathed a collective sigh of relief. The doctor stayed for lunch then checked Jonas' progress before leaving. He called Mark to his buggy just before he left.

"Your work here is done, son," he said quietly, "Your own family has been waiting for you to come home, so I think it is time. The Goss's will see that the chores get done here until Jonas can do them again. I think within a week he'll be around enough to do most anything that needs doing."

Mark sighed and looked at the house. "I had thought I'd stay the week at least but I will stay just a couple more days."

"Well, a couple more days would be alright. Shall I tell your family to expect you by Saturday next then?" The doctor looked at his nephew. "It wouldn't be good for you to stay here too much longer for your own sake."

Mark looked at the doctor, "What do you mean, Uncle?"

"This isn't your family, son. You have a family that needs you just as much," the doctor said quietly. "You are a married man with responsibilities of your own."

Mark stammered, "But she's all alone… I mean, they're alone out here with Jonas not up to taking care of them."

"Son, don't let your feelings get confused here. You came out to help out, not stay." Dr. Mitchell made himself as comfortable as possible in his buggy seat, "I'll tell your wife to expect you by Saturday. You've done a fine job here Mark, but the job is done. Good-bye son, see you soon." The doctor snapped the reins on his horse and his rig sped the doctor off to his next stop, leaving Mark standing in the yard.

Rose was standing on the porch when Mark came back to the house. She waved at the doctor's buggy but he wasn't looking back. "That man sure is a good man. I imagine you are mighty proud of your uncle."

"I am," Mark said quietly, "He's a smart old bird, too, nothing passes unnoticed with him."

Rose wondered what Mark meant by that as she followed him back into the house. Lydia was sitting in the rocking chair holding one baby and Jonas was sitting on the settee holding the other. "Look at you two, spoiling those babies by holding them too much!" Rose scolded in jest.

"When is it Betsy and my turns?" She laughed and sat down by Jonas who grudgingly gave her the baby he was holding. Rose looked at the neck. "Oh, I've got Samuel. Granny loves you, boy," she cooed to the sleeping baby. It was a wonderful, tender day.

* * *

On Friday of that week Mark was in turmoil for reasons he didn't fully understand. He knew intellectually what he had to do but something in his heart didn't want to. He was going home the next day. Home, it was strange to not associate love with home. Here in this strangers home he had felt more love than he had for years. Was he going crazy?

Lydia went to the root cellar just after breakfast to get some apples for a pie. Mark observed her slip in the mud on the way and his heart nearly stopped. He rushed from the wood pile he'd been working on and helped her up. "Are you alright?" he asked hugging her to him.

She pushed him away, "Mark, I'm fine. You don't have to worry. I won't break. The danger is past. I might have been hurt, or the boys, before I had them but I'm back to being a rugged farm girl. I can take a few spills. Don't concern yourself about me." She laughed and continued into the root cellar. She lit a candle and started to dig in the straw for apples. She didn't notice that Mark had followed her. She let out a little gasp when she turned around and found him standing there. "I said I was fine. I'm just getting some apples for baking."

Mark was overcome with emotion and stepped forward and swept her into his arms. "Lydia, I can't hide how I feel any more," he breathed hotly, "I just can't." He kissed her solidly once, then looked at her surprised face then kissed her again softly, with all the passion he was feeling. She was motionless until he let her slip from his arms.

She sat down on a barrel and put her hands to her flush face. "Mark, I don't know what to say." She breathed heavily, his kiss had been a surprise, not that he had kissed her but that she found it exciting and strangely pleasant. "This is not right. Not for either of us. You are a married man with children. I am a married woman with two brand new babies. This is just not right."

Mark knelt down beside her and touched the tears running down her cheeks, "I don't know what to do."

"You have to go today, not tomorrow and don't come back." Lydia said quietly. "I have to tell you that unnerved me. I really liked you kissing me and I don't know why. I don't love you, I love Zack but he's so far away now…" Lydia put her head in her hands.

"I don't know why people fall in love, but I have fallen love with you," Mark bit his lip, "I know it's wrong but…"

Lydia put her hand over his mouth lightly. "Mark, you need to go today. I want to always remember your kindness and friendship. I don't want to spoil that memory with pain. Please Mark," she pleaded, "be strong for both of us and our children."

Mark inhaled deeply. "I'll get the apples for you. You go on in. I think I'll be going later today. I can see I am not needed here anymore." He got up and turned to look for the fruit. Lydia got up and stood beside him for a moment. He looked into her eyes and she into his. Then she walked slowly out of the root cellar towards the house but changed her mind and went to Jonas cabin.

"Can I come," she called to Jonas, "I'd like to come for a visit."

"Sure, Miss Lydia, I am glad to have your company. Would you like tea? I have some made."

"That would be nice, thank you." Lydia sat down and looked around the room. It struck her strange that she had never been in his home before. It was just one room but it was very much him. He had a bed at the back with a lace coverlet. There were curtains at the windows and a tablecloth on the small table by the window. Several books were stacked on the shelf above the table. There were several nice cups and saucers on the shelf with a tin of tea and sugar. He was very much the Englishman. She nodded her thanks when he served her tea in one of his fancy cups.

Jonas noticed the tear stains on her cheeks, "Are you sad about something, Miss Lydia?"

Lydia looked at him, "I don't think I rightly understand men. Do you, Jonas?"

Jonas laughed, "Well, being one, I would hope I do a bit. What man in particular don't you understand?"

Lydia couldn't decide, "Zack is off somewhere in the middle of this country. He doesn't even know we had two babies. How could he do that? How could he not wait and take us with him?"

Jonas shook his head, "You told him to go. Men are pretty straight thinkers for the most part, they take it as a directive, not a test, when a woman tells them to do something."

"What do you mean a test?"

"You told him to go west. He thought you wanted him to go, he didn't know it was a test of his loyalty or feelings for you. But you saw it as a test to see if he'd put you first. You said go, he went. Had you said "You can go or you can stay with me until after the baby is born and then we'll all go" he might have made a different choice."

Lydia looked shocked, "So you say it was my fault?"

"Fault? No, you were doing what you thought best for him. Now you're thinking of what would have been best for you. There is neither right nor wrong, a thing is what it is. Choices, once made, have to be lived with. That's what you're doing now. Living with the choices you helped make."

Lydia sipped the last of her tea and wiped her face with her coat sleeve. "I will have to give a lot of thought to what you've just told me. I never thought about things in that way."

Jonas patted her hand, "I'm just an old man who has watched people and their relationships. That's one advantage to being black, no one ever thinks you are intelligent enough to see or understand what they say and do."

"People who think that of you are making a big mistake," she laughed. "Thanks for talking with me, Jonas. I feel a lot better.

Then she got up and headed back for the house feeling much better, that is, until she saw Mark saddling up his horse. She joined Rose on the porch as they both waved good-bye to their friend. Rose yelled to Mark that he was always welcome to come visit. Lydia felt sure she would never see him again. Somehow that hurt a little.

Chapter 19
Polk County, Oregon—November 1866

It had rained steadily for six days. A lot of rain wasn't unusual for the area, but this was not the off and on kind of rain. It poured hard. Cleveland had really never seen water stand in his pasture before, but it did now. As he stood on his porch he could see just how his land was shaped. His little valley wasn't level as he'd always thought it was, but was rather a lopsided bowl with the deepest part of the bowl being down by the road where you came onto his place. It gently sloped back to where the house was. Then in back of the house it sloped fairly quickly down to the creek. Across the fields from the house it was about six or seven feet lower than the house. He was glad he'd buried his ma and pa on the hillside, rather than in the pasture. He guessed where he was standing must be about ten to fifteen feet higher than that lowest corner. The barn was just a couple feet lower than the house. The outhouse over the rise just beyond the garden was on the same level as the house. It gave him a chill, thinking about the Willamette being just a few miles away. It had never flooded as far as his place but, there was always the chance.

It had been a week or two since Cleveland had finished the Brunk barn. He'd been working on several furniture pieces to supplement his income. He'd managed quite well, which pleased him. He and Cork never went hungry. He ran to the workshop, deciding there really wasn't anything he could do about the rain. He opened the barn door so the animals could go into the smaller pasture but none of them ventured out for more than a second or two. They were content to just eat hay and stay dry. Cleveland couldn't blame them for that.

Several times during the day Cleveland looked at the growing pond developing at the far corner of his property. Late in the afternoon he put on his poncho and walked down to assess the problem. He looked for any possible way to drain the water away but couldn't see any answer. He just hoped it would stop raining soon so the water could just dry up, even if it might take awhile. He walked back to the house and went to see how the creek was doing. In the summer and most of the year the little spring fed creek was nothing more that a pleasant little waterway with a few pools deep enough for a bath or washing your clothes. This day, however, it was quite a little torrent. It was over its usual banks already. It was running smooth, brown and fast. It was menacing. There would be no throwing a stick into the water for Cork today. "Come on, girl," he said pulling her back, "This is no place to play today." He eyed the raging water and calculated how much chance of flooding into his land there was. "I don't think it could ever come up this high." He was relieved to see there was at least ten feet or more to the top of the rise by his house and five or six feet at the lowest point near the edge of his property. "Surely it couldn't get that high," he told Cork as they went back to the house to prepare their dinner.

It got dark early that night, before they had finished eating, in fact. Cleveland had to go to the barn and tend the animals and shut things up by lantern light. It wasn't overly cold but the driving rain sent a chill through him as he hurried back inside his warm house. Cork shook herself hard and then went to lay in front of the fire. Cleveland dried his hair and arms on a towel. He took his boots off and put them by the fire, angled to dry out the wet insides. He took a blanket off his bed and sat with Cork by the fire. It was a good night to stay in.

Cleveland woke up with a start. He looked around. Cork was also listening. The fire was nothing but embers so they must have been asleep for quite awhile. Cleveland lit a candle and looked at the clock. It was never very accurate but it was close enough. The clock said it was three a.m. Cleveland strained to hear what had woke him. Outside the wind was howling more furiously than he'd ever heard before. Limbs and flying debris was hitting the house. Cleveland sighed, "We must have heard a tree branch hitting the house, Cork." He was trying to reassure himself as much as he was trying to calm the dog. He stoked up the fire and added a few pieces of kindling which caught on immediately. He added a couple logs. The light and warmth made things seem better immediately. He curled back up in the chair and wrapped the blanket around him. He dozed off and on for over an hour. Cork finally lay back down but she kept her eyes open.

Suddenly a jolt rocked the house. It felt like an earthquake and sounded like the devil himself was coming. Cork jumped up, barking and whirling around. Cleveland hurried into his pants and boots. He donned his poncho and took the lantern outside. He couldn't see anything in the horizontal rain that pelted him with tiny shards of ice. He made his way to the barn and felt reassured that everything was safe there. He checked the outside of the house and found no damage so he decided he could wait for daylight to see what had happened. He went back into the house and built a fire in the cooking stove. Coffee, bacon and biscuits were ready in no time. Cleveland was uneasy but he figured he'd better eat while he could. Cork was a little nervous but ate her biscuit and bacon anyway.

Cleveland sipped his coffee as he watched for the first telltale signs of daylight. He couldn't see much through the rain that blew in under the porch roof and fogged the window by the eating table. "Nasty day again, Cork," Cleveland sighed. He strained to see out across the land but couldn't make out any familiar landmarks. It was well after five when the first gray highlights appeared in the black clouds overhead. Cleveland went out on the porch and strained to find the answer to his worries. He was shocked to see that there was water covering the all the pasture to the east and half the of the one on the right and it was still rising. If it kept up it would reach the barn in no time. "Is it the Willamette?" he yelled into the wind. He ran to the top of the bank to look down at the creek. He then saw the trouble. A fairly large oak tree had fallen into the creek making a dam of sorts that sent the water into his pasture. He looked at the tree, it had broken in half in the middle so if he could just pull part of it free of the stream the water would return to its channel.

Cleveland ran for the barn and harnessed up the two mules. He attached long leads to a yoke made especially for hauling and pulling stumps. He took them down by the creek. Both animals were obviously frightened, but Cleveland tied them to a bush and dove into the icy water to attach the ropes. It took several tries to get a rope to hold in a spot he could reach. The branches were like daggers sticking up everywhere, one wrong move and he'd impale himself. He cut his hands and legs several times in his attempts. Finally he had a substantial amount of rope tied to the tree. He crawled out of the water near the end of his strength. He slapped the reins over the back of the mules, he yelled "Come on, pull General! Molly, pull!"

The two mules strained against the ropes, Cleveland pulled, too, with all the strength he had left. The first try only budged the top end of the log a little, but it did move enough to allow the water to change course. Cleveland rested himself and the mules a few minutes. When he could breathe again he lined them all up and tried the pull again. This time the log gave enough that the water itself became an ally. The log bounced through and over the water, until it was up on the bank near Cleveland. With a whoosh the roiling water in the little stream found a new path for itself and directed its flood toward the waiting Willamette. Cleveland lay back on the hillside for a few minutes until the rain beating on his face became unbearable. He took the mules back to the barn and dried them off. He gave each of them an extra measure of feed. "You both did so well," he said, stroking both of the animals. He petted the cows too, before going into the house, it helped reassure them they were going to be alright.

Once back in the house Cleveland tended his wounds. He had several pretty deep cuts on his legs where he'd banged up against the log under the water. His left hand had a puncture wound from one of the torn off limb spikes. He put iodine on the wound, then did a little war dance until the pain subsided. Cork danced around with him, thinking it was some sort of game. He found some dry clothes and changed, hanging his wet ones by the fire. The rain and creek had pretty well washed his clothes so he felt they just needed to be dried.

The rain continued the rest of the day but by evening the storm had all but blown itself out. In the growing darkness Cleveland could see that his fields were still under water. Only a little pasture just beyond the barn was spared. That presented a new problem for him. He'd counted on the pastures to provide some feed for his animals but now he'd have to buy more hay to get them through the winter. He'd have to find work.

In the morning he surveyed the damage. From his porch he could see that more than half of his land was under water. The road to his house was probably under four feet or more at the lowest point. An awful thought crossed his mind, Thanksgiving was just a little over a week away, he was going to have dinner at the Brunk farm. "What if the water isn't gone and I can't get out of here? Mary! "Cleveland wailed.

Cork looked at her master. She could sense his dismay. She got a stick and brought it to him but he wasn't in a playing mood. He checked the animals and they were alright. He walked around the little land that wasn't under water. The outhouse roof had a big limb poking out of it but that was easily fixed. A couple shingles on the house roof need to be replaced, easy enough. The back side of his unused hen house was hanging on only one of its two hinges. The root cellar had about a foot of water in it so Cleveland put the few vegetables he had up on boxes. He took a bucket and bailed out as much of the water as he could. When it was down to just a wet floor he called it good.

Cleveland spent the day chopping up the branches that littered the ground everywhere. He mended the roof of both buildings, his house and outhouse. After fixing the chicken coop he was just about to check how deep the water was on his road when a wagon appeared at the main road. "Hello Cleveland, you all right?" A man called.

Cleveland waved, he recognized Fred Wiggins' rig. "I'm alright, just got a little water. Your place alright?" Cleveland yelled back, he waded closer to Fred. He stopped when the water reached his waist.

"Got water a foot deep in my house. Not as bad as it was in '61 when I thought I'd lose the place, but bad enough that I'm going into town for a couple days. You want to come with me?" Fred yelled.

"No, but thanks for the offer," Cleveland yelled back, "No problem with my house. I got food enough to wait it out. It will go down soon, I hope."

"Yeah, doesn't take long usually. Just need a few days without rain." Fred scratched his head and looked at the sky, "It may not rain again for a day or two."

"Hope not," Cleveland yelled back.

"You take care of yourself now, son," Fred said as he gently urged his two horses on, "I'll come back by with some supplies in a couple days."

"I'd appreciate that Fred, thanks." Cleveland called as he began wading out of the water. He looked back as Fred drove out of sight. He'd been wrong, there was probably more than five feet of water at the lower end of the pasture. Not much had drained back into the creek, either. He was soaked again from wading in the water. He slogged over to where the creek had entered the pasture. The creek bank was now above the stream and the water in the pasture. Seemed that he'd have to dig a trench to empty the water back into the creek. That would not be an easy task, but one that had to be done. He got a shovel and began the arduous work. By sunset he had made very little progress. His trench was only about five feet long of the twenty five feet he needed. He gave up for the day, took care of the stock and went to fix his and Cork's dinner.

He made a fine ham stew. Cork loved her cup of stew meat and vegetables but it was that bone that sent her into a delightful roll and bark. She played with the smooth bone for several minutes before settling down to enjoy it. Cleveland laughed, he was exhausted but she could still make him smile. He rinsed off his dishes and settled down for the night. He sat in his chair for a few minutes, but remembered how he'd fallen asleep there, so he opted to drag his cot out by the fire. Good thing he did because he was asleep in no time.

The next morning he ate a cold breakfast of leftover ham stew and then headed for the trench work. He had just started when he heard the splashing of horses. He was surprised to see Jose Morales and Martin Johnson riding up. They were hired hands for the Porterfield's.

"Porterfield was worried about, you boy," Jose said as he slid off his wet horse. "Thought maybe the river got you."

Johnson looked back at the water they just came through, "Looks like it almost did."

Cleveland reached out and shook each of their hands, "It was a tree falling in the creek that caused most of the damage." Cleveland walked to the top of the bank overlooking the creek, the men followed. "That tree dammed the creek over there. I got the mules and pulled half of the tree over here that let most of the water go back down the regular way. But I still got all that water in my pasture. I'm trying to dig a trench over there to let some of the water go back into the creek."

"Well, we can help with that," Jose said as he took off his coat and rolled up his sleeves. "Little work won't kill us."

Cleveland nodded, and the three men went to work. By just after noon the trench was finished and water was flowing back into the stream. Cleveland made coffee and biscuits for the men. "I want you to tell Mr. Porterfield how much I appreciate you men coming to help me."

"Was Mrs. Porterfield actually, she worries a lot about you."

"Mrs. Porterfield?"

"Yeah, she thinks you're just a kid and you're going to get hurt or something out here alone." Jose looked around and then at Cleveland, "I don't think you're a kid. I think you're a man and you can take care of yourself. You prove it all the time. I knew Truit and his wife, he said you're one of the best workers he'd ever worked with."

Cleveland sighed, "I miss them. They were good people."

"I miss them, too. My sister knew Mrs. Jens in California. She comes from a prominent family who were dismayed when she married a gringo."

"Funny about people, isn't it," Cleveland observed, "Everyone has a prejudice about something."

Jose laughed, "You got that right amigo."

"Well, I guess we'd best be getting back. Porterfields will be glad you're doing all right and that the main river didn't get this far." Johnson reached out and shook Cleveland's hand again before getting on his horse. Jose walked over and hugged Cleveland then ran and jumped over the back of his horse into his saddle. The two men waded out into the water towards the main road.

"Water's down quite a bit already," Johnson yelled back, "the horses don't have to swim it this time."

"That's good news," Cleveland called after them. Maybe there was hope he'd get to the Brunks' for Thanksgiving after all. He was dying to see Mary Brunk again.

* * *

Cleveland still had water standing in the lowest corner of his east field, but his road was now clear of the flood by Thanksgiving Day. It was a muddy mess though, all of his formerly lush pasture was useless. The mules and cows had trouble walking around in the muck. They were having to be fed hay and grain still to get by. Cleveland had finished and sold his special orders of furniture so he did have that little money put aside, but feed for him and the animals for the winter would come dear. He needed to find work soon. He tried to put that out of his mind as he rode Molly to the Brunk farm just before noon. Dinner was scheduled for one o'clock and he would rather show up early than a minute late.

It was a clear crisp day with a sharp little breeze that cut right through his Sunday go-to-meeting clothes. He'd bathed in the creek that morning even though the water was extremely cold. Even used the good smelling soap his mother used to use. He wanted to be at his best. He brushed his teeth twice. His shoes wouldn't have taken a shine even if he knew how to do that so he just brushed the mud off and wiped them down with a little lard. They didn't exactly shine but they looked better than they had. He urged Molly along, as he shivered under his poncho.

It took a little longer to get there this day because in places the road had been damaged by the wind and rain storm. In a couple places trees had come down and been sawed up and moved but leaving damage on the roadway. He could see that the family was just sitting down at the table when he tied Molly up out front at the hitching rail out side the family cooking room, which was a nice sized building just a short distance from the main house. "Sorry girl," said as he threw his poncho over her to keep her warm, "I'll take you to the barn later." He hurried to the door and knocked.

"You are right on time," Mrs. Brunk said with a smile as she opened the door of the kitchen.

Mr. Brunk hadn't said grace yet so he waited as Cleveland found a seat and made himself comfortable. He didn't smile but simply bowed his head, "Lord, we have come through a terrible storm. It reminds us that we are not in control of our fate. We trust you in all things, Father, to do what is in our best interest. We are grateful for your provision and guidance over this last year. Help our crops grow, our children to be wise and our friends to be many. In the name of the Lord Jesus Christ. Amen."

Finally Mr. Brunk smiled, first at this wife then at Cleveland, "Well, son, we were beginning to worry. Thought maybe the flooding had kept you from coming. Did you have any damage to your farm?"

"Just a little, my pastures had several feet of water standing in them when a tree dammed up the little creek that runs behind my house. The windfall caused the creek to overflow right at me. But the water is down considerable now. Mr. Porterfield from over the other side of Buena Vista, sent a couple of his hands to help me make a trench that drained the water for the most part. Time is just doing the rest. Wouldn't like to see another storm like that one soon. You have any damage here, Mr. Brunk?"

Harrison Brunk laughed, "Your barn stood up well. We lost a window in the main house and a couple of fruit trees blew down but no water damage, we're on high ground here."

Cleveland enjoyed being included in the conversations as they passed one overflowing dish after another around the table. There were eleven Brunk children, as well as Mr. and Mrs. Brunk, a young couple who were distant cousins from back east on their honeymoon, and three ranch hands, making it a lot of people sitting at three large eating tables. One was the normal family table and two were two wide planks over saw horses with benches on either side. All the eating tables were covered with nice table cloths. The food was wonderful, but Cleveland didn't want to let on how hungry he was. He seldom had enough to eat on any given day and it was so tempting to just take large servings of whatever went by. He tried to put on his best manners. Mrs. Brunk urged him not to be shy. Oh, how he wanted not to be shy!

Mary and the older daughters helped serve everything. Finally the meal came to an end with a wide array of pies. Cleveland took one piece of mince and one of the apple pie he knew Mary had made. He noticed she smiled when he purposely took a piece of "her" special pie. His heart raced so, he hardly tasted the luscious pastry.

Mr. Brunk stood up and thanked everyone for coming. He invited the men into the house for a glass of wine while the ladies cleaned up the dishes and dealt with the leftovers. Cleveland noticed some of the Brunk boys were staying to help with the chores. He wondered if he should, too, but he took one more look at Mary and it made him bold. He was going to talk to Mr. Brunk.

The interior of the house was warm and inviting. It was divided right down the middle with a central hall and the stairway to the upstairs. On either side of the entrance hall there were equal sized rooms. One side had a sitting room with two small bedrooms off of it. The other side had the formal parlor with two more small rooms off it. On one side Mr. Brunk used one of the rooms for an office and the other was his and Mrs. Brunk's bedroom. There was a fireplace in the parlor and one in the sitting room.

The men sat with their glass of wine in the parlor on the west side of the house. Cleveland had never had a glass of wine before, just the little sip one got with communion on Sunday. He hardly knew what to do with it. He watched Mr. Brunk to see if you just drank it or what. Mr. Brunk smelled it first then took tiny sips, sitting his glass down often to make a point with his hand gestures.

Cleveland put his small glass to his lips and took his first sip. It was awful, almost bitter. It smelled awful too. He tried not to show his disappointment as he smiled and entered into the laughter of a joke he didn't really hear.

"Like the wine, boy?" Mr. Brunk asked him, "Grow the grapes and make it myself here on the farm."

Cleveland tried to look sincere, "It's the best I've ever had, sir."

Mr. Brunk smiled and then went back to telling some story about an elk he'd seen. Cleveland's mind wandered back to the kitchen. He hoped Mary would come in soon so he could see her once more, just to steel his nerve. With her help he could do anything. He absent-mindedly picked up his wine and downed the whole glass. It hit his stomach like a fist! First it burned then it soured. He tried not to act like anything was out of the ordinary but he was afraid he was going to be sick. Cleveland needed some air, quick. He excused himself and headed for the privy. Once in the cold air outside, he felt much better. He stood on the porch for a few minutes until he began to feel better. It was odd, now it was a kind of nice feeling in the pit of his stomach. The heat had turned to warmth and he was feeling much better. "Hum," thinking to himself, "Maybe wine is one of those things you like after you get used to it." Smiling, he went back inside to see if a second glass was as bad as the first. By the third glass of wine, he didn't care what it tasted like.

Late in the afternoon people started leaving and Cleveland knew it was now or never. "Mr. Brunk I wonder if I might have a word with you outside on the porch," he asked, feeling buoyed up by the wine.

Mr. Brunk's eyebrows went up momentarily but he smiled and excused himself from a couple people still sitting around and followed the young man to the porch. "What can I do for you, son? Are you ready to leave?"

"Mr. Brunk," he started feeling actually brave, "I would like your permission to court your daughter, Mary."

Mr. Brunk's mouth fell open, then he sighed and put his hand on Cleveland's shoulder, "I was young once myself so I understand. But, my boy, I don't think she's the one for you at all. In the end though, it's Mary's choice. I'll go get her and if she wants you to come calling, you have my blessing." The older man shook his head as he headed for the kitchen building. Cleveland found the railing of the porch and sat down. The cold air was helping him feel a little more alert.

In a few minutes Mary Brunk came up on the porch. She shivered even though she had a thick shawl over her head and shoulders. "Cleveland, my father told me that you'd like to come see me sometime." She puckered up her lips and for a moment Cleveland thought she might want him to kiss her, his heart skipped a couple beats. Then she sighed and looked him directly in the eyes, "You are a very nice boy. That's the problem for us. You are what, sixteen?"

"I'm nearly eighteen," he said defensively.

"Well, all right you're "nearly" eighteen. That means you are seventeen and I am twenty. If it were the other way round we wouldn't be having this conversation because," she smiled, "You are cute as can be and I think any girl would be happy to have you courting her."

Cleveland was confused, was she saying she liked him? For some reason he was having trouble hearing and understanding everything she was saying. His head was a little achy and it felt like the porch was moving at times.

"Cleveland, I would consider it an honor to have you as my friend but the plain truth is I'm just too old for you and the young men I've been seeing are years older than you. You're going to find a girl someday who will be the one for you. I'm sorry, my friend, I can't let you come calling on me in that way. You are welcome to visit my family anytime, though, and if you let me know ahead of your visit, I'll bake a pie for you."

Cleveland took a deep breath, "I think I'm going to be sick," he wheezed, "I need to go home."

"Cleveland, I didn't mean to upset you so much," Mary said putting her hand out to touch him but he pushed her hand away.

"I know you don't want me to be your beau, I heard you. But you're wrong, I'm not too young. I'm more of a man than any city man. I work hard and earn my own way. I'll show you who's too young. You'll regret missing your chance." Cleveland whirled around and stumbled off the porch. Molly protested a little at the sloppy way he got up into the saddle but obediently trotted off toward home at his urging.

Cleveland didn't remember much about the trip home but he was grateful Molly knew the way well because he had major blank spots in his memory about the whole ride. All he could remember as he put the mule in her stall and fed the others was the fool he'd made of himself in front of the woman he loved. Cleveland was sure he would never be able to face any of the Brunk family again. "Oh my head," he wailed several times while he got his evening chores done. He vowed then and there never to touch wine again, his mother was right, the Good Book was right!

His house was cold and dark inside. No heat remained from the morning cook fire. Cleveland fed a cold biscuit to Cork and laid down on his bed for a moment, hoping to stop the ringing in his ears and pounding in his head. It was morning when he opened his eyes again and even Cork was shivering.

Chapter 20
Sedalia, Missouri—November 1866

Sheriff Oroville came to the Grandville farm two days after the shooting incident with some news. Zack and Ten Trees were just finishing their breakfast of oatmeal with raisins and side pork when he arrived.

"Morning boys," the sheriff said, twitching his grey handlebar moustache back and forth. The man appeared to be in his late sixties, but he looked fit and strong.

Zack stood up and shook the extended hand, "I'm Zack Grant and this is Ted LaClair. We're the freighters for Bill Zumwalt."

"Yeah, my deputy told me about your trouble. Mr. Zumwalt doing all right?" Zack nodded, although he hadn't checked that day yet. "Good, good." The sheriff reached into his vest pocket and took out an envelope, "This is the reward money you got coming to you. And," he smiled, "You get a bonus. When we contacted the sheriff where the horse was stolen, he said the people who reported the horse stolen had moved back to New York, so he and I decided the horse is yours."

Zack's mouth dropped open, he knew what that horse must be worth. "Well, that is a bonus."

The sheriff stayed for a cup of coffee before moving on to other business. He'd brought the palomino with him, so Zack took charge of the animal, giving him a good examination. He was sound, a little underweight but some rest and good food would set him right again. Zack washed and brushed the horse. "So, whose horse is he?" he said to Ten Trees.

Ten Trees shook his head, "You shot the guy who stole him, but Bill was wounded so maybe him having the horse is fair. But if you two can't decide, I'd take him. I've never owned a horse of my own." Ten Trees stroked the horse's nose.

"We'll talk it over with Bill when he gets out of the doctors. Right now let's just feed and take care of this big boy." Zack said as he combed the long, silky, white tail.

Bill was moved to the Grandville farm several days later. Zack and Ten Trees took bunks in the main room and gave Bill the small single room in the back of Hope's barn. It seemed the injury had taken a lot out of Bill and he was very discouraged. For the first time, his age really showed. He even complained about the lumps in the cot mattress. "I'd be better off sleeping on the floor." Ten Trees went to the barn and got straw to fill in the rough places on Bill's bed and it seemed to help some.

Hope came to the barn with some soup and biscuits for their lunch on the first day Bill was there, and when Bill complained in foul terms about the soup being too salty, she lit into him good. "Listen mister, you keep your opinions to yourself unless you want to say it in a decent way. I don't mind you being here in my place and I'm trying to be hospitable but don't push me. You understand me?" She towered over him.

Bill looked shocked, no woman had ever dressed him down since his momma when he was in knee britches. He nodded, feeling more than a little foolish.

Hope smiled then, "I'll try not to put so much salt in any soup I bring for you after this. Let me know how long you plan to stay, boys." She turned and left the barn.

Bill sat up in his bed and shook his head. "The doctor says that I am not going to be able to go on being a freighter. My knee is shattered and I'll have a stiff leg for the rest of my life. He thinks I ought to go to St. Louis where they have doctors who might be able to repair it enough so I can walk without crutches, but I'm going to have to find something else to do."

Ten Trees and Zack looked at each other. Both of their lives had just changed, too. "So what do you want us to do?" Ten Trees asked.

"I'm going to pay you your wages to this point with a bonus. I guess you're just on your own now, the two of you. Make your own plans and good luck to you." Bill said sadly.

"What do you plan to do, Bill?" Zack sat down on the edge of the cot.

"Well, I'll stay here until I can get around good on my crutches. Then I'll sell the freight wagon and horses, take the steamer back down the Missouri and go to St. Louis. I got a brother who lives near there, so I might look him up and stay there while I see about the surgery the doctor was talking about. I'll be alright. I got a little money saved, and I own a small piece of land in Kentucky I could go back to." Bill looked at Zack, then Ten Trees, "Any ideas what you'll do?"

"My plan was always to go west," Zack said with a sigh, "I'm still headed that direction. Guess I'll go to Independence and see if I can hook up with any wagon trains headed out."

Ten Trees shook his head, "Don't know. I might go west, too," he looked at Zack. "Want company?"

Zack smiled and shook Ten Trees hand, "I would be proud to have you joining me."

Ten Trees turned to Bill again, "We got some things to talk about dividing up. There was a reward of two hundred and fifty dollars for that McCord man. And we were given the horse."

Bill looked surprised, "Well now." He thought a minute, "What do you think, Zack?"

"Ten Trees was saying he'd never had a horse and thought the palomino might be a nice one, but that's a fancy horse, better for a gentleman on Sunday's than riding over the Rockies. I bet we could sell it for enough to split three ways and still get a great horse for Ten Trees." He looked to see if there was any change of expression on the Indian's face, there wasn't.

"That sounds practical," Bill nodded, "Okay with you Ten Trees?"

"Yes, it is." Ten Trees walked to the little window as a stiff breeze rattled the panes. "We'd better do it quickly. The time to go west is getting short."

Within a week, a buyer was found for the horse and the three men had said their good-byes. Zack and Ten Trees rode on to Independence and the beginning of the west. They were a little disappointed to find that it had been a couple months since the last wagon train had left and that there wouldn't be another until at least March or April, if the weather was mild. They stayed in a small boardinghouse for a night to decide what to do.

The two sat at a café mulling over their options. "Zack, I think we could make it to at least Fort Laramie before hard winter sets in. I know how to hunt and I think if we're careful we could do it."

"I don't know Ten Trees," Zack shook his head, "What if one of us is hurt or Indians…" he remembered who he was speaking to. "You know what I mean."

"I do. Plains Indians are some of the most fierce people you'll ever meet."

"We could go south to the stageline and go to California."

"That'd take another three weeks to get there."

"I still think we could make it to Fort Laramie before the heavy snows. I got this book with all the routes clearly marked out. People have been making this trip for years now." Ten Trees held up a copy of a book called The Prairie Traveler. "This guy wrote this book when he was in the Army."

Zack took the book and thumbed through it. "It does look possible but I'm just not sure. Just the two of us? We could disappear and no one would ever know what happened to us."

"You got this far, have a little faith you'll get the rest of the way." Ten Trees said softly, "the Great Spirit protects us in life and in death."

"God is with us, Emmanuel," Zack said absently, remembering something his mother had always said.

"I am willing to do whatever you want to," Ten Trees sighed. "I have no home anymore so, I'm just drifting."

"I thought you had some people in Kansas?"

"Some cousins, yes but even there I am without a home. They look like Indians and I don't. I am but I am not, it's a tough fence to sit on." Ten Trees sipped more coffee. "I have always thought of going back to

Canada. I think things have changed there a bit and maybe I would fit in there better. I could become a trapper like my father and his father were."

"I hear the trapping's pretty played out."

"There is always Alaska."

"Too cold for me."

"You have never felt the warmth of a buffalo or a grizzly bear coat. When I was a child my mother made me clothes out of all these wonderful hides my father brought in. I was never cold then."

"You'll have to show me how to hunt for buffalo, if we see any."

"If we cross the prairie to Fort Laramie you will see plenty."

"Let's get a good night sleep and decide in the morning what we're going to do my friend."

Neither of them slept too well that night but in the morning they both had made up their minds. They were headed for Fort Laramie. They bought a pack mule, as many supplies as they could carry, and set off.

A day out of Independence Ten Trees changed into his buckskins and for the first time he actually looked like an Indian. "Now I feel better," he laughed, "I want my relatives to recognize me if we run into any. We're just a hundred miles or so south of the place they call home."

"Do you want to go find them?"

"Nah, someday maybe, but today we've got to press on to Fort Laramie. The snow will come soon and we don't want to be caught out in it."

They rode on. Ten Trees was good at keeping a low profile as they rode. He was fully aware of the Cheyenne and Arapaho battles that had taken place in recent years. So was Zack. In Independence, they had been warned several times as they were buying their supplies.

At night they camped in gullies or in a grove of trees, anywhere that would be a little shelter from the constant wind and offer a bit of cover. There was little or no game to be seen as they rode. Hardtack and jerky was a tedious diet but it served its purpose.

Finally, about twenty miles from Fort Kearney, Ten Trees killed a small deer and they had fresh meat for their dinner. They settled down at sunset in a small gulch, under a large over-hanging rock ledge by a small stream. In moments they had a fire going and meat sizzling in the frying pan.

"Nothing better than a nice venison steak," Ten Trees said as he licked his fingers.

"Or two steaks," Zack laughed, "I swear you can eat! For such a thin man, Ten Trees, you eat twice as much as I can."

Ten Trees laughed again and leaned over and poked at the fire with a stick. "Zack, just stay loose and keep eating. We've got visitors." He leaned back and waved at the shadows beyond the firelight. He said something in a language Zack didn't understand, then turned to Zack, "Stay calm, they're not in war paint."

Two old Indians came into the light of the fire. Zack had never seen so many wrinkles on a human being in his life as on the old man who sat down across from him. The other Indian was a woman, probably his wife, and nearly as old. She walked to the fire and took two pieces of meat from the pan and offered them to the old man. After he chose his piece, she took the other and sat at the edge of the lighted area around them. They chewed noisily, trying to get through the tough meat with the few teeth they had left. It was a difficult process but they managed to get the food soft enough to swallow. They rubbed the fat left on their hands over their hands and arms. Zack couldn't do anything but watch with fascination. Ten Trees offered more meat but they declined with an up-raised hand. Without much fanfare, the old couple got up and went off into the night. The next morning when Zack went to get water from the little creek nearby, the tracks told him that there had been twenty or more Indians on ponies just a few yards from them. He called Ten Trees who examined the tracks. It seemed that the old couple were just scouts to see what they were up to.

"Arapahos," Ten Tree said with a nod, "We were fortunate, my friend, that we had something of value to offer them. Food is always good."

"Did you know there were more Indians?"

"Nah," Ten Trees shook his head.

"Don't you ever get scared of dying out here like this?"

"My grandfather was very smart, he always saw the way of the world as a natural thing. He used to say we are all a part of something bigger than ourselves whether we know it or not. We will live and we will die. Most of us will never leave a trace on the earth, we will just go into the dust and be forgotten. But he said the dust of the earth is a funny thing, it covers all the land, it nourishes the grass that feeds the buffalo and deer that we eat. So as we become one with the earth, we become one with everything else. No person is ever unimportant to the Great Spirit and dying is just a part of living."

"I'm not anxious to go "into the dust" and become one with the earth myself," Zack said as he nervously looked around. "Do you think they're watching us?"

"Nah," Ten Trees laughed, "I think from the tracks they've moved on. But I wouldn't want to stay around here just in case they come back this way. No telling what kind of mood they might be in later if their hunting doesn't go well."

There was no argument from Zack. They quickly loaded their gear and headed on into the clear bright morning. It wasn't much comfort to him to see Ten Trees stop and scan the hillsides every so often. Both of them knew they weren't safe anywhere in this country. They had to stay vigilant.

Zack felt sick to his stomach. He had never felt so close to death in his life. He thought of Lydia and the baby. In just a month his child would be born. Would he die without ever seeing his child? The thought somehow left an ominous foreboding in his mind. He tried to shake the thought all the way to the Fort. But try as he might he couldn't forget it, he could only bury it in the worries of the day and his aching heart.

* * *

Fort Kearney was a tense place. It was clear they had suffered many losses in the short time the Fort had been in existence. Talk at the Wheatley eating house, just outside of the main fort area, was of all the deaths and people leaving, going back east instead of west and of course, the Indians. Ten Trees had wisely changed back into his white man's clothes just before they reached the fort.

"Glen Woods left here one morning to go hunting and a couple days later he was found out by the Little Muddy. Remember that, Mr. Andrews?" Mr. Wheatley said as he poured coffee to a customer.

Ten Trees and Zack sat by a window in the sod building with a low ceiling. It was warm and dry in the strange building even though it did smell like damp earth. They ordered bread and stew, which was all that was being served. A pleasant woman who identified herself as Mrs. Wheatley served them. "You boys are new here, aren't you? Just come in on a wagon train?"

"No, just the two of us." Ten Trees said as he tested the stew. He didn't say anything, but it was pretty tasteless.

Zack tried his bowl and found it the same, Ten Trees made a venison stew twice as good but at least this was hot and ample. Hot food was good no matter what, so he had two bowls, then settled back to listen to the talk over a couple cups of coffee. "So what kinds of trouble have you been having with the Indians?" he inquired.

Wheatley got a chair and drew it up by Zack and Ten Trees."We've had a couple small raids on the Fort. Old Joe Donaldson died chasing a batch of the dirty coyotes off. Some others were just out in the wrong place when they were killed like that old miner," he turned to his wife. "What was his name?"

"Can't remember, darling," she shook her head. "I think the saddest thing, though, was when Pierre Gassoux got killed, left that Indian wife with five children. She was from some tribe a long ways away from here and now with all the Indian trouble, no one goes near her. Only thing she can do is clean up at the hospital to earn enough to scrape by."

"These are indeed bad times to be going around the country without an escort, gentlemen." Mr. Wheatley said shaking his head.

"We might stay the winter when we get to Fort Laramie." Ten Trees said quietly.

"I think there's a troop riding out tomorrow to Fort Laramie. I think one of the men who eats breakfast with us said something about being transferred." Mrs. Wheatley added, "Maybe you could ride with them?"

"We'll look into that, ma'am. Thank you," Zack flipped two bits onto the table and so did Ten Trees as they got up and left the soddie.

They got their horses and led them into the main fort area to what looked like the headquarters. A young sergeant in a freshly ironed uniform greeted them coldly. He said it was not their policy to let civilians, ride along but they would be leaving in three days if they wanted to wait and ride behind them. Zack thanked the young man and they left.

They went to the general store, which was more of a warehouse than a shop, for supplies. As they were going in a young Indian woman was just coming out. She didn't look up but stood aside so they could enter. Ten Trees said something to her in a soft guttural voice. She looked up startled that someone would speak to her in her own language. She quietly replied immediately. They talked for a couple minutes and then Ten Trees followed her outside where they talked until Zack came out of the store with two bags of food and other supplies. The woman looked down, said a couple things and then hurried off.

"That the Gassoux widow?"

Ten Trees nodded, "She's had a pretty rough time of it here."

When they were back on their horses they talked over the options. They decided to head on out. By nightfall they were miles from the Fort. They found a place to camp, that was a little protected from the wind by a stand of willows. The night was clear but the weather had changed. "I smell snow in the air," Ten Trees said when he got up the next morning he'd slept in his store bought clothes but put on his buckskins back on. The air held his breath in a fog. "We need to get to Fort Laramie as soon as possible. If a blizzard comes we might be in real trouble."

It did snow later that day, but it was only a dusting. There was very little on the ground but it was enough to leave tracks. Ten Tree was relieved when the snow changed over to rain. He didn't like leaving tracks if he didn't have to. The rain was not heavy but cold. Zack could feel himself becoming chilled and was glad when they found an ideal place to camp, even though it was still quite early. Ten Trees found a cave that was large enough for the horses and the men. Zack built a fire and in no time they were all warm. It was a pleasant evening and Zack slept better than he had in days. When he woke up, however, he was in for a big surprise.

Ten Trees was standing behind the fire still fully dressed in his buckskins. He was looking at the mouth of their cave. Zack was laying on his side facing Ten Trees so he slowly rolled over to see what he was seeing. He had to really hold on to his nerves as he faced the two Indians standing in the entrance, their two paint ponies right behind them. They were as magnificent as they were frightening. Zack slowly got up and stood next to Ten Trees. That foreboding came back and he had to swallow hard not to scream.

Zack's mind raced. He was flooded with thoughts, random and odd. He looked at the two men who were as still as statues. The shorter one wore buckskins with fringes up the side, and headdress of feathers that crowned him like a king, the other man was tall and strong looking. The taller man's eyes burned with hatred but the other man's face asked questions without saying a word. It was obvious who the chief was. Zack looked beyond the Indians at the horses. They, too, were beautiful. Zack looked down and saw a torn hoof on one of the spotted ponies.

Zack leaned towards Ten Trees, "Ask if I can fix that horse's hoof?"

Ten Trees looked surprised but did as Zack asked. Ten Trees used Indian sign language to convey his message. The chief must have understood what he said because he moved aside a step or two. Zack quickly got a couple tools from his pack and went to work. He clipped and smoothed the hoof and cleaned the center out. He checked the other hooves while he was at it. Then he went back and stood by Ten Trees.

"Do we have anything we could give him as a gift?" Ten Trees whispered. "This is a big war chief and it is appropriate to give an important gift."

Zack thought a minute, then remembered the halter piece he had made for his child's pony someday. He could always make another if he was alive, which was the question right now. Would they live through this? "I have something. Tell him I'm giving him a big gift."

Ten Trees nodded and relayed the message while Zack got his gift. "This is the eye of the mighty mountain lion to watch over you and give you strength and courage during battles." Zack said as he handed the halter with the head piece in the center. The rock in the center caught the firelight and sparkled. The chief seemed pleased and said something to the other Indian and then turned to Zack.

He looked at his horse and then at Zack. "Thank you," he said in understandable English.

The chief made several remarks to the other man who walked over to Zack's horse. At first Zack thought they meant to take their horses, meaning almost certain death for them but instead the Indian man painted a symbol on the horse. Then the two of them left.

Ten Trees let out a long sigh and sat down on the ground. "My God, Zack! Do you know what just happened?"

"I think you are going to tell me we're very lucky." Zack said as he began to take up his bed roll.

"We were more than lucky, my friend." Ten Trees shook his head. "I'm pretty sure that was Red Cloud. I'm not too sure who that young one was, but I think it might have been Crazy Horse. Probably not many white men have ever met them and lived to tell about it. Especially not now when they've been betrayed so often."

"We didn't mean them any harm so they must not have considered us a threat. Or maybe it's because you're an Indian."

"They could care less about a mostly white Indian of the Sac Fox Nation." Ten Trees shook his head, "I think the Great Spirit has spared us. I think I just became a *very* religious man."

"I saw lots of men become religious when they were facing the barrel of a rifle when I fought in the war," Zack said wistfully, "I was hoping to find a peaceful place. Guess this isn't it either. Let's get out of here before they change their mind and come back."

"Whatever you do, Zack, don't wash that print off your horse. I think they've given us a pass through their territory."

Zack looked at the mark that was sort of half-hand print and half moon with splotches. Didn't mean anything to him but if it would get them through to Fort Laramie he welcomed it.

Chapter 21
East Tennessee—December 1866

By the time Dr. Mitchell paid his next visit the babies were gaining weight, laughing and cooing like any other six week olds. Lydia herself looked as if she'd never had any babies, her figure was back and so was her ability to laugh. She'd thrown herself into being a mother, getting each day's chores done and helping Jonas. Rose was doing better and needed little or no help, although a constant cough nagged her. Dr. Mitchell listened to her lungs each time he visited, and checked the babies over. He'd stopped examining Lydia, however, because in his words she was "fit as a fiddle." No mention was ever made of Mark, except that he'd taken his family and moved to Lexington.

Days after the doctor's visit Eddie Goss came riding into the yard one bright afternoon. "Hey the house," he yelled, "Got mail for you."

Rose and Lydia came running, "I hope it's from Zack," they almost sang out in unison. Jonas heard the commotion and hurried to the house from his cabin. His cat, Goldie, hopped right behind him.

There were three letters, two from Zack and one from Lydia's sister, Ellen. "Which should I read first?" Lydia asked excitedly.

"Well, when were they mailed? Read the oldest first." Rose advised.

Lydia looked at the envelopes and saw that there was one from Stone Hill, Missouri and one from Four Mile Settlement that were just a week apart. She held them to her breast, he **was** thinking of her often it seemed.

Her sister's letter was dated the week after the first of Zack's letters. So she arranged her letters as they walked into the house. Jonas was now using just a cane, so he could hold one baby as he settled into a chair in front of the fireplace. Rose gathered the other baby, little Pete, in the folds of her skirt on the floor as she got comfortable to listen to the letters. Goldie came and flopped over on her back next to the baby between Rose's knees. The cat purred contentedly despite the occasional little hand or foot making contact with its body. Eddie helped himself to a glass of buttermilk and joined the family. When everyone looked ready Lydia began.

> *"Four Mile Settlement,*
> *Sometime in September, 1866*
>
> *My dearest Wife and Mother and Jonas,*
>
> *I ran into some bad luck in Memphis. Was really sick for a few days. Took a good deal of money for the doctor and board while I recovered so couldn't take the stage as planned. I found a job as a freighter and we are hauling goods all over the countryside.*
>
> *My plans are to do this work until we get to Independence, Missouri then hire out with some wagon train to cross the prairie into Oregon or Washington. I work with Bill Zumwalt and Ten Trees LaClair. Ten Trees is an Indian with light hair and blue eyes, lest he told you, you'd never know he was Indian.*
>
> *I miss you and hope things on the farm are going well. The country here is pretty.*
>
> *The roads have been barely passable but Bill has four strong horses pulling the wagon. We eat regular.*
>
> *I guess that is all for now. My love always,*
> *Zack"*

Lydia carefully folded the letter and put it back into the envelope. She knew she would read it over and over again later. Carefully she took up the letter from her sister.

"Dear Lydia and family,

We have been meaning to come and see you and the babies for sometime. Thanks for sending the wire letting us know of their birth. My pregnancy didn't go all that well. I lost baby just a short spell after Zack was here. Took us all awhile to get over that. Now we got new trouble. Our step-mother had sent a letter from a lawyer saying she wants us to sell the farm give her the profits. As father's widow she feels she is owed his property. After she left him and us? Can you believe that? We need to get a lawyer but we don't have any money for one. Roy is selling off some of our cows just to keep us going and now this. When it comes down to it, the farm is as much yours as it is mine. What do you think we should do?

Sorry to trouble you with this but we need to do something pretty soon. Her lawyer has given us just three months to decide. Any ideas you have would be appreciated.

Your loving sister,
Ellen"

"Did we send them a wire about the babies?" Lydia asked Rose.

"Must have been Mark or Dr. Mitchell," Rose said thoughtfully, "I remembered one of them, can't remember which right now, asked if there was anyone we should tell about the birth."

"Hum-m-m," Lydia said, "too bad about their baby. It would have made four for them." She looked at her two babies, both sleeping sweetly, and sighed. "Wonder what they'll do about our family farm?" She mulled that over a moment, she'd never thought about having an interest in the farm. She'd always thought of it as Ellen and Roy's.

"Read the other letter," Eddie urged. Everyone looked at him in surprise, the mail really didn't concern him but he was caught up in their family now.

Lydia unfolded the rough little sheet of paper.

"October 1866
Dearest Wife, mother and friends,

We are in Stone Hill, Missouri and we have just picked up a shipment of wine to take to the railhead at Rolla. I tasted the wine and it wasn't nearly as good as the hard cider that we made at home.

It was raining hard several times this week making the roads miserable. We are pushing on through the Missouri countryside. It's pretty but its not Tennessee. I have a beautiful image of our farm and all of you standing on the porch that day I left. It never leaves my mind. I look forward to the day I can stand with you again on a new porch out west with our baby. Hope the time is going well and you will have an easy time of it Liddy. There isn't a day that I don't wish I could turn back but I've come too far now.

We aren't stopping for long so got to find a place to post this. God bless you all.

My love and best regards,
Zack

Lydia swallowed the lump in her throat and folded the letter back into its envelope. Her emotions were tearing away at her. Her husband didn't even know that he was the father of two beautiful little boys and there wasn't any way to tell him.

"Let's write a letter to him," Jonas suggested. "He said he was going to Independence to follow the wagon trains. They all go a specific way, passing through several of the frontier forts. If we write two or three letters and send them to each of the forts, one of them might reach him."

Rose smiled and picked up the sleeping baby weighing her down. "I think that's a great idea. Let's each write a page and put them in each of the envelopes. Nothing too heavy though, because it will cost a fortune to send." She got up and gently laid Pete in the cradle. Jonas brought Sam over and laid him at the other end. Rose looked down at her two grandsons, "We're going to need to make beds for each of them soon, they are growing so."

Jonas laughed, "I'm ahead of you there, Miss Rose. I have been working on two little beds for the youngsters. They will have sides until they're old enough to get up on their own."

Rose hugged Jonas, "What would we do without you, my friend."

Lydia hurriedly found several sheets of thin paper and they took turns using the quill pen and ink stand. Chores for the day were all but forgotten. The letters were the first priority. It turned out to be harder than she thought to write her letters. How did she say all the things she felt, the love, the anger, the joy, all of it confined to one page. It took her all afternoon to finish her first letter. She mulled over ideas during the times she nursed her babies. She talked to herself while she changed diapers. Even during meals Rose, Jonas and Lydia seemed lost in their own worlds. Only young Eddie babbled on, talking almost to himself.

By sunset the letters were written, and Eddie left with their precious cargo and several dollars to post them. Lydia watched from the window as Eddie rode off toward his home. He'd promised to take the letters to the valley store first thing tomorrow. All her hopes and dreams went with the delicate sheets of news for Zack. "Oh Lord," she prayed silently, "Let the letters reach him somewhere."

* * *

Lydia kept herself busy with things to keep her mind occupied. Winter was upon them with the first snow. It was beautiful when the world was all white and pristine but it could be deadly. A simple cold could take a baby with no effort. A slip or fall could trap a person outside long enough to freeze to death. It was a time to take great caution about the things you normally took for granted. Had they put up enough food to get through until the next crop? Did they have enough wood stacked? With Zack gone and Jonas laid up for so long, they only had half the meat in the smoke house that they normally did going into winter. Would it be enough? There were lean, hard days ahead of them. They rationed themselves automatically, meals were adequate but not ample.

The house was kept warm but never too warm. Jonas moved into a corner of the main room so as not to need to heat his little cabin as well as the main house. The doors were kept shut on the barn until after sunup and closed before sundown to help the animals keep warm.

December had come in quietly, at first a few snowflakes and then the snow became inches, followed by feet. There were days that were sunny and almost warm, but then it would begin again. Mid-month a warm rain began and lasted almost a week, taking most of the snow away. The rain left a muddy mess. Several times Jonas slipped and fell trying to get to and from the barn. He spent most of his day tending to the horses, the three cows they had and feeding the goats. The chickens quit laying but still needed to be fed. Days were short and went by quickly.

Christmas Eve came on the heels of another snowstorm. The wind howled in morning and continued until just about seven o'clock. Rose lit a candle and read the Christmas story to her sleeping grandchildren, Jonas and Lydia. They celebrated the night by toasting each other and the baby Jesus with hot cocoa, a little treat Rose had saved since summer for a special occasion. After Rose and Jonas went to bed, Lydia sat by the fire and remembered that sweet first Christmas she had shared with Zack.

Lydia could see him in his tattered uniform. He'd come that very day to buy extra horses for his unit. It had been late, so her father had asked him to stay for dinner at least on Christmas Eve with his family. Her father had let her and Ellen decorate the house with the ornaments from the attic that had been her mother's, one of the few boxes her step-mother hadn't thrown out. It had been magical. Zack was young and dashing, she was young and as pretty as she ever would be. He seemed drawn to her immediately and she to him. Several times during dinner she found him staring at her. Maybe it was the candlelight on the table, maybe it was her father reading the Christmas story, perhaps it was walking with Zack to his horse when he touched her face with his hand. Whatever it was, it was powerful. She would never forget that night if she lived to be a hundred. She shook her head, would she have married him if she had of known he would leave her alone like this?

A baby cried, then another, both demanding to be fed. Their little calls brought her out of her daydreams. Yes, marrying Zack had been the right thing. If she hadn't, she wouldn't be the mother of those babies. She smiled as she walked to the new men in her life

Chapter 22
Polk County, Oregon—December 1866

Cleveland stood on his front porch late in the day, ignoring the cold, wet breeze that swirled around him. He just stood staring into the distance. Cork shivered at his side. Things seemed bleak, like the slate gray sky overhead. It had been two weeks since Cleveland had any work. And it was the day before Christmas and he was alone. The intermittent rain that had gone on for days didn't help his mood.

The only good thing to look forward to was being invited to the Porterfield's for dinner the next day. For once he would have enough to eat. Since the flooding of his pasture in November he'd had to feed the livestock more hay and grain. The extra money for feed had meant a pretty bland diet for him and the dog. For the last week they'd only small portions of beans and ham twice a day. If he didn't find work soon, even the ham might be out of reach. Cleveland reached down to pet Cork. It pained him to feel her ribs, like he could feel his own. She didn't insist on playing, instead was as quiet as he was. Tonight he would make sure she got more than her share of their meager fare.

Cleveland started to go inside when he heard a rider coming. He turned to see who it was.

"Hello the house," the rider called. "Cleveland, I got a Christmas present for you."

Cleveland walked out into the yard and held out his hand as soon as he recognized the rider, it was Tom Munson, one of the hands from the Brunk house. "Well Mr. Munson, what brings you clear out here?"

The middle aged man got down from his horse and untied a couple large bags from his saddle. "Miss Brunk said that she had promised you a pie for Christmas so she asked me to bring this to you. Mrs. Brunk also sent along some things. They just wanted to wish you a merry Christmas, son." He smiled and handed the heavy bags to Cleveland.

Cork was jumping around excitedly and Cleveland had to push her down with his knee.

"Would you like to come in for some tea?"

"No, got to get back before dark." Tom hopped back on his horse and tipped his hat. "I'll be wishing you a blessed Christmas, son." He whirled and started off.

"Thank the Brunk family for me, and wish them a Merry Christmas from me."

"I'll do that," Tom called back from half-way down the lane.

"Oh, and thank you for making the trip out here," Cleveland yelled but wasn't sure the man heard him as he was nearly out of sight.

Cleveland hurried into the house and lit a candle. His mouth was watering thinking there might be a treasure of food in the offering. "Cork, looks like our Christmas Eve dinner will be better than we thought." He was delighted to see that the pie had made the trip, flattened but intact. Besides the pie, there was a dozen oatmeal and raisin cookies, a half dozen hard-boiled eggs, a small loaf of fruitcake, a tin of cocoa and three wrapped packages. Cleveland ignored the presents. He peeled two of the eggs, then sliced the apple pie into four pieces. He got Cork's plate and put a half-slice of pie and one of the eggs on it.

"I'm not sure pie is all that good for you, Cork, but you deserve a good meal so I hope this doesn't upset you." He put the plate down and the grateful dog made short work of every crumb of the pie and egg. Cleveland fixed the same for himself and finished it nearly as fast as the dog. When their immediate hunger was satisfied, Cork and Cleveland settled down in front of the fire and began working on the cookies. Within minutes the cookies were all gone too. Cork had three and Cleveland the rest. It felt good to both of them to have a full stomach.

"Wasn't a steak or potatoes, girl, but it did taste pretty darn good didn't it?" Cleveland asked the dog as he wiped crumbs from the fur around her mouth. He started to get up when he heard a knock on the door.

"Hello," he said, cautiously opening the door.

"Hello my boy," Reverend Murphy and his Missus, as well as about six other people had arrived. The others had remained in the large farm wagon sitting on bales of straw. Cleveland had been so preoccupied with the food he hadn't heard them arrive.

Cleveland started to say something but the minister put his hand up and motioned to the people in the wagon. One of the men put a fiddle to his chin and the group began to sing choruses of "Hark the Herald Angels Sing," "O Little Town of Bethlehem," and lastly "Silent Night."

Cleveland stood on the porch with Cork at his side. He didn't even notice the cold wind and light rain. The carolers didn't seem to mind the weather, either. Cleveland clapped his hands and smiled, "That was right pretty. Thank you so much for coming by. Would you like to come in and warm up?"

"No, we got three more stops before we head back to town. We are just out wishing members of the flock a Merry Christmas," Reverend Murphy said as he helped his wife back up into the front seat of the wagon. Then he walked to the back and got a small wooden crate. "This is for you, my boy, Merry Christmas." He didn't say anything else as he plunked the box into Cleveland's arms, whirled around and got back into the wagon and happily went off into the gathering night.

"Thank you and Merry Christmas everyone," Cleveland called out as they disappeared into the darkness.

"Cork, can you believe this, girl? We didn't have enough for dinner now we have more than we need. It's a miracle." He took the box in and put it on the table to see what new treasures they had. "Oh my," he sighed, "this is wonderful." He held a bag of coffee out to show Cork. She sniffed but didn't find it particularly interesting. "We've been out of coffee for a week," Cleveland explained. "Oh, here is something that may interest you." Mrs. Murphy always asked about Cork on Sundays. She knew the dog was Cleveland's only companion, so in her thoughtfulness she had wrapped a large soup bone with good bits of meat still attached and put it into the box. Cork was her old self when she saw the bone. "Merry Christmas, my friend," Cleveland said gently patting her on the head as he handed her the bone. She grabbed it and headed for the warm rug in front of the fire. The slurping and crunching noises that filled the room nearly brought tears to Cleveland's eyes. He loved her to be happy.

The box also contained a bar of soap, tins of beef, chicken, a jug of milk, vegetables, a bag of potatoes, a bag of onions, a bag of carrots, baking soda, a small bag of flour, and three oranges. It was a treasure chest indeed. Cleveland couldn't hardly peel one of the oranges fast enough. It had been a long time since he'd had fresh fruit. Its tart sweetness was better than the pie he'd just eaten.

What had started out as a dismal Christmas Eve had turned out to be anything but dismal. He was full and content. Two things he hadn't been in a long time. All at once he remembered the presents. He brought them over to his cot and looked at them for a minute or two. Just last year his mother had been with him. The presents reminded him of her and how she always made sure he had at least two gifts every Christmas, no matter how poor they were. He'd always made her something, nothing special, just something. Their last time together he'd made her a fancy little trivet out of wood to sit hot pots on. He'd also saved up his money and bought her a comb with a pretty, mother of pearl handle. She really seemed to like that but had said it was the extra effort it took that really touched her. He was glad he'd been able to make her happy. He took a deep breath and then shook off the pain of those memories.

Cleveland shook the first package and heard a soft thud. "Must be clothes," he said to Cork.

Carefully he untied the little string that was holding it. The plain red paper slipped away from the box, drifting slowly to the floor. "Well see, I was right." He looked at the dark brown, knitted mittens and scarf that were in the package. There was also a little note, "For my friend, Merry Christmas, Mary Brunk." He felt embarrassed all over again. He'd made such a fool of himself in front of her and the Brunk family. They obviously didn't hold it against him, though. He smiled, opening the second package. "Oh, this is nice," Cleveland said holding up a new blue shirt. The card said that it was from Mr. and Mrs. Brunk. The third package was heavier than the other two but smaller. It turned out to be three books, a Bible, a cookbook, and a journal to write in. "That's amazing. I don't think they knew I buried ma's Bible with her. They couldn't have known I didn't have one. The cookbook, well, first you have to have something to cook. Maybe I can learn though. What do you think, Cork? Want something more than ham and beans?" He lay down on the rug and wrestled the dog for a few minutes. Both of them fell asleep there in front of the fire, happier than they had been in months.

* * *

Cleveland didn't want to but he had to leave Cork at home on Christmas day. It was just too wet to take her along. Neither of them had been happy about that but it had to be. She'd been a muddy mess by the time they got to the Porterfield's. Cleveland had to send her back several times before she finally accepted his orders. She lay on the porch looking so miserable as he rode off that he thought about not going.

It wasn't raining but it had rained during the night and looked like it might start again at any moment. Since it was a Tuesday they weren't having a church service that day. Most folks were just getting together for a big dinner. He was glad the Porterfield family always included him in their celebrations. They'd become a second family to him. Old Molly nearly knew the route by heart.

He arrived about half an hour early. Once Molly was in a stall in the barn, Cleveland headed for the house. A buckboard behind two mules and a phaeton buggy hitched to two fancy horses were tied up out front. He'd never seen either of the rigs before and wondered who else was here.

Cleveland knocked and walked into the kitchen. Mrs. Porterfield was busily preparing food with the help of two other women. "Morning, Mrs. Porterfield," he stammered as one of the other women whirled past him with a plate of steaming hot food.

"Cleveland my boy, just in time. Grab a plate and carry it into the other room."

He did as he was instructed. He grabbed a bowl full of bean salad and hurried into the main room of the house where a huge table of lumber over sawhorses had been set up. Several men and Mrs. Porterfield's elderly mother were sitting around the fireplace. Mr. Porterfield came over and got Cleveland by the arm and ushered him over to the men's group. "Those women put you right to work I see," he laughed. "Gentleman, this is young Cleveland Taylor, owns a small place just north of Buena Vista." He pointed to each of the four older men one by one. "This is George Ash, he's got a place on the Luckiamute. This is Sandy Bridges, he's a traveling salesman who's been a long time friend. This is Brick Millhouser, a distant cousin of mine from Seattle. That's his wife Esse and daughter Nina helping out in the kitchen. And last but not least, this is Del Gabriel, a circuit preacher on his way to Seattle." Cleveland shook hands with each of the men.

"Cleveland had the misfortune of losing his mother just last spring, lost his father a year or two before that. He's a sharp hand with carpentry tools though, makes his living that way." Mr. Porterfield pointed to a chair. "That's the chair he made my Missus."

Cleveland was pleased with the oohs and ahs from the five men sitting there as they looked over the chair. "Wouldn't mind having a chair like that myself," George Ash said, half squinting at Cleveland. "What would you charge me to make one for me?"

"Let's not talk work today," Mr. Porterfield interrupted, "Today we're going to eat and be joyful." He laughed and the older men settled down to talk about their favorite thing, politics.

Cleveland really didn't know much about politics, so he just listened. He was, however, very grateful when Mrs. Porterfield finally announced that dinner was ready. The three full time ranch hands came in to join the rest of the guests for dinner.

When everyone had found a chair or a place on a bench, Mr. Porterfield stood, read Luke 2: 1-7 from the family Bible, *"And it came to pass in those days that a decree went out from Caesar Augustus that all the world should be registered. This census first took place while Quirinius was governing Syria. So all went to be registered, everyone to his own city. Joseph also went up from Galilee out of the city of Nazareth, into Judea, to the city of David which is also called Bethlehem because he was of the house and lineage of David, to be registered with Mary, his betrothed wife, who was with child. So it was, that while they were there the days were completed for her to be delivered. And she brought forth her firstborn Son, and wrapped Him in swaddling cloths, and laid Him in a manger, because there was no room at the inn."* Mr. Porterfield closed the Bible, laying it aside. "May we always have room in our hearts and at our table for all those who worship Christ, the new born King. Amen." He sat down and smiled, "Well, let's see if these women folk have cooked anything fit to eat."

Mrs. Porterfield sat a huge turkey on a platter in front of her husband, "I think we did. Please do the honors, father." Mr. Porterfield stood back up to begin slicing the bird. In moments, platters of every kind of delicacy passed in front of Cleveland. It made him as dizzy as the wine at Thanksgiving had. When his plate could hold no more Cleveland began to eat. It was heavenly!

When he'd wiped his plate with the last of his biscuit Cleveland finally looked up. He was surprised to see that the young woman sitting across from his was watching him with amusement. "You really must have been hungry." She laughed softly. "Hello, I'm Nina." She waved long slender fingers at him.

Cleveland swallowed. He knew she wasn't being rude, but it was embarrassing to be noticed eating so much. He tried to say something clever but nothing came to mind so he just said, "It was such good food, I couldn't help myself."

Mrs. Porterfield laughed, "Cleveland always eats like that Nina. He's still growing and works like a horse. He needs all the fuel he can get."

"What is it you do, Cleveland?" the young woman asked softly.

Cleveland looked at her and realized she wasn't much older than him. She had dark curly hair framing a soft, pretty face. Her eyes were bright blue, her mouth small with full bowed lips. "I'm a carpenter," he said, struggling with a dry mouth and throat for some reason.

"Oh, what do you build?"

"Lots of things. I helped repair the Christian School in Monmouth, helped build the Brunk family barn, helped with several houses or anything I'm asked to work on. In my spare time, I make furniture pieces like that chair over there," he pointed to the other end of the room.

"What are you working on now?" Nina continued.

Cleveland shrugged, "I'm always looking for work. I usually work with a crew from Independence, but they've been idle for a couple weeks. I guess I'll have to go out tomorrow and look for something to do until they start back up."

George Ash had a mouthful of food when he over heard Cleveland and Nina. He washed his food down with a bigger sip of apple cider. "Listen boy, if you're looking for work, I got a lot of wind damage in that storm last month. My barn is fixing to fall down if I don't do something soon. It's more than I can rightly do by myself. I'd be willing to pay you going wages for helping me out."

"I can come tomorrow and see what needs to be done," Cleveland said around the two people sitting between them.

"That would be just fine! Before we leave today I'll tell you how to get to my place."

Cleveland nodded, and everyone went back to eating. Cleveland couldn't believe his good luck. Just yesterday he had nothing much to eat, no prospects for work and now he had a week's worth of food for himself and Cork, plus a job. He felt it just couldn't get any more astonishing but the day still had a couple surprises for him.

It took nearly two hours for everyone to get to the point they just had to leave the table. Everyone helped the women carry the leftovers to the kitchen. The men settled in again in front of the fireplace to wait for the womenfolk. The hired hands left to go back to work, on-going chores were part of farm life.

In a half hour or so Nina came into the living room, coming straight to Cleveland. "Mrs. Porterfield thinks I ought to ask you to show me around the farm. She said you know the farm as well as the hired hands."

Cleveland stood up, looking for help from Mr. Porterfield but all he got was a smile and wave off, "You young people go take a walk. We'll keep the fire going and continue our debate about who's going to win the election."

Cleveland followed Nina to the front door. They both put on ponchos that were hanging by the front door for anyone to use when they went outside. It was a good thing they had put on the extra clothing for warmth because the weather had definitely gotten colder.

They walked briskly to the barn. "This is a pretty nice barn." Cleveland said lamely. "Better than mine anyway."

"I guess barns come in all sizes and shapes, don't they."

"Do you have a barn?"

"No we live in the city," Nina said quietly, "our horses are kept at the livery stable at the end of the street. They have a barn and an exercise area that doubles as a show ring for horse shows."

"What do they do at a horse show?"

"Fancy riding or sometimes contests using the horses to go around obstacles and things." Nina wrinkled up her nose, "A horse still smells like a horse though, no matter how pretty it is or how well it performs."

Cleveland had never thought about how things smelled. He walked over to Molly, she didn't smell any way except the way she always did. "This is my mule, Molly," he said while stroking her neck.

"Do you have a horse, too?"

"No, just two mules, two cows and a dog."

"Oh a dog, what kind is it? We have a dog at home, her name is Willow. She's an Irish Setter. Have you ever seen an Irish Setter, Cleveland?"

"Can't say I have. Cork is just a dog, my ma thought she might be some kind of Collie mix."

"An Irish Setter is a fair sized dog with long silky red hair. When she runs she just shimmers." Nina walked to the door of the barn, "I think it's going to snow. It feels cold enough, don't you think? Do you have a girlfriend, Cleveland?"

Cleveland found it annoying that Nina asked questions without giving him time to answer them. "I don't think it's cold enough to snow. And no, I don't have a girlfriend."

She turned and smiled at him. "You're awfully cute, Cleveland. I can imagine the girls around here pester you all the time, wanting to be your girl."

Now the conversation was making him uncomfortable. He couldn't tell if she was making fun of him or flirting. Either way he wanted to run. Cleveland walked over next to her and looked out the door. "Maybe you're right, it might be getting ready to snow. I think I should leave and get my chores done before it starts." He started to walk out of the barn when Nina surprised him by grabbing his arm and dragging him back further into the barn. "What?" he said concerned.

She smiled and quickly kissed him lightly on the lips. He was too surprised to do anything but stand there. Nina seized the moment and kissed him again, this time for a longer time and with more passion. For a minute Cleveland felt like he might faint as she stood leaning against him. He wanted to kiss her back but knew that would be a mistake. He finally stepped back and wheezed, "What on earth did you do that for?"

"Just wanted to see if I'd like it," she said with a twisted little smile, "Didn't like it at all." She walked around him towards the house, stopping once to look back at his white, drawn face, "Well, maybe I did like it, a little bit." She laughed and ran on into the house.

Cleveland stayed in the barn for a few minutes gathering his shattered emotions and trying to cool his crimson face. He saddled Molly for the ride home, debating wether he should go back into the house and thank the Porterfields. It crossed his mind that Nina might be in there right at that moment telling everyone that he'd kissed her. He shuddered at the thought. Finally good manners won out and he headed for the house to thank the family for their invitation.

Cleveland was pleased to find Mrs. Porterfield in the kitchen alone when he entered the room. "Mrs. Porterfield, I want to thank you for all the fine food today and the good company. I need to go home now." He said almost in a panic.

Mrs. Porterfield hugged him, "I hope that you'll come here often, son," she stood back and motioned for him to follow her back into the main room. "Come on we're not done here."

Cleveland was reluctant to see Nina again but he was relieved that she just pretended nothing at all had happened between them. Mr. Porterfield nodded to his wife as they crossed the room and stepped out onto the porch for a few minutes. When he came back he was carrying a large crate full of chickens.

"Merry Christmas, Cleveland," the Porterfields chimed together.

"We knew you'd been saving up for a flock of chickens for some time so we thought we'd get you started. We think there are four laying hens and a rooster in here." He sat the crate down and counted the moving targets again, "Yes, I think that's what we have here."

Cleveland was stunned, what an amazing gift. "Are you sure, I mean that's an expensive gift…I don't…"

"Don't think a thing about it. I'll have my man bring these down and put them in your coop first thing tomorrow."

"I have to put the wire fence up first. I have the wire, just didn't have a reason to put it up yet. Could you keep them until Saturday?"

"Saturday it will be." Mr. Porterfield hugged Cleveland.

Cleveland bid everyone farewell and headed off to the barn to get Molly. Mrs. Porterfield handed him a box of leftovers before he left for "later." It had turned out to be a magnificent Christmas. He felt far from alone as he had just twenty four hours ago. He'd been kissed by a pretty girl. He had food for him and Cork, he had the promise of work and now he had chickens that he hoped meant hard boiled eggs anytime he wanted them. Life was good.

Chapter 23
Fort Laramie—February 1867

It had been snowing lightly when Ten Trees and Zack arrived at the Fort. By the time they had found a place to stay and stable their horses and the mule, a full blown blizzard descended upon them. The quarters available were pretty marginal. An old barracks like building was used to house single men. There were six sets of bunk beds lining the walls. A small pot bellied stove sat in the middle and two small eating tables on either side of the stove made up the furnishings. There was a front door that opened to the path that took a man to the main fort. The back door lead one way to the woodpile and other to the outhouse. For water and washing up, the Laramie River was just twenty yards beyond the woodpile.

Luckily there were only three other men in the quarters so Ten Trees and Zack took a set of bunks at one end of the building, away from the others. The three others seemed friendly enough. One, named Joe Hopine, was a skinny little salesman from New York. He was heading to California to go into mining but had became ill on the trail, and he so had stayed behind when his wagon train left. He was hoping to start off with the next train through. Zack wondered to himself if Joe would make it that long, though, because the man still had a really bad cough. The second man was Alex Maynard. He'd been a surveyor with the army but his job was done so he'd be heading back with the troops that were due to be replaced soon. The last man, a large, heavy-set man named Lars Johansen, was also from the last wagon train. He had lost his wagon in an Indian attack. His wife and son had been killed. He, too, planned to return east with the soldiers.

As the wind howled outside the men settled down for a long siege. The little stove struggled valiantly to give enough heat that the men didn't freeze to death. The weather got vicious. The wind driven snow was so deep at times that they had to tie a rope to the door and one to the wood pile and one to the outhouse, so no one would get lost on the way to either. Days went by, and food was meager, usually cold biscuits for breakfast, with watery stew for lunch and dinner. To pass the time, the men played cards or told stories of their childhoods. Daylight was short, so they often went to bed after dinner. A week, then two went by.

Finally, the wind died down. A few days later the troops from Fort Kearney arrived. They had been delayed by an Indian attack that had left several settlers and many troops dead. The talk was all about the new threats. It was very unsettling. Alex and Lars got permission to ride with the soldiers when they returned to Fort Kearney instead of having to ride behind. That relieved them both. Ten Trees was quietly listening as they made their plans and packed up what little they had. The soldiers were leaving the next morning.

Zack and Ten Trees took a walk along the ice-covered Laramie River to see if there was any game to be had. The wind had scoured the snow off the river and most flat patches of land. Here and there in the gullies there were huge drifts of snow, but mostly it was just hard frozen earth. The cold was bitter. Neither of them had heavy enough clothing for this kind of weather. Their hunting trip would have to be short. They saw a deer, but it bounded away before they had a chance to even get a shot off. Ten Trees managed to get a couple rabbits, at least. Zack had to admit Ten Trees was quite a hunter. They walked briskly back to the lodge with their feast for the night.

"You're mighty quiet, Ten Trees," Zack said as they hurried along.

"I'm going to go back to Fort Kearney," Ten Trees said without emotion. "I told you I would get you to Fort Laramie and we are here."

"I thought you were going west?"

"Hum," Ten Trees said, "I was thinking of taking Mrs. Gassoux back to her people, if she wants to go. She's only twenty three and has five children. She was only a child when she was taken." He looked at Zack and smiled, "And she's not bad looking."

Zack laughed, "You are brave to take on a woman with five children." Zack felt a sudden pang of guilt. His own child should be born by this time.

Ten Trees shook his head, "You've always been white. They fought a war to free black men and bad as it was for them, it's been just as bad or worse for the Indian. We are seen as the enemy. There's a saying that you hear along the trails all the time, "The only good Indian is a dead Indian."

"Yeah, I've heard that but I've never said it," Zack answered.

"You're more sensitive than most," Ten Trees said nodding, "but one man's opinion isn't enough. Don't know how long it will take to change things for my people in general."

Zack didn't know what to say so he just kept silent for the rest of way to the barrack. He was really glad when they finally stepped in out of the cold. The tips of his fingers were nearly numb. He tore off his thin gloves and held his hands over the stove. The other three men were playing a hand of cards. "We got some rabbits for a send off dinner tonight." Zack said cheerful, "Ted's decided to go back with you."

"We'll welcome the company, Ted," Joe said, "And the extra gun, too, in case we have to fight any dirty red skins."

Ten Trees just looked at Zack for a brief moment, then took the rabbits and prepared them for the stew. Zack continued to warm himself by the fire for a few more minutes. "I'll go get some more wood," he said heading for the back door. Before he could leave, however, the front door opened and a young soldier stepped quickly inside.

"Howdy men," the corporal said, "one of you men Zachary Grant?"

"That would be me," Zack said cautiously.

"Got a letter for you, came to Fort Kearney but we was coming here so we brought it along."

He walked across the floor and handed it to Zack, then he turned and left with a nod to each of them.

"It's from my family," Zack said in astonishment. He forgot all about going for the wood, instead he peeled off his coat, hat and gloves. He took the letter to his bunk and sat looking at it with tears in his eyes. Ten Trees quietly went to get the evening wood supply.

Zack took a deep breath and gently opened the small envelope. His eyes were so misted that he couldn't see the writing for a moment. The letter consisted of three small sheets of thin paper with writing on each side. He wiped his eyes with his sleeve and took the first sheet of paper. He glanced down and saw that it was from his mother. He sorted the pages so that the one from Lydia was first, then his mother, then the one from Jonas. He sighed and settled back on his pillow to read the mail.

December 12, 1866
My Dearest Husband,

We are all praying our letters reach you. We have no idea where you are but we have faith that you are well. We are all very well. There is much to tell you and not much room to say it all. You have a surprise coming my love, you have two sons. Peter and Samuel were born last month. They weren't very big but have grown well in the last few weeks. They don't look much alike. Sam is much bigger than Pete, eats more, cries more.

Your mother said Sam favors me and Pete looks like you. The doctor said I came through real well and should not have any problems having other babies. I can't wait for you to come home so we can add to our family. I am praying that day is soon.

Jonas broke his leg but is on the mend, he can tell you about that. The winter has set in. We have had some snow already. The Goss boy has come up and cut wood for us so we'll have plenty for what's to come. Your mother and I have been canning, making quilts and things. It makes the day go by quicker.

My sister Ellen says they may lose the farm to my step-mother. That is a hard situation.

I never thought about it before but I guess I have an interest in that home place too. I wish you were here to help us sort that out.

Be safe, know that we love you. Most of all come back to us soon or send for us. I never want you to leave me again. I didn't realize how lonely it would be without you.

Thank goodness for your mother and Jonas, they have been cheerful and so helpful with Pete and Sam. We all love you.

God bless you my husband,
Yours always,
Liddy"

Zack read his mother's letter and the one from Jonas. He sat for a few moments in stunned silence, then he realized the others in the room were looking at him. He smiled, making one more pass with his sleeve over his tear stained face. "I got two boys, Peter and Samuel. My wife had twins."

Ten Trees jumped up in the air and let out a howl, then remembered how that would sound to the others, "That is great news my friend," he said running over to pat Zack on the shoulders. Joe and Alex came over and shook Zack's hand. Lars continued to sit at the table, finally putting his head in his hands, sobbing.

Zack got up and followed the others back to the table. "I had a son," Lars choked out, "His name was also Peter. He was only four." The others patted him on the back, trying to console him.

"This is a hard country, if the Indians don't get you then illness might," Joe tried to sound comforting.

"We never know the why of things but my mother always used to say things happen for a reason. She likes to quote Job's troubles." Zack said quietly, "I never actually found it all that understandable but I think the gist of it was if we remain faithful, though we lose everything, in the end God will make it right with us somehow."

Lars looked at Zack, clearly in pain, "We must have had the same momma. Mine said the same. Through the loss of my father, a second husband and three children she remained faithful to God, trusting it would work out."

"Did it work out?" Joe asked skeptically.

Lars shrugged, "Well, she married for the third time and was happy until she died at age 57. She lived to see four grandchildren, including my boy Peter. I sometimes dream that they are all together in a better place than this."

"Well, wouldn't take much to be better than this," Alex laughed.

Lars laughed softly, "Got that right. I'm sorry men, I didn't mean to dampen your happy news, Zack. Congratulations, twin boys, that's really great." He stood up and shook Zack's hand.

Ten Trees finished putting the rabbit stew fixings in the pot. Its fragrance filled the room and by the time it was ready for eating, everyone was in a happier mood. But it was only superficial because the next day would bring many changes. Ten Trees and the others knew that a lot of Indians lay between the forts as well as unpredictable weather. It was a very dangerous time to be going anywhere. Every day in the wilderness had it's own peril.

The morning came extremely cold and clear. Ten Trees stoically packed up what little he had and prepared to leave. "You keep the pack mule," he said to Zack without emotion. "I'll get a wagon back at Fort Kearney."

Zack nodded, hesitantly following him out the door and to the stables. He watched as his friend saddled his horse and started to get on him. Ten Trees turned and closed the distance between them. The two men hugged. "May the Great Spirit protect you and deliver you to the land you seek."

"And you, my friend," Zack said, "Oh yes, I nearly forgot. Will you post this for me?" Zack held out a small envelope.

Ten Trees took the letter and put it into his saddlebag. He didn't say anything else. He simply got on his horse and rode out of the livery stable. Alex and Lars were waiting just out side for him. They waved to Zack and headed off to the main part of the fort where the army troops were assembling. Zack stood by the edge of the parade grounds to watch the goings on. Within a few minutes Zack saw the column of soldiers and his friends riding off across the river to the east. He watched as long as he could, but finally the bitter cold sent him back inside the nearly empty barracks. Joe was taking an afternoon nap, coughing without waking up. The room wasn't very big but it felt huge and empty without his friend. He made a pot of coffee and sat down to re-read his letters.

* * *

The bad weather came back with a vengeance. Snow piled up everywhere, the wood supply dwindled. The food supply was also scant. Zack wasn't the hunter that Ten Trees had been so even an occasional rabbit was a treat. Joe was not a hunter, besides not being well enough to go foraging for wood. Zack was puzzled what a man like him was doing out in this rugged land.

One afternoon they got a new boarder. When the front door opened, both Zack and Joe yelled to shut the door quickly. The wind could suck the warmth from the room in seconds. It took a moment for Zack's eyes to re-adjust to room light again after the glaring white of the snow through the open door. He was surprised at the man who had joined them. He was covered in animal skins. Without a word, he looked around then walked to a bunk closest to the fire and began to unwrap himself. It took several layers of robes before a man in buckskins finally emerged.

"My name is Frenchy Longworth," he said as he walked over and extended a hand to Zack.

"I'm a trapper from up north." Frenchy was a short stocky man, his face was pock marked and his skin was dark and weathered like old leather, but he looked as strong as an ox, with huge biceps and large hands that showed evidence of hard work. There was no way of telling how old he might be.

Zack shook his hand and smiled, "I'm Zack Grant and that's Joe Hopine."

Joe started to extend his hand but had another round of coughing and had to return to his bunk. Frenchy looked at Zack and nodded, both of them knew that Joe was probably not going to make it through this winter, but that was life on the frontier. Only the strong could survive, and then not even all of them.

"I've got some coffee on," Zack said pointing to the pot. "Joe, you want some?" Joe shook his head.

Frenchy drew up a chair as Zack brought two mugs of coffee to the table. "Where you from, Frenchy?"

"From up near the border with Canada. I'm Canadian," he smiled, "Half anyway. I guess you'd call me a half-breed. My mother is Sioux. My father was a Canadian trapper."

"I had a friend, Ten Trees, who was also part French and part Indian. He helped me get out here. He was here until just a few days ago, went back to Fort Kearney."

"Are you talking about Ted?" Joe croaked between coughs.

"Yes, he always went by Ted when we were in white settlements, but his name was Ten Trees. He was of the Sac Fox nation."

"Well, I'll be," Joe shook his head, "he had blue eyes and looked absolutely white to me."

"Does it make a difference," Zack asked, "That he was Indian?"

"It would have to Lars," Joe said shaking his head, "Brother, would it have. Now there they are, riding to Kearney together like kin."

"Guess that's why he kept it to himself."

Frenchy laughed, "That's why I stay out of the civilized world. I know what people would think of me. I look Indian. I ain't ashamed of it, either. My mother's people treat me as one of them, unlike my father's people." He sipped his coffee. "This is good, not strong enough but good. That's one thing my father taught me was how to make coffee strong."

"We take turns making the food here, you can make the next pot of coffee. We don't have a lot of food but we share what we have."

Frenchy laughed again, "I got food. I'll bring it in." He got up and threw a hide over himself and went out again. In just a few minutes he was back with a bundle. He walked over and pulled the wraps off of it. It turned out to be a frozen block of meat. Frenchy pried three large pieces loose, "Here, you can cook these for us tonight." He rewrapped the meat and took it outside to find a safe place to stash it. By the time he came back Zack had the pan on the stove and the steaks were nearly thawed. Both Joe and Zack hadn't had a steak of anything in such a long time they never even thought to ask what might be in the pan.

After they had eaten and had another pot of stronger coffee the three of them sat contentedly around the one small candle on the table. "Could you tell what you were eating?"

Zack looked at Joe and shook his head, "Thought it was elk or maybe moose, tasted a little strong for deer."

"It was a bear," Frenchy said with a twisted grin. "Killed a grizzly just about ten miles from here." He rolled up his sleeve to reveal a couple half healed big puncture wounds on his upper arm. "He didn't go easy. Took four arrows then finally a knife to the brain through an eye to take him down. I ate his liver on the spot. It's the best when it's still warm."

Zack felt a little queasy thinking about eating raw liver but he tried not to show it, "I hear liver is good for a person."

"Supposed to make you more of a man," Frenchy laughed wickedly, "If you know what I mean?"

"We get it," Joe said with a half smile.

"Probably do you some good, build up your blood, Joe." Frenchy said. "I think there is a little chunk of that left in the bundle."

"I'll pass thank you, but the steak was absolutely wonderful," Joe yawned, "I'm going to turn in. Thanks again for the food, Frenchy." He got up and walked to his bunk. Within moments Joe was snoring in between bouts of coughing.

"He doesn't sound good," Frenchy said quietly, leaning across the table towards Zack.

"I know, I think he's got consumption. I don't remember many people surviving that."

Zack said quietly leaning towards Frenchy. "What are you doing here in Laramie, Frenchy?"

"I came looking for you," Frenchy said in a near whisper.

Zack looked surprised, "Me? We don't know each other. Why would you be looking for me?"

"I didn't know your name, but I knew your horse."

"My horse?" Zack said in disbelief, "You know my horse? Why would you..." Zack remembered the hand printed symbol that was still on his horse's flank. "You know who put that symbol on my horse?"

Frenchy nodded, "We have mutual friends." Frenchy looked over to reassure himself Joe was fast asleep. "I was sent to take you to Fort Hall."

"What?"

"Our mutual friends want me to make sure you get to Fort Hall."

"I don't understand why," Zack said still trying to grasp what Frenchy was saying but the half-breed put his hand up to silence him.

"Tomorrow I will take you and your pack animal with as many supplies as you can afford and we will head west. I will keep you safe and guide you as far as Fort Hall." Frenchy looked at Joe again. "We go at first light, no other discussion." He got up and stretched. "I haven't slept on a real bed in a long time." He went over and flopped down on the thin horsehair pad that served as a mattress, "Ah, this is nice."

Zack laughed softly, "It must have been a long time since you slept in a real bed if you think that is nice."

"To tell the truth, I ain't never slept in a white man's bed but I always heard they were soft so I didn't want to say anything against my first one. This is hard as a rock!"

Zack nodded and headed for his bunk, "You can say that again." Zack gathered up his clothes and put them into his small valise. It would not take long to pack up in the morning.

After coffee, biscuits and another bear steak, in the morning, Frenchy and Zack stopped at the company store, then headed west. Zack couldn't help wonder why he'd been given this escort yet he knew he shouldn't question the reason, but just accept the helping hand.

The going was hard, snow was everywhere and it was so cold. Frenchy had draped Zack and his horse and mule in furs that kept the frigid wind from reaching their skins. They had to fight for every step in snow often up to the bellies of the animals. The short hours of daylight were followed by long cold nights but somehow Frenchy knew where to camp, often in the well at the base of a tall fir tree. Sometimes he'd know of a cave or find a fallen tree that had created an artificial cave.

Frenchy's hunting skills provided food for them. Even high in the mountains he was able to track and find game. He kept them moving steadily along until at last they came down on the west side of a high mountain pass. A broad valley lay before them, French pointed off towards the river that was on the horizon. "That's Fort Hall down there by the river." Frenchy brought a bag of provisions from his horse and tied it on the pack mule. Then he turned to go back the way he'd come without a word.

"Wait," Zack said, "I want to know why you've done this? Why did you bring me out here in the middle of winter at no little danger to yourself?"

"Let's just say that Red Cloud promised you safe passage through his territory. If you stayed in Laramie, you might have been at risk." Frenchy grinned wickedly, "All white men look alike to an Indian you know. There is big talk of war." Frenchy brought his horse along side of Zack's. He reached out with the sleeve of his bear skin robe and rubbed vigorously at the painted symbol on Zack's horse. Within seconds it was gone. He looked Zack in the eyes, "Don't come back this way again. Red Cloud has returned your gift ten-fold. He feels no need to protect you now." He wheeled his horse around and headed towards the east. "Good luck, Zack."

"And to you. Thank Red Cloud for me." Zack waved, sighed, then began the next leg of his journey.

* * *

Fort Hall provided a much needed place to rest for a few days and pick up a couple odd jobs of shoeing horses. With a little extra money, Zack was able to buy supplies to continue on his trek west. It took a week of following the Snake River to reach Farewell Bend.

It was cold and windy, but hadn't snowed in a month. It was a pretty dismal looking place, but it did have a store and a ferry to cross the river. More than a dozen wagons were camped out around the small valley near the crossing. The steep walls of the canyon beyond the crossing seemed ominous.

Zack tied up his animals out of the wind at the side of the store and went in. There was a couple of tables at one side of the room, so he went and sat down. A man in a white apron came over and brought the coffee pot with a large tin mug. "Figure you're wanting some coffee?"

"You got that right." Zack said gratefully. "Got anything to eat?"

"Rabbit stew or biscuits and gravy."

"Biscuits and gravy sounds good."

"Be right back," the man turned and looked at Zack, "That will be two bits."

Zack fished around in his shirt pocket and bought out one of his three remaining coins and put it on the table. The man nodded and went off to get the food. It was a time when money was very scarce, Zack had found that most everyone in this part of the county preferred to trade in gold dust, which was hard to come by, too.

The meal had sounded better than it turned out to be, but it was hot and certainly ample. Zack was having a second cup of coffee, when two other men came in. They were tired looking and dirty, but friendly. They came and joined Zack at his table. The older of the two men introduced himself as Eldon Reid and his friend as Fred Swell. The two were miners who'd been mining north of Fort Boise, but hadn't had much luck. They were traveling on to Baker City because they'd heard about several rich strikes.

"I'm kind of headed the same direction, I'm going to the Willamette Valley," Zack said, "Maybe we could travel together, at least to Baker City."

"Sounds good to me, safety in numbers," Fred said, around swigs of hot coffee.

The men sat for awhile chatting about how far they'd come and from where. Each had different reasons, but here they were in the same place; broke, a long way from their families, and still searching. Fred pointed to the wagons outside the store, "Those poor souls have a long tough haul to Baker City. I've heard stories that there's thousands of graves, between here and there. The early wagon trains ran into poor water, ran out of food, got caught in bad weather, and met more than a few Indians. We're lucky, it's all pretty easy on horseback now."

Zack shuttered to think of how hard it must have been twenty years earlier, in the time of the first wagon trains. "Things are changing so fast, next thing you know they'll put a bridge across this river and plow a road right up the hill."

"Yeah, it will become just like Pennsylvania." Eldon said looking away sadly.

INTO THE DUST

Zack finished his coffee and purchased a little more feed for his animals. He didn't have enough money to buy anything for himself though. He'd have to hunt for his meals. The other two men did the same. Once outside they cast one more look at the wagons and the tired looking people, huddled around their fires. The riders headed for the ferry.

The ferry ride was a strained one. The river was running pretty high, even though the spring floods hadn't come yet, according to the ferry operator. The horses didn't like it any more than the men did, but mercifully it didn't take too long. Once across, they started up the legendary Burnt River Canyon. There was still large snow drifts to navigate around, but they still made good progress. They camped after about ten miles in a small sheltered grove of willows.

Zack got snow out of a drift to melt for their coffee. Eldon had some dried elk meat for their dinner. It wasn't much, but it was enough. Their fire brought warmth and reassurance, as they bedded down for the night. Coyotes howled in the distance reminding them they were never alone.

No one said much, they had all seen the graves, the broken wagon wheels, the various bits and pieces left behind by people who'd come upon hard luck. It was like traveling through a grave yard in a way. It was a place they all wanted to pass through quickly.

At first light they broke camp, without coffee. Within three more days of hard traveling, they reached the Power River Valley and Baker City. Much to Zack and Eldon's surprise, Fred had found something long the trail one time when he'd gone off to relieve himself. He'd found a very pretty gold chain and some other small gold items in a small brown bag. The bag looked like it had been there for years. He was able to sell the little find in Baker City for enough to resupply himself and Eldon. He even gave Zack a share. Fortune was seeming to smile upon them.

Zack bid his traveling companions good-bye in Fort Sumpter and continued up the Old Oregon Trail through Granite, Ukiah and finally through the Blue Mountain Range. He'd been lucky enough to buy deer jerky in Fort Sumpter and it got him through to Cecil.

He found a stable to rest the horse and mule. The stable owner let Zack sleep in the hay loft. It was warm and fresh smelling despite the horses down below. It was easy to sleep, and Zack did. After about ten hours of sleep, Zack was ready to continue with his push west. He sold the mule to the stable owner for enough gold dust to see him down the Columbia. Zack headed west with renewed hope.

Chapter 24
East Tennessee—February 1867

Lydia had just bathed the boys when Eddie Goss came riding into the yard. Even over the happy noises the babies were making she could hear him clattering up the porch stairs calling her name.

"I'm in the house," she called out to him.

Eddie threw open the door and practically ran to her with his hands outstretched, "you got two more letters Liddy."

Lydia turned and finished dressing the babies, "just put them on the side board until I'm through here." It surprised her that somehow getting letters made her a little angry. A nagging question haunted her: how, if he loved her, could Zack stay away from his sons and her so long? She took a deep breath and placed the boys on a blanket on the floor. She handed the tub of water to Eddie, "Would you throw this out back?" He looked a little disappointed but took the tin of water. "I'll wait for you before I read the letters." That seemed to make all the difference. The teenager ran for the back door, letting it slam behind him. Lydia laughed and sat down in her rocker next to the fire. It seemed still cool in the house even though the cookstove and fireplace both were going. February had seen little snow but many of days below freezing so far. She sighed, "Can't wait for spring again."

Eddie was back in just moments. Rose came in right behind him. At the same time Jonas came in the front door. "I guess you're all here to hear what the letters have to say." Lydia laughed, they were addressed to her but the mail always belonged to the whole family. Everyone found a close place to sit. Eddie plopped down next to the babies on the floor, Rose took the rocker next to Lydia and Jonas pulled up a table chair. When everyone was ready, Lydia opened the first letter.

"October 29, 1866
Sedalia, Missouri
Dearest wife, mother and friends,

We're hit some bad luck. Bill was wounded in a hold up attempt and I had to shoot the bandit. I thought all the killing was behind me in the war but I guess human nature being what it is, never changes. Bill is doing alright but not able to ride right now so we are not sure of what's going to happen. Ten Trees and I are staying at a farm for a few days to get things worked out. The horse is still doing well and I'm eating regular. I still don't have enough money saved up to send for you but hope that will happen soon.

I miss you all more than words can say. I hope the harvest went well and you have plenty of hams and game in the cellar for winter. I'm praying God will keep you all safe.

Yours always with love,
Zack."

Lydia refolded the letter and put it in her apron pocket. She felt exhausted. She looked at Rose who's face was white.

"I had known there would be dangers along the journey. I am glad that Zack can take care of himself." Rose said trying to put a positive face over her fears.

Lydia reached over and patted her mother-in-law's hands, she understood because she felt the same. "Let's see what the other letter says."

INTO THE DUST

"November 10, 1866
Independence, Missouri
Dearest wife, mother and friends,

We got some more bad news. Bill has to return to the east to recover and see some special kind of doctor. He's sold his wagon and team, paid us off and so we are on our own. We missed the last of the wagon trains for the year so Ten Trees and I are going as far as we can on our own before winter sets in too hard. We'll winter over at one of the forts along the way.

One good thing, we got a reward of sorts for killing that bandit. There was a reward and we got a horse he'd stolen. Turned out to be a valuable one so we sold it to give us enough money to outfit ourselves well for the trip. We're setting out almost immediately so I wanted to let you know.

I know you only got another month until the baby is born. I think about that every day. I'm working on a little head piece for the first pony he'll have. I dream about all the things we'll do as a family and pray the time will pass quickly until we're together again.

Got to get some rest for the early start we're going to make. Please know I love you and miss each and everyone of you.

My love always,
Zack

"I'm glad that Indian fellow, Ten Trees, is with Zack. I'd hate to think of him trying to make his way himself. I've heard the winters in the terrorities can be mighty bad."

Lydia got up and walked to the window. She could feel the cold draft coming in from around the panes. She absent mindedly tucked the cloth chinking back into the gaps, smiling slightly as she felt the draft stop. "Those letters were written months ago. It's hard to know where he is right now. There's no way of knowing if he's sick or even alive today."

Rose got up and came up beside Lydia, she put her arms around her shoulders, "Don't lose hope, daughter," she comforted, "Don't lose hope."

The two women looked out at the yard bathed in sunlight yet frost covered. The hillside glistened with ice crystals on everything. Lydia felt as though her life was covered in ice, too. It was bitter cold and she felt lifeless. One of the babies began to protest it's hunger; Lydia looked at her sons and began to thaw. At least, she had her sons with her, that alone was enough to give her purpose. She began to unbutton her shirt as she picked up her first baby to feed. She sat with her back to the fire and quietly rocked as she nursed little Sam. When he was full and asleep, Pete took his place. In a few minutes both boys were full and sleeping contentedly. Lydia put them into the small bed Jonas had made for them in Lydia's room.

When she came back into the main room she found the family and Eddie looking at a sheet of paper he'd laid out on the eating table. "What's this?" she asked as she joined them.

"It's a map of the territories. I got it from Mr. Fleshman who teaches school in the next valley. I told him I'd bring it back after I showed it to you."

Lydia stared at the map intently. "I don't think I've ever seen this kind of map before."

"This is one of the newest maps available," Eddie said, pointing to the little label in the corner, "It's only a few years old, see 1853."

"It shows the Oregon Territory and some of the forts along the way," Jonas said softly.

All of them stared quietly as Lydia put her finger on Independence, Missouri. The map showed many roads leading up to Independence, but then she moved her finger slowly into the area with no roads beyond that. There were several forts and many rivers indicated on map. She traced several rivers to the forts that were built on them. There was nothing in between the forts to indicate what lay out there except one's imagination. Lydia shook her head, there was no way of knowing what had happened to Zack, which way he'd gone, where he'd wound up or even if he was on his way home. It had been half a year ago she'd watched him ride away from her. So much that had happened to her that had changed who she was; had the same happened to him? Would they be so different when they finally re-united that it wouldn't work out? The ice returned to her soul and she took her finger off of the paper. "It's an awfully big wilderness, isn't it?"

Everyone stood and looked at the map for a few more seconds. "Thank your Mr. Fleshman for letting us see this map. It's very interesting and it gives us a rough idea, at least, where Zack is."

Rose managed a smile as she rolled the map back up and handed it to Eddie.

Eddie took the map and put his hat back on. "I'd best be getting back down to our place. Dad said we got a sick cow that has to be watched today. Beast probably ate something wrong." He accepted a couple cookies to eat on the way home and was quickly gone.

Rose, Lydia and Jonas went back to the morning's work. Throwing themselves into the familiar routines helped them get through the days. Sometimes they were able to go for minutes, even hours without worrying about Zack.

Lydia felt the full range of emotions from anger to sadness to despair throughout the day. She was glad to get Zack's letters, but they didn't always bring her joy. By the end of the day, however, she had re-read the letters at least three times. That night she fell asleep dreaming of the first few months she and Zack had spent together, a joyous, loving time.

* * *

Days turned into weeks and by the end of February it had snowed again, thawed again and turned everything to a muddy mess. Lydia found it harder everyday to carry the boys back and forth from their beds to the living room. She complained to Rose with a laugh, "This must be why mothers are anxious for the children to grow up. They get mighty heavy after awhile."

Rose laughed as she looked over from the sideboard where she was kneading bread. "Those are pretty small babies. When Zack was a baby, he was big as both of those boys combined."

"They sure take after their daddy, the way they're growing." Lydia sighed. She put the boys down on a blanket. Peter immediately rolled over on his stomach and raised himself on elbows. "Look Rose," Lydia said in surprise, "he rolled over on his own."

"Looks like that's going to be the one to watch, he'll be getting into all kinds of mischief before long." Rose went back to her bread making chores.

Lydia rolled a second blanket up to make a barrier to keep Peter from rolling off the quilt they were lying on. Samuel just lay contentedly playing with his toes after he'd pulled off his bootie. Lydia couldn't help but wonder what the boys would be like as they got older, would they both be like Zack or would they favor her side of the family? She allowed herself a couple more minutes of daydreaming before she stood up and went to help with the weekly bread making. She grabbed the grease and prepared the pans for the dough to rise in. Rose divided the dough into loaves and places a portion into each of the six pans. There was a small amount of dough leftover that she rolled out into a long rope and cut it into eight or nine pieces, "Good biscuits for dinner," Rose said.

"Maybe we could make biscuits and gravy for dinner. Jonas likes that, with a lot of sausage in it," Lydia offered.

"Sounds good to me, something easy is always nice." Rose wiped her hands on her apron as Lydia covered the dough to let it rise. Rose heard footsteps on the porch, "Must be Jonas coming up for a cup of tea. I'll put the pot on." She crossed over to the stove and looked in the water bucket. "Oh, we need more water. I'll go get it."

"Let me, Rose, you sit down and rest. You can keep an eye on the boys." Lydia grabbed the water bucket and headed for the back door, but a knock on the front door stopped her. "I wonder who that is?"

Rose moved to the fireplace and took down the rifle. Lydia moved uneasily to the door and peeked out the window. "Oh," Lydia was almost speechless, "It's a friend, Rose." She slowly opened the door.

Mark Fellowes stood on the porch, his blond hair hanging loosely around his handsome but weary face. "Hello, Lydia," he said quietly, then looked beyond her to Rose, "Rose. I was just down in the valley and thought I'd ride up and visit for a spell."

Rose came up beside Lydia with a broad grin on her face, "Please come in." She took Mark's arm and led him into the house. He noticed Lydia was holding the pail.

"Can I get the water for you?"

"No, no," Lydia said, "it's no bother at all. You make yourself comfortable. You must be tired after your ride up the hill. I'll be right back with water for tea." She almost ran to the well, going off the front porch then around the house.

In minutes she was back in with the water and Rose busied herself with setting up for tea. Jonas came up from the barn. "I saw you ride up Mister Mark. It's good to see you again." The two men shook hands.

"You look like you mended with no ill effects," Mark said looking Jonas up and down. Then he looked at Lydia, "Just like you came through your difficult pregnancy with no problems. One would never know you were old enough to be the mother of two fine boys." He looked over at the boys playing on the floor. "May I?" He nodded towards the babies.

Lydia nodded and Mark went over and bent down, picking up Samuel first, then Peter. The boys didn't protest but did look to their mother several times as the stranger looked them over. "Mighty fine. Both of them." Peter rolled over several times, making Mark laugh. "That one's a lively little guy."

Lydia came over and placed Peter in the middle of the quilt again. "Rose thinks he'll be into mischief before Samuel will."

Lydia's hair was hanging loose and it passed over Mark's hand as he got up from playing with the boys. He let out a small involuntary gasp as the electricity rippled through his body. Lydia heard him and couldn't help but feel her heart beat faster. She immediately moved away from him as he went back to the eating table and took a sip of the tea that Rose had poured for him.

Jonas was the first to speak again, "So what brings you out this way. Mark? We'd heard you moved up north."

Mark nodded sadly, "I never mentioned it when I was here last fall but my wife had been ill for sometime. I thought maybe by moving back closer to my wife's family in West Virginia she'd feel better, but when we got there she decided she no longer wanted to be married to me. We divorced in January. She moved back in with her parents. Her mother was ill and they had a big farm to run so she felt they needed her more than me and the children did. I've bought a little place just outside of Knoxville for my family. Got a young couple helping me out there. The woman serves as a nanny for the children and the husband helps me farm. It works pretty well." He looked at Lydia briefly and then at Rose and Jonas. "I got a problem that I wanted to talk to you three about. There was a man who came to our farm looking for work. He's an older black man, he was turned out of his home of many years when the white owner died. The carpetbagger who took over the plantation got rid of all the blacks. He's a hard working man and I would have liked to take him on, but it's not safe in Knoxville for him right now nor for anyone willing to take in the displaced souls from the deep South. I was wondering with Zack gone if you could use another hand here?"

Jonas looked at Rose, "Well… I am not sure."

Rose looked down at her tea cup, "I expect we could use the help this spring with all the planting and more tree cutting. But it would only be temporary because I'm sure that Zack will be home by summer."

Lydia looked at Rose, did she really think Zack would be coming home that soon? "Yes, I think we could use the help at least through the spring, until Zack gets home." It sounded so good to say Zack would be coming home. Was it too much to hope for?

Mark smiled, "Well then, I'll let him know and you can expect him within a couple weeks or so."

Jonas got up and shook Mark's hand again, "That's mighty nice of you to try to help this man. I heard horror stories about the treatment of the men and women when they were kicked out of the plantations. What's his name?"

"Deben Claypool. Claypool was the name of the old plantation owner when he was brought to the farm. He can't remember his name before that. Lots of folks lost their true identity during those awful years. Times aren't much better now but they are free."

Rose scoffed, "Free, but still hunted and hurt."

"We aren't going to change people's attitudes overnight," Mark sighed, "It might take a hundred years to get it right."

"I wonder if we'll ever get to a point where we live as brothers, like the

Bible says we should," Rose said softly as she sipped her tea. "I'm going out to the root cellar to get some potatoes for a soup for lunch, will you stay for lunch?"

"Only if I can do some chores to earn my keep." Mark laughed.

"Well then you and Lydia go get the potatoes and gather the eggs, I'll watch the boys."

Lydia winced, she didn't relish being alone ever again with Mark, not that she didn't trust him. It was herself she questioned. But still she smiled and led the way out of the house. It was a cold, crisp morning. The ground was just turning mushy as it thawed once again. It was easy to lose one's footing, so Mark took her arm and led the way to the chicken coop. Once inside he couldn't contain himself, he grabbed Lydia and kissed her hard. She couldn't stop herself from kissing him back. It was a breathless moment that sent her head spinning.

Mark let go of her and stepped back, "I am so sorry, Lydia. I haven't stopped thinking about you for a minute since I left here. I know you wanted me not to come back but I just couldn't help myself. When Deben needed a place to go, I jumped at the excuse to come up here so I could see you."

Lydia turned and started feeling around in the hen's nesting boxes. She found several eggs before she said anything, "Mark, this is totally wrong, but I know what you are saying. I've given a lot of thought to you, too." She put her hand up as he started towards her. "We will not do this."

She walked ahead of him to the root cellar. He held the basket up as she fished three large potatoes and a few carrots out of the sawdust. When he put the basket down he again put his arms around her and kissed her slowly with all the passion he had. She fell into his arms and returned his kiss wholeheartedly. Both of them knew this truly would be the last time. Mark stepped back and wiped tears from his eyes. Lydia reached up and wiped a couple wet lines from Mark's face. "I will remember you with affection all of my life, Mark. Remember me kindly, too. We just have different paths to walk. Maybe someday if God wills it, we'll find each other again, but I doubt it."

"If you ever do need me or want to come to me, I'll be in Knoxville." Mark sighed and kissed her fingers.

"Don't wait for me. Find someone and be happy. I've got a husband that I'll be with again someday and two sons. My life is full, be happy for me."

"I'll try." He started to kiss her again but she put her hand on his lips.

Mark cleared his throat, "Please tell Rose that I changed my mind and decided I'd better get on to make it down the hill before it starts to get too muddy to travel."

"I will," Lydia swallowed hard, "I wish you God's speed, Mark. I will pray that you find happiness and someone to love soon."

"That will be hard when I love someone already," he said as he looked deeply into her eyes. Then he whirled around and left her standing in the dark cellar. She waited until she heard his horse's hoof beats leaving the yard before she walked slowly back to the house.

Rose didn't even ask where Mark had gone.

"He said he wanted to get down the hill before the trail became to muddy," Lydia said quietly, "he won't be back again."

"That's probably best," Rose said with a sad knowing smile as she took the eggs and vegetables from Lydia. Lydia knew Rose had figured out why Mark had really come to the farm and she felt ashamed. Oh, how she wished that Zack had never left her. Why had such temptation come into her life?

Chapter 25
Polk County, Oregon—February 1867

The sun rose stubbornly, and the day was bright but extremely cold. Frost stayed in the shadows until well after noon. Cleveland busied himself with chores in the house and barn before tending to the outdoor needs. He hadn't worked for several days so he was a little worried about his income again, but he tried to not think much about that. He had enough to last the month out if he was careful and kept their needs simple; he and Cork had learned to do quite well on oatmeal in the morning and potatoes and ham at night. Usually bread was a luxury but they did have an occasional biscuit without jam or butter though. Surely things would open up in March and he'd find more jobs.

The work on George Ash's barn had not been as extensive as first thought and only took three weeks to complete. He'd made one wash stand for a lady from his church since Christmas but had no other furniture orders. Finding out what it's like to be a grown up had been an eye-opener to Cleveland. He realized what his father must have felt being responsible for a wife and children through hard times. He missed his father and mother, wishing often that he could tell them how much he appreciated all they did for him, especially now that he understood what they must have gone through coming to Oregon, feeding the family, building the place. Early in the afternoon he walked over to his parents graves and took his hat off, even though it was in a shaded spot and still frost covered.

"Ma and Pa, I'm not sure if you are still within earshot or not, but I just want you to know not a day goes by that I don't think about you. I hope whereever the Lord has taken you is a pretty place and you are together and happy there." He whispered as he looked up. Tears welled up in his eyes and for a moment he couldn't see anything but a blur of moving tree limbs and cold blue sky. He shook his head and looked at the wooden crosses at the head of the graves. Limbs had been blown down and near knocked his father's over. Cleveland set about clearing the debris from away from the area. He was just tossing the last piece of fallen wood away when a shot rang out across his property. He quickly ducked behind a tree trying to see where the shot had come from.

It took his eyes a moment to refocus in the bright sunlight but finally as he looked around he could see clearly. At first Cleveland didn't see anything but then a small movement caught his eye. Then horror hit him like a sledgehammer. "Cork," he screamed as he dashed out of the safety of the trees. He ran as hard as his rubbery legs would carry him to the middle of his pasture where he saw her. He stopped suddenly as he neared her, "Cork girl," he gasped. He dropped down beside the dog, who lay motionless.

She raised her head slightly and looked at Cleveland, for a moment only, then her eyes went dim and with one painful breath she was gone. Cleveland screamed into the air, "Cork, don't leave me!" He scooped the lifeless dog up into his arms, ignoring her blood dripping down across his shirt. He cried with the abandon of one who'd lost everything. He was so distraught he didn't notice the two men on horseback ride up quietly behind him.

One of the horses whinnied and Cleveland whirled around. One of the men, a man with a scar on his cheek, had a rifle in his hand. The scar pulled his left eye down slightly giving him a menacing look. The other man was thin and dirty looking, he was glancing nervously back and forth between Cleveland and the mean-eyed man. The nervous man was the first one to speak.

"Sorry son, Jake here thought your dog was a coyote," he shrugged, "No law against shooting a coyote."

The scarred man, Jake, looked around the farm yard and then looked towards where Cleveland had come out of the woods. He saw the two graves on the hillside, "You all by yourself here, boy?"

Cleveland looked down at Cork and laid her gently down on the ground, and then drew himself up as tall as he could to face her killer. "She didn't look anything like a coyote, mister."

The man swung his rifle over his saddle in front of him and turned his horse a little so that the barrel was clearly pointing at Cleveland. The other man quickly jumped down and got between the two of them. "Boy, it did look like a varmint from a distance. This was just an accident. Let it go," the nervous man pleaded.

Cleveland started to take a step forward, but the man stopped him and whispered in his ear, "Let me help you bury the dog boy. I don't want to be burying you, too. You just don't know what this man is apt to do, if you cross him."

Cleveland glared at the man, then took another look at the scar faced man. He could see it was true, that man would not hesitate to kill him. He hadn't really believed Cork was a coyote, he just like to kill things. It probably gave him pleasure to kill animals, or for that matter, people. His dad had talked about the gunslingers they'd seen in some of the frontier towns that would just as soon shoot you as look at you. Many of them had killed cats, dogs or Indians just for sport. Cleveland pushed the man back, "I can bury my own dog." He stood his ground as he glared at the intruders.

The skinny man got back on his horse, "Let's go Jake, no need to hang around here. You can see the kid's got nothing of value."

The scarred man looked again at the graves, then at Cleveland. "Sorry, kid," he said with a sneer. He fished around in his coat pocket and tossed a coin on the ground in front of Cleveland. "Buy yourself another dog." He pulled roughly on the reins of his horse and immediately the two men galloped off Cleveland's property. Cleveland quickly picked up the coin and threw it at the retreating riders.

Cleveland ran for the house and grabbed his father's old Sharps rifle and headed for the end of the pasture, but the men were completely out of sight. He went back to Cork and fell across her body, crying for his loss as he had never done for his mother and father. He couldn't help himself. The man was gone and the boy who'd lost so much was all there was. It was more than half an hour before he could contain himself enough to get the shovel and think about where he was going to put this sweet, gentle creature who had gotten him through the worst of times. They had played, grieved, starved and recovered together, and now he was alone, really alone for the first time.

It didn't seem right to bury her with his parents although he thought about it. He decided instead to place her where the sunlight came through the trees by the creek, it was her favorite spot to lay in the summer while he washed his clothes. He'd always try to remember her that way, warm and content to be where ever he was. More than his muscles ached as he dug the hole and lined it with sweet smelling pine boughs.

He had just gone back to the pasture and picked his dog up when two more riders came galloping into his yard. The badge pinned to the coat of the older rider told Cleveland who these men were. "Hello young man," the sheriff said as he got off his horse and looked at Cork. "What happened, son?"

Cleveland had to swallow hard to keep from crying again, "Two men just an hour or so ago," he choked, "Said he thought she was a coyote." Tears again came and Cleveland was unable to stop them, "She never did look like a...."

The sheriff's deputy got off his horse and took the dog from Cleveland, "Where are you going to bury her, son?"

"I dug a hole over there by the creek," Cleveland pointed and the deputy carried Cork to the ground Cleveland had prepared.

"I'm Sheriff Liggett, son, most people call me Joe." He patted the shaking boy on the shoulder, "Are you the only one home?"

"My folks are both gone," Cleveland pointed to the graves. "This is my farm."

The sheriff eyed the boy, "How old are you, son?"

Cleveland stiffened, "I'm eighteen, sir. I've been living here on my own for two years."

The sheriff nodded, "Can you tell me anything about these men?" He looked knowingly as his deputy rejoined them.

"One had a scar on his face," Cleveland ran his finger over his cheek to indicate where it had been. "The other was a skinny guy, smelled like he hadn't washed in a very long time. They rode off towards Buena Vista."

"Sounds like them," the deputy said with a nod.

"We're looking for two men who've been breaking into houses and stealing whatever they can find. Roughed up one old lady who happened to be home alone. Did these two men take anything from you?"

"No, in fact, they gave me something," Cleveland walked a few feet up the dirt road until he found the coin he'd thrown. "The guy who shot Cork threw this at me and told me to buy another dog."

The sheriff took the coin, "A fifty dollar gold piece. Is that on the list of things we know were taken?" He asked the deputy who looked at a slip of paper he'd taken from his saddle bag.

The deputy nodded. The sheriff looked at Cleveland, "Well son, there's no way to prove this is the same fifty dollar gold piece that was stolen earlier, but we're going to have to take it with us. There was a twenty dollar reward though for the return of the goods so you can have at least ten for return of this. Deputy, give him ten dollars."

The deputy had a slightly surprised look on his face but did as he was told. They both got back on their horses, "I don't imagine that those men will come around here again. But if they do, you play it safe and get out quickly, send someone to Dallas to let us know they've been seen again. Sorry about your dog, boy." He tipped his hat and they rode off.

Cleveland went to where Cork was now buried. He made a little covering of river stones over her grave and piled flat stones on end around the edge. After it was finished, he lay down on top of the mound of rock and cried until well after dark. Finally the cold reached his bones and he went inside and built a small fire in the fire place. Then he burned the shirt he'd been wearing that had Cork's blood all over it. He didn't bother to eat, he simply slept. His mother always had said things would be better in the morning after a good night's rest. He prayed she was right.

Chapter 26
The Dalles, Oregon, on the Columbia River—April 1867

Zack wiped the salty sweat from his around his mouth. He'd been working for two days shoeing horses and even though the weather outside was wet and cold, it was hot enough to work without a shirt in the blacksmith's shop and livery stable. The work was hard and the hours long. It was taking all he had left to make it through the day. Poor food and exposure to the elements had left him pretty weak, but he needed the work if he was going to make it on to the Willamette Valley. He felt fortunate to have a skill that had earned him a little money here and in Fort Hall. He tried not to think about Fort Hall as he worked, but it plagued him. He couldn't help but remember that black chapter in his journey west.

Fort Hall had been a bustling place, lots of miners and people settling down around in the area. Many of the pioneers headed west had decided that this valley was as far as they were going. He'd found work the first day he'd been there in a livery shop, making harness and shoeing horses. He'd only planned to work a week to earn enough money for the next leg of his trek but on his third day he made what he considered one of the biggest mistakes of his life. He'd been in a couple saloons and had a beer a couple times in his life, so he felt it was no big deal to go to the one near the little boardinghouse he'd take a room in.

The beer was flat, probably made right on the premises but it was cold and tasted passable. Zack had looked around the room and noticed a young woman in a pretty yellow dress watching him. She smiled and he smiled. Immediately she walked toward him swaying her hips in a provocative way. She was prettier than Lydia and probably younger. For some reason at that moment he couldn't remember what Lydia looked like exactly.

"Hello there, fella," the young woman said softly as she came and stood next to Zack so their arms were touching.

Zack felt immediately uncomfortable having her stand so near, "Hello," he said in a choked voice, which made her laugh softly. "Who are you?"

"Lucy Ann's my name. What's yours?"

"Zack," he said hesitantly.

Lucy Ann turned to more or less face Zack, "So, Zack, what brings you to Fort Hall?"

"Just passing through, going on to Oregon."

She smiled again and moved closer to Zack in such a way that her knee was between his and the bar. "So have you got a girl in town, Zack?"

Zack looked at her, she was young but somehow hard, her face was covered in a thick face powder, "How old are you, Lucy Ann?"

"Old enough," she said with a sly smile, "I can do lots of things to make a man happy."

Zack started to move away from her intruding knee but she grabbed his collar and brought him close to her and kissed him. For a moment he resisted, then all the loneliness flooded his being and he found himself returning the kiss. Longing ached throughout his body, his hand found its way to Lucy Ann's waist and he held her tight.

"I got a tent out back, Zack, I think you'd enjoy coming home with me tonight," Lucy Ann breathed in his ear. "I can tell you like me." She moved her leg in between his.

Zack stood frozen for a moment, he couldn't believe he was actually thinking about going to the tent with her. He felt like he was going to throw up. He had a wife and two children counting on him, what was he doing? He pushed Lucy Ann back away from him gently, "I'm a married man, Lucy Ann."

She laughed, "Most of my men friends are, but their wives are either back east or just not exciting anymore." She touched his cheek with a soft hand, "I won't tell, if you don't. Come on we'll just have a little fun. What do you say? Only two dollars for the whole night."

Zack looked at her again, "How old are you really, Lucy Ann?"

She turned to the bar with disgust, "I'm fifteen, if it's any of your business."

"Why are you doing this?"

"My momma left me here in Fort Hall when she ran off with a miner. My father and older brother had been killed on the wagon train coming here. Didn't seem to be much else for me to do. I've gotten pretty good at my job in the last year." She looked sad for a moment, then turned to Zack with a twisted smile and tilt of her head, "I sure would like to show you how good I am."

Zack backed away from her. He put a quarter on the counter for his beer and handed her five dollars. "Get yourself out of here while there's still time to save yourself, girl. This is no life for anyone." He turned and vowed never to go in a saloon again.

That next morning Zack left Fort Hall, ashamed that several times during the night he woke up thinking of Lucy Ann and what she'd offered. He was tempted, and he knew if he'd stayed in town he might have gone back. At the blacksmith shop, he hammered with all his strength, trying to forget how close he'd come to ruination.

The last horse of the day, just after dark, was a huge old draft animal. When Zack saw the Belgian he thought he was going to have to have help, but the horse was so good natured and had been shoed so many times already that he was no problem. It was just that he was so big! It took the last little bit of stamina he had to finish the job. After Zack put the horse back in its stall, he went straight to the small room just behind the fireplace forge that served as his bunk room.

One wall of his room was the back of the fireplace, and so at least it was warm and dry. There was one tiny window but it was already dark outside, so he had to light the small candle that came with the room. Zack could hear and smell the horses in their stalls at the other end of the blacksmith shop, but it didn't matter, he was so tired he could sleep through anything. His straw filled mat on a slat board rack was more comfortable than the rocky plains, so that didn't bother him either. The blacksmith had provided a water pitcher and basin so Zack took sponge baths every night. Zack hadn't had any money to buy food so he'd been pretty much doing without until he got his first pay. He'd come into town with a little jerky left that he'd made go a long way. He was out of even that now. At least his horse was being fed well here in the blacksmiths stables.

Zack was nearly in bed when he heard a small knock on the door. He put his shirt back on and answered the door. An elderly woman was standing there with a fair sized basket under her arm. "Good evening, Mr. Grant. My son, the blacksmith, told me you were staying in the shop. I figured you didn't have a place to cook for yourself. I brought you a couple things." She handed him the basket, "You can just leave it outside the door and I'll come back and get it tomorrow." She smiled and turned around and was gone.

"Thank you, ma'am," Zack called after her in disbelief. He took the basket to his bed, sat down on the edge and gently lifted one corner of the towel covering the contents. His mouth watered at the smells wafting up at him. It was not a disappointment! There were three pieces of fried chicken, three biscuits, a small jug of milk and two pieces of apple pie. Zack could hardly believe it. He quickly ate a piece of pie, followed by a biscuit and chicken leg. It was odd to have a full stomach, odd and a little uncomfortable for some reason. He drank the milk and re-covered the food. There was enough for breakfast and dinner of the next day if he was careful. He lay down feeling renewed and within minutes he was sleeping contentedly.

The next morning Zack was awakened by the sunlight streaming in the small window, hitting him directly in the face. It was strange to see the sunshine after days of rain and gray leaden skies. He dressed and hurried to get to work. The blacksmith was a friendly, bald man everyone called Smithy. He must have been in his mid forties already but strong as an ox. Smithy was already there getting the hot fire going. "Morning," he said with a nod.

"Morning Smithy," Zack said grabbing a lead rope to go get the first horse for shoeing. "Sure did appreciate your mother bringing food over last night. She's a mighty good cook."

Smithy laughed, "You must be pretty hungry to think she's a good cook. Usually burns everything or undercooks it. Can't seem to ever get it right. Your wife a good cook, Zack?"

"She surely is, so is my mother. I guess I had it really good at home. I really miss them."

"What made you come west, Zack?"

"Seemed like the thing to do at the time. I thought I'd get out here and make a fortune and send for my family. Didn't realize how hard just getting out here would be."

"It takes a lot of work and sweat to make it out here in the new country but it can be done. Maybe not overnight but it can be done. I think you'll do fine when you find your own place." Smithy went back to work, pounding on the heated metal. Zack got the first animal and the day was off and running.

At the end of the week the blacksmith was caught up again and Zack received his pay. Smithy's mother brought over a sack of fried chicken and biscuits for the road and Zack set off again for that promised land, the Willamette Valley. He was full of hope that he'd find his heart's desire there, although he'd come to realize even there, life would not be easy.

* * *

Zack reached McMinnville on a rainy Tuesday. It was a bustling little village that he'd heard had at least three blacksmith shops. Surely he could find some work there. Work had yet to materialize for him anywhere yet so he was beginning to feel hopeless again. He tried all three shops but no luck. He camped near the Yamhill River, but couldn't even find enough dry tinder to make a fire last more than a few minutes. Finally he gave up and slept under a tree in a damp bedroll. He woke up shivering. After bathing in the river, he headed on down the valley.

On Thursday he found a farmer near the little community of Bethel who gave him a few days work shoeing horses and fixing harnesses. He was allowed to sleep in the hay loft and feed his horse. The farmer gave him dinner and breakfast both days so that helped.

Zack was finished with the work on Saturday but since the next day was Sunday the farmer invited Zack to stay over until Monday and go to church in Spring Valley with the family. Zack hesitated but finally decided to take the man up on the offer. The farmer had three small boys, his wife and his handicapped brother living on the farm. It was all the two mules he owned could do to pull the wagon with the family and Zack up and over the hill to the little country church.

There was a potluck after services and Zack enjoyed the fellowship time. He sat with the family and heard all the stories about how each of the families had struggled to get to Oregon and find their place. Zack was impressed with the hardships the earliest pioneers had endured to settle this land that now bustled with cities and industries. It seemed in many ways like it had always been settled, not like the frontier anymore at all. There were steamships on the river, ferries here and there, stage lines, hotels. It was all quite civilized.

Unfortunately, politics were hot topics in this part of the country, too, Some of the talk reminded him of all the things he'd left Tennessee to get away from. People in Oregon were divided over the issues that had started the war and some still were looking for someone to blame. A couple of the men said it was the democrats, others blamed the blacks, others said it was God's will. At one point, the discussion got too much for Zack and he excused himself and went outside.

It was cool outside, but at least the rain had stopped for a couple days. The air was crisp and daffodils dotted the hillside around the church with the hint of spring that encouraged him. The view from the church was breathtaking in a quiet way. You could see across the a portion of the valley to the low rolling hills to the north. Towering above them Mt. Hood stood, a gently rising cone of snow-covered beauty. He took a deep breath and prayed, "Lord, help me find my destiny here, I've come so far, take me the rest of the way to whatever you have planned for me and my family."

Shortly it was time to return to the farm. It had been a pleasant day, but it had also been a sad one in several ways. First it reminded him of how much he missed his own family and secondly, it became clear to him that the problems caused by the Civil War couldn't be run from, no matter how far you went.

The next morning after breakfast Zack headed for Salem. He took his nervous horse on the ferry that crossed the Willamette just north of town. Salem was a busy place, several hotels were available as well as livery stables. He found one close to the ferry and left his horse. The "Western Hotel" had a big sign out front advertising reasonable room rates and "A table Spread with the Best the Country Affords." Zack went in and paid his six dollars for a week's board and room. "Surely I'll have a job by the end of the week."

He was given a room key and a set of towels and sheets. His room was on the second floor in the back. It was small but adequate having a double bed, night stand with a basin and pitcher, a dresser with two small drawers and a coat rack. There was also a small table and chair by the window. A printed card on the table announced that "The bath house was downstairs, just outside of the back door. Men could use the bath house from 6:00 p.m. to 9:00 p.m., women and children from 8:00 a.m. to 11:00 a.m., sign up at the front desk for a half hour time. The necessarys were just beyond the bath house, one for women and one for men. Meals were available from 8:00 a.m. to 6:00 p.m. Coffee could be brought to the rooms but all dishes needed to be returned to the kitchen."

Zack put the rough sheets on his bed and spread the two blankets he found over the bed. There was water already in the pitcher so he washed his face. It was still before noon so he walked out on the street to look around. He found a newspaper stand and bought a paper. He was disappointed there were no jobs listed. He went back to the hotel to have lunch.

The food turned out to be pretty plain and simple. Lunch was a thin soup of navy bean and ham with bread and coffee. It didn't seem satisfying at all but he had two bowls of the soup anyway. Zack stopped at the front desk to talk to the clerk about where he might look for work and sign up for a turn in the bathhouse. Zack was pleased to see the sheet laying on the counter so he didn't have to ask. Surprisingly there was only one name on the list, despite the fact the hotel seemed quite fully occupied. Not many people believed in daily bathing but he liked to when ever the opportunity presented itself. He put himself down for seven p.m., just before he usually went to bed.

The young man behind the counter was delicate looking, Zack observed he probably never had worked at anything harder than what he was doing now. "Excuse me I'm new in town and I'm looking for work. Have you heard about anything?" Zack said in a friendly manner.

The young man looked at him with disdain, "What kind of work do you do?"

Zack shrugged, "I'm a good farrier and I can also make and repair harnesses or do leather work."

"Well, I don't know of anything around here. We have lots of stables in town, though, you might start with them." He thought a moment then added, "I have heard of a tannery in Dallas. We have a stage that runs to Dallas on Monday, Wednesday and Friday from the hotel. You missed the one today but you might try them."

"I actually know someone in the Independence area that I thought I would look up if I don't find something here soon. And I have a horse so I don't need to worry about the stage. Thanks for the information though." Zack shook the young man's hand and then set out to visit the stables in the area. By dinnertime he had made the rounds of several of the shops and found nothing available and no leads. He felt the nagging fingers of fear and disappointment closing around his stomach again.

At last it was dinner time and he went to the dining room, hoping that dinner was better and more substantial than lunch had been. To his delight it was. The meal was a generous portion of turkey, mashed potatoes and gravy, with peas and carrots in a butter sauce. With two servings of bread and butter and three cups of tea he finally felt full and hopeful again. No dessert was offered but it didn't matter he was content.

After dinner he took his half hour turn in the bath house, which turned out to be an eight by ten, nearly empty room. A large watering trough served as a tub and a small cookstove provided a way to heat water. The "tub" had a plug in one end to drain water out of. Two or three teakettles for heating water sat next to the stove. Water was supplied by a hand pump at one end of the trough. Zack thought it was all pretty modern.

Within minutes, he had water heated and three or four inches of water in the trough. He poured the hot water into the cold and then eased himself down into the tepid bath. There was a communal bar of pine soap that felt good to his skin. He took a moment or two after he'd dried himself off to wash his two spare pairs of socks, his extra pair of long-johns and his other shirt. After wringing the clothing out he draped them over a chair near the fire while he redressed and drained the tub. He was a little embarrassed at the color of the water he'd just been in. It was a muddy color, like a creek after a spring rain. "I really must have needed that bath," he laughed to himself. After getting another pail of water to rinse out the tub, he went back to his room with his damp clothing.

Zack hung his laundry up as best as he could around the room. His clothes smelled a little like a wet dog but at least they were cleaner than they had been. He lay down on his bed and felt contented. He had eaten three times in a single day for the first time in a long time and he was sleeping on clean sheets. Surely this was the start of something good.

Chapter 27
East Tennessee—April 1867

Spring was warm in the air. Birds were raucously announcing their joy. Flowers were beginning to show, first the daffodils and crocus and soon the cherry and apple trees would blossom. It was a precious time of year. Pete and Sam were trying their best to stand, Pete is doing better than Sam. They were happy babies, always jabbering and rough housing with each other. Lydia was thankful there were two of them to keep each other company, but in other ways it made her sad because she felt like she was so alone. Often she would try to remember what Zack looked like and couldn't quite bring his face into focus in her mind. More than once, though, she could remember the face of Mark Fellowes. She had to shake off those memories as soon as she realized she was thinking about him again.

Rose seemed to be feeling better as weather improved. She had had several rough times during the winter with her cough but was much more comfortable now. Jonas had mended completely from his injury, and Deben Claypool had come to stay and help with the spring work.

Deben had turned out to be a bit of a surprise. He was very black yet had piercing blue gray eyes and light colored, straight hair. He seemed older than Jonas and at first he was not terribly friendly. Jonas and Deben usually had their breakfast in Jonas's cabin, and Rose would bring their lunch to the barn where they worked most of the day. The family, including Jonas, tried to make him feel at home but it had taken a month before he would take suppers in the kitchen with them. Finally he joined them but seemed afraid to enter into the conversations. He would just eat and speak politely when spoken to. Evening meals remained a fairly tense event for several days. Finally one evening over dinner Rose got Deben to understand he was not a slave but a hired helper. It did take a little work though.

"Deben, I can't tell you how much we appreciate you coming to help Jonas this spring," Rose said with a smile. Deben nodded, kept his head down and continued to eat.

Rose looked at Lydia, who then looked at Deben, "We don't want to pry, Deben, but we'd like to know how you got your name and where you come from."

Deben looked up at Lydia, then Rose. He lowered his head, "My momma gave me the name Deben and Claypool was the name of the man who owned us. He'd owned my momma since she was a girl. I never knew who my father was. We lived on a plantation in Georgia for awhile and then I got shipped to another farm in Louisiana where I worked in the field when I was fairly young.

Never saw my momma again. I heard she died about ten years after I left though. When I got old enough I worked in the kitchen and gardens. I was working there when the war started. The old owner of the farm died and the Yankee who bought it after the war didn't want any of us…colored…staying around." He sighed, "I tried to find work here and there but most often nobody wanted me because I'm not young and strong. I thought maybe Master Fellowes wanted me at his farm, but he sent me here."

Rose reached across the table and patted Deben's hand. "Mark didn't send you here because he didn't want you. He sent you to us because we needed you and he thought so much of you, he knew you'd be someone we'd like and trust."

Deben looked up a little surprised, then looked at Jonas who nodded and smiled. "That's right. We do need your help. Mister Zack is gone and the farm is more than I can handle on my own. We got spring planting for the garden coming up, cutting the wood for next winter, white washing the house, tending the new calves that are due anytime. Why we really need you! You are not a slave here, you are a free man. And this is a job! Miss Rose and Miss Lydia are fine bosses, too." He smiled and waved his hand across the table, "And they are good cooks, too."

Deben looked at the table then smiled, revealing strong white teeth. "I have never thought of myself as a free man. I was born a slave and thought I'd die one. I will try my best to be worthy of your trust and do the best I can do to help out around here."

"We can't ask any more of you than that," Rose said with a smile. The family went back to their meal with renewed appetites.

* * *

Jonas and Lydia took the wagon to the valley store for supplies as soon as the snow was gone. It was a bumpy ride over the pot-holed road. The winter had been hard on the already poor roadway. It was barely a goat path, rutted deeply by the wagons. Lydia was glad she hadn't brought Rose or the babies. She felt bruised by the time they reached the store. She had made some hand-stitched items that the store owner often bought from her. It added only a dollar or two to her account, but everything helped. Zack had left them enough money to get through the winter but that had been quickly used up and now they were counting pennies. The farm would have to produce the majority of their food from now on, and they'd have to barter for the rest with other neighbors. She tried not to worry as she entered the store.

Freda Watson was behind the counter and her husband was on a ladder putting bolts of cloth up on high shelves when Jonas and Lydia came through the front door. "Morning, Mrs. Grant," Freda called out cheerfully. "We haven't seen much of you lately. How are those boys doing?"

"They're both fine, Freda, growing like weeds though. I need to make them all kinds of new clothes." Lydia walked around the store looking at everything, but mostly noticing the prices that seemed to have risen considerably since the last time she was here. She put her little package of cloth goods on the counter, "I've made some aprons, a few potholders and three sets of pillow cases."

Lydia waited as the plump woman behind the counter looked each item over. Freda looked up at her husband and smiled, "Jimmy, look at these lovely things that Lydia made. I think we can use them, don't you?"

Jim Watson joined his wife and ran his hand over the work Lydia had brought in, "Mighty fine workmanship, Lydia. We never have trouble selling what you make. I think we can give you," he paused and looked at his wife, "I think we can give you fifty cents for each of the aprons and a dollar for each set of pillow cases. The potholders aren't a big seller so we can only give you a dollar for the whole stack. Let's see...that would come to five dollars. Would that be alright?"

"Oh yes, that would be quite fine," Lydia beamed, proud to have her work admired but also happy to have five dollars more to spend on the things they needed. It took her no time at all to pick out two lengths of cloth for shirts for the boys, a tin of buttons, twenty pounds of flour, ten pounds of bacon, five pounds of sugar, a twenty pound bag of potatoes, five pounds of carrots, two boxes of matches, three boxes of candles, and some wax for sealing jam. Jonas got three bags of grain for the horses, too. As a gift, Jim Watson threw in two cans of pie cherries and four apples.

Freda happily chattered away as she helped Lydia and Jonas load their wagon for the trip home. Just at the last moment Jim came rushing out of the store, "I almost forgot this. You have a letter here from your husband." He helped Lydia up into the wagon seat then handed her the letter.

"Hope it's good news."

Lydia put the letter in her pocket and Jonas started off toward home. Lydia waved at the Watson's just before they went back into their store. She could feel the letter in her pocket. For such a little thing it began to feel as though it weighed a ton. Her heart was bursting to know what it said but her head couldn't bring herself to open it just yet. Several times she caught Jonas casting a glance toward her pocket. He seemed torn, too. "I'll wait until we get home so we can all hear it together," she said loudly over the creaking of the wagon and harnesses as the wagon and road jostled them along.

Jonas nodded, "Probably couldn't read it, bouncing around like this."

Lydia was grateful that he agreed. Neither of them mentioned it again until they got back to the farm. Rose was waiting on the porch with lunch ready. Even though the day was cool it was pleasant so they opted to eat outside on the steps. Deben came up from the barn and joined them. "We'll unload the wagon after we eat," Jonas said as the older man joined them. "Miss Lydia got a letter."

A look of excitement that came over Rose's face. "Is it from Zack?"

Lydia hadn't actually looked at the letter yet, "I think so." She pulled it out of its hiding place and looked at it. Immediately she recognized the tight little handwriting of her husband, "Yes, it's from Zack." She looked around at the expectant faces, "I guess I'd better read this so we can get on with lunch." She looked over at her boys who were sitting on a blanket, chewing on thick slices of well-toasted bread. Goldie was sitting next to Sam, hoping for a dropped bit of crust. The boys had no idea how important the letter was to all of them, because they had no clue as to who their father was. It made her mad and sad all at the same time. She looked back at the letter and for one instant she thought of tearing it into a thousand little pieces. Instead she gently opened it, then unfolded the two small pages and began to read to her family.

"Fort Laramie
February 18, 1867
Dearest wife, sons and family,

I got your letter and was so amazed and happy to find out that we have twin boys. You did so well my darling. I will have to make this letter quick because Ten Tree's decided to return to Fort Kearney with a troop of soldiers whose tour of duty is up here. He is leaving in a few minutes and I want him to take this letter with him. I will miss him, he has saved me from many perils along the way. He also is a good hunter and I will miss the game he always found.

I hope that you are well and that the boys are doing well. I know you are taking wonderful care of our sons. I feel ashamed sometimes that I am not there providing for you. I pray everyday for your safety and health. I also pray that Oregon will be all that we've hoped it would be. I will be looking up Reverend Elder when I get there. He was the preacher for awhile at the Valley Church. I think his wife was from our area. I heard they settled in Independence, Oregon so he might be able to help me get some work.

We met some fearsome Indians along the trail but we were not harmed. One of them actually helped us get here. I had been making a beaded headdress for the Sam or Pete's first pony. As a gesture of good will I gave it to this Indian Chief and he repaid us with safe passage through his territory. Ten Trees said we were very lucky.

Even though winter has hit us hard here, I am well. I share a barracks with three other men and we manage to find enough to eat to each day. I hope the wagon trains start coming soon so I can push on to Oregon, I am very anxious to get there and send for you.

My love to all, God bless you and keep you safe,
Zack."

Lydia refolded the letter and reached for the pot of tea Rose had brought out. She poured some of the strong liquid in everyone's cups. No one said anything as they quietly began to take their sandwiches and tea. Only the babies made any sound at all. They played and smeared toast all over themselves and the blanket.

After they finished their meal Deben and Jonas unloaded the wagon, foodstuff into the house and grain to the barn. Lydia watched as the men led the horses pulling the wagon down the hill. "Rose, do you think Oregon is going to be as good as here?"

Rose shook her head, "I don't think it's going to be much different than here because it's the people that make a place. Every place has its good and bad points. Here we got rocks instead of good top soil, maybe the land will be better in Oregon and we'll be able to grow more crops." Rose walked to the edge of the porch, "But my husband is buried over there, and his father and mother as well as three of my children. I don't think I could leave them. Oh, I know they're gone but it's a comfort to me to be able to see where they're buried. I want to join them someday. I think I'm too old and too set in these hills to ever leave." She wiped tears from her eyes, "I thought I could when Zack left, but I'm not as sure as I was then. The more I think about it the less I think I can."

Lydia crossed the porch and held her mother-in-law. "I know what you mean. I felt that way when I left my family's farm but somehow coming here seemed right because Zack was here. I think I can go anywhere he is."

Rose managed a smile, "That's the way it should be, daughter. We go where our men are, no matter what." She looked off across the clearing to the small family graveyard, "My man is here."

Lydia stood for a few minutes thinking about where Zack was. Could she really join him someday in Oregon? Or would it be best if he came back to her, here in his home place where his family had always been? What was best for her boys? It gave her a headache trying to think too much about her situation, so she busied herself with the daily chores. Life was hard enough without burdening oneself with what might be. "Just deal with today," she chided herself. "There's plenty to keep a person worn out."

Chapter 28
South of Independence, Oregon—April 1867

Cleveland was pleased that his birthday fell on a day that he wasn't working. The work crew was between building jobs for three days so it gave him time to ride into Dallas. At eighteen he was now considered an adult by the law, so he needed to go put the farm in his own name and pay his taxes.

Dallas was quite a little city as Cleveland rode into it mid-morning. The wide street in front of the courthouse was filled with activities of all kinds. There were freight wagons bringing in goods to the general stores, and a couple drovers driving their cattle right down the middle of the street. Several buggies carrying men and women were coming and going amid the chaos. Cleveland looked at all the choices. A person could shop at one of two mercantile stores or eat at one of the restaurants in the hotels. There were also a couple saloons on Main Street, across the street from the courthouse and a few idle men were standing around looking at passers-by. Cleveland wasn't looking for any kind of trouble so he steered his mule to the other side of the street and continued on until he saw what he was looking for. He stopped outside a small, whitewashed building that had a shingle out front, "James Layton Collins, Attorney at Law."

Cleveland had heard that Mr. Collins specialized in land claims and land dealings so he'd decided on seeing him rather than the other lawyers in town. He dusted himself off and took his hat off to slick his hair back out of his eyes. Hat in hand he entered the small office. Mr. Collins was sitting at a large desk at the back of the room. There were tall windows on either side of the room, that seemed to focus the light right over the desk. Three small wooden chairs and a small wood stove filled what was left of the floor space. The back wall of the office was lined with shelves full of books. Cleveland was impressed by the number of books in that one place.

Mr. Collins stood up and came over to Cleveland, "Can I help you, son?"

Cleveland almost forgot why he'd came. James Collins had piercing blue eyes that just seemed to hold a person spellbound. He towered over Cleveland as the two stood for a moment sizing each other up. Finally the twitch of Collins' full moustache broke the spell. "I need to put my farm in my name." Cleveland blurted out hurriedly.

"Well, I see. Who's name is it in now, Mr.....?"

"Oh sorry sir," Cleveland extended his hand, "I'm Cleveland Taylor. My father was Alex Taylor. He died sometime back, my ma died a couple years back and I waited until now to come because I'm eighteen now. I've been working the farm since my dad died, living there and taking care of things."

"Do you have any other family that have claim to it?"

"I have two sisters that I haven't seen or heard from in ten years. Wouldn't have a clue how to find them, either."

James Collins made a few notes on paper, "Where exactly is your farm?"

Cleveland explained as best he could where the farm was. Collins unrolled a survey map of the county and together they tried to pinpoint the area. "I will need to go to the courthouse and find the original deed to the property, then we can proceed. Will you be staying in town?"

"I can stay tonight if need be." Cleveland smiled. He thought it might be fun to stay in a hotel for the first time in his life and eat in another restaurant.

"Come back at three today and I will have found out what papers we will need to file. It may be that we need to post this for three weeks to give anyone who has claim against your property time to step forward. If there were any debts or others listed on the title you might have to settle with them or sell the farm for mutual benefit."

"You mean I might lose my farm?" Cleveland said in shock.

"I sincerely hope it doesn't come to that, but let me see what we find before we start to worry, my young friend. We will discuss my fee when we meet this afternoon. Usually I charge from five to ten dollars if it isn't too complicated." They shook hands again at the door and Cleveland stepped outside.

Cleveland was on the verge of panic. He had never thought of ever losing his farm. He'd worked so hard. He walked his mule over to the livery stable and, after making sure she was fed and watered he headed for the larger of the two hotels. He had saved up twenty five dollars because he knew lawyers charged, but the money didn't seem as important as it had before.

The hotel lobby had a small counter that blocked the entrance to their small café and the stairs to the second floor. No one was at the counter when he first went in, so he stood for a few moments looking at the lacy curtains on the windows and lace doilies draped over the small tables at either side of the counter. A small vase of flowers graced the counter along with a log book and pen.

On the wall behind the counter there was a painting of a bowl of flowers and a calendar.

"What can I do for you, Sir?"

Cleveland was surprised to see a boy of twelve or thirteen take his position behind the counter. "I would like a room for the night, please."

"Certainly sir," the boy looked at a small rack of keys. "Will it be just you?"

"Yes, I'm traveling alone."

"Very well, sir we have a choice of a room facing the street or one on the back side of the building that looks out over the alley. The one on the alley is a little quieter, and is only a dollar instead of one dollar and fifty cents. Of course, breakfast and dinner come with either of the rooms. Lunch is fifty cents extra."

Cleveland thought briefly, "I'll take the one on the front of the building. It's my birthday, so I'll live it up a bit."

The boy smiled, "Very good, sir. Please sign our guest book." He put a key down next to the pen on the counter. Cleveland signed his name and then handed two dollars to the boy. After he pocketed his change Cleveland asked, "Are you serving lunch in the dining room now?"

"Yes sir, my mother's the cook and she's a really good one." The boy stepped around the corner of the counter and with a grand gesture ushered Cleveland into the small dining room. Two or three others were already having lunch even though it was only a little after eleven in the morning. Cleveland seated himself by one of the three windows that faced the street. He loved watching all the hubbub.

A young woman in a bright white apron came to the table with a list of choices for his lunch. "We have two different lunches today beings as how its a weekday. Weekends we have more of a family style meal. You can have a cold roast lamb sandwich on wheat bread with a bowl of lamb stew, or you can have a two pieces of cold fried chicken and potato salad. Both come with your choice of milk, buttermilk, coffee or tea, an apple or two oatmeal cookies."

"I think I'll try the lamb, with milk to drink," Cleveland said, his mouth watering.

In moments he had his lunch and it was not disappointing. The boy at the counter had been right: his mother was an excellent cook. He lingered over the sweet milk with his cookies until the last bit of both were gone. He hadn't eaten so well in a long time. There hadn't been many opportunities to visit with the Porterfields and there hadn't been any church socials so he'd been pretty much fixing for himself. Since the loss of Cork, eating and cooking hadn't seemed so important. He shook himself, he got melancholy whenever he thought of the senseless killing of his dog.

After lunch he walked the length of the main street then went down and sat for awhile on the banks of the Rickreall Creek. It was a nice little stream. Here and there people were fishing, a couple people were catching fair sized trout. Cleveland wished he'd had his fishing pole along. He found himself a grassy spot, free of poison oak, and sat down. He was surprised when a child threw a rock into the creek with a loud "kerthump" and he realized he'd been asleep. He jumped up and hurried back up town, hoping he hadn't missed his appointment with Mr. Collins.

It was five minutes past three when Cleveland reentered the law office. Mr. Collins looked at his watch then at Cleveland. "Sorry sir," Cleveland said with a shrug, "I went for a walk by the creek and fell asleep."

James Collins smiled, "I don't blame you. It's a right nice day out there." He shuffled through a couple papers and then motioned for Cleveland to sit down. "I have some good news for you, young man. I found your father's deed and it seems that he had already put your name on it with him, so all we have to do is sign a couple papers stating that your father is deceased and that you are now sole owner."

Cleveland couldn't believe what he was hearing, "He put my name on the deed with him?"

The lawyer nodded, "He must have known he wasn't in good health because he did that several years after his original deed was filed."

It took a few minutes to absorb what the lawyer had just said. His father knew he was ill? Why didn't he tell Cleveland and his mother? She had been as shocked as he was when his father died. "I didn't know that."

"You need to sign these three papers," Collins laid the pages in front of Cleveland and pointed to lines marked with an "X". "I will take these back to the courthouse this very afternoon and get them entered into the record. You can come by in the morning about ten and I will have the final papers you will need. You'll need to go to the courthouse and pay last years taxes, which was twelve dollars." He stood up and shook Cleveland's hand. "This was certainly easier than it might have been. My fee will be five dollars." He smiled. "I will see you in the morning."

Cleveland paid his fee and left quickly. He still was reeling from the idea his father knew he was going to die, yet told no one. It was a long time ago, but still it was hard to know now. Cleveland went back to the hotel to clean up a bit before supper and to look at his hotel room. It was still his birthday, but still sometimes the hurts of his life came back to haunt him and take the fun out of things. He sighed, "Maybe that's what comes with being a grown man."

INTO THE DUST

* * *

Cleveland was putting up a door jamb for the front door on a two-story house in Independence. The work had gone slowly, and the day had been surprisingly hot for late April. It was a relief when Harve, the crew boss, called time out for lunch. Everyone went to a shady spot to eat whatever they had brought. Cleveland went to his mule and made sure she had water and a handful of grain. He led her around for a few minutes before hitching her back to the tree, then he sat down to eat his hard boiled egg and slice of bread. It wasn't much, but it was his usual fare. It only took a minute or two to finish his meager meal then he sat in the shade and rested. He closed his eyes for a moment and didn't notice Harve and another man walk up.

"Cleve," Harve said loudly.

Cleveland jumped, hitting the mule on the leg. She kicked out at him in surprise. He narrowly missed her flying hoof. "Whoa girl," he said as he tried to calm her down. He got up and looked at Harve and the stranger.

"Cleveland this is, Zack Grant. He's a friend of Reverend Elder. I told him I'd give him a try as a laborer with us. He's a horseman, not a builder, but he's willing to work and that's what we need right now." He turned to Zack, "This fellow looks young, but don't let that fool you. He's a master carpenter and can work circles around most of us here. You'd do well to do as he asks you to, he knows what he's talking about. You'll be his helper for the rest of the week and then we'll see where we are. You okay with that?"

Zack smiled at Cleveland. "I think that is just fine."

Cleveland looked at Harve. He was pleased that the boss thought so highly of him, but he wasn't sure he was ready to be training people who were older than he. Cleveland eyed Zack for a moment. He was taller than Cleveland but probably didn't weigh as much. He had obviously seen some hard times, his face was thin and lined. He looked to be thirty but might not be that old. His hands were big and strong, though. "You ready to get to work?" Cleveland said hesitantly.

"Let's do it," Zack said and stood aside to let Cleveland lead the way.

Cleveland was pleased as the afternoon wore on. Zack wasn't used to carpentry work but he was a quick learner and fell easily into helping his younger work mate. Harve checked at the end of the day to see if Zack would work out and Cleveland said, "Well, he put in a good afternoon of work. I think if he comes back, he'll be just fine."

The next morning when Cleveland got to the work site just after sunup, Zack was sitting on the porch eating an apple. He smiled when he saw Cleveland and waved. The mornings work passed quickly, Zack turned out to be a great help to Cleveland. At lunchtime the two sat together and shared the lunch that Reverend Elder's wife had prepared for Zack.

"Mrs. Elder must have thought I am starving to death," Zack laughed. "She packed enough here for a week. Probably more than I had to eat most of the time I was crossing the country."

"You came across recently?"

"Got to Oregon just this month." Zack said around a piece of apple pie.

"Bet you got stories to tell," Cleveland said with interest.

Zack nodded his head and kept eating. When he finished he wiped his mouth on his sleeve and sat thinking for a moment. "I came out by myself to find a job, a place and a future for my family. I got a wife and two boys in Tennessee. They're staying with my mother on the family farm."

Cleveland didn't know what to say so he just waited to hear more but before Zack could continue the lunch time was over and they were back at the seemingly endless work of finishing a house. It was hard, backbreaking work but Zack didn't complain. Cleveland appreciated that even more when he saw the blisters on Zack's hands. There was something about this newcomer that Cleveland liked, maybe he reminded him of himself in some ways.

As Cleveland prepared to leave Zack came over and asked a couple questions. "You know I've been staying with Reverend Elder and his family, but that isn't very comfortable for them. I wondered if you know someone who might have a room to rent or a boarding house in the area? I don't really have any money until I get paid here so I need something kind of cheap."

Cleveland thought a moment, then looked out towards his own farm.

"Well, I got a farm south of town. It's just me and I got a bedroom that was my ma's that I don't use. I guess you could stay with me for a few days until you get your pay. You could help with the chores for your keep."

Zack looked a little surprised, "You don't live with your folks?"

Cleveland shook his head, "My pa died several years ago and my ma just a couple after him. So it's just me. I did have an old dog but…."he couldn't finish that thought.

"If you're sure it wouldn't put you out I'd be right pleased to help with chores on your farm."

Cleveland smiled, "It's fine with me."

"I'll tell Reverend Elder I'll be staying with you then starting tomorrow after work." He held out his hand, "I really appreciate that, Cleveland."

After shaking Zack's hand, Cleveland climbed on the mule and headed home. He wondered if he'd done the right thing, inviting a near stranger to share his home for a spell. But the thought of having someone to talk to for awhile seemed mighty pleasant, so maybe it would work out for a few days.

* * *

It was a little hard to sleep the first couple nights Zack slept in the bedroom that had been Cleveland's ma's. Zack snored something awful. They laughed about it but it was a problem. Finally Cleveland moved his cot back into the alcove away from the fireplace in the front room and he couldn't hear Zack quite as much. Finally Cleveland got used to it and slept well.

At the end of the week Zack got his first pay. After a stop at the store the two returned to the farm and fixed a real meal of steak, potatoes with biscuits and gravy. Zack was a pretty good cook, much to Cleveland's delight.

"What do you do for fun on weekends?" Zack asked casually as they relaxed on the porch after dinner.

"Fun?" Cleveland hadn't ever thought of doing something for fun.

"What do you like to do?" Zack pressed.

"Well, when Cork was with me I used to take her down to the river and we'd go fishing. I never really cared much for fish but she liked to swim and chase frogs."

"You really loved that dog, didn't you?" Zack said softly.

"She was the only one here with me when ma died. She made me laugh and gave me a reason to come home." Cleveland sighed. "Guess I'm silly for caring about a dog so much."

"Nonsense, she was a good and faithful friend," Zack reached over and patted Cleveland on the shoulder. "We don't find many in our lives who accept us unconditionally and ask for nothing more than to be fed and housed in return. They are devoted to us, man nor beast." Zack sprawled out on his back and looked up at the first stars appearing in the purple haze of the evening. "Hard to believe I'm so far from my family yet they might be looking at the same stars I am."

Cleveland looked up, "Do you suppose they are thinking about you as much as you think about them? You talk about them a lot."

Zack sat up, suddenly he was lonely again. "I do miss them. This has not been anything like I thought it would be. I've been gone for over six months now. I thought I'd been all established by now, sending for my family any day but here I am with just a few dollars in my pocket and a temporary job."

"It will get better, you'll get your own place and send for your family soon. I am sure of it."

Zack looked at Cleveland, "I guess I should be looking for a place now that I've gotten paid. I really do appreciate you letting me stay with you until I got on my feet."

Cleveland turned away, he didn't want Zack to see the tears welling up in his eyes. "You know you're welcome to stay. I mean, it's been working out pretty well. You cook better than I do and your help with catching up with some of the repairs here has been a god-send for me."

Zack sat a moment. "I don't want to wear out my welcome. I think you're a great kid, Cleveland. In many ways you remind me of my brother Joshua, except he wasn't really fond of me. He was the farmer and I wasn't. He always thought I didn't care enough about the farm, didn't do my share of the chores."

"I've never found you to shy away from any chores."

Zack reached out and patted Cleveland's shoulder, "This isn't as big as our family farm. This is manageable for two men who really want to do something else. Your father was right, a small farm is enough for a tradesman. It's enough to provide a cow or two, some chickens but not so much you have to be here twenty four hours a day. You've got a good place here, Cleve."

"I really wish you'd consider staying on here. Someday you'll buy a place of your own out here but for right now you'd be more than welcome to stay."

Zack thought about it for a few minutes, "I won't say that doesn't sound good to me. I have enjoyed having someone to talk with and share work with. There are some things I've seen around here that I could help you with."

"What things?"

"You got a couple natural springs here on the place. I thought I could use those for a project I have in mind. Maybe make you a big surprise."

Cleveland laughed, "Now for sure you have to stay. I am looking forward having a surprise."

The two men laughed and shared stories of their experiences into the night. When Cleveland finally settled into his cot he was still smiling. For the first time in a long time, he fell asleep in a state of near contentment.

Chapter 29
East Tennessee—Early July 1867

Lydia sat on the front porch and swatted flies. It was only ten in the morning but it was just too hot to be in the house with the doors closed so the alternative was to sit outside in the shade and deal with the nuisance of the bugs. The boys were napping on a blanket near her. They were under a layer of netting so did not notice the buzzing insects as she did. Sometimes she envied her boys, there was always someone to look after them and take care of them. Rose and Deben had gone down to the well house to get more water for lemonade, and Jonas was tending to the animals with the Goss boy tagging along. Eddy had come just after sunrise with the mail and a couple bags of supplies. Lydia was glad for the few minutes alone. She wasn't sure why, but she was in a bad mood. The letter from Zack lay beside her on the step unopened. Anger, anticipation, and loneliness boiled up in her chest. Tears came hot and heavy as she reached for the letter and finally opened it.

"Independence, Oregon
April 25, 1867
Dearest Wife and family,

I trust this finds you all well. I have finally made it to Oregon and got a job. I am working as a carpenter's helper building houses. I have been fortunate to meet a young man, Cleveland Taylor, who has a small spread just south of town and he has given me room and tucker for helping around his farm. He lost his parents several years ago and has been on his own since. He's a real nice kid, whole lot like my brother was as a boy. I think you'd really like him.

This has been a much different trip than I thought it would be. It seems it will take quite a bit of working to save up enough to buy a decent farm. I saw a pretty one nearly like ours back there but it was over a thousand dollars. Needless to say, I didn't have more than two dollars when I got here. Reverend Elder and his Mrs. was kind enough to let me stay with them until I got this job and place with Cleve.

The country is pretty here, much like Tennessee but without the rocks. The Willamette Valley is huge. The ground is good too. They can grow just about anything they have a mind to. Cleveland doesn't know much about raising a garden but I can teach him.

Liddy, my darling, I can see now that this is going to take some time. I hate being apart from you but there is no way I can come get you all yet. I hope it is not too hard waiting there on the farm. I want to have a nest egg enough to at least put a down payment on a place of our own and enough money for all your passages out here.

You can see it's going to be a longer time being without one another than I thought. It hurts me now to know that my boys will be three or four before I get to see them. I admit that I was foolish to chase this dream. It's a great place but not worth the price you are having to pay. Please forgive me and understand my intentions were good. I promise to work as hard as a man can to make this all happen as quickly as possible.

You are always on my mind my beloved wife, mother and Jonas.

*Godspeed,
Zack"*

Lydia put the letter down on the step and buried her head in her hands for a few moments. Then the anger won out. "Eddy," she yelled down to the barn.

The boy peeked out of the barn door, "Yes Miss Liddy?"

"Don't leave until I finish a letter to Zack," she replied, "I want you to post it for me."

The boy waved his agreement as Lydia whirled and went to get her writing materials. In seconds she was back on the porch, her quill pen flying between the ink well and the paper. Each word she put on it dug deeper into the rough surface of the thin sheets of linen. She finished the piece just before the boys woke up for their lunch. She started to fold the letter. After biting her lip for a moment she reached into her sewing basket, retrieving her scissors. With determination she whacked off a long stand of hair and tucked it between the sheets of paper. In a second the letter was in its envelope and addressed to "Zack Grant, Care of Cleveland Taylor, Independence, Oregon." with a sigh of frustration she hurried down to the barn and gave her work to Eddy, "Post this today for me will you?"

"Sure, Miss Liddy," Eddy tipped his hat and headed for his mule. She stood and watched as he went down the winding road.

"You look like you could fry an egg on your head," Jonas observed.

"I am a little heated," Lydia admitted. "Zack's letter said he was working in Oregon but it might be a long time before he could send for us. Isn't that just the way a man thinks? He thinks he's got to have it all before we come out there or he comes home. I wouldn't care if we lived in a mud hut if we were together."

Jonas walked over to her and smiled knowingly. "I know you miss him and you really didn't understand why he had to go. But you know the good book says God moves in mysterious ways and sometimes we got to just trust in the end everything will work out. You'll be happy again, I just know it."

Lydia shrugged, "I wish I could believe that but right now it's hard to do."

"You all coming up for lunch?" Rose called from the front porch.

"We're coming, Miss Rose," Jonas answered. He looked at Lydia, "You got them beautiful boys waiting for their lunch."

Lydia smiled at the black man with his infectious smile. "You always know what to say to bring me back to reality." They laughed and walked up the hill to the house.

* * *

For a week Lydia worried over what Zack would think when he got her letter, feeling at times bitter and other times remorseful. Nothing seemed right. Pete got a cold and was fussy, Sam soon caught the cold, then so did Lydia. It was a miserably hot July, too, making matters worse. She bathed the boys every few hours to help keep their fevers down but there wasn't anything she could do about the hot days. They all got through it but it took all her energy. By the time the hacking cough was gone she had lost five or six pounds and felt as weak as a newborn kitten. Rose had fixed most of the meals for the whole two weeks Lydia was sick and was getting tired, too. Jonas and Deben did as much as they could of the chores in and out of the house but everyone was at the edge of what they could take.

One evening just as the sun was setting a wagon pulled up in the yard. Rose and Lydia stood on the porch and Jonas and Deben went to the foot of the stairs. None of them recognized the thin young man, nor the woman and half-grown boy who got out of the wagon, no one until the man turned and looked at Rose. "Momma?" he said softly.

Rose's jaw dropped! "Joshua?" she said breathlessly.

The young man held out his arms as his mother came down the stairs. Joshua turned to Jonas, "Don't you recognize me either my friend?"

"My stars, Mister Joshua, it has been so long and you've changed considerably." Jonas reached out and shook Joshua's hand, but Joshua drew him into a bear hug just as his mother approached and joined in the embrace.

"Liddy, come here," Rose called. "This is your brother-in-law. My son Josh."

"Well, I figured that out by now." Liddy said as she came to join the group.

"So Zack got married too," Joshua said shaking Lydia's hand, "This is my wife Susan and her brother, Brett."

Rose looked at the pretty young woman with light colored curls pecking out under a straw bonnet. "Well, darling, welcome to your husband's home."

Joshua looked around. "So where is my brother Zack?"

Rose looked at Lydia who looked away for a moment. "That's a long story. We'll talk over some late supper. I imagine you've been on the road a piece and haven't eaten?"

"No ma'am, we haven't," Brett chimed in hopefully.

"Come on in the house and we'll see what we can find," Lydia said. "Jonas, would you and Deben come in, too, after you put their rig and horses in the barn?"

"Will do, Miss Liddy, don't tell too much until we get there." Jonas and Deben hurried to get their work done so they could get back to the house.

"Who's Deben, Ma?" Joshua asked as he helped his wife into the house.

"That too is a long story, but most simply he's a friend of our doctor's nephew. He was turned out of a plantation down south and had no where to go, so he's been helping us here with the farm and the children."

"Children?" Susan asked.

"Zack and I have twin boys," Lydia said proudly. "I've already put them down for the night but I think I could be forgiven for getting them up for a little while."

"That's alright, sister Lydia," Susan said softly, "I think we're going to turn in pretty soon ourselves. We've been up since way before sunrise. I'm really tired." She smiled at her husband then Lydia, "Your boys are going to have a cousin by Christmas."

Rose rushed over and hugged Susan, "What great news."

Within a few minutes a pot of coffee had been made, cold slabs of ham put on slices of thick bread, and fresh strawberries with cream were ready for an evening celebration. Everyone settled down in the living room, including Jonas and Deben to hear all the news. "Well, it's hard to know where to start," Joshua said, "I guess I was just a foolish boy when I went off to do my part in the war. I got to the army headquarters but no one was there, they'd moved somewhere so I never did join up. Instead I found myself in Boston sailing out on a merchant ship." He stopped to smile at Susan who had fallen asleep in the rocking chair. "That's how I met Susan.

Her father was the Captain of the ship. He wasn't too keen on us marrying because she was only seventeen and I was eighteen at the time, but it was good that we did because he was killed in an accident while we were in England. Her ma had died when she was only nine or ten. Brett here is twelve so we've become a family of three, soon to be four." He looked at Lydia, "So, now you tell me about Zack."

Lydia tried to tell the tale as calmly as she could, praying her anger wouldn't come through as it had off and on for so long. It took two cups of coffee before she had brought Joshua up-to-date. Rose nodded often, obviously reliving the details herself.

Joshua shook his head, "I always felt that Zack wasn't cut out to be a farmer. He always had a wandering foot." He looked at Jonas. "I have some very interesting news for you my dear friend. While I was in England I looked up that old Lord Bently you worked for when you were brought out of Africa. I was all prepared to give him the devil for what he done to you. It turns out though that he tried to look for you when he found out what his overseer had done. He was really upset, had the man fired and wanted to make things right with you. He said you were never a slave but a hired man. He sent me home with some money for you. He also set up an account with his bank in England that will pay you a yearly salary for the rest of your life. He said he also thinks he knows where your wife and child might be, and he would be willing to help you try to find them if you want him too."

Tears began to flow down Jonas face. "Oh my God," he choked, "I can't believe this."

Rose went and put her arms around Jonas. "I can't imagine you ever leaving us but for a good reason and this seems like the best of reasons." Her tears mingled with his, "You have been the dearest friend a body could have, but I know this has always been an ache in your heart. You must go and try to find your family."

Jonas was so overcome he couldn't speak, he simply got up and hugged Joshua and motioned for Deben to follow. Deben quietly said good night and they left the room through the back door. Rose looked at her son with pride, "You've made that man so happy. I can't imagine how vindicated he must feel."

"He can take one of the ships in Susan's father's line to England anytime he wants to go. I know the English Lord will help him. He seemed really genuinely concerned about what had happened."

Lydia smiled at Joshua and his sleeping wife. "I'll make up some pallets here on the floor so you can all get a good night's sleep. I think Susan and the boy are too tired for any more visiting tonight." She got up and returned with three thick quilts to put down as bedding and some sheets for covers. "It's a hot night so you probably won't need much more than this."

Rose helped Lydia smooth out the make shift beds. "You are home to stay, aren't you Joshua?" Rose said hopefully.

"Well, I wasn't sure ma," Joshua looked at Lydia. "I thought maybe if Zack were farming the place I'd try to find a place nearby to buy and set up my own farm."

"Nonsense, son," Rose shook her head, "This is your farm too. Zack would have loved to have you here helping us even if it had worked out that he stayed, but now it looks like he's not planning to come back for quite a spell." She hesitated and added softly, "If at all."

"Since it's that way, ma, I would like to stay and help you run the farm. It could make a good living for all of us. I think there is going to be good money in a new crop, tobacco. I seen some farms not far from here already growing it. We could clear some more land and see if that would grow here."

Rose sat on the floor a moment and smiled at her son, "It's good to hear you talk about improving the place. Zack was just content to get by here. His heart was never in the farm. Always thinking about making a business out of his horse shoeing and leather work."

Lydia finished the work and laid a fire in the cookstove for morning breakfast. It wasn't lost on her what Rose was saying. It was painful to hear, but true. Zack just wasn't a farmer and didn't really want to be. She tried not to show the discomfort she was beginning to feel, trying to shake off the worry about what or where that left her and her boys in this family if Joshua and his family were here to stay.

"In the morning we'll move Zack's boys' bed into my room and Lydia can sleep with me, leaving you two the bigger bedroom," Rose said joyfully, "Oh, I am so happy to have you home." She hugged Joshua again before taking Lydia's arm and heading for the bedrooms. Lydia wasn't too pleased at Rose's giving her family's room away so easily. For the first time ever she felt like a guest in this house, a house that had been hers when Zack was home. Again she felt like someone was pushing her out, just as it was when she was a child when her step-mother displaced her in her father's home and affections. Anger was coming more easily every day to Lydia and she didn't feel better for it.

* * *

As Jonas prepared to leave for England, Lydia realized just how lonely it would be for her without his wise council. As for the rest of the family, Rose was so caught up in Joshua being home that she seldom even played with the twins anymore. Susan and her brother took to doing most of the chores in the house so there wasn't much for Lydia to do, either. Joshua loved the farm and took right up where he'd left off years ago. It made him happy to be back on the land, Lydia couldn't fault him for that. In fact, often she wished Zack had been more like his brother.

The awful day came when Jonas did go. He didn't linger, instead he took his breakfast, gave Brett some last minute instructions on how to take care of his cat, Goldie. Brett and Goldie had taken right up with each other, so Jonas felt better about having to leave her behind. He left before sunrise on a clear bright day, before anyone had time for tears. Rose had given him a horse so he wouldn't have to walk. He left each of them a note of thanks and pledged to let them know how everything turned out and if he found his family. He took Deben with him. The elderly man had decided to go north to a place he'd heard about where black folks had formed their own town. He thought he might find someone he knew. It was on the way to Boston where Jonas would catch the ship to England and beyond. When everyone was up and realized what had happened, they sat around the breakfast table in stunned silence. One by one they read the letters that Jonas had left. They were happy for their friends, but it did leave a huge empty spot at their table.

The only good thing that came out of Jonas and Deben leaving was now there was another room to fix up. Lydia and Rose cleaned for two or three days getting Jonas' rustic cabin floor to nearly shine. Susan helped put up batting on the walls and then cover it with wall paper. It made a fairly warm room. They painted the chairs, table and wash stand, then washed blankets, sheets and made new coverlets and window coverings. When they had finished they had a nice sized room with two attractive sleeping areas separated by a willow screen. It was decided that since Lydia helped with the cooking early in the morning she would take Rose's bedroom. Brett and Rose would share the cabin. Lydia protested, "I could take the cabin with the boys."

"No, you need to be in here to get breakfast started and the boys need to be nearby," Rose said putting her hand up. "Now Brett, do you think you can stand sharing a room with your Grandma Rose?"

Brett smiled, "I think I can, Grandma Rose. That is if you don't snore any louder than Joshua."

Everyone laughed and returned to the day's chores. For awhile the new arrangement seemed to work well. Everyone was in good humor and Lydia thought maybe it would be alright after all. But then Pete got sick again and the doctor had to come. The baby had the measles and had to be quarantined. Lydia and the boys were quickly moved to the cabin, the doctor fearing for Susan and her unborn child. It was tense during the following two weeks as Sam quickly followed with the dreaded spots. Rose brought meals to the cabin but didn't come in. Lydia had the small woodstove Jonas used to keep the cabin warm so that wasn't a problem, but the isolation with two sick boys was.

Resentment began to grow again, whether she wanted it or not.

When it was clear no one else was going to get the measles, Rose helped Lydia wash all the bedding and air the room. She did not, however, offer to move back into the cabin herself. Lydia knew she had to get off the farm for awhile or she might go crazy. Finally she made up her mind to do that very thing. She announced that she would like to go visit her sister in Knoxville and asked Joshua to drive them in the wagon. No one objected, in fact it seemed to her that the idea was met with relief.

Two days later she loaded her clothes, a few belongings, the boys and their supplies into the wagon with everyone's help. They all were tearful as Joshua drove the wagon out of the yard. Lydia looked back as they neared the first bend in the road. Rose was walking back towards the house with her arm around Susan, just as she had with her when Zack left. A chill swept through Lydia as she looked at the house, the yard, the fields and barns. At that moment she knew she would never come back here. This was a part of a past that didn't exist for her anymore. Wherever Zack might be was her home now, even though she had no idea how she would get there or if he might come for her. The future was uncertain but there wasn't anything for her anymore in this part of Tennessee, she did know. She sighed and turned to look ahead. Sometime in the days to come, surely there was someone to love her and her children. She was hopeful it would be Zack.

Chapter 30
Salem, Oregon—July 4, 1867

Cleveland could hardly control his excitement. He'd never dreamed of actually having fun again. His life had been about work and keeping up the farm for longer than he could remember. Sure he'd had some fun as a child, but that seemed like a lifetime ago. But here he stood on the edge of what promised to be a great day. Zack and Cleveland had money in their pockets and since the 4th was on a Thursday, four days off. They didn't have to go back to work until Monday. It was a true holiday! According to the Salem Daily Record this was going to be one huge celebration.

Zack pushed Cleveland ahead of him. "Come on boy, we got to get a good place to see this parade." They wound their way through the crowd of men in fancy suits, women in their finest linen or silk dresses and children all spruced up like they were going to church. It was a very festive day. In the distance they could hear music playing so they knew the event was underway. Finally they found themselves a fairly good spot behind some children seated on the ground on Court Street. They looked up and down the street while they waited. "Quite a crowd. Seems everybody likes a good parade."

Cleveland laughed and started to say something, but the cheering crowd drowned him out as a wagon pulled by four beautiful white horses came by them. The sign said "Grand Marshal." It was followed by several men on horses decorated with all kinds of flowers. Then sign bearers announced the "Aurora Pioneer Brass Band." They were loud but good. Cleveland cheered as they broke into a lively rendition of "Yankee Doodle." Zack just stood quietly; that song had bad memories attached to it for him but he knew this was a different time and place. He was pleased when the next selection was "My Old Kentucy Home." Everyone quieted down as the flag of the United States passed by. Several people removed their hats, others put their hands across their hearts. Several old soldiers, some wearing Union uniforms and a couple in Confederate ones marched by. People remained quiet and thoughtful as they passed. Then those from the war with Mexico passed by. The mood lifted when the fire wagon came into view, pulled by six big work horses. It was followed by all kinds of modern fire fighting equipment like the huge reel of hoses drawn by a brace of mules. Other fire departments and men came next, followed by several groups of men in baseball uniforms.

"You ever play baseball?" Zack asked Cleveland over the din, he shook his head. "Me neither. Maybe we can go see how it's done."

There were many in the procession who were just decked out in fancy clothes, several wagons full of people waving to the crowds and throwing pennies or candy to the children. The final wagon was filled with so many flowers it looked like there was no room for people, but somehow there was a man playing a fiddle and a woman singing at the top of her lungs. The crowd lining the streets filled in behind the wagon and became a part of the event themselves. Zack and Cleveland weren't going to miss out on the fun either, joining right in with all the other watchers. Soon they found themselves at Marion Square where a big stage had been set up right in the middle of the park. Zack and Cleveland found themselves an open spot and sat on the grass to hear the program. Everyone else did the same.

The afternoon passed quickly as they first heard music by a band, then singing by a glee club. There was a prayer and more singing, then some official read the Declaration of Independence, which brought shouts and amens from the crowd. There were windy speeches by several people, more singing and more speeches. Cleveland's mind began to wander as he grew hungry. Luckily there were vendors coming through the park with sausages and peanuts. A couple rounds of everything they could find made Zack and Cleveland perk up. It was about three when the afternoon festivities downtown finally drew to a close. Cleveland and Zack quickly made their way to the fairgrounds. "You ever see a horse race, Zack?"

"Yeah, saw several in Knoxville. It's amazing how fast a horse can run on a track. They don't move very quickly when you got them hooked to a plow or riding cross country but on a track for a short spurt they can really go."

Cleveland was surprised to see you could look at the horses before the race and then bet on who you thought would win. It was amazing. They didn't bet on the first race but did guess who they thought might win. Zack was right about his choice, but Cleveland's pick came in dead last. They laughed and decided to spend a dollar each on a bet. It seemed a lot of money, but when the horse Cleveland picked came in third he got four dollars in return. Cleveland split the winnings with Zack and they went back downtown to find themselves a steak dinner.

On the way they passed one of the many saloons in town. "You ever had liquor?" Cleveland asked with a smile.

"A few times. Jonas and I made some hard apple cider that was pretty good. A neighbor or two would bring a little corn liquor by sometimes. But then there was the not so pleasant kinds. Some stuff the guys in the army made, a wild kind of whiskey from potatoes, would kill you if you had more than a sip. Then I had some wine and it was pretty strong, too. I had a little beer, in an occasional stop on the way here." He started to say something else but just then the doors on the saloon flew open and two men wrestled out onto the sidewalk cursing and hurling fists at each other. In their unawareness of anyone else, they managed to knock Cleveland off the sidewalk. Zack rushed over and pulled his friend to safety. They stood openmouthed as the fight continued. Several men staggered out of the bar and joined in the fray. Zack pushed Cleveland to the other side of the street. "We'd better stay out of that one. It's not our fight and fights never end well."

They watched as a couple sheriff deputies arrived and broke up the fight. One of the men took a swing at one of the officers and was promptly hit over the head with a heavy night stick. The man slumped to the ground with blood oozing out of a gash across his forehead. "Did he kill him?" Cleveland whispered.

"No, I don't think so, but let's get out of here before someone sees us watching," Zack darted down an alley and Cleveland followed. Their light, happy mood disappeared for a few minutes until they were safely on the next street and away from the scene they'd just witnessed. "Let's find that restaurant and eat before anything else happens."

"I'm with you there. This is turning kind of wild." Luckily there were lots of eating places to choose from and within minutes they had found one that boasted "Home cooking like your mother used to make." It looked clean and affordable so they went in. The menu was simple, served family style but it was well worth the dollar-fifty it cost.

It was nearly sunset by the time they'd finished their steak, fried potatoes, and sliced tomatoes. Then there was apple pie for dessert! They decided to take the ferry across the Willamette before dark. The fare on the Salem Ferry had gone up to twenty five cents for a horse and rider, but it was better than trying to ford the river, even if it wasn't as high as it had been in the spring. They were nearly the last ones to cross that night. They found themselves a nice bank to see the last of the day's activities. They waited in the growing dark. Neither of them said much as they sat there. Cleveland's mule and Zack's horse found some grass where they were tethered, so they were content. All at once a burst of color filled the sky, followed by a loud boom. The animals jumped and needed to be calmed before they understood they were in no danger. The bright colors and blooming patterns that exploded across the sky lasted for several minutes. From everywhere they could hear the delighted cries from children and laughter from adults. When three or four of the fireworks went off at one time they knew that was the finale. They led their mounts to the road home and slowly made their way back to the farm.

It was a warm, star filled night though the moon wasn't up yet. Still, it was easy making the trip back to the farm, a good end to a mostly great day.

***

During the next week after work, they busied themselves working on projects to improve the farm. Zack had found at least two springs on the place and suspected there were more than that. He and Cleveland built a small building just beyond the garden in back of the house. It was built sort of into the hillside where Zack knew there was water. After the shell of the building was finished Zack shooed Cleveland away so he could finish it himself as a surprise. Cleveland thought that was funny but didn't protest too much. He trusted Zack with anything and everything.

Cleveland had several orders for furniture, two dressers, a table and some chairs so it kept him busy in his wood shop. One by one the pieces were finished and when Cleveland had a wagon full to deliver, he asked Zack to go along. Zack was happy to do that with him on a day they had off between houses they were working on.

Mrs. Logan, in the neighboring community of Suver, was delighted with Cleveland's work. The table and four chairs he'd made looked just beautiful in her main room. He'd made it out of a light pine and oiled it until it shined. Mr. Logan was paying Cleveland when something occurred to Zack. "You wouldn't need any horses shod, or any harnesses repaired, would you, Mr. Logan? That's what I do best."

Mr. Logan looked surprised, "Well, I usually have to go into Buena Vista to get those things done. What do you charge, son?"

"I take what you think is fair, sir."

Mr. Logan looked thoughtful for a moment. "I do have two horses that haven't been tended in a couple weeks because my back is sore from all the work in the fields." He motioned for Zack to follow him. Zack grabbed his little bag of tools out of the wagon and followed Logan.

Cleveland was surprised. He hadn't seen Zack put the tools in the wagon, but he was pleased that this was working out for him, too. "Zack, I have to deliver one other piece of furniture. It's not over two miles from here. I could deliver it and be back in an hour. Is that enough time?"

"That's just perfect, Cleveland," Zack waved and smiled.

Cleveland tipped his hat to Mrs. Logan and rode out of the farm yard.

As he bumped along the road he thought about maybe combining his furniture making and Zack's horse shoeing and tack business. He let himself day dream a bit, wondering if they could make a living doing that without having to work for someone else. After he returned to the Logan farm and picked up Zack he shared his daydreams.

"What do you think Zack? Think we could make a living doing our own work?"

Zack looked wistful for a moment, "Sounds nice, Cleve. I'd like nothing better, but right now I got to do everything I can to get my family out here. I just want to take on any kind of work so's I can do that. That's the first thing I got to do. So far, working as a carpenter helper I've only saved up twenty dollars. I figure it's going to cost at least five hundred to get Lydia, my mother and my boys out here. I don't rightly know if Jonas will want to come. It's not much better for blacks out here than Tennessee."

"Yeah, I've heard talk from some of the people who came from the South. They just can't get over it."

"I'm from the south and I'm trying. I never understood why we got in such a mess in the first place. Don't know who or how it started but nobody should ever thought they could own people's very lives. Why Jonas, an educated, well spoken man, was taken away and sold. Can't imagine how painful that was."

"Hard to imagine, isn't it." Cleveland shook his head, "But even where my folks came from was divided over the issue. My grandmother was from Georgia."

"People feel the same about other people too, like the Indians and the Mexicans. Even Christian people sometimes get caught up in the hating, they use the Bible against people even. I've heard preachers talk about Indians like they were the devil himself."

Cleveland pondered that a minute, "My momma used to say there were those who said they were Christians and then theres those who are. Usually you can tell the difference by what comes out of their mouth. She always said Jesus died for all men, not just the whiter ones."

"Amen, brother, amen!" Both men settled down into their own thoughts as they rode on into the afternoon.

* * *

The following Saturday after the men got paid, Zack asked Cleveland to go do the shopping at the store by himself. He wanted to get home and finish his surprise. Cleveland again thought it funny but agreed. Zack got on his horse and trotted out of town. Cleveland watched in amusement until Zack was out of sight. He bought all the essentials, bacon, coffee, beans and flour, plus a couple of little extras like a new work shirt and new pair of socks. As an afterthought he splurged on two new towels. The ones he and Zack used were nearly threadbare. He loaded his supplies on to Molly and they gently trotted off towards home. Cleveland hoped he'd given Zack enough time. He vowed to himself to act pleased no matter how silly it really was.

When Cleveland crested the hill to come down into his farm he was surprised to see a thin wisp of smoke coming from the stove pipe of the small shed they had built. It had been a very hot day, he couldn't imagine why Zack had built a fire on a warm afternoon like this but he guessed it was part of the surprise. Cleveland rode up to the barn and put the supplies down. He took the saddle and halter off Molly and turned her out into the pasture. She kicked up her heels and headed for the big watering trough. Cleveland put his supplies in the house then went out the back door. "I'm home," he yelled. He didn't see Zack anywhere for a minute, then the door on the shed opened and Zack motioned for him to come.

Cleveland wasn't sure what he would find in the little wooden building but it meant a lot to Zack so he didn't hesitate. It was all he could do to keep from laughing at his friend acting so childish. "So what is this big surprise?" He walked through the door into the very warm room. "Why on earth do you have a fire going?" He looked around the room. It was only about eight feet by eight feet, rough wood on the walls, two pipes running into a water barrel in one corner opposite the small stove with a big black wrought iron pot sitting on top. On the wall nearest the stove there were a row of pegs. Across from that was a watering trough on braces, about a foot off the floor. "Oh, well now, what is all this?"

"This is your bathhouse. Here's how it works," Zack walked over and pointed to the barrel. "See, one of these pipes is tapped into that little spring behind the building. It doesn't run very fast so I thought it needed a little help. This pipe leads to the roof and so when it rains I got a board that will direct all the rainwater into the barrel. What you do then is take three buckets of water like this," Zack got the first bucket and dumped it into the trough. He repeated the action two more times. "Then you take the pot of hot water and add it to the mix." When he was through he refilled the big kettle and sat it back on the stove. "Now all you have to do is strip off and have the best bath you've ever had. Then when you're done you can wash your clothes in the same water and use a fresh bucket of water to rinse them with. The pegs over there are to hang your clothes to dry. There's a plug you pull down at the end of the bath that let's the water out through a pipe that runs out to the garden. Now you have all the modern conveniences a man could ask for!"

"I didn't ask for this," Cleveland laughed. "I don't know if I'm going to like taking a bath in a trough."

"Listen, you try it then we'll talk about it. Go on now you take your bath then yell when you're done. While you're bathing I'll start supper, then after we eat I'll take my bath." Zack slapped Cleveland on the back as he left the room. "There's some good smelling pine soap there, use all you want, after a day of sweating like we put in, you need it."

"And you don't?" Cleveland laughed as Zack closed the door.

Cleveland stood and looked at the contraption his friend had rigged up. He tested it to make sure it would take his weight. When he was confident he wouldn't wind up on the floor in a wet mess he took his clothes off and threw them on the floor. The water was not too warm, just tepid but on a hot day like it was it felt good. He sat down in the water making it come up nearly over his legs. "Probably one more bucket of water or one more pot of hot water would make it even better," he said aloud to himself. He lathered up with the fragrant soap. The fresh, clean smell contrasted with the dirty clothes on the floor, Zack had been right, he had smelled pretty rank. He washed every part of himself, then sat a few moments enjoying the luxury of not having to wipe mud off his clean body as he did every time he bathed in the creek. This had been a good surprise. He reluctantly stepped out of the bath and picked up his work clothes. The soapy water in the trough immediately turned murky brown. It took several minutes to get the clothes washed thoroughly. Cleveland got a bucket of water from the barrel and rinsed the soap out of his clothing. He let the bath water drain out of the basin before using the rinse water to clean out the trough. He wrung his clothes out and hung them on the hooks as instructed. It would be nice to find dry clothes in the morning. There was a small channel under the row of hooks to catch the drippings from wet things. Zack had thought of everything. Cleveland wrapped his towel around himself and headed for the main house.

"I guess that was better than I thought it would be," Cleveland beamed as he came into the main room. The smell of eggs frying filled his senses and all of a sudden he was very hungry.

"Told you. When I had my first bath in a room like that I knew I wanted to build one in my house someday. It was good practice for me to work out the details for you, so when I build one for Liddy it will be even better." He looked at Cleveland, "Get some clothes on, boy. Can't eat in your birthday suit, least not at my table."

Cleveland laughed and did as he was told.

"You think about Liddy all the time, don't you?"

"Can't help it."

Cleveland sat down at the eating table and Zack brought him a plate of fried eggs and potatoes with a couple biscuits. "Man, is that what I smelled like?" he made a face and fanned the air as Zack came near.

"You were even worse, I took a bath yesterday in the creek because it was so hot. You hadn't bathed since Wednesday."

"Does Liddy bathe everyday?" Cleveland asked quietly. "I don't know anything about women, except my ma and I never really paid much attention to her, as a woman I mean."

Zack laughed, "Women folk are different. They like to be clean, they can take a whole bath with a cloth and soap every morning and every night, making them smell sweet all the time. Even when they sweat, and they do, they still smell better than any man does."

"Was Liddy the only woman you were ever with?"

"Well, now you're getting kind of personal," Zack laughed and looked at Cleveland, "But you're my friend and I know you're asking because you ain't got a pa to ask these things of, so I'll try to answer you the best I can. I have sort of been with a couple other women. Nothing like being married, but I have kissed a girl or two in my time. What about you? You been kissed?"

Cleveland blushed, "Yeah, I've been kissed. I didn't kiss her, but boy she sure did kiss me. Wasn't all that bad either."

Zack laughed, "Oh, its never all that bad. But there are times you got to be careful about how and who you kiss. Decent girls don't expect you to kiss them unless you are thinking about marrying them. And girls who don't care if you kiss them without thinking about marriage probably aren't decent girls. Do you know what I'm saying?"

"I do," Cleveland ate the rest of his meal quickly. "My momma always told me it was better to marry a woman who was a good helpmate in your life than one that was too pretty or too proud to work hard."

"I guess I'm lucky because I got the best of both, I got a pretty wife who is willing to work hard."

"Tell me about what it's like to be married? Start from the beginning and tell me how you met Liddy and how you worked up the nerve to ask her to marry you."

Zack laughed, "Let me go take my bath then let's sit out on the porch where its cooler and I'll tell you everything you want to know." He started out the back door, "Well almost everything. There's just some things that are private between a man and a woman. Those things are part of your education a woman will have to teach you someday."

Cleveland watched the door close behind Zack. "And those things I wonder about most of all," he sighed.

Chapter 31
Knoxville, Tennessee—September 1867

Lydia finished the laundry early in the day. With five active children under one roof the washing was a twice, sometimes three times a week chore. Her boys, still not quite a year old, were crawling and trying to walk, requiring constant watching. Her oldest nephew, Virgil, was seven and able to watch the others while she hung clothes out on the line. But he wandered off the moment she came back into the house. Ellen busied herself with the cooking most of the day.

As the days grew shorter, everyone spent more time in the house making it easy to get in each other's way, even though the family farm home was big. Ellen hadn't totally recovered from the loss of her fourth child. Every so often she would break down in to long crying jags, straining everyone's nerves. Lydia often put her boys in the wheel barrow and walked to the end of the yard and back. The boys thought they were having a great time, but Lydia just did it to work off a little steam and clear her head. On rare days when all the children took a nap at the same time Lydia would walk out in the small patch of woods near the creek. She'd done that many times as a child but never appreciated it as much as she did now. There was a crisp smell in the air, clean and dry, fall was coming early. Several trees had already dropped their leaves, covering the floor of the woods in bright golds and reds.

On one bright morning, a fancy gig pulled into the yard pulled by a sleek black mare decked out in silver harnesses and a fancy jeweled head piece draped between her ears. A short, greasy looking man dressed as garishly as his horse got out and came to the door of the house. Lydia and Ellen came out onto the porch as Roy came from the barn. "Good day, I am Addison Barnes, Solicitor for Mrs. Violet Beaumont. She has a claim against this property and is planning to sue for the sale of this property since she was the wife of your father at the time of his unfortunate death." He took a piece of paper from his jacket that he handed to Roy. "This is a summons to appear in court on Tuesday, November 12, 1867. I would suggest that you have two choices. You can settle this out of court by selling the property and giving my client the proceeds from that sale, or you can get a lawyer and meet us in court to let a judge decide this matter." He tipped his bowler hat and quickly walked back to his carriage and left at a fast trot.

Roy looked at the paper. "We can't afford a lawyer." He sighed and handed the paper to Ellen. "This is your and Rose's farm. I really hate to see you lose it to some scheming woman whose only interest is the money. The land means a lot to me and I had dreamed of leaving it to our kids someday." He shrugged. "But then on the other hand, we got three kids and maybe none of them are going to be farmers." He walked off the porch. "Well that's my say, this is really up to the two of you if you want to fight her on this."

Ellen looked at Lydia, "What can we do?"

"I don't have any money for a lawyer. Do you?"

"I got a little money left that our father left me. It might be enough to at least talk to a lawyer and see what can be done."

Lydia thought a moment, "Let's go into to town tomorrow and see what we can find out. If you don't mind spending that money, let's do it."

"All right. I'll have Roy ride over to the Dawson's farm and ask those two older girls of their's to come stay with the children while Roy takes us into town tomorrow." Ellen headed for the barn to involve Roy in their plans.

* * *

Two days later Roy, Ellen and Lydia sat down at the eating table after dinner had been cleared away, the dishes done and the children in bed. It had been a gloomy household since their trip into town to visit with a lawyer. It seemed that everything was against them keeping the farm. It appeared that the best that could happen was selling the farm with Lydia and Ellen receiving part of the money from the sale as next of kin, since no will had been found. It didn't seem likely that their family farm would stay in the family.

Roy sighed as he sat down next to his wife. He patted her on the back and looked at Lydia. "Well gals, what do you want to do?"

Lydia looked at her sister, then her brother-in-law. "Roy, you have an equal say in this. It's been your hard work that has kept this farm in the family. Yesterday the lawyer said since the war these farms aren't worth the sweat we put into them, but you've poured your life into this place, your children were born here. You have equal say about what we do."

"It was that damn war," Ellen sobbed, "we've lost so much because of that. We lost the business, everything."

"You can't change what happened yesterday, honey," Roy said comforting his wife. "We have to think about what to do now."

Everyone sat for a few minutes in silence. "What about doing a little gold mining in California?" Roy said quietly, "I hear they are still finding occasional veins, there and there are lots of jobs. Maybe we could earn enough in a year to come back and pay Violet off?"

Lydia's eyes grew wide, California was very close to Oregon. "How would we get there?"

"We could sell the stock off for enough to pay for our tickets out there. There's stage lines and railroads now that we can take to get there fairly quickly."

"We'd all go, right, Roy?" Ellen said with a hint of fear in her voice.

"Yes," he smiled reassuringly. "I wouldn't go without you and the kids." He looked a Lydia, "And you and your boys, too."

Lydia smiled to be included, "It would be a hard trip but I would give anything to go with you."

"Let's contact that Barnes fellow and make Violet an offer. Let's tell him we could sell the farm for next to nothing now, meaning his client would get nothing or he could give us six months to a year to raise enough money to double what she could get by selling our farm." Roy suggested.

"That sounds good to me." Ellen said squeezing Roy's hand. "Do you really think we can do it?"

"Lydia, are you in agreement?" Roy asked.

"I am, for sure."

"Then tomorrow I'm going to go into town and see what the man can come up with."

Everyone sighed hopefully and went back to finishing the last of the chores for the day. Lydia found herself humming for the first time in a long time. She didn't want to think too much about what might happen but she couldn't help daydream about being reunited with Zack.

* * *

The word finally got back from Lydia's step-mother; they would be given ten months to raise enough money to buy her share in the farm. Lydia and Ellen were overjoyed, yet apprehensive. There was so much to do before they could get underway to California.

Roy contacted Alfred Jenkins, a friend from their church who'd lost an arm in the war, to stay at the farm while they were gone just to make sure it was kept safe. Alfred was widowed and lived alone in a small boarding house in town. He was happy about the prospect of living on a farm again, even if he wouldn't be doing more than making sure the hay got cut and brought in. Roy arranged to sell all their horses, cows and rabbits off to neighbors but left their small herd of goats and two mules for Alfred to watch over. Their two dogs, both old, would stay behind, too.

Ellen, with Lydia's help, washed all the clothing and bedding they would be taking. They had one suitcase each and two large trunks that would be going along. For the first few days of the trip there would be plenty of food that they prepared and kept in a large basket. It was amazing how much it would take to travel with five children and three adults. They would have their hands full just keeping track of their belongings. But they never hesitated; the prize was worth winning and so they prepared as if going into battle, hoping every moment it was the right thing to do.

Finally, after two weeks of preparation, they were ready to jump off. The eight of them stood on the front porch of their family home for a few minutes in the early light of a crisp morning and looked around one last time. Roy took Ellen's hand and bowed his head. Ellen reached out to Lydia and all of them prayed for a moment silently, then Roy said softly, "Lord, our future is in your hands. Guide us, protect us and prosper us. Amen."

Alfred had already moved to the farm so he brought the wagon around hitched to the two mules and after everyone was onboard, drove them to the railroad station in town. Within a few hours they were rattling and rocking across Tennessee to Memphis. Lydia felt stronger and more sure as each mile passed. This was the route Zack had taken just a little over a year ago, and now she was on her way to join him. It just felt right. The boys slept next to her, lulled to sleep by the rolling of the train. The next month was going to be a hard trip she realized but it would be worth it to be reunited with Zack. She had to hold on to that thought!

* * *

Memphis turned out to be a noisy, confusing place. The railroads were crowded and the news was not good. Several Indian raids in the north had interrupted the train schedules and there was some uncertainty by the railroads themselves as to whether to allow families to travel by rail at the time. Luckily there was a second option. Roy was able to buy tickets for all of them on the Wells Fargo Stage Line and in two days they would be heading west again using the southern route. The stages were running at regular intervals now and seemed like the safest option for a family. It was tentatively good news. Lydia wasn't sure how the trip would go for the five children, but it would only be for three weeks so that was something to be thankful for.

The big day arrived and they all loaded themselves into the dusty coach. It was a tight squeeze. There was supposedly enough room for eight passengers. Roy had thought they were going to have the coach to themselves, but it turned out that the ticket agent had sold two other seats in the wagon since Lydia's babies weren't being charged a fare, he expected them to be held during the trip to San Diego, California. It was uncomfortable from the start for everyone.

The other two passengers were a middle aged, tired looking sewing machine salesman, Donald Beemer and a willowy younger man on the way to join his father in the gold fields. His name was Hank Friday. Both of them seemed uncomfortable at first around the women and children but relaxed and tried to get as comfortable as possible as the driver and the guard pushed the six horses through the day. About six or seven hours into the day they made their first stop. The driver announced they would only be stopping long enough to eat and change horses, less than twenty five minutes. If anyone needed to use the necessary or eat it was now.

It was hard to get the children out of the coach and into the little house that served as the station. Men were hurriedly changing the horses and everyone lined up to use the privy. The children coughed at the dust billowing up around their ankles as they walked. An old man and woman brought coffee in small cups to each of them and offered a sandwich of coarse bread and butter with jam of some unfamiliar fruit. It wasn't much, but it at least stopped their stomachs from rumbling. In no time at all the driver was yelling for everyone to be back on board. Lydia carried the boys, one on each hip back to the waiting wagon as quickly as she could. She got a stern look from the driver as she more or less threw the boys to Roy and climbed in last. She wasn't even seated when the coach lurched back on to the rutted trail at full speed. It hurt when she fell against the side of the bench on the way to sitting down.

All through the day they pushed on and on. It was getting dark when they stopped again, eight or more hours later. The routine was the same, alight quickly, go to the privy, eat whatever was offered and be back on the coach with in twenty or so minutes. By the third and fourth stop, it didn't matter what there was to eat, everyone was so exhausted they couldn't have guessed what it was anyway. The children had passed beyond fussy to barely conscious. It was a relief when they all fell soundly asleep despite the loud snoring of Mr. Beemer. Lydia couldn't move under the weight of her sleeping boys. At times when they hit a rock in the road, one of the children's head would bounce into her ribs, nearly knocking the breath out of her. She imagined when she finally got to see herself again she would be black and blue under her once lovely yellow traveling suit.

Shortly after daybreak they pulled into a station and the driver announced this would be the breakfast stop and they would have an hour to rest up and have breakfast. The children reluctantly woke up and Lydia followed Ellen out of the wagon. Hank offered to carry one of the boys into to the small house that served as the way station. Lydia was grateful for the small bit of help. She could hardly walk she was so stiff and sore from being battered through the night.

The little house turned out to be just that—a little house. It had one large room in front and a small room off to the back. The caretaker's wife offered the women a chance to wash up in the small room in the back. Ellen and Lydia took the children to the back of the building, and were pleased to see two pitchers and basins waiting. Lydia washed her face and hands, then washed the boys face and hands too, then changed their diapers and washed out the diapers before throwing out the water through a small back door. She hung the wet nappies over a porch railing. She could see the necessary down the hill from the house, so she asked Ellen to watch the boys while she took a turn.

Soon she was back and took the boys from Ellen, who then took her turn going down the hill. Breakfast was sourdough biscuits, ham and coffee. It wasn't much, but there was enough to satisfy their hunger. The children wanted to go back to sleep, but Ellen and Lydia tried to keep them awake until it was time to get back on the wagon, which seemed to come much too soon. The driver announced the stage would be leaving in five minutes. He gave a direct look at Lydia and repeated the deadline. She immediately gathered up the boys and headed for the coach, vowing never to be last again. At least this time she wasn't. Hank helped her onto the coach and then put one of the twins across his lap. The baby immediately went back to sleep. Lydia nodded her thanks to Hank and settled back as the vehicle creaked out again. This time she slept and soon became oblivious to all the jolts and shaking going on.

Lydia was surprised when she did open her eyes again. The land had changed from scrubby trees to more of an open prairie. There were colorful rock outcrops and shallow broad rivers they passed by and through. It was very beautiful in a stark way. Ellen's children were unusually quiet, as if trying to be brave and endure this unexpectedly hard ride to the unknown. Lydia couldn't tell whether it was fear or sadness but they were quiet. Her boys were fussy once in awhile but between Hank and herself, they were able to keep them occupied.

And so it went for the first week of the journey. But then the unexpected happened and they hit the first serious problem of the trip. Their coach broke an axle five miles from their next stop of the day. It was mid-day and hot as the driver set out on one of the horses to bring back help. By the time he returned with a wagon, everyone on the coach was feeling sick from the lack of water and the heat, especially the children. They were all loaded into a buckboard and taken to the station. Cots had been set up in a small barn for the women and children, the men were supposed to stay in the small lean-to horse barn. It was hard to tell which was worse, the enclosed barn with only one door to let in fresh air, or the horse stalls outside that had just a bit of straw over the dirt. The way station keeper was an elderly man who only knew how to cook beans and rice, so that's what they were offered for dinner that night and the next morning, too. It took two trips to the broken wagon to bring their luggage. Shortly after breakfast they were told that there was no way to repair the coach so they would have to stay until the next stage came by and hope there was room for them. The alternative was to take another stage that was going to come through heading to Santa Fe, New Mexico that would connect to the one going to Virginia City and then to Sacramento. Everyone was disappointed, but there wasn't anything to do but wait and pray as the heat of the desert began to climb. At least the older children didn't seem to mind, they played games with the tumbleweeds and found ways to enjoy themselves.

There was a small stream close by, so Ellen and Lydia took the opportunity to bathe for the first time in weeks. Then they washed all the dirty clothes they had all been wearing for days and changed into clean ones. It was a small blessing but one that was appreciated. Lydia couldn't imagine how bad she must have smelled.

A day, then two passed before the first stage pulled in. There were five passengers on the stage and none of them wanted to get off to let the family on. There was enough room for Hank and Mr. Beemer, so they left. Lydia was sorry to see Hank go, he'd been very helpful with the children and she would miss that. But it wasn't his place to help her, she thought bitterly, Zack should be here with his family. She shook that thought from her mind and tried to replace it with her dream of seeing him again.

Later that same day, the stage to Santa Fe pulled in with an older couple as its only passengers. Mr. Zellig and his wife were delighted to share the coach with the family. It was quickly discovered they had six children and fourteen grandchildren, so were quite comfortable with noise and care of youngsters. The choice was settled, they were headed to Santa Fe. Everyone loaded themselves into the coach and were off again. Lydia watched the world of new sights pass by through the open windows. During the day, if there wasn't too much dust, they kept the leather window coverings rolled up. It was beautiful but lonely country. A couple of times she saw Indians in the distance, sitting atop painted ponies, just watching the coach go by. She wondered if there was any danger from natives along this route. None ever came close to the coach, however, so after a few miles she relaxed, dozing for a few minutes at a time. She let herself daydream a bit about seeing the man she loved again. It startled her a little that she couldn't clearly remember his face, but she looked at her boys and then she could remember what he looked like. They were the only photo of him she needed to see.

Chapter 32
October 1867, Bethel, Oregon— Northern Polk County

Cleveland couldn't believe that he'd let Zack talk him into this wild goose chase. It was a gray, cold day to boot, but at least it wasn't raining for the time being. Zack's horse traveled easier and quicker than Cleveland's Molly so he had to push her hard to keep up with his friend.

They'd come through Independence and Rickreall before sunrise, soon the were winding their way over the rough, muddy roads that wove themselves in between the big farms and orchards that lined the valley floor. "I can't see why we're doing this," Cleveland complained.

Zack looked back with a smile. "I read all about this farm that's for sale and I just got to see it for myself, it sounded so good."

"But you can't afford a place of your own right now. You said so yourself."

Zack fetched a torn piece of newspaper from his pocket, "Listen to this, Cleve, it really sounds great," he tried to hold the paper steady as he slowed the horse a bit. "Valuable Farm for Sale. Near the Bethel School. This farm consists of 150 acres, all fenced and 60 under cultivation. It is well watered with springs and has a good orchard. Value of $2,000 part of which can be secured by mortgage on the place." He looked back at Cleveland. "Doesn't that sound just what I'm looking for?"

"Oh, you shouldn't believe everything you read in the American Union."

Zack just shook his head, "You got a place, Cleve. I got to find a place that I can bring my family to." He urged his horse on.

Cleveland sighed. He knew the truth of that but he really didn't want his friend to move this far from him. This was an all day trip, up and back, he probably would be so tied up with his family and farm that Zack'd never get down to see him. Cleveland began to feel that sense of loss again. He tried to shake it, but he was having a hard time working up any enthusiasm about this trip to see the farm listed in the paper.

Finally they reached the store in Bethel. Zack made a couple inquiries about the Clark place and was told how to get there. A Mr. Jones was living on the property and would show them around. It didn't take more than twenty minutes to ride up the little draw behind the small town to the farm. They stopped to take it in just as they came through the front gate at the upper end of the place. It was hillier than Cleveland would like but that didn't seem to bother Zack. "Looks like my land in Tennessee, it was on a hillside too. This has some good bottom land down there and lots of fir and oak. The orchard is between the small barn and the main living building. House isn't much, but it has potential." Zack said more to himself than to Cleveland.

"House looks small as mine."

Zack smiled at Cleveland, "You got a right nice house, Cleve. It would be quite comfortable for four or five people and could be added on to real easy." Zack urged the horse on, Cleveland lagged behind slightly.

Zack hopped off his horse and knocked on the door. There was no answer but a voice called from the orchard grove. "What you fellas want?" An old man came up the hill with a bucket full of apples.

"Saw the ad in the paper and thought I'd come look at the farm." Zack said.

The man put the bucket down on the porch. "Well son, sorry to tell you that advert was in the paper for two months. The owner just didn't take it out when it sold. Sold it two weeks ago to some family coming from the east, won't even be here until March."

Cleveland saw Zack's shoulders slump. "It looks like someone's getting a good place. Sorry to have troubled you, Mr. Jones." Zack started to turn his horse.

"Sorry you had to ride all the way out here to be disappointed. You fellas can take all the apples and pears you want out of the orchard. No sense letting them go to waste, I can't eat them all."

Cleveland finally heard something to be happy about, "Thanks Mr. Jones. We'll do that."

The old man went over to the other side of the porch and came back with a gunny sack bag and handed it to Cleveland. "Take all you want now." Then he turned and went back inside.

Zack followed Cleveland to the trees. It only took a few minutes to fill the bag with fruit, which would make a nice treat for many weeks to come. "At least the trip wasn't a total waste." Cleveland said trying to cheer Zack up. Zack managed a smile but his heart wasn't in it. He remained quiet for several miles, but he got over it and was his old self again. At least Cleveland got so see a part of the county he hadn't seen for quite a time, so that was something.

* * *

The Oregon State Fair, even the name sounded grand. Cleveland couldn't believe their luck. They didn't have to work on Saturday, the last day of the fair, and they were given a bonus Friday with their pay. It seemed like a great time to celebrate. Cleveland had never been to any kind of a fair so this was all new to him. They arrived in Salem mid-morning and were astonished by the size of the events. There was a row of food booths, a row of game booths and all kinds of displays of one kind or another. Cleveland just couldn't believe how much there was to do and see. They watched several horse races before they stopped and sampled a few of the food choices. It was heady stuff; corn on the cob, dripping in butter, fried chicken and candy covered apples.

They walked through barns full of beautiful animals. Several people from Polk County had won ribbons, so Zack and Cleveland stopped when they saw a name and congratulated them on their winning. F.B. Frayer of Bethel had a three year old bull that took second place in its division. A Mr. Delos of Buena Vista had a bull calf that took first. When they came to the horse barns Zack had a bright idea. He quickly searched through the stalls until he found winners from Polk County.

The first one he found was a Mr. Frederick of Salt Creek whose colt had taken second place. Zack struck up a conversation with the man. Cleveland just watched, wondering what Zack was up to. Soon it became apparent. Zack told Mr. Frederick of his horse shoeing and tack work and offered to come to his farm anytime he needed some work. The horse owner seemed pleased with that and asked Zack to come the following week. Zack found a couple mule owners, too, a Mr. Clark from Dallas and J. S. Cooper of Lincoln. Most everyone seemed pleased by his offer to come by and do the work at their farms, although a Mr. Yocom said he had a hired hand at his place who took care of all the work at his place.

As they were leaving the last barn Zack seemed pleased. "I figure that if I can get one or two side jobs a week in addition to my carpenter's job I can save up four or five hundred dollars in a year." Then he sighed, "God, a year sounds like a long time."

"It will pass quickly," Cleveland said trying to cheer his friend up. "Didn't this last year go fast?"

Zack shuttered, "Yeah, too fast. My boys are nearly a year old now and I've never seen them."

Cleveland looked around and spotted something that might cheer Zack up. "Look at that, Zack." He pointed at a sideshow wagon that promised several unusual things like a three foot lady and a man with alligator skin. "Do you want to go in and see the freaks?"

Zack shook his head, "I saw too many people with misfortunes during the war. People without faces, arms or legs. I don't like to look at the misery of other human beings, I got enough of my own." He walked off towards their horses. "Let's go home before it gets too late. We got to feed the stock and get ready for church tomorrow. We haven't been to church in a month. I think I need to be praying for a miracle to get my family out here."

Cleveland followed along. Maybe church would be good for both of them. He missed seeing the Porterfields and some of the other people who had helped him in his time of need.

INTO THE DUST

* * *

The month passed quickly. The two men worked week days at carpentry from sunup to sundown, Monday through Saturday noon. Saturday afternoon and most of Sunday they went from farm to farm, Cleveland fixing fences, mending furniture or building cabinets and Zack working on horses or harnesses.

One Saturday, Cleveland had been feeling poorly all week with a cold that just wanted to hang on so he opted to go home instead of going with Zack on his rounds. Cleveland finished the chores around the farm and started a pot of stew for dinner then laid down on his cot and fell fast asleep. He was dreaming about a field of corn for some reason when his dream changed into one of Cork. He could feel her warm "kisses" gently stroking his cheek and he could smell that distinctly doggy smell. He smiled in his dream and then felt that ache of missing her. The dream persisted and he slowly opened his eyes. About six inches from his face was a pair of bright blue eyes, one ringed in black and one set in a sea of white. A lightening fast pink tongue was trying to reach him. "What?"

Zack laughed. "Well, nobody is going mistake this little critter for a coyote!"

Cleveland sat up and looked at Zack holding the half grown puppy. "Where did you get that and why?"

"It's for you," Zack handed the wriggling little creature to Cleveland. "One of the farms had a litter of pups from their two sheep dogs. They said these are the brightest dogs around, can bring in the stock, keep varmints out and learn to understand you better than your best friend." Zack smiled. "Which in your case would be me."

Cleveland looked down at the dog. Besides the black ring around one eye, it was mostly white with one patch of black behind it's right ear and a couple dark spots on it's back. It quieted down and studied Cleveland as much as he studied it. It wasn't Cork, but it was a cute little thing. He'd never had a puppy before, "What do you feed a pup?"

"Same as you fed your last dog, just cut it up a bit more." Zack laughed. "You look like you've just had your first child. It's about four months old, so it will grow up quickly and not be a problem."

"What will we call her?"

"Well, first, it's a boy dog."

"Oh," Cleveland held the puppy up for a look. "Sorry fella. He's mighty smart you say? Maybe we ought to give him some sort of impressive name like Ulysses."

"Hey, I can't even say that let alone spell it. Keep it simple."

"Okay, we'll call him Blue 'cause of his eyes."

"Blue it is! Might be a good thing to keep him in the barn until he's house broken. We can make a place for him out there."

Cleveland looked at the dog and caught a light in the pup's eyes. Did he understand what was being said? Cleveland was a little hesitant to use Cork's old dish for the puppy, but it was all he had so he ladled out a nice helping of the stew they were having for dinner, chopped it up fine and put it down. It was apparent that getting Blue to eat would not be a problem. A healthy belch and the pup trotted over to the door and looked at Cleveland. It was uncanny, it was just the way Cork had always announced her need to go out. It would seem house breaking was not going to be an issue, either.

The next morning, Blue and Cleveland got up early and went to the barn. The young dog instinctively lay down and watched the cows and mules as Cleveland let them out into the pasture. He was too young to run behind them but Cleveland could see he wanted to. "Someday boy, you'll help me at night bring the stock in. I can see you'll be good at that."

Cleveland decided on a good place to build a small straw-lined pen to put Blue in during the day while they were at work. He'd be safer there than just on his own. Coyotes were known to take pups and kittens, even small calves if they could get them alone. "You won't like this boy but it's to protect you. I'll work on this today but first let's go get some breakfast."

The little dog walked ahead of Cleveland as if he knew exactly what they were going to do. He stopped and took care of his business before they went inside. Cleveland laughed as Blue hopped from one step to the next, going up onto the porch. This little guy had lots of spunk.

After breakfast, Zack washed his clothes and hung them up in the bath shack. Cleveland worked on the enclosure for the puppy. He didn't even notice Zack get his shoeing tools and head out to the pasture where the mules were. The puppy nipped at his pant legs as he assembled the boards into a nice, two foot high enclosure. He fashioned a removable lid with leather hinges so nothing could get in from the top and a simple latch lock for the front. He was nearly done when he heard a bray from one of the mules and a scream of pain from Zack.

Cleveland ran out of the barn and saw the General standing over Zack's prone body. The old mule was still kicking a little. Cleveland rushed into the pasture, Blue right on his heels. Cleveland let out an involuntary scream of his own. Zack was bleeding from this temple and side, his shoeing tools lay all around him. Cleveland quickly got a long board from the wood shop and carefully rolled the unconscious Zack onto it. It was hard work but he managed to get his friend into the house. Blue was whimpering and trying to get comfort from Cleveland but there was no time for that right then. Cleveland grabbed the puppy and put him in the newly finished pen in the barn. He then saddled up Zack's horse, which was faster than the mules, and rode hard into Buena Vista to get the doctor. Within three quarters of an hour they were back

The doctor examined Zack careful while he was still on the floor, then with Cleveland's help wrapped the wound on Zack's side. "This is going to be black and blue from his shoulder down to his hips, so don't worry about that. He's got a couple broken ribs for sure, so he won't be moving much for quite a spell. His head wound is pretty deep and he may loose his right eye. You can see the hoof print the mule made right here." The doctor pointed out the telltale curve that came off Zack's forehead and crossed over to his cheek bone. "Got a concussion, most likely. Let's ease him up into the bed and put a couple pillows under his head."

It wasn't easy but they managed the task. Zack moaned a couple times but never woke completely up. "What do you think, Doctor? Will he pull through?" Cleveland was afraid of the answer.

"He's young and strong. People have survived much worse. He won't be working for awhile though, he'll have to be in bed for probably a month or more. Are you up to taking care of him?"

"Sure, I can do that. He's like a brother to me."

"I'll come back tomorrow afternoon and see how he's doing." The doctor walked out on the porch, then to his buggy. He had a second bag under the front seat. He got a small bottle of medicine. "This will help with the pain. Give him a teaspoon full once every six hours but don't give it to him until he's fully awake and is talking to you." A sharp, shrill howl interrupted his instructions. "What on earth is that?"

"We got a new puppy yesterday. It didn't want to be put in the barn when I went to get you."

"Hum, well just watch Zack. Try to get him to eat a little broth or thin oatmeal, nothing heavy." The doctor climbed into his buggy and started off, "See you tomorrow."

"Thanks again, Doctor." Cleveland called after him on the way to get Blue. The little dog bolted towards the house the minute he was let out of his enclosure. Cleveland followed, and when he opened the door, the dog made a beeline for the bed where Zack lay moaning. Cleveland lifted him up so he could see Zack and the puppy wiggled his way out of Cleveland's grasp, landing softly on the bed next to Zack. Blue gently licked at Zack's forehead around the bandage over the swollen wound. Zack moaned and seemed to relax as the little white bundle laid down next to his face. It seemed that Blue had chosen who he wanted to love best. Cleveland realized he and the dog might be friends but it was Zack he'd decided to love. Somehow that was all right.

Two days later Zack began to come around, though his eyes were swollen shut still. Other than trips outside to relieve himself or to eat, Blue had stayed by Zack's side all the time. "Cleve," Zack wheezed, "How am I doing?"

"You've got some broken ribs, you're really bruised on you left side, you got a hoof print on your face, and you've slept more than you've been awake for the last couple days but other than that you're doing pretty good." Cleveland tried to mask the worry he felt.

"You been working?"

"Nah, I told the boss what happened and that I couldn't come back until you were fully awake and could kind of help yourself a bit. Going to be awhile until you're up and around. Doctor said might take a month before you can do much more than walk to the necessary or bath house. Hope you get to take a bath soon though, you're getting kind of ripe."

"Thanks a lot, friend," Zack could feel Blue sitting next to him. "What's he doing up here?"

"He hasn't left your side since the accident. He's decided he's your dog and that's just fine with me. He and I get along fine, but it's you he wants to be his papa."

Zack tried to look through his one good eye at Cleveland, "Sorry about that. Didn't know that would happen." He groaned as a wave of pain rolled through his body. "I was so foolish."

"I thought about killing that cursed mule," Cleveland said angrily. "Might still do it."

"Wasn't the mule's fault, was mine. I thought I could do that in the pasture, not in the barn in a stall. Just took a bird flying by at the wrong time to spook him and when I touched him to lift his foot he kicked out. Really got me. I've done that a hundred times and just takes one time of not doing what I should to get in trouble." He sighed and eased into a different position on the pillow. Blue moved right with him.

Cleveland went to the stove and got some stew that he'd made earlier. He skimmed off the broth and brought a cup to Zack. It was hard to spoon it into his mouth, but Cleveland managed to do it. Zack coughed a little as he ate, but he wanted to eat and get well so he made every effort to help his friend.

"Zack, you got a letter all the way from Tennessee. I think it's from your wife."

Weakly Zachary turned his head and tried to focus on his young friend. "I got a letter?" He coughed slightly. "Come on and read it to me. Please." He wheezed. He tried to sit up but it was no use. Cleveland rushed over and put an extra tick pillow under his head. Zachary smiled in appreciation and then closed his blackened eyes and settled back into the bedding. "Please, read it to me, Cleve."

Cleveland smiled and pulled up a stool next to the bed. Gently he loosened the seal on the letter, handling it like it was breakable, then chided himself that if the letter had made it all the way to Oregon, his opening it wouldn't hurt it. He carefully unfolded the three-inch square of paper inside. He let out an astonished gasp as he reached the center.

"What is it, Cleve?" Zachary said in a worried voice. "Is something wrong?"

"No, Zack, I was just surprised." He held out the paper toward his friend but saw that Zachary wasn't even trying to see out of his swollen eyes. "It's about the prettiest thing I've ever seen. It's a long lock of hair. It's so soft and shiny." Cleve stoked the silky strand for a second and then gently touched Zachary's face with it. "Must be your wife's?"

"Is it dark reddish brown with sprinkles of copper dancing through it?" Zachary shuddered at the touch of the hair on his cheek.

"Yes, and so soft," Cleve whispered with a tear in his eye for some reason.

Zachary choked back a wave of pain and pushed Cleve's hand away from his face with his good left hand. "Please read the letter."

"Sure," Cleveland reluctantly placed the lock of hair on the bed next to Zachary. "It's good my momma made sure I got my reading every night so I can read. It would have been a shame to see this beautiful handwriting and not know what it says." Cleveland marveled at the letter, having never gotten one himself.

Zachary half-laughed then spoke through gritted teeth, "Are you going to ever read the letter to me?"

"Sure," he gulped then began to read, touching each word as he went. Cleveland hesitated, it felt almost like he was sharing a secret between lovers,

> *"July 28, 1867,*
> *My dearest Zachary,*
>
> *I just got your letter written in April and I am very distressed. I know that I said I understood, and agreed with the reasons for you to leave. I am not faulting you at all for that, but so much time has passed and now it seems that it will take even longer. I can't help but be wondering why you have not come back. The children are growing so fast and they need their pa, just like I need my husband. Every night when I lay alone in our bed I wonder if you are thinking about me too. We had so little time together and we have been apart so long.*

INTO THE DUST

I trust you with my life. You are a good man, honest, and hard working. I know that you wanted to make a new life for the children, me and your mother. I understand that, but I want you to know that isn't what matters to me. It would be fine with me if we never own a place that makes us a living. I'll sew clothes for people, bake or clean to help earn money. Anywhere with you is home. I want you with me. I am so lonely without you.

The boys wear me out, they are so full of energy. Samuel seems to be catching on to things quicker than Peter is but they are both bright. Samuel sits up on his own. Peter still is trying. He's the one who wants to be held as much as possible. Your mother says Peter looks like you as a child and Samuel seems to have the same color of hair as I do. Both your sons need a father who is with them every step of the way.

Jonas is clearing rocks for a bigger garden. Jonas has a friend, Deben Claypool, that has come to stay. It's obvious that Deben had a white daddy, he's colored but he's got light eyes and sort of sandy colored hair but dark skin. He was turned out of a plantation with nothing but the clothes on his back. He's very quiet, probably seen some hard times. He seems happy to have room and board for his work. We're glad for his help, Jonas wasn't up to doing the work alone. We all need you here. The garden is poor this year, so we have to make sure to harvest and can everything available. The rocks just seem to keep coming up out of the ground, wish the corn and pumpkin would come up so well.

We had a couple of visitors last week. They said the railroad is going to go clear to California someday soon. Maybe you could come home on the railroad and it wouldn't take you nearly a year like getting to Oregon did.

I hope this finds you in good health. I am in very good health my darling husband, the boys are too, we are just lonely and tired of the way things are now. Please come home or send for us. We need to be together as soon as possible.

I remain your devoted wife,
Liddy"

Cleveland carefully re-folded the letter and put it into its envelope. His face burned a bit, hearing about how hard life was for Lydia and the children without his friend there. He felt bad that he'd been so selfish in wanting Zack to stay with him to ease his own loneliness.

Zack motioned for Cleveland to come closer. "I want you to write to my wife for me. I am not going to be able to write for some time and I want her to know why." He hesitated for a moment, "I also have a bigger favor to ask. You are like a brother to me and you are a decent young man who I would trust with everything I hold dear which is my family." He took a few deep breaths. "If anything should happen to me I want you to promise you will take care of my family. It might mean you have to go back to Tennessee to make sure they're provided for and but I need to know someone will be there for them." He squinted again at Cleveland, "Would you do that for me? I know that's a lot to ask but I wouldn't trust anyone else."

Cleveland looked down for a moment lost in his thoughts then he looked at his friend, "What kind of talk is this? Nothing's going to happen to you. You'll get through this and take care of your family yourself."

"Would you promise me?"

Cleveland shrugged, "If you'll stop badgering me, of course I'll promise."

"Thank you, Cleve," Zack came close to dozing off, then woke up again. "Get an envelope and paper out of my little stationary box would you. I want to write that letter now."

Cleveland did as he was asked. He was very apprehensive when Zack made Cleveland write down the promise he'd made. Zack's wife would probably think it was the dumbest thing she'd ever heard but it seemed to appease Zack, making it easier for him to finally lay back and sleep. Cleveland took the puppy and fed him, then took him out for one last time before turning in. Blue curled up next to Zack and sighed. Cleveland smiled as he turned out the lamp and left the room.

Chapter 33
Virginia City, Nevada—December 1867

Lydia stood on the porch of the boardinghouse they were staying at, looking at the high, snow covered mountains to the west. It seemed ironic that when they set out, the trip was only supposed to take three weeks or so, unlike the near year it had taken Zack to get to Oregon. Now, it looked like it might take just as long for them to make their journey. She sighed and walked back into the house to return to her duties of taking care of five children.

The doctor was just finishing his exam of Ellen when Lydia entered the bedroom. "She looks like she's doing fine, probably needs to rest another two weeks, maybe three and then she'll be able to continue on your way." The doctor looked at Lydia and could see the strain taking it's toll, "You need to get some rest, my dear," he said kindly.

"Hard to do with five active children in a two rooms," she managed a small laugh.

Ellen lay quietly looking out the window until the doctor packed up his kit and left. Tears were running down her cheeks but she didn't say anything. In the other room the children were happily unaware of her pain as they played and tumbled with each other. "Is Roy back yet?" she asked when the door closed behind the doctor. She turned and put her hands out for Lydia.

Lydia rushed to her sister and gathered her up in her arms as Ellen cried, "oh Liddy, he said this was bad. He said I probably won't be able to have children ever again."

"That's too bad, Ellen," Lydia felt her sister's anguish. It had crossed her mind that she might not have any other children either. "We shouldn't have come on this awful trip. Why didn't you tell us you were expecting again?"

"You and Roy had such a good plan to save the farm and I wanted so to keep it in the family. I thought I was stronger than this, I guess."

Lydia shook her head and eased Ellen back into the pillows, "You are more precious any day than that farm. This was a close call. We thought we might lose you and nothing would be worth that."

Ellen smiled through her tears, "you are a dear sister Liddy, I don't know what I'd do without you and Roy." Ellen looked at the frost on the window, "Where is Roy?"

"He said he found some temporary work. He's been gone since breakfast. I think he's doing that so we won't have to use up our nest egg while we're here. You talk about dear people, he really puts himself out for this family."

"I am lucky, aren't I," Ellen said quietly. "I have three beautiful children, a loving husband and two nephews, plus a great sister."

"It helps to count one's blessings every so often to remind us that bad things happen but life goes on." Lydia dipped a cloth into the basin of water she'd poured that morning and gently wiped her sister's face. "You try to rest now. I can hear the kids getting tired, so I've got to go put a foot down." Lydia laughed and quietly left the room as her sister allowed her eyes to close.

* * *

Christmas came and went in an unremarkable fashion. Roy had managed to get a couple toys for each of the children and some toilet water for Ellen and Lydia. The women had sewn new outfits for the children and a shirt for Roy. They had a very good dinner on Christmas day at the boarding house but there wasn't much joy in it. Ellen's recovery was going slowly and it looked like it would be at least two weeks more before they could push on. Ellen often offered to stay behind but Roy and Lydia wouldn't hear of it.

Finally in mid-January the doctor hesitantly pronounced Ellen fit for travel. The pass was just barely passable. Early snows had melted a bit and there was a lull in the storms that often swept across the Sierra's. The stage line had put sled runners on the coach but somehow it was still a bumpy ride. Ellen never complained, however. The children huddled together to stay warm. The only source of heat in the coach was a bucket of coals they put in the coach twice a day when they stopped to change horses. The cold challenged the clothing and blankets they had. Finally though, they came down out of the mountains into the flat Sacramento Valley. At the first stop, they changed coaches, into one with wheels again to finish the journey into Sacramento.

Roy found a small hotel for them to stay at a few days to decide where they would go from that point, and to let Ellen rest. Lydia was grateful that their rooms were on the back side of the building and there was a nice grassy area behind it for the children to play in. Winter and being cooped up in the stage had made the children bundles of pent-up energy. The weather was very pleasant and dry.

Lydia took the children out to the back area to play. She put a quilt down on the ground and put her two boys down. They were walking but not very steady yet, so she sat down with them. Virgil, Ellen's oldest went running through the grass with his sister and brother right behind him.

Lydia laughed to see them so happy after such a hard time. She stopped laughing though when Virgil let out a scream. Lydia grabbed her two boys and ran for Virgil. "What happened Virgil?"

The wide-eyed youngster was protecting his brother and sister, pushing them slowly back, "Auntie, there's the biggest spider I ever saw." He pointed to a small rock and sure enough there was a huge hairy spider sunning itself on the rock.

Virgil's scream had not only brought Lydia running it brought almost everyone in the hotel. The owner, a short, balding man brought a shotgun as he came. "What is it boy? Are you snake bit?"

"It's a giant spider, scared the boy," Lydia said quickly and pointed.

The innkeeper sighed, "Oh, that's just a tarantula. Got a mean bite if you accidently scare 'em but not too poisonous and usually not aggressive. You leave them alone, they leave you alone." He turned to the children and glanced at the parents. "You folks aren't from around here so I'd best tell you we got rattlesnakes, scorpions and these big spiders but we also got some nastier spiders. We got black widows with a little red hourglass on their bellies and large brown ones, both of them can kill a person so be watchful. If I were you, I'd keep the children pretty close to the building and don't go sticking your hands around rocks at all."

The people who'd come to see what had happened dispersed as quickly as they had arrived. Lydia looked at Ellen's pale face. "Do you need a doctor?"

"No, I was just so frightened when I heard the scream. For a moment I thought I might lose another child...." she collapsed in tears, then fainted dead away.

Roy grabbed Ellen up in his arms, "Lydia, I'll get her in bed and you stay with the kids. I'll find the doctor."

Lydia hurried all the children inside. An air of uncertainly hung over them like a fog. Lydia felt herself on the verge of falling apart herself but she knew she had to remain strong for the children. It was an ordeal waiting for Roy to find one to the town's doctors. Finally though he did come back with a doctor in tow. Roy waited with the children while Lydia attended the doctor during his exam of Ellen. The doctor, a young, slender man in his early thirties, didn't say much as he completed his exam except, "Mrs. Jackman, you are fine, you just need a little more rest. Your husband told me about what you went through in Virginia City. I think it was ill advised to have you travel so soon. But not to worry, just rest." He smiled and patted Ellen on the arm and with a nod of his head to Lydia, they left the room.

Once they were outside of the room and the door was closed he pulled Roy and Lydia aside and spoked quietly. "Mrs. Jackman is anemic, she's very pale and I fear her blood is weak. She needs rest, lots of good food to build her up again. We have a lot of fruit here, make sure she eats plenty of it. How far were you planning to travel?"

Roy looked at Lydia, "I guess we are going on to Oregon."

"I suggest that you don't do it overland, that would be too hard on

Mrs. Jackman, the jarring of another stage coach would not be good. There are ships that sail regularly from San Francisco to Astoria or even Portland. Do you have family there?"

Lydia said quietly, "My husband is close to there, I believe."

"I have a cousin who lives in Oregon City. I wrote to him and told him we might be coming his way," Roy added. "I think we could stay with them for awhile."

Lydia was surprised, she didn't know Roy had family in Oregon too. "You never mentioned knowing someone in Oregon?"

Roy just shrugged. "Just didn't seem that important, till now." Roy turned to the doctor, "How long do you think we should wait before moving on?"

The doctor thought a moment or two, "At least two weeks, maybe a month. I'll come back in ten days and see how she's doing. My instructions in the meantime are plenty of fruit, meat and sunshine. A short daily walk will help her build up her appetite and strength, but don't overdo it even if she thinks she's up to it." The doctor packed up his supplies, accepted five dollars from Roy and left.

Roy and Lydia just stood silently for a few minutes. "I think I'll write to my cousin." Roy said, "Let him know we're coming. He's got a farm so probably room enough for us all. Then I'll go make some inquiries about the boat trip to Oregon the doctor recommended"

Lydia sighed, "I wanted to surprise Zack but I think by this time he'll be worrying about why he hasn't heard from me so I'll write to him too and tell him I'm coming." She looked at the children who were uncommonly quiet. Lydia went to them and gathered them all into her arms for a hug, "Well, children we're going to have a week or two here to explore the town. Then we may get to go out on the ocean in a big ship. How does that sound?"

"What's the ocean?" Toby asked sweetly.

"It's like a lake," Virgil said with the authority of an elder brother, "a really big lake."

"Everything is big out here in California," Darcy said, "Like the spiders."

Lydia laughed and took Darcy into her lap, "I'm not crazy about spiders, that one scared me, too." In a few minutes the children were happily playing again, this time just on the back porch of the hotel. It would be a long time before they would venture out into the fields or grass by themselves again.

It turned out to be a good week for the family. The doctor had been right there was an abundance of fruit and foods to be had; even though it was out of season for most things, people had stored the summer's bounty in root cellars where it kept very well. Sweet oranges were everyone's favorite. Ellen's color improved and her energy returned. By the end of the week the doctor was pleased with her progress and gave his blessings for her continuing on their journey.

Roy had given up the idea of seeking their fortunes in the gold fields. He was more concerned about getting Ellen to a place where they could start over. When he thought he might lose Ellen, the farm in Tennessee didn't seem as important as it once did. It didn't take much to convince Lydia and Ellen either, they knew he was right.

The trip to San Francisco went very smoothly. There were actually dry roads that were nearly worn smooth. Everyone one of them gasp at the sight of the Pacific Ocean. Virgil had been right—it was a very, very big lake. Lydia had a few moments of hesitation when she realized that they would be sailing out into that wide dark water. She'd never been on anything bigger than a ferry that crossed a river. She forced herself to think of the prize that lay at the end of the trail. She would be with Zack again. She only hoped he would be pleased she came.

Chapter 34
South of Independence—December 1867

Cleveland stood alone with Blue, the two of them remained next to the grave long after the other few mourners had left. Not too many people had come to know Zack in the short time he'd been in Polk County, so his passing didn't hit them as hard as it had Cleveland. In his heart he'd lost the only brother he'd ever known. From the time they met, it felt to him like they'd known each other forever. Now his brother lay next to Cleveland's mother and father. Cleveland looked around the farm. Everyone he'd ever really loved died here, he wondered for a few moments whether he should stay, it seemed such a sad place.

Cleveland walked over to the porch and sat down. Blue laid down next to the new grave for a few minutes more and then came over and sat on the porch near, but not next to, Cleveland. Both of them were still looking at the place were their friend had been placed just two hours before.

It was hard to believe. Zack seemed to be getting better. He was able to eat, sit up and had begun to take short walks outside. Just two weeks ago he'd come out and sat on the edge of the porch where they were sitting now. A week ago Zack had caught a slight cold but it didn't seem all that serious. Then suddenly the cough got really bad. After a couple days of listening to Zack struggle for his breath during one of the coughing fits, Cleveland had gone for the doctor but by the time he got back it was already too late to change anything. Pneumonia the doctor called it. Zack died just four days later.

Cleveland sat on the porch until the last bit of light disappeared from the gray sky. He hadn't even noticed that it had started to drizzle. Blue moved out of the misting rain but Cleveland remained where he was until a breeze chilled him. He shuddered to think of how hard Zack's death was by pneumonia. He got up and went into the house. Blue followed him closely now, it was well past his usual meal time but Cleveland hadn't even thought of that. Cleveland went to the fireplace and built a fire. Blue went over to his empty bowl and sat down watching the young man bring warmth into the cabin. Finally Cleveland turned and saw the dog sitting next to his feeding plate, he laughed slightly. "You sure can make yourself understood Blue."

There was enough rabbit stew left over from the night before to heat up for the two of them. One of the women from his church had brought a loaf of bread and a pie for him. No one else brought anything though, it wasn't like it was when his mother died. No one thought of him as a poor orphaned child anymore. He was a man on his own for sure now.

It took a few minutes to heat up the old kitchen stove, but soon the top of the range was ready enough to warm up their dinner. He picked up the old plate, then tested the stew with a spoon and when it was warm enough for Blue, Cleveland took a slice of bread and tore it into pieces, poured a cupful of the stew over it and put it down. In seconds it was gone. Blue trotted off to settle in on the rug in front of the fire. He didn't seem to need company, just a warm place to sleep and food. Blue was nothing like Cork. Cork had loved life wholeheartedly, acting like a puppy until the day she was killed. She had also openly loved Cleveland! Blue seemed to think of him more like a servant, someone there to feed him, house him and let him out when he needed. Blue wasn't an unpleasant dog, just a distant one. Maybe it was the breed. Whatever it was, there wasn't much playfulness in Blue even though he was only half grown. The other odd thing about Blue was that he always seemed to be studying everything, learning how things worked, and how he just moved upon command, never having to be asked twice to do something, remembering everything he was told. It was at times a little unnerving, he was submissive and willing, but somehow always independent. The two of them had come to respect each other, at least that was something.

Cleveland ate the rest of the stew right from the pot when it was a bit warmer. He ate a couple slices of bread but he hardly noticed them. The fire in the stove died down slowly. Cleveland didn't care, he was done cooking for the night. He was tired, a kind of tired that comes with loss. There were a couple pots in need of washing but he was too tired to bother. He put a keeper log on the fireplace and went to the outhouse for one last time. Blue trotted along dutifully, taking care of himself along the way.

Once back in the house, Cleveland closed the bedroom door where Zack had died. He would have to put away Zack's things sometime but not for a few days at least. He went to his old familiar cot, moving it out closer to the fireplace as defense against the chill of a wet December night. Blue watched from the rug but didn't move. Cleveland stripped off his over clothes, opting to sleep in his wool long johns. He pulled his blanket up over him and tried to sleep, but it was hard to do. He heard the house creak, the wind blow softly against the windows. He looked at Blue who was able to sleep easily. He felt so alone again. Each time someone he cared about died, it got harder to take. His mother had always said dying was a part of living. It was, but for the ones left living it was almost unbearable. Sometime during that long night he did fall asleep. He was surprised the next morning to find Blue sleeping on the end of his bed, nested in a fold of his blanket.

* * *

Christmas came and went without fanfare. Cleveland did attend services on Christmas day but didn't stay for the dessert following. It was a Wednesday and he had an offer of a job the next day that he felt he needed to take since he hadn't worked steady since Zack was injured and money was really getting tight. There were no presents this year except for a bone with a little meat on it for Blue.

The work was usually pretty sporadic during the winter so any job was welcome. This time he would be helping tear down a barn near Eloa that had been burned beyond repair. With any luck he'd be asked to stay on and help rebuild the structure. As it turned out he was asked and that brought in a fair amount of income for the next few weeks. Blue got a good soup bone at least once a week and they had bacon several times. Food seemed to become the indicator of how well they were doing; if they had enough money they ate well, otherwise it was beans and biscuits.

The days melted into one another. Cleveland found himself guiding Molly through the dark going and coming from the work site. He didn't like leaving Blue alone, but Blue didn't seem to care one way or the other. He, unlike Cork, never offered to go with Cleveland; however he would come with tail wagging if invited. Several times on a fair Sunday afternoon Cleveland bundled up and went down to the river to do a little fishing. Blue always got to go with him. The dog loved swimming in the water and chasing small things like frogs along the muddy banks. It was one of the few times Cleveland ever saw the dog enjoy himself with abandon. Cleveland laughed at the dog's antics but didn't like the muddy footprints all over the porch or the wet dog smell in the house that lasted long after the dog was completely dry.

When the job on the barn came to an end Cleveland received an offer to work with his old boss, Harve. This time it would just be the two of them, adding a room and more cabinets to a house they had built earlier. The Mercer family was expecting another child, their sixth. It was perfect timing, Cleveland needed to work, and seeing his mentor and friend would be an added bonus.

One night after supper, in mid-January, Cleveland finally found the energy and strength to go into the bedroom to put away Zack's things. There wasn't much but still it had to be done. Cleveland let Blue come with him. The dog seemed to sense why they were there. He watched each move Cleveland made as he folded the few clothes Zack had left behind and put them into a satchel. There was the little box with the writing materials and Lydia's address. Cleveland took the box to the eating table and sat looking at it for a moment. He remembered his promise to Zack. Cleveland shook his head. "How in the world am I going to keep that promise?"

Slowly he took a couple sheets of paper and an envelope out of the box. He brought a lamp to the table and began to write. He poured out his sorrow at Zack's death, he also poured out his love for his friend and his friend's family. He explained how he'd promised Zack to take care of his family and he was honor bound to do so. Cleveland told Lydia his whole life history, gave a full account of his farm and his abilities and how he'd be more than happy to have her and the boys come to Oregon and if she found him the least bit worthy, he'd like to marry her. He pledged to take care of her and the boys as Zack would have. Cleveland had to fight back tears as he wrote the letter, he had no idea of how the idea would set with her, he just had to be honest and be willing to do whatever it took to honor his word.

The letter with the lock of beautiful auburn hair was still there in the writing box but Cleveland couldn't bear to look at it again. He thought his heart might break at the feel of it against his hand. He finished his letter and then put the box and the bag of clothing up in the rafters above the bedroom. He washed up and built the night fire in the fireplace. He looked several times at his letter, all ready to be posted and wondered if he was doing the right thing. Lydia probably wouldn't care about his promise. Maybe she'd think he was just a crazy kid, and maybe she was right. In a funny way he felt all along he was falling in love with her. Listening to Zack talk about her, seeing the her hair, feeling it's silky softness, somehow she became very real to him, she became his Liddy, too. He shook his head, "Maybe I am crazy." Blue reminded him of the need to just keep carrying on by going to the door and waiting to be let out for one last time.

He also wrote a short note to Zack's parents. He was surprised that it was as hard to write as the one to Lydia had been. He knew what it felt like to lose someone you loved.

The next day he posted his letters as he was going to work. It would be hard to wait to see what her answer might be if she did answer. It might be months before he heard from her, he just couldn't let himself get his hopes up. Cleveland tried to live in the moment but every so often he would drift into daydreaming about what she might say to his proposal in the same letter he'd told her that her husband had died. He knew it would be some time before he even could expect to hear anything, but he could try to be optimistic. It somehow helped him get through the empty days, thinking about what she might say, especially if against all reason she said yes.

* * *

"Cleve?" Harve said with a question in his voice.

Cleveland was startled, he hadn't realized he dozed off. Even in the cold, unheated shed they were taking their lunch break in the boy was having trouble staying awake. "Sorry, didn't realize I'd fallen asleep. Haven't been sleeping too well lately. Got a lot on my mind."

"Sounds like you got woman trouble, boy," Harve said teasingly, "You got a little sweetie here in town? Is it that girl who used to come round where we were working?"

"No," Cleveland said laughing, "I haven't seen her in a long time." He shook his head, "It's more complicated than that by a long sight."

"Can't be all that bad, young handsome man like you should have your pick of the eligible girls around here."

Cleveland looked off into the distance, "No, there's no one around here for me. I made a promise." He looked down, he couldn't bring himself to tell Harve about his promise to Zack. He'd just think he was a dumb kid. "I made a promise to a friend and I just don't know how I'm going to keep it."

Harve looked serious, "Oh, well if it ain't illegal or immoral you'll figure out a way. You just got to give things time. And time is what we don't have right now. We need to get back out into the cold and work on till quitting time. I think that will be early tonight because I think I feel snow coming. My knees and back always ache when it get's just the right amount of cold and moisture going to snow."

"I heard about people being able to tell weather by their bones." Cleveland laughed, "Really old people."

"Hey!" Harve took a playful swing at the younger man. "Smart mouthed kid."

Harve was right. By the time Cleveland reached home there was a light dusting of snow. The snowstorm ended as quickly as it started though. The temperature began to drop sharply, so Cleveland brought the stock in and started the small wood stove in the shop area. It was enough to make it a little less cold, but not exactly warm. Blue patiently followed Cleveland, footstep for footstep, waiting his turn for feeding and a little pat on the head.

Blue and Cleveland settled in for the night in front of the fire after their dinner. They had come to a point where everything seemed in place. The two of them had learned to live comfortably together. It wasn't a joyous relationship, but it was pleasant enough. Cleveland didn't feel alone at least when he came home, and that was something.

The next morning when he got up, Cleveland went out on the porch while Blue trotted off to relieve himself. It was a strangely glorious morning. There was a freezing fog settling in over the land. As far as you could see the trees were white against a dark sky. The air was filled with tiny shining ice crystals as the fog froze. It was so beautiful it made him feel almost breathless. The tiny shards of ice felt like little pin pricks as they hit and melted on his skin. The trees seemed huge and everything, down to the grass was clothed in white. As a weak sun tried to break through the fog, the crystals in the air glowed like glass. It was the prettiest thing Cleveland had ever seen.

He stood there, ignoring the cold just to watch the sight. Blue came back to the house and insisted on being let in but Cleveland let him wait. Soon the sun won out over the fog and the magical scene slowly melted away.

Cleveland returned to his routine of feeding the animals and readying himself for work. By seven thirty he was on Molly and riding for town. This was his life, but he hoped someday there would be someone to share it, maybe even someone with beautiful auburn hair.

Chapter 35
Somewhere off the Oregon Coast—March 1868

Lydia looked out over the rolling sea. Just a hint of the rugged coast line of Oregon could be seen on the horizon as the ship rolled up on top of a swell. She hoped that her misery would soon be over and they would be on dry land again. Over and over she had vowed never to set foot on an ocean-going ship. Her sister and most of the children were still in the cabin too sick to even come topside. Only Roy and Toby seemed immune to the sea sickness that had overtaken most of the family. Lydia imagined she could never eat again. Surely her whole digestive system must be ruined for life from the excessive heaving she had done over the rail of the ship.

Roy took turns checking on her on deck then going below to check on the rest of the family. It was certainly not a pleasant trip. Lydia couldn't see how a stagecoach ride to Oregon could have been any worse on Ellen either. The only good thing was that Ellen made the entire trip in a bunk. It was only taking five days but with the not being able to keep anything down, it seemed like an eternity. Several times an hour Lydia would return to the cabin to check on her children but they were sleeping through most of the journey, mercifully. She worried they weren't eating enough but could understand why. She prayed a few days wouldn't cause lasting problems for any of them.

It was raining hard as the ship neared the mouth of the Columbia.

Huge waves rolled in on either side of the ship, pulling it first one way and then another. Lydia was forced to go below by a burley crewman who yelled something quite rude about a "Bloody woman was just in the way. Serve 'er right to be swept over the side." She couldn't see who he was talking to, but she knew who he was talking about. On the way down the stairs to the galley she was thrown off balance when the ship lurched. She wound up at the bottom of the steps with one leg twisted back under her. When she tried to get up she screamed in pain. One of the cook's young helpers came running and got her to her feet. She steadied herself and found it hurt to put her weight on the injured leg. The boy helped her to her cabin through the quaking ship. Once inside her room she hobbled over to her bunk and more or less fell in. Ellen and Roy were holding their children in a bunk across the room and her two boys were in the bunk next to hers. Everyone had a terrified look on their faces, even Roy this time. It was hard just to stay in the bunks, let alone do it when you were so sick to your stomach.

The ship was moaning and straining against the waves and pressure of crossing the bar. It felt like it never would end. Even her boys were roused from their stupor and started to cry. She got up, holding on to everything she could to steady herself to get to them. She was just about there when all of a sudden it stopped. There was no violent rolling and pitching, just a gentle sway front to back.

She crawled into the bunk with the boys and sat holding them. It was almost eerie. The old ship no longer seemed to be straining. For a moment she wondered if they were still even moving.

There was a knock on her door, "Everyone alright in there?"

Roy looked at everyone, "Just a bruise or two, nothing serious." He yelled back to whoever asked.

"We'll send the ship's doctor around to check on those bruises after he sees to an injured crewman. Please stay in your cabin until he gives you the word you're okay to go on deck. We made it over the breakwater just fine. It's raining, so watch your step if you get topside, it will be a might slippery. But we're on the Columbia now." Footsteps trailed off down the hall to other passenger's rooms.

"Are you and the boys alright over there, Lydia?" Ellen asked weakly.

"I fell down the stairs coming down and I thought for a minute I might have broken my leg, but I think it's just bruised as Roy said. What about you?"

"Virgil's got a knot on his forehead from hitting the upper berth. Couldn't hold on to him during one of those big drops the ship made. I think I might have to change my pants, that was such a hard jolt." Roy laughed.

Ellen tried to laugh but was too weak. "We should be to Portland by tomorrow. It will be so good to get off this ship and see land again."

"I agree. I've decided this is my one and only trip out on the ocean," Lydia said as the boys began to settle down again.

Within a few minutes the steward came around with tea, a pot of honey and hot biscuits. "The captain says this is good to settle your stomachs. It will help you regain your strength."

Roy gave tea laced with the honey to Ellen and the children. In the calmer waters of the river they all found it easier to take a little nourishment. Lydia even gave the babies the tea and honey concoction. They liked it, even having seconds. It was amazing how fast they seemed to be recovering from the ordeal. Most everyone only took a couple of the biscuits except Toby. He ate three or four.

It was nearly an hour before the doctor came by. He'd had several fairly serious injuries to treat before them. A crewman had been thrown against a chain, removing a good deal of skin from his shoulder, a passenger had slipped and broken an ankle, and another passenger had been cut on the hand when a lamp in their cabin broke.

The doctor looked first at the lump on Virgil's head. It didn't seem to be too bad but he advised Ellen and Roy to watch the boy and make sure he didn't go to sleep for several hours. Other than putting some cold compresses on the bump, he said there wasn't much too do for it but let time heal it. Since it didn't seem too painful for the boy, he didn't prescribe any pain medicine.

Then he turned to Lydia. He pulled the curtain in the middle of the cabin that separated the cabin at night for modesty's sake. Lydia lifted her skirts and pulled up her pantaloons. Her leg had turned a bright red from just above her knee to her ankle and was swelling. "Ah, my dear, I am going to get some ice packs on this. You will have a nasty bruise for several days." He felt the leg, bending it several times. He took off her laced up shoe to make sure she could wiggle her toes. "Well, the good news is that nothing seems to be broken, but I would advise you not to put much weight on this leg for at least three weeks, or until the bruise is gone. This was as close to a serious accident as you could come without actually breaking something." He pulled her dress back down and opened the curtain. He walked over to Roy.

"You will need to arrange for a cart for your sister-in-law, or at the very least some crutches. She should not walk from the ship to whereever you are going." He looked at Ellen, whom he'd come to see several times during the trip. "And that would be good for your wife too, she needs at least two weeks of bedrest before doing anything as strenuous as taking care of the children or a household. Do you have someone to help?"

"I hope so," Roy sighed.

"Good," the doctor said as he closed up his bag and left to check on his other patients. "I will stop by tomorrow just before we get off the ship and check everyone out before going on shore. The steward will come soon with some ice packs for Mrs. Grant's leg."

Roy closed the door behind the doctor and looked around the room at his ailing wife and wounded sister-in-law. Lydia could see tears in his eyes. She couldn't bear it. Whatever dreams he'd had were lost for the moment in having to take care of the whole family. It hardly seemed fair. The anger started to rise again in her soul, why wasn't Zack here to take care of her and the boys. She turned and buried her head in a pillow. The boys fell asleep peacefully and finally their mother did too.

* * *

Just before sunrise a rousing knock on the door woke the whole family. "We'll be tying up to the dock in Portland in just a couple hours. Pack your gear before that please and be ready to get off the ship within a hour of our lowering the gangplank." The voice continued on down the hall knocking on doors as he went with the same announcement.

Lydia limped over and helped Ellen get dressed and to a chair, then hurriedly dressed herself as Roy dressed and began dressing the children. They didn't have much baggage with them so packing their things didn't take much time at all. As promised the ship's doctor came by to give Virgil one last look as well as Lydia. The lump on the boy's head had gone down considerably and he was showing no worse for wear. Lydia's leg had gone from a bright red to various shades of purple and there was a broken vein near the top of where her high laced shoe had cut into her in the fall. The doctor advised more cold packs and staying off her feet as much as possible, then he left. The family looked one last time around the room for anything they might have missed. Seeing nothing, they headed for the deck to get their first glimpse of Portland.

Men were scampering about on the deck so they pressed themselves back against the cabin walls to stay out of the way. Portland was a big, noisy place. From the ship's vantage point, it looked almost as big as Knoxville, but not nearly as clean and civilized. The streets were not paved and wooden sidewalks lined all the muddy streets. It was still raining lightly so it was hard to see very much. A fog hung low over the heavy forests just beyond the town.

One of the ship's officers came over to Roy. "I have taken the liberty to send one of the officers ahead to secure rooms for you and your party since your women folk are feeling poorly according to the doctor. I hope that they recover soon. Since they were injured on our ship we feel it is only right to offer you two nights lodging to rest up on the company sir." He looked around and saw the passenger gangplank being lowered. "If you'll wait here sir, my man will be back with a rig and take you to the accommodations shortly."

Roy smiled, "Thank you kindly, sir. That is very generous of you. We accept gratefully."

Ellen turned to Lydia, "Isn't that thoughtful of the ship's company?"

Lydia shrugged, "I think they were worried we'd sue them."

Ellen laughed tiredly, "You're just getting cynical. There are still good people out there."

They were all pretty wet by the time the reached the hotel. The ship's man had secured two rooms for them at a fairly decent hotel on the far edge of the town. "You'll like it out here better," he explained, "When the rain stops it gets pretty rank in town with horses, cows and people in the streets, if you know what I mean. Near the harbor is a rough place too, lots of saloons and not very suitable for the children." He brought their bags in and set everything in the hotel's lobby.

"I thought it smelled bad because of the rain," Roy laughed.

"It gets worse, believe me!" the young man said in all seriousness. "Good day ladies, have a successful journey from here on out."

"Thank you," Roy said as the young officer left.

A woman working at the registration desk smiled, "You've already been signed in. Here are your keys to the rooms. Breakfast and dinner are included. We serve breakfast in the café from six until nine, dinner is from five to seven. For lunch we just put a tray of sandwiches and fruit on the side board over there and you can come get what you'd like. We've put a pitcher of fresh water in your rooms to wash up with. There is a bath house about a block down the street. They offer women's baths from one in the afternoon to three and men's baths from six in the morning until noon.

I have a coupon for one bath each for you, too." She smiled and handed all the things to Roy.

Roy nodded and looked around, there were stairs to the upper floors immediately to their left.

"Your rooms are on this floor next to the back door." The woman pointed, "We thought with the children it would be quieter for the rest of the guests. We don't often get children."

"Thank you," Ellen said, "I appreciate not having to climb any stairs."

"The necessary is just up the hill in the back." The clerk added as the family wearily made their way down the hall.

Their rooms were surprisingly big. Lydia took the room with one double bed and a single cot. She would put both boys in the bed and take the cot herself. Roy and Ellen had a room with two double beds and a cot. The boys could sleep in one double bed, Roy and Ellen in one and Darcy could have the cot. The beds took up most of the room so there wasn't much else as far as furniture went; no dressers only hooks on the wall to hang things, but there was a wash stand with a basin and pitcher as promised atop a commode that had the night pot in it. Each room also had a couple kitchen chairs to sit on and a small table with an oil lamp. They were very clean rooms, too. There was several small brown towels by the basin and fresh sheets on each bed ready to put on.

"I'm very hungry," Toby whined.

Roy looked at his pocket watch, "They should still be serving breakfast. Let's all go and get something to eat."

Ellen waved her hand, "I really don't think I could. I'm so dirty, too. I need that bath before I go anywhere."

"Well, I think we'll go, dirty or not." Lydia said boldly. "For the first time in days I am hungry although my legs feel so rubbery. I can still feel the ship rocking under me." She managed to hop around on one leg while trying not to put much weight on her injured one.

"They say it takes a couple days to get over that, to get your land legs back," Roy said.

"Roy you could bring me back some of that tea and honey, that was very gentle on my stomach," Ellen said as she washed the children's hands in the basin.

"We surely can do that," he motioned to the children. "Come on, be as quiet as possible. They don't get many children remember, so they expect you to behave well."

Lydia washed her boys' faces and hands then, led them to the small one room café off the main entrance to the hotel. She had to use the wall to help her limp into the dining area. There were several people, mostly men, lingering over cups of coffee as they entered. They looked quite the bedraggled mess as the seven of them moved chairs and tables around so they could sit together.

The waitress came over. "You have lovely children," she smiled as she greeted them.

"We aren't too lovely today. We just got in on the ship that docked this morning and all of us had a pretty hard time on the ocean." Lydia grimaced. "My sister is still ill and couldn't join us. So we'll want to take some tea with honey back to our rooms for her."

"Sure we can do that. Sorry to hear you had a rough crossing. Where did you come from?"

"Well, we started out in Knoxville, Tennessee," Roy said with a sigh, "But we got on the ship in San Francisco."

"Winter is a rough time to travel on the Pacific, that's for sure." The waitress took a pad from her pocket. "What can I get for you folks? We have eggs, bacon, potatoes and coffee. There's oatmeal with raisins for the children if you'd like. And we have goat's milk, lots of vitamins."

"Oh, the oatmeal sounds good for the boys," Lydia said thinking for a moment, "And for me, too, with some scrambled eggs on the side."

Roy and his children ordered everything. The waitress laughed softly and headed off for the kitchen. Within moments she was back with the first platter. The children quickly finished their milk and oatmeal. It was good to see everyone able to eat again. The twins ate their oatmeal and scrambled eggs without complaint. By the time the meal was over Lydia felt like a new person! Nothing short of a real bath would do now.

The front counter clerk came up to Lydia as she was heading down the hall. She had a pretty cane with a small silver head with her. "A gentleman stayed with us last year for a couple weeks. When he left he forgot this. We've held on to it in case he returned but he's not come back so I don't see any harm in you using this. It will sure make it easier to get around."

"Yes, thank you," Lydia gratefully took the cane. It did make it much better. Roy took the tea and a couple small biscuits to Ellen. Lydia went to her room with the boys and put them down for a nap. She hadn't intended to take one herself but she lay down on the cot and fell fast asleep. It was nearly noon when Roy knocked lightly on her door.

"Lydia, I'm going to get a tray of sandwiches for us can I bring you some too?"

"Yes please," Lydia said opening the door. "I'll come over and join you and Ellen if that's okay."

"Sure, everyone is awake in there."

Ellen looked better than she had in days, she even had a little color in her cheeks. "Did you take a nap? We all did, felt wonderful not to be bounced around."

Lydia sat her boys down on the floor where the other children were playing with a box of marbles. "Don't let them put any of the marbles in their mouths."

"Virgil said he saw Pete swallow one already Aunt Liddy," Toby said innocently.

"Is that true?" Lydia said in shock.

"No, I was just funning Toby."

Lydia laughed, "Good."

Everyone took the rest of the day just to relax and get a feel for the ground again. The rain continued through much of the day making even the trips to the necessary unpleasant so it seemed a good thing to just to stay inside. By dinner time Ellen was feeling strong enough to join the family in the dining room although she still couldn't eat much. Lydia found she could get around quite well with the cane.

The next morning Roy rented a horse and rode out to Oregon City to find his cousin and see where they went from the hotel. Lydia and Ellen managed to get the children and themselves to the bath house, which turned out to be a small building sitting off behind another hotel. They were given four towels for the seven of them, one bar of soap and a little sweet smelling powder. The bath room held two large tin tubs with high backs. A Chinese woman poured pails of hot water into each of the tubs and stood by to see if more would be needed. Lydia tested the water and added one pail of cold water from a large cask that was sitting in the room. Then it was just right. She quickly bathed the boys. Ellen's children stripped off and took a bath in the other tub, the boys first then Ellen and Darcy. There was a curtain separating the two tub areas so it did provide a little privacy. Lydia put her boys at one end of the tub and lowered herself down into the water. It was a tight fit but they all managed well. It was heavenly to wash herself all over, even her hair. It felt like she had only been in her bath for a few minutes, but soon the Chinese lady announced, "Hour over."

"Thank you," Lydia said as she accepted a towel to wrap around herself. She lifted the boys out of the bath and dried them off thoroughly. She was still a little damp when she dressed herself but it was wonderful still. Even her leg felt better for being in the water. She was grateful for the good smelling powder. For the first time in a long time she remembered the smell of flowers. It was quite a pleasant experience.

Ellen seemed to enjoy the morning too, although it tired her out considerably. By the time they got back to the hotel all Ellen wanted to do was take a nap. Lydia offered to take the children into her room while

Ellen rested before lunch. Ellen actually slept through lunch, sleeping until just before dinner when Roy returned.

"Well it's not quite as we'd hoped but it won't be all that bad. My cousin, Moss, has five kids of his own and one on the way so their house is pretty crowded. But he just recently bought a farm adjoining his. Seems the family there had tried to make the farm work but when the wife died the neighbor decided to take his two children back to Maryland to be with his folks. The acquired place has a small, three room house that we can have for as long as we need. We can use the garden spot, hunt on the land or do whatever else we need. Moss said there's a little furniture in it but he'll get in touch with his church and see what they can come up with. Maybe even have a welcoming party for us."

Ellen looked sad again. "We had such a beautiful place back in Tennessee. Can't hardly bear the idea of being squatters on someone else's land."

"We were going to lose that place anyway, hon," Roy said stroking her hair. "I know this isn't what we hoped for but we'll make it work. We got to have faith."

"Faith," Ellen looked up with tears welling up, "That's mighty easy to say, hard to live out."

He held her to his chest and the children became quiet. They came over to the bed and put their arms around their mother and father. Lydia picked up her boys and went back to her room and wept. She had no idea what to believe anymore. She thought about Zack for a moment then pushed that thought out of her mind. She would find him soon enough, when she could walk up to him proudly, not limping and looking pitiful.

The rain stopped the next day so Roy rented a buckboard and a couple mules and they headed to their next stop. The small farm just northeast of Oregon City was located in beautiful, wooded country. Here and there several acres had been cleared for farms and roads. Moss Graham and his wife Evie greeted them with open arms when the wagon pulled into their yard. It was a small house they lived in, but it seemed large in love and family. Children ran out of the house hugging their cousins by marriage like long lost friends. Evie was at least five months along so she didn't help with getting the children down from the buckboard but did hug everyone. A large lunch had been prepared in their honor so immediately everyone fell into helping get things on the table. The children ate their lunch on a table that had been set up on the covered front porch. Even though the sun was out it was a little cold, but they didn't seem mind eating with their coats on.

After loading the buckboard with blankets, food plus small things like dishes, pots and pans they headed off towards the other house. Moss followed in his wagon with some furniture he'd come up with from the neighbors. The house turned out to be in quite a pretty setting. They rounded a stand of trees to see a small trail leading up to the house that sat atop a small knoll. The barn was down the hill about a hundred yards. Three or four acres of land had already been cleared in front of the house so it had a good view. In fact, when they reached the house they were surprised to see a majestic white capped mountain to the east. It looked as tall as the ones they'd seen in the Sierras. "That's Mt. Hood," Moss said proudly. "Got a great view from here. I am thinking someday of building a big house up here for us. The one we're in now doesn't have that view. Got a better well though. This one is adequate for most of the year but get's a little slow in July and August."

Ellen and Lydia were pleasantly surprised to find the house was bigger inside than it looked and had been left very clean. The one big room in the house ran the entire width of one end of the house. A fireplace of river stone was in one front corner of the room, plus at the back, there was a decent cookstove, a long table and two benches. Straight cross the room from the front door was a back door that had a small attached covered porch. Some wood was cut and stored there already. Roy checked the stove pipe and found it clean enough to go ahead and build a fire. "I'll get some water so we can think about making some coffee."

The women and children continued exploring their new home. The other two rooms off to one side were bedrooms, the front one considerably smaller than the other. Each had a wood framed double bed but no mattresses on them. Along the wall in the larger sleeping room, were a pair of ships bunks, stacked one on top of each other. There was also a small loft in the larger bedroom that could be reached by a ladder framework attached to the cabin wall. In the loft there were two wooden cots tucked under the slope of the roof. "I'll take the front bed room, Ellen. I can make pallets on the floor for the boys," Lydia said. "This room looks big enough for your whole family." Ellen nodded in agreement.

Moss helped Roy bring in the water then the two men unloaded the supplies off the wagons. The women got the fire going. The older children went out side on the small front porch and stood not knowing whether they should move or not. "Mr. Moss, are there big spiders here?" Virgil asked.

"Why no son, but we do have some bear and mountain lions, so don't go into the woods or too far from the cabin. You can play from here to the barn without too much worry."

With that the children let out whoops and started running for the barn to explore. "Wish I had their energy."

Moss had brought three cotton ticks for the bunks and two double tied mattress for the beds.

There was an assortment of quilts and a few sheets, some mended many times but all clean. Roy had picked up some staples from the general store in Oregon City so they had food enough for a few days to get them started. Evie had thrown in enough cloth to cover the table so in no time the place seemed more homey, but still stark. Lydia could tell by the look on her sister's face that all she could see was their beautiful home farm in Tennessee. Ellen walked out to look at the mountains and the farm. Lydia joined her for a moment.

"It is pretty here isn't it." Ellen said quietly.

"Yes," Lydia hugged her sister, "We'll get through this. Somehow everything will work out the way it's meant to. Roy's right: we have to have faith."

Ellen sighed and they walked back inside to start dinner. Moss brought in two or three wooden chairs and a small chest of drawers. It was a meager start but at least they had a place to stay, food to eat and they were all still together. That was something to be grateful for.

Over the next several days a steady stream of neighbors dropped by with all kinds of food and furniture to help them settle in. By week's end they had more things than they could store. They'd even been given a milk goat with a kid and a pair of mules hitched to an old farm wagon. Roy got a job on a neighboring farm, plowing and planting so there was a little money coming in. Life wasn't easy but it was a start, at least.

Chapter 36
Independence, Oregon—March 1868

Cleveland ate his hard boiled egg and slice of bread as he walked to the post office. He and Harve seldom took more than twenty minutes for their lunch, especially on cold, rainy days like this one, so he didn't want to be late getting back.

The Lyon's building now housed the post office and looked like a beacon of hope in the bleakness of the day. Cleveland stepped inside and closed the door behind him. The small pot-bellied stove was almost too warm. Cleveland went up to the window. "Morning, Mr. Mervin," Cleveland said taking off his hat. "Anything for me?"

The bespectacled man beyond the opening peered over his glasses and smiled. "Just a catalog and your newspaper." The man handed the two pieces of mail to Cleveland. "You've been in here nearly everyday for the last week Cleve. Expecting something important?"

Cleveland sighed, "Yeah, kind of anyway." He wasn't sure if he would hear from Lydia. One could only imagine how hard his news had been for her. Cleveland wasn't sure he'd ever hear from her but he'd given himself six months. If by that time he hadn't heard from her he'd make the trip to Tennessee to make sure she and the boys were alright and being well taken care of. He'd promised and to him that was a sacred oath. "Thanks, Mr. Mervin. See ya."

Somehow the walk back to the work site was slower and more

unpleasant. Usually the weather didn't bother him but today it fit his mood. Even Harve knew something was wrong. As they worked along side of each other Cleveland was very quiet.

"Are you going to tell me what's eating you, boy?" Harve asked quietly as he swung his hammer in a steady rate. "Is it that promise you said you made some time back?"

Cleveland cast a glance at his boss and friend, he had no one else to talk to so he took a chance on Harve. "Sort of." He swallowed hard and picked up a piece of lumber and held in place while Harve anchored it down. When he could let go of the plank he blurted out his promise and what he'd done. "I promised Zack Grant to take care of his wife and children just before he died, so I wrote to her and asked her to marry me."

Harve dropped his hammer in surprise, "You asked his widow to marry you?"

"Well, I couldn't see any better way to take care of her than to bring her out her and marry her so I could do that."

Harve shook his head, "Son, I'm not sure what you'd expect but I think any woman would consider that was a crazy notion."

"My ma used to say people on the trail got married for all kinds of reasons, not just love. If there was a widow with children she often just married an available man."

"I think things may have changed a little since those days," Harve said as he picked up his hammer and started working again. "I really don't know what to tell you. I think that was a pretty rash thing to do. You don't know her at all, maybe there was a reason Zack left her and come out here on his own."

Cleveland felt a little anger rising for the first time ever at his friend. "There was nothing like that. He had good reasons for leaving when he did. He loved Lydia and she is a good woman."

"Lydia is it?" Harve shook his head. "I think you've taken a mighty big chance, boy. She could take you up on your offer and suddenly you'll be having, what three extra mouths to feed? You know how tough just getting by has been. It's a big responsibility to take on a woman and another man's children."

Cleveland cringed a bit, put that way it did seem foolhardy to make such an offer to a complete stranger, but he was a man of his word. He had faith that whatever happened he would somehow rise to the challenge. He had come so far, he knew he had the strength, with God's help, to do what he had to do. He decided there was no use talking about it anymore with anyone else. He would probably get the same response so he just went back to work and didn't say anything more about the subject. He was glad though when the end of the day came, more ached than his back. Once again the world seemed big and he seemed so alone.

* * *

Three weeks later Cleveland again visited the post office. He'd stopped going more than once a week, beginning to feel that it was a futile trip yet unable to give up all hope. It was a sunny day but still pretty cold so the warm building was pleasant to step into. Mr. Marvin saw him come in and smiled. "Cleveland, good thing you came in. I got a letter for that friend of yours Zack Grant. Guess someone doesn't know about him dying. It's addressed in care of you so I'll give it to you so you can write to them and let them know. There's also one for you."

Cleveland swallowed hard as he took the letter, he recognized Lydia's handwriting on one of the letters. The other was from Zack's mother. "Thanks, Mr. Marvin, I'll do that." He took the letter outside, debating if he should open it or not. He tucked it into his shirt pocket and went back to work. All afternoon he kept touching the place where the letter was near his heart. It began to almost weigh him down.

He could hardly get home fast enough, urging a complaining Molly to her fastest speed. When Cleveland reached home he quickly fed the stock and Blue. He left collecting the eggs until after he read the letter. He brought a lamp over to the eating table and with trembling hands opened the small delicate piece of mail. Taking a deep breath he began to read it aloud.

*"Sacramento, California
January 23, 1868
Dearest Husband,*

I know you will be shocked to learn that the children and I are on the way to join you in Oregon. Many things have changed since the last time I wrote to you. Your brother came home with his family, so your mother is being well cared for on the farm. Jonas went back to England to begin the search for his wife and child. My step-mother has given Ellen and I six months to raise the money to buy her interest in the farm, so I am traveling with Roy and Ellen. Ellen is not well so we have been making slow progress. We were going to stop here in California so Roy could do some mining but with Ellen's condition we decided to press on to Oregon. Roy has some family near Portland we will try to stay with for a while before coming to Independence.

I was hoping to surprise you my love, but I knew you'd be worried if you didn't hear from me soon. I haven't heard from you, of course, since we've been crossing the country. What an adventure this has been, we will have so much to talk about. The three of us are well, the boys continue to grow well. They are walking and talking a bit.

We will be staying another few weeks in California so Ellen will rest up, then we plan on taking a ship to Portland. The doctor thought that would be easier on her than traveling by stage as we did to get here. If all goes well I will see you sometime in mid-April. I hope this is pleasing news to you my darling. Give my best to Cleveland.

*Your loving wife,
Liddy"*

Tears were running down his cheeks as he laid the letter down. She was coming in just a few weeks and she didn't know Zack was gone. She was coming full of love and hope. Cleveland put his head in his folded arms. "My God, why do I have to be the one to break her heart?"

Blue came up beside Cleveland and put his head into his lap. "Boy, we've got trouble," Cleveland said as he sat up and stroked the dog's head. Cleveland reached for the other letter and opened it.

"Dear Cleveland,

Thank you for letting us know what happened to Zack. It was a terrible thing but we are glad he had a good friend to take care of him during his final days. I had a terrible strong feeling when he rode off for Oregon I might never see him again and it looks like that was the case.

Lydia and her sister's family had just sent word that they were going to California to mine for gold in hopes of saving the family farm a couple weeks before we got your letter. There was no way I could let her know of this terrible situation but I will write to her as soon as she sends me an address.

Again thank you for your kindness to my son. God bless you.

Sincerely,
Rose Grant"

Cleveland looked around the room. It hadn't been really cleaned since his mother died. Zack didn't care much about housekeeping, and neither did he. But with Lydia coming, Cleveland decided he'd best clean it down to the floors. Maybe even put up some paper on the walls. He'd seen the Porterfield house fixed up the way Mrs. Porterfield thought was pretty. He decided to do it right away, as it would help him take his mind off the coming storm he'd have to face.

Over the next few days Cleveland stopped at the store almost every night on his way home. Mrs. Woods, the clerk, told him the red checked cloth made a table seem festive so he got that. He picked up some real dishes, not the tin plates he was used to eating off of, and some real cups, not tin ones. He got several gallons of white wash and some more pine soap for the bath house. On Sundays he worked from daybreak to sundown sprucing up his place. It felt the most important thing he had to do. He wanted the place to be charming and inviting to a lady like Lydia.

He'd gotten in the habit of taking his smaller wagon to work in case he thought of something else to add to his place. Cleveland also began stopping by the dock on his way home at night to check with the ferryman, on those days when the sidewheeler brought passengers and supplies to town from down river. One boat came down the river in the mornings and another one came up the river in the evenings. After a few days the ferryman got perturbed, and more or less told Cleveland to quit pestering him. From then on, Cleveland only came to the top of the hill and watched the passengers who got off the boat. After a week or so he stopped doing that when he realized a few people had began to talk about his odd behavior. He was a mess, he knew that. He could hardly eat or sleep. His mind played out every scenario imaginable, but no matter what he hoped for he knew it probably wouldn't work out well.

Chapter 37
Oregon City, Oregon—April 1868

Lydia fixed her bonnet for the fourth or fifth time. "Are you sure I look alright?"

Ellen tweaked the hat for her sister one more time. "I wish you'd wait and let me go with you. I can't believe you want to go to Independence by yourself." They stood by the wagon as the sun came up. "We should have just sent for Zack a long time ago. He should be coming to you."

"Don't be silly. It's not more than a day upriver and I'll be there by supper time." Lydia smiled trying to hide her own fears. "And besides, this is the way I wanted it. I wanted to surprise him by getting all the way to Oregon, to him, by myself. I wanted him to think of me as strong and able." She didn't say it, but she was thinking, "In case he doesn't want me anymore, I want him to think I'll be fine on my own."

"Well, you kiss that lucky man of yours for me," Ellen said as she hugged her sister a last time. Tears were in both their eyes. They both knew that this could go terribly wrong. Ellen said several times she had a bad feeling about Zack. Lydia tried to put those warnings out of her mind, even though Ellen's feelings turned out right a good share of the time. Lydia hadn't heard from Zack in months. He might have even moved on from Independence for all they knew. Lydia was leaving the boys with Ellen and Roy just in case there were any problems.

"Now, I will be back by the end of the week," Lydia smiled bravely,

"And I hope Zack will be with me and we'll work things out." A sharp whistle blast signaled it was time to leave the dock, just above the falls in Oregon City. "I'll be back sooner if there is any problems. Pray for us." Lydia waved as she took her place along the railing aboard the ship. Her leg had pretty well healed, but it was still a little discolored and sore. She hoped she wouldn't have to do a lot of walking when she reached Independence. It didn't matter to her though. If this was the last distance she had to go to close the gap between her and Zack, it was worth any pain and effort.

The ship steamed easily up the wide Willamette. Spring rains had pushed the river to near flood stage, so they were fighting quite a current, but still they made steady progress. The boat stopped one or two times to let people on and off, even though Lydia would have preferred it plow straight on to Independence. Because of dealing with the currents, the boat was a little late arriving in Independence. It was about five thirty when she finally stepped out on the shore, grateful that the ride up the river had not been nearly as rough as the one on the sea. When she asked if the boatman knew Zack Grant or Cleveland Taylor, she was elated when the man told her where to find Cleveland. The young man had been working on a house not too far from where they were and might still be there. She gathered her bag and headed immediately to the location.

She saw several streets running north and south. As directed, she went over three streets past the main street of the town, turned left and walked to the edge of town. Lydia's heart beat wildly as she saw a young man hitching up a mule to a wagon, as though he was getting ready to leave the work site for the day. She approached him nervously. "Excuse me. Are you Cleveland Taylor?"

Cleveland turned around and nearly fainted. He knew immediately who she was. Her beautiful auburn hair was curled around her head with a couple long locks hanging softly to one side beneath a small straw brimmed hat. "Liddy," he stammered, "I mean Mrs. Grant—Lydia I mean."

She laughed softly, "Please call me Liddy."

Cleveland took a deep breath, for the hour of his death seemed to have arrived. He was happy, sad, sick, everything a human being could feel, he felt in that moment. "I am glad to meet you." It was trite but all he could think of. He took in everything about her in a flash; she was just slightly shorter than he was, thin but healthy looking, beautiful in her own way with clear skin, bright smile and that hair. He knew for sure now he was in love, yet this might be the hardest day of his life. He wanted to run, throw up and cry, but he held his ground as his stomach knotted, churned and his heart pounded all the way into his head.

"It's nice to meet you, too, Cleveland. Zack said some very nice things about you in his letters." Lydia looked around, "Where is my husband?"

Cleveland sighed. She didn't know and this didn't seem the place to tell her. "I'll take you to him. He's out at my farm." He offered her his hand and helped her into the wagon. It wasn't very comfortable but it was better than the large buckboard. He put her valise in the seat between them as they headed out of town.

"This is such beautiful county, Cleveland," Lydia said lightly. "No wonder people like it here. In a way, it reminds me of the valley around Knoxville where I grew up."

"That's what Zack said," Cleveland said softly.

After a couple miles, Lydia shifted her weight several times, her leg was beginning to throb again bumping along in the buggy. It seemed to her that Cleveland was unwilling to talk much about Zack. Maybe there was something wrong! Her mind began to run through the possibilities.

Just as they turned off the main road, Cleveland stopped the rig and got out to come around to her side, "I'd like to show you my favorite view of my farm." She gratefully took his hand for help out of the rough riding wagon.

Cleveland led Lydia to the little stone bench he'd made where they could see the whole property. She was happy to sit and look at it for a moment, but she was still a little perplexed by his reluctance to talk about Zack. Finally the worst thing that might have happened popped into her mind. "Cleveland has Zack taken up with another woman?"

Cleveland's jaw dropped, "No, no! Miss Lydia," he took her hand in his and sat down next to her. "Liddy, it is obvious to me that you didn't get any of my letters. I got the letter you sent from Sacramento, so I knew you were coming but I didn't have any way to get in touch with you. Zack would never cheat on you, he loved you with everything he had. It's just that," he swallowed hard, "he died of pneumonia just before Christmas." He felt her start to tremble.

"What?" she said in disbelief.

Cleveland pointed off across the field to the little family grave yard. "I buried him over there, next to my ma and pa."

Lydia got to her feet unsteadily. All her worry, all the dangers they'd come through, all her hopes simply gone. She started walking down the road, around the pasture towards the graves on the hillside. Cleveland followed a few feet behind her.

Cleveland shoved his curly hair back out of his eyes, tucking it securely under his hat as he stood in agony, watching the woman he loved, kneel and cry over the grave of her husband, a man he also loved. It was as if time itself was standing still, the very air seemed heavy, and hard to pull into his lungs. He felt so helpless; never in his nineteen years had he been in so much pain. He had known more than his share of loss in this harsh world, but nothing had prepared him for this torment. It had been less than two hours since he and Lydia had finally met. It had been a confusing, painful ride to his farm and now he faced the worst part.

Lydia Grant felt her world had been shattered with a few simple words. "Your husband is dead." After more than a year of waiting to rejoin him, the hardships of coming so far, the loneliness, the terrors, the longing, here she was 22, a mother, a widow and all alone in the world. She couldn't stop shaking. She hardly felt the young man lifting her to her feet. Without meaning to she clung to him, feeling somehow safe as he put his arms around her as she soaked his shirt with her tears. The world was spinning, she could feel the breeze through loose wisps of her hair, his hands smoothing them down, his cheek against hers. She was oddly comforted by the touch of another person right at that moment. Lydia fought to catch her breath as she looked up into to the man's eyes. She discovered that he was crying too, their lives intertwined in that moment of shared grief. Lydia could tell Cleveland had loved Zack and she smiled to comfort him, but he moved beyond that and kissed her gently. Lydia went limp at the sensation his kiss sent through her, she couldn't move, couldn't think. Why was he doing that? Darkness closed in over her like a smothering blanket and she felt the ground go out from beneath her feet.

Cleveland felt Lydia go completely limp in his arms. "My God Lydia, forgive me," he yelled as he lowered her to the ground to make sure she was still breathing. Lightly touching her neck he felt her steady pulse and breathed a sigh of relief. He quickly picked her up and carried her to the house. She was amazingly light. Her beautiful auburn hair came loose from its pins and flowed in the fading sunlight. It was as beautiful as Cleveland had known it would be. As he carried her, Lydia's hair swirled across his shoulder and against his neck, sending shivers through his entire body. Suddenly he realized that he needed to put her down and move away while he still could.

Cleveland gently laid Lydia down on the living room settee. He loosed the top button of her high starched collar down to the small pulsating "v" of her neck but didn't trust himself to go any further. He quickly got a cool washcloth and washed her tear-stained face. After rinsing the cloth in cool water, he softly laid it down across her forehead and went to the table. There he buried his head in his arms. "Zack! Zack, I will try to do what I promised," he said hoarsely.

Blue, Zack's dog, sat next to the couch and Lydia, not moving, only watching. Cleveland could tell he understood her grief. Though he couldn't express it, the dog knew the same heartache. The dog instantly bonded to Lydia, just the way he'd chosen Zack.

Lydia listened, and she watched Cleveland through veiled eyes. She had come around shortly after Cleveland put her on the hard bench, but she didn't have the strength to move or the clarity to respond to what had happened. She welcomed the unattended moments to regain herself. She quietly sat up, and although the room was still spinning a little, she was feeling stronger by the minute. "What promise?" she asked quietly.

Cleveland whirled around, startled. "I promised," he stammered, "I promised Zack that I would take care of you," he looked down for a moment, "and the boys." The young man was going to make the speech of his life and it was going to take all the courage he could muster but he had to and he knew it was now or never. "I know this will be hard to hear, especially since you just found about Zack. It seems you didn't get any of my letters," he sighed. "I want you to marry me, Miss Lydia. I want you and the boys to come live here with me. Zack would have wanted that. He was my best friend, the brother I never had. We'd planned to maybe farm together or start a business. I'm as a good carpenter as he was good with horses and tack. What you don't know, though," Cleveland swallowed hard, "Is that over the time Zack lived here, he talked about you so much that I came to love you as much as he did. When he died, thinking of you kept me going. I was saving up money to come to Tennessee to get you when I got the letter saying you were on your way."

Lydia sat wordless, her whole body ached and her mind screamed for this day to be over. In the space of an hour she'd learned that her old life was destroyed and a new one was being offered by a near stranger. Lydia could tell Cleveland was a decent young man and she didn't want to hurt him, but what he was saying just didn't make any sense to her. She couldn't think clearly and for a moment she thought she might faint. Then she realized she hadn't eaten anything that day and it was nearly sundown. "Do you have anything to eat?"

Cleveland gasped, "of course." He was shocked he hadn't even thought about her being hungry. "I'll be right back." He ran out the back door to the root cellar. Within a few minutes he was back with a jug of buttermilk and a slice of ham. He fetched two biscuits from the flour cupboard, put the ham and bread on a plate and brought it to her, along with a cup of milk.

Lydia sipped the cool, lumpy buttermilk and ate one of his biscuits. She wondered as she bit into the slightly stale biscuit if that was all the boy had. Her stomach revolted at the ham and she couldn't eat more than a couple bites but she was able to finish the milk. She felt stronger after even that small amount of food. "Thank you, Cleveland," she forced a smile and handed the dishes back to him. She looked around the room. It was a well-built house she could tell, bigger than the one back in Oregon City probably. A woman hadn't lived there a long time obviously, yet the house was very clean. She looked at Cleveland, he was young but his face showed he was grown. His body was well muscled and lean, she had felt his strength as he'd held her. She could see why Zack had liked him so. He was very close in age and general looks to Joshua, Zack's younger brother.

She looked at the strange dog who was staring at her in the most intense way. "That's an unusual dog. It has blue eyes!" Lydia stroked the dog's head a couple times and it lay down at her feet.

"That's why Zack named him Blue, 'cause of his eyes. He's a sheep-herding dog of some kind. Really bright but not too playful. He took to Zack right off and he seems to taken to you, too."

"So Blue was Zack's dog?"

"Yes. He tolerates me just fine but he mourned Zack for weeks." Cleveland got up and started toward the cookstove. "I'll fix you a proper supper as soon as I get the fire going, Miss Lydia." Cleveland said shyly.

"I probably should go back to town, Cleveland," Lydia started to get up but felt dizzy again. She plopped back down on the bench.

"I got a perfectly good room in there, was my ma's. Got a new bed in it. I got rid of the other one when…"He got a catch in his throat.

Lydia looked at him, "When Zack died in it?"

Cleveland nodded as he started to put wood in the black cookstove. Lydia held onto the side of the bench as she regained her balance. "Tell you what, Cleveland, why don't you build the fire and I'll make us some dinner if you show me where your supplies are. Would that be all right?"

Cleveland looked at her, studying everything about her face. He had dreamed of this moment for so long, yet lived in fear it would never happen. Now here she was so close but it might still all be a dream. "I'd be right happy to do that.," he stammered. "There are some canned goods in the cupboard there, and some meat in the root cellar out back, Miss Lydia."

She managed a small smile. "Please remember to call me Liddy. My…" She couldn't finish her sentence, tears came flooding back. She put her hand up as Cleveland started towards her. "Please, I'll be fine. It's just all so new to me."

Cleveland stopped and nodded, "Zack always called you Liddy. I know how you must have loved him. He was a wonderful man." Cleveland stood awkwardly for a moment, then went out the back door. "I'll get a couple more pieces of wood."

Lydia looked around the room for a few moments then went back out onto the front porch. Blue quietly accompanied her. She could look across the pasture to the spot on the hillside where there were three graves. Rose had said it was somehow comforting to know that a person could see those they loved and lost everyday. They didn't seem so far away like that. Tears came to her eyes unbidden again. She couldn't really remember what Zack looked like anymore, it had been so long since she had seen him. A mule brayed and she looked towards the barn. Cleveland was putting the animals into the barn for the night feeding. He went about his work so naturally, one by one he led he animals in, gently talking to them, stroking their backs as they went. His young body was strong and his hands sure. She felt a cool breeze sweep across the porch ruffling her hair. Her gaze went from Cleveland to the graves again. She didn't try to check the tears, nor stop the shaking.

Lydia had more questions than she had answers at that moment, everything seemed uncertain. A coyote howled in the distance, its voice added sadness to the dying of another day. What unknown forces had worked against them? Had fate conspired against them to cause the three of them to be brought together like this, or was there a bigger plan? It was hard to know where it might end. She finally went back inside to fix dinner. She wasn't at her best, but she managed to make a hash of potatoes, onions and ham that Cleveland claimed was the best thing he'd had since his ma died. They talked some as they ate, but Lydia was so exhausted she couldn't think of much to say. After they ate she cleaned up the few dishes and the skillet she'd used, setting them to dry on a towel on counter.

Cleveland went outside for a few minutes then came back in. "Liddy, I fixed a bath for you. I figure you're pretty tired and maybe would like to clean up before bed. Zack built that bathhouse as a surprise for me last fall. He said he was going to build one for you someday, a real fancy one." He stepped aside as she walked out the back door. Then he led the way to the building, and once they were inside he showed her how clever Zack had been and how well it all worked.

"Zack built this with his own hands," Lydia said as she ran her hands across the top of the bath trough. She picked up the bar of soap and smiled, pine soap, Zack's favorite. She could sense him all over this farm.

"I'll leave you to enjoy the bath," Cleveland said as he left the room and closed the door. He walked down to the creek and took his bath. Even though the water was a little muddy and cold, it still was refreshing to his aching body. He dried off and hurried back to the house. Blue had remained on the step of the bathhouse and came in when Lydia did.

Lydia had wrapped her towel around her head, covering her beautiful hair. She went over by the fireplace and began to dry her hair by first running her fingers through it, then taking a brush. As Cleveland watched he realized how much he'd like to be running his fingers through her hair, wielding that brush as it made stroke after stroke. He finally had to look away before he tormented himself. Finally he heard Lydia sigh.

"I'm really tired, Cleveland," she got up and headed for the bedroom. "Thank you for being such a good friend to my husband and being so kind to me." She went into the bedroom and closed the door. Blue scratched on the door until she opened it slightly and let him in. "I guess it's all right to let him in, isn't it?"

"Yes, he'll sleep through the night most of the time. If he needs to go out, he'll let you know."

"Thanks again then," she said and closed the door behind the dog.

Cleveland left his cot in the corner alcove and quickly got into bed himself. He had a hard time falling asleep but finally managed somehow. Things were still up in the air, but he'd spoke his piece and now it was all up to Lydia. She was everything he'd dreamed of, and more. He wanted her to stay, but was man enough to let her go if need be. Life seemed so unfair.

When Cleveland woke up the next morning, Lydia already had coffee on and was making pancakes, something he hadn't had in years. She fried the batter in bacon grease, sending the tantalizing aroma all over the house. He quickly dressed and went to feed the animals before he had his breakfast. It was all on the table when he came back in. Blue was already licking his paws as he always did after his meals. "I see you got your food first as usual." Cleveland laughed as he patted the dog's head.

"Hope you like this," Lydia said as she pushed a plate of food towards him and then sat down with a small plate for herself.

Cleveland thought he'd died and gone to heaven, the food was wonderful. The bacon drippings made the johnnycakes crisp and light.

The thick bacon was fried to perfection and the coffee was strong. She knew how to cook for a man for sure. "I haven't had anything so good in years! Thank you."

They didn't talk much as they ate, nor did they look at each other much. Cleveland lingered over a second cup of coffee as Lydia cleaned up the dishes. "I'd like to go to the ferry when you go to work this morning, Cleveland. I've got to get back to Oregon City and my children."

Cleveland instantly felt his stomach churn. "Alright, Liddy." He struggled not to let his feelings show. "I'd be happy to take you." He finished his coffee and headed out to get the stock ready for the day. In just a few minutes he had the wagon out front of the house waiting for Lydia.

Lydia put her satchel on the buggy seat and then knelt down to stroke Blue's head a few times before getting into the rig. "Good bye, boy," she sighed. "You have such beautiful eyes. I bet my boys would just love you." She stood up and the dog went back to the porch and put his head between his paws, as though he understood she was saying goodbye to him, maybe forever.

Cleveland thought he and Blue were both too sad for words. It pained him as he watched Lydia gather wildflowers and put them on Zack's grave before coming to get in the wagon. He helped her up into the seat, but couldn't say anything that would make a difference. It seemed she had made up her mind and was leaving him. They rode into town in silence. At the ferry landing, Cleveland helped her down and put her bag next to her.

Cleveland pulled a small leather bag out of his pocket, "This is for you, Liddy."

Lydia looked into the bag and was surprised to see more than fifty dollars. "Cleveland, I can't take this from you." She started to hand it back but Cleveland up his hand up.

"That's money Zack was saving up to bring you out here. I paid the doctor out of it and that is what was left." Cleveland remembered something else. "Oh yes, that horse at my place is yours, too. I just got two mules myself."

Lydia smiled, "You keep the horse. I know that Zack would want you to have it."

"I could sell it and send you the money."

"No, you keep it." Lydia looked down the hill to the dock where the ship would be coming in. "Well, thank you again for your kindness, Cleveland," Lydia said with a shaky voice.

Cleveland sighed, he wanted to throw her back in the wagon and take her right back to his place; he wanted to grab her in his arms and kiss her until she agreed to stay. He wanted to, but his ma had raised him better than that and he knew that would never do, so he just decided to plead his case one more time. "Miss Lydia, I know it was sudden that I asked you to marry me out of the blue like that, but I want you to know it wasn't an empty offer." He took his hat off and rolled it around in his hands nervously. "I want to be a good husband for you and a father to your boys. I think if you gave me a chance, you'd come to love me, at least a little." He looked deeply into her eyes. It broke his heart to see her tears forming again. "I'm sorry. I never want to make you cry." He stepped ever so slightly closer to whisper to her even though no one was anywhere close to them. "I love you, Liddy and I would do anything for you and I'd never leave you 'cept in a coffin."

Lydia looked surprised at his words, why hadn't Zack felt that way? "Cleveland," she pushed him back to arm's length. "Cleveland, you are a very decent young man and I believe you. I do appreciate how you feel but I'm so much older than you and I have two children."

"Age means nothing," Cleveland scoffed. "Besides you can't be much more than a couple years older than me. And as far as the boys go, well, they need a father and I'm volunteering."

"I just don't see how this could work," Lydia shook her head. "In fact I think it's probably the worst thing you could do. You have so much to offer a woman, Cleveland, you need to find a woman and have your own children."

"Please, at least tell me you'll think about it," Cleveland pleaded.

Lydia shook her head, she was so tired and utterly confused that she would do whatever it took to get him to quit pressing. "Of course I will think about, Cleveland," she stepped forward and kissed him on the cheek, "Go to work now and thank you again." She stepped back and picked up her bag and walked to the edge of the ferry landing where there was a bench to sit on to wait. She purposely didn't look back; she felt if she did Cleveland would never leave. When she finally cast a glance behind her, she was relieved to see he had left. She didn't think to look further up the hill, where he was still watching her. His heart leaped with hope when she turned to see if he was still there. He watched until the ferry came, she got on and it pulled away. Only as the boat left the river bank did she see him sitting at the top of the hill. He looked so alone as he sat there and for some reason it broke her heart.

Chapter 38
Oregon City, Oregon—May 1868

Lydia folded the clothes that she'd just brought in from the line. Her back was aching from the morning washing and hanging of clothes, but she was through now. Ellen was busy at the stove baking bread. Their lives had settled into a routine and things were going pretty smoothly. Everyone was well and busy, but somehow no one was happy. Lydia was glad for the hard life they led, being exhausted every day made it easier not to think. After the last piece of children's shirts was hung on the hooks she took a moment to rest on the front porch. Roy would be coming home from work in a few minutes, they'd eat and then it would be bath time for the children, cleaning up and chores for the animals before turning in. The days were full, that was a blessing.

When Lydia saw Roy coming up the path she knew something was wrong. He usually never pushed the mules, especially at the end of the day but today he was coming very quickly. "Ellen," Lydia yelled as she stood up, "Come out here!"

Ellen immediately joined Lydia on the porch as she wiped her flour covered hands on her apron, "What is it?"

Lydia pointed to Roy, "Something must be the matter. Roy's really driving those mules."

Ellen hurried out to meet the wagon. "What's the matter, Roy, you hurt?"

Roy jumped down from the wagon and hugged Ellen. "I'm not hurt, honey, I am happy!" Then Roy, who was never one to be rowdy, let out a tremendous war hoop and started twirling Ellen around until she was dizzy. The children heard their father and came running, even the twins toddled out to the porch. Lydia put her hands over her mouth as she laughed out loud at Roy's antics.

Ellen finally got Roy to stop. "Roy you're acting crazy! What has happened? Did you find gold?"

"Better than that! Listen to this," Roy retrieved a letter out of his pocket. "This is from your step-mother's lawyer."

"How can that be something to celebrate about?" Lydia said soberly.

"Just listen," Roy said waving her to be silent, "He says that she died unexpectedly. She and your father had never divorced, so she was his widow at the time of her death. Since she had no kin except her husband's family, her estate was left to us. He said there were no further claims against our farm and he enclosed a check for seven hundred dollars that was left after all her debts were satisfied. Isn't that something? She tried to take away everything we had but instead we wound up with everything she had."

"God does work in mysterious ways," Ellen breathed in astonishment. "What does that mean?"

Roy hugged his wife, "It means we can go home! The farm is ours, as it always was!"

The children shouted for joy and ran to join the family embrace. Everyone was overjoyed except Lydia. Something inside her was still torn and raging but she couldn't quite tell what. Roy saw that she hadn't joined them and untangled himself from his family. "I almost forgot, Liddy. There were three other letters there that were for you. The man I left at our farm forwarded everything that came."

Lydia walked over and took the letters, "Virgil, would you watch the twins so I can read these in peace?" The boy nodded and herded the babies back into the house. "Thanks honey," she called after him. She looked at Roy and Ellen still hugging and laughing. She wished she felt that way, the way she'd hoped it would be when she saw Zack again. She shook her head, that was the past now.

She went down to the barn and sat on a log next to the corral and looked at the letters. The first was from Zack. It was written by Cleveland but dictated by Zack right after he had been hurt. He told her that he had asked Cleveland to take care of her and the boys. She understood how binding that must have felt to the young man as he watched his dearest friend die.

The second letter was from Cleveland shortly after Zack had died. He poured out his heart to her, pledging to do as he had promised Zack. He wanted her and the boys to know that. The third letter was from him too, but this time he wasn't speaking of his promise so much as his need for her and the boys to be the family he wanted. He knew that it wasn't the best way for a man and a woman to start out, but with commitment and God's help they could make a good life for themselves. And once again he said something that had haunted her since they met; He said he would never leave her for any reason save death. As far as she could remember, Zack had never said or felt that; he was able to leave her and not regret it enough to come home. Lydia re-read all the letters and then sat for awhile thinking about what she needed to do. She walked back to the house to help with dinner.

Ellen and Roy were all atwitter with making plans for their return to Tennessee. Lydia listened but didn't join in. Finally Ellen noticed Lydia's silence and took a deep breath to ask the hard questions. "Sister you are going home with us, aren't you? You know you are more than welcome to live on the farm until you remarry."

Lydia looked shocked, Ellen had said "remarry." Of course that would be expected of her, she was young and had children who needed a father. It was right to remarry. She thought for a moment about Mark. Her cheeks burned as she thought of his kiss, but somehow he didn't seem right for her and her children. He had three children of his own that he didn't seem particularly attached to. She wanted a man who could love her and her children, and never leave them. The words in Cleveland's letter floated across her mind. "This may seem a little strange to you. It is a bit surprising to me too, but I think I am going to stay here in Oregon. It may be the wrong thing to do but I believe I will marry Cleveland Taylor, if his offer was sincere."

Ellen looked at Roy, "You really don't know him, sister!"

"I thought I knew Zack and look how that turned out," Lydia sighed.

"Zack was a good man, he just had a wandering foot," Roy said quietly.

"Zack was a very good man and I loved him," Lydia said flatly. "But I guess I want someone who doesn't have a "wandering foot" as you call it. Cleveland says he'd never leave me and that sounds very good to me."

Roy smiled at Ellen, "So when are we having a wedding? We'd like to be here for that but we're mighty anxious to get home." Ellen took his hand and laughed in joy.

"I'll write to Cleveland and see when we could all come. He'll have to line up a preacher but I don't think that'd take too long. I'd like you to see the farm and where we'll be so you'll always have a picture in your mind of where the boys and I are."

Ellen got up and hugged her sister. "You are so special to me. I will pray everyday of my life for you and your boys."

* * *

Harve and Cleveland had just started working together on a barn just south of Monmouth. Harve had watched Cleveland going through the motions and still doing superior work but his attitude was so gloomy he couldn't take it anymore. "Boy, if you don't get over this I might have to fire you."

Cleveland looked shocked, "What do you mean? Get over what?"

"Ever since you met Zack's widow, you've been acting like you're a mule who's eaten too much sweet grass."

Cleveland laughed, "I ain't acting that bad."

"You might be acting worse. Boy, you've got to settle this thing once and for all. It was a foolish thing in the first place. Your friend Zack shouldn't never of asked a silly thing like that of you, making you promise to take care of his wife and children. Then her showing up here like that," Harve shook his head.

"She didn't know he was dead," Cleveland said sternly.

"Well, you need to either go after her or forget her," Harve picked up his tools and headed on to a new spot. "That's all there is to it. You know it."

Cleveland did. Quietly he took his tools to another spot and started to work. All through the day he kept to himself, thinking of what Harve had said. He chided himself for being so stupid. Maybe he had pressed her too hard. Maybe if he'd given her more time she would have considered the idea in a better light but it was too late now. She was gone and he hadn't heard from her since she left. It was all over. For all he knew she'd found someone else by now or had even left Oregon. He made up his mind that if he hadn't heard from her by the end of the month, he would do everything in his power to forget her and forget all this ever happened. He wondered if it was within his power though, as much in love as he was.

Mid-week Cleveland had to go into Independence to get some extra wood and supplies so he stopped by the post office. He was surprised and yet apprehensive when he saw he had a letter from Lydia. It was from Oregon City so she hadn't left the state yet, that was good. He took it back to his wagon and found a shady spot, away from anyone seeing him as he read his letter. His hand shook as he opened the small envelope.

"*Dear Cleveland,*

I want to thank you again for all the kindness you have shown me and the consideration. Your farm is a lovely place and you have done well for yourself there.

Something wonderful happened for my sister's family. Our family farm in Tennessee is once again theirs so they are planning to return home soon. They are very excited about that.

This is hard for me to say Cleveland, but I do believe you when you say you want to take care of me and the boys. I do believe that you would never leave us and I do believe we could work out a good life together. So what I guess I am asking is if you still want to marry me and be a father to my sons? This in no way obligates you to anything. If you have changed your mind I will understand. I will always think well of you no matter what you decide.

If you would like to continue with this plan please let me know when. I would like my sister and her family to come be a part of it and see where we will be living before they leave.

You would have to arrange for a minister and a place for us to be married but I don't expect anything fancy. Just let me know when and where, I will be there.

There is no big hurry to make this decision but my sister and her husband are talking about taking the stage to California by the end of June and taking the train home from there. I would need to make arrangements to go with them as soon as possible if I am not going to stay here.

Again, thank you for your kindness and I await hearing from you.

Sincerely yours,
Lydia"

Cleveland let out a loud shout of joy. He looked around but really didn't care if anyone was close enough to hear. She had said yes, maybe not as enthusiastically as he'd hoped but none-the-less she had said yes. On the way back to the work site Cleveland stopped to talk to Reverend Murphy who was overjoyed for him, and he promised to perform the ceremony at any time. Cleveland quickly calculated how long it would take for his letter to get to Lydia, her to get up river to him and came up with a date. "How about a week from Friday?"

"Sounds good to me, boy," Rev. Murphy laughed.

"Could I borrow a pen, envelope and some paper?" Cleveland nearly pleaded.

"Of course," the minister fetched the supplies for Cleveland, "You write your intended and I'll post it for you today. I have to go to the post office myself anyway."

Cleveland dashed off just a few sentences, and hurriedly sealed the letter in its envelope. He addressed it and gave it to the minister with a big smile, "I can't remember being so happy."

Reverend Murphy reached out and shook his hand, "It's about time some happiness came your way, son. You're a special soul. This woman is a lucky bride."

"Thanks for those kind words, Reverend. I got to get back to work. Harve will think I run out on him." He tipped his hat and slapped the reins across the mules' backs. He nearly flew back to where Harve was.

"Hey," he yelled as he popped down off the wagon and ran to hug his surprised boss, "Guess what? She said yes. I'm getting married a week from Friday. Will you be my best man?"

"Whoa, boy," Harve laughed, pushing him back, "You're way too anxious to load yourself down with a family. What about her husband; Won't knowing she loved him always stand between you? Do you really know what you're getting yourself into?"

Cleveland laughed, "Yeah I do. I'm getting a ready made family that I already belong to in a way. I don't have any problem that she loved him before she knew me; Heck, I loved him before I met her. Zack was like my brother so she and I can always love him together."

Harve shook his head, "Well, I can see there's no talking sense to you." He held out his hand and shook Cleveland's, "So I guess the only thing to do is wish you all the luck in the world and stand up with you when you do this thing."

* * *

The boat seemed to take forever. The river wasn't nearly as high as it was the first time Lydia had made the trip. The water wasn't running as swiftly against the boat so they weren't running late but still it seemed to be going slower than usual. Ellen and Roy walked around the deck several times admiring the scenery but Lydia stayed in the front of the boat waiting to see Independence. The boys played quietly on the deck beside her. The other children lay beside her twins and drew on pieces of paper. The day was pleasant enough. All along the shore rhodies and azaleas were in bloom, some daffodils were sprinkled here and there. It was beautiful but Lydia's mind was too full of other things to even take much notice.

Finally about four twenty in the afternoon, half an hour ahead of schedule, the boat rounded the bend and there was Independence. Lydia called excitedly to Ellen, "Sister, we're here."

Ellen and Roy each picked up one of the twins as the other children gathered with them beside Lydia. She scanned ahead to see if she could see Cleveland, but she couldn't, which disturbed her a little. As they got closer to the dock she shrank inside when she couldn't see him anywhere. Surely he hadn't forgotten to come get her. She began to worry then she saw the buggy, a nice shiny one all decorated with flowers, waiting by the landing. Her hopes rose again. Lydia and her family hurried down the gangplank as soon as it was lowered.

"Afternoon folks," a tall middle-aged man said as he approached, "I'm Harve Bauer, the best man at a wedding this day at the Taylor farm. I've come to pick-up the bride and party." He smiled as he offered his hand to Roy and then the women, "Would I be right in assuming one of you two ladies is that bride?"

Lydia laughed, "It's me." She felt young and giddy. What fun this was as well as sweet!

A second wagon had to be hired to carry Lydia's two large trunks, as the family took up all the room in the buggy. The ride was a little tight but they managed fairly comfortably. There was a great air of expectation as they traveled the few miles to the farm. When they topped the hill to turn off the main road she asked Harve to stop. She had the family climb out and go to the spot where she'd first seen the whole farm. It was as beautiful as she remembered.

"This is a lovely place," Ellen said softly.

"I want you to always remember me standing there on that porch," Lydia said, "Standing there and being happy. Please always remember me that way." Lydia turned and hugged her sister.

"I'm not sure but I think there's some happy people already standing on that porch down there. We'd better get on over there."

Lydia laughed and the adults along with the twins got back in the wagon while the other children decided to run to the house themselves. It only took a few minutes to pull up in front of the house. Several neighbors had gathered and there was a well decorated table in the front yard with all kinds of food. Standing on the porch the minister, dressed in a long black robe, was looking serious and official next to Cleveland, who was beaming from ear to ear. The minister held Cleveland back as Harve helped Lydia down and walked with her to the porch. Then Harve went and stood slightly behind Cleveland.

Ellen and Roy held the twins while their children gathered behind them. The minister raised his hand for silence from the group. When everyone had settled quietly, he began, "Welcome to Polk County, Lydia. You have certainly won the heart of a wonderful young man. I hope you'll be very happy here. Are you ready to begin?"

Lydia looked at Cleveland; she wasn't totally sure this was the right thing to do but she was totally sure she wanted to. "Yes, I am ready to begin."

The official part of the service took only about ten minutes from the "Dearly Beloved" to the "you may kiss the bride" but it seemed much longer than that to Lydia and Cleveland. It was hard to tell who was shaking harder when they finally got to that kiss. Cleveland kissed her gently but had a hard time letting her go. She smiled at him as their lips parted and then surprised him by giving him a solid kiss. They turned to the friends and family assembled as the minister announced, "Friends, I'd like you to greet Mr. and Mrs. Cleveland Taylor." Everyone cheered and started lining up to introduce themselves to Lydia and congratulate the couple. When everyone had made the round, someone shouted, "let's eat!" The mood became jubilant and the feast began.

Lydia introduced her family to Cleveland and then he gave them a quick tour of the farm. It was more festive than Lydia had imagined their wedding would be. Someone broke out a fiddle and struck up a lively rendition of *Listen to the Mockingbird* followed by *Jennie with the Light Brown Hair* to make the day even more special. As the sun began it's descent people started to leave for their homes. Only the Porterfields lingered behind to help clean up. Lydia had to say a tearful goodbye to her sister and her family. Harve took them back into town to spend the night at a hotel so they could catch the first ship down river in the morning. It was joyous yet sad to say goodbye, but somehow she knew she would see them again.

They waved until the buggy was completely out of sight. Lydia and Mrs. Porterfield cleared away the leftover food. There was enough food such as fried chicken and corn on the cob to have for dinner the next day.

The two women washed up the dishes while Cleveland and Mr. Porterfield took care of the stock and chickens. After the Porterfields left, Lydia took the boys to the bath house to get them ready for bed. When she brought them back in to put on their night clothes, she noticed that Cleveland had made them each a small wooden framed bed in the alcove where the cot used to be. She blushed when she realized that Cleveland wouldn't be sleeping on that cot in the alcove that night, or any other night.

It was a warm evening so Lydia took the boys back out on the porch until Cleveland was done in the barn. The twilight lingered, filling the sky with shades of mauve and purple. Lydia looked off across the field where Zack lay. Somehow she knew even though this was not what he'd planned, it would be fine with him, those he loved to be together. It was all right, everything was all right. Cleveland came up and hesitantly put his arm around her waist. She felt him relax when she leaned against him.

"Liddy look," Cleveland said calling her attention to the other end of the porch where the twins were playing with Blue. He was loving it. The dog was acting like a puppy, something he'd never done before. The boys giggled as Blue licked their faces. Blue lay down and let the children crawl all over him, even tolerating it when they grabbed handfuls of hair. The dog seemed truly happy for the first time in his life. "I guess it's official, we're a family now."